The
Beauty Curse

By
Rose Horobin

MAPLE
PUBLISHERS

The Beauty Curse

Author: Rose Horobin

First Published in 2024 *(Wife Number Three)*
First Published in 2025 *(The Beauty Curse)*

ISBN 978-1-83538-504-3 (Paperback)
      978-1-83538-505-0 (E-Book)

Book Cover by: David Fletcher

Book Layout by:
      White Magic Studios
      www.whitemagicstudios.co.uk

Published by:
      Maple Publishers
      Fairbourne Drive, Atterbury,
      Milton Keynes,
      MK10 9RG, UK
      www.maplepublishers.com

CHAPTER ONE

Thursday 3rd March 2022

Luke snuggled under the duvet to avoid the cold air of the room as he gazed at photos on his mobile phone. His perfect woman to stare at, and dream about, when he wanted. A woman with an exquisitely beautiful face and wavy brown hair that he knew would flow through his fingers, like satin, if he were lucky enough to touch it. Mesmerising, large blue eyes framed by long black lashes. A soft red mouth made more enticing by her smile or her laughter. A mouth that he could stare at forever. She was small in height, about five-foot-four inches, which made her super cute. It made him feel tall and manly when he was able to stand next to her. He hoped her body was shapely with rounded breasts, small waist and curvaceous bottom. This was hard to discern during the winter months when she wore belted macs or padded coats. Luke yearned for the spring and summer months when her body would be visible without a top layer of clothing for warmth.

Luke shivered with excitement. His ideal woman was captured in many images on his mobile phone. But this woman was not a famous movie star who lived in Hollywood. This woman lived in his local area and shopped in the same supermarket as him. If he were patient, clever and cunning, he could stand a chance of getting to know her and making her his.

Luke's daydreaming was interrupted by the loud voice of his father who entered the room. 'Luke, get out of bed, I won't tell you again,' Jez Milner ordered his son. 'You know I wanted you and Russ to help me lay this new patio. Russ has been out there for over an hour. But there's no sign of you. You need to get up.'

Luke's father stood at the side of his bed, hands on hips, anger on his face as he stared at his son. Luke pretended to be asleep, hoping his father would just go away. The area around the bed was littered with crumpled beer cans and a pizza box. The room had a musty, malty, sweet aroma. Jez moved away from the bed to pull open the mid-grey curtains, and as sunlight trickled in, particles of dust were seen floating in the air. A pile of discarded clothes lay scattered around the bed; jeans, grubby T-shirts, assorted socks and underpants.

'Ok, Luke, you lazy git. This room's a mess. I know you're not asleep, just pretending,' Jez shouted, as he stomped back over to the bed, pulled back the duvet and grabbed the mobile phone out of Luke's hand. 'You've probably been getting off looking at images of young women on those porn websites. I've told you that if you want a woman, you need to get out there and find one.' Jez touched the phone's screen and photos of Luke's secret crush were revealed to him. 'Blimey, she's pretty. If you're aiming for this level of beauty, you are doomed to disappointment. Do as the rest of us do, pick an average looking one, and they'll be forever grateful.'

Still firmly closing his eyes and ignoring his father's blather, Luke sighed softly. His father was all talk. Yeah, he could agree that his mother had been average; in looks, intelligence and educational attainment. Two CSE's (whatever these were), one in art and one in domestic science which was cooking, apparently. These culinary skills were never demonstrated in the actual mediocre meals she prepared according to his father's description of burnt sausages and semi-raw roast chicken. In other areas, she must have excelled as she developed a reputation with the local men for being a high achiever in terms of her sexual expertise. His father's 'average' wife had not shown any inclination to be forever grateful to her husband for choosing her. After ten years of marriage she scarpered to Turkey to live with a waiter she'd met on a two week holiday.

Luke would admit to having a habit of watching porn. It was the only way he ever got to see naked females and he researched the websites carefully to establish the type of woman he wanted in his life. He was not going to settle for a grateful Miss Average. Porn sites were useful for all this as they spelt out the realities of the female form. When he had first explored these sites as a teenager he expected wall-to-wall female perfection. This was not the case at all. After years of scrutiny, he had seen many examples and rejected many, many possibilities. His chosen female could not be obese, so no heavy breasts, no rolling tummy or thunder thighs. Not too skinny, no twiglet arms and barely-there breasts. Not too tall, as he was of medium height and he wanted a woman who was shorter than him. What he desired was a natural beauty with smooth skin and a beautiful face who smelt of delicate perfumes. Luke often explored the perfume counters at high-end stores, pretending he was buying for a girlfriend. He'd acquired a number of paper strips drenched in perfumes that he would sniff in bed at night to select a favourite. His preferred choice was Versace's *Bright Crystal* and there was a bottle of it in his bedside cabinet. Just dabbing it on his wrist last thing at night would send him to sleep dreaming about 'his girl'. He imagined smelling the perfume on her soft skin when they made love for the first time.

By now, Luke sensed his father's growing impatience and knew that he would become irate if he was ignored. Generally, his father was easy-going but he had specifically wanted Luke's help today with laying the patio so that the job would get done quicker. But Luke did not want to leave his warm bed to spend hours outside in the cold. Perhaps his father would just go away?

This question was swiftly answered as the duvet was ripped off, exposing his body to the cold air in the room. 'Right, I made it clear I wanted your help today. Get up now or you'll find out you're not too big for a clout,' his father commanded, in the low, gruff tone of voice that would brook no argument.

Luke tentatively opened his eyes to see his father's reddened, flabby face glaring at him. 'Ok, ok. I'm getting up now. It's really annoying though. We're having a couple of days off in the week, a bit of a rest from work, and you want me to help lay a patio. I just want a long weekend so I can chill out and do some writing.'

Jez's irritation with his son grew. 'We don't all get what we want in life, son. I want you to pull you weight in return for living rent free. So jump to it.'

Knowing that he was not going to win this battle, Luke conceded, 'Ok, give me ten minutes and I'll be down to help.'

'Good, that's the right attitude. Getting into some physical work always takes your mind off women. If you just want sex, do what your brother does and go on them dating app thingies. Russ seems to do fairly well. Mind you, I expect the women aren't much to write home about,' his father prattled on.

'Ok, dad, as I said, I'll be down in ten,' Luke sighed, sitting up in bed, shivering from the cold air on his body, as he was naked except for a pair of boxer shorts. Jeez, it was mortifying at twenty-five-years old to be getting dating advice from a man whose wife left him years ago.

To Luke, his father and his brother were failures in terms of relationships with women. Luke was not going to settle for less than perfect. This had always been a problem in the past. He'd had a couple of brief relationships with girls over the years, no longer than for a few weeks, as they quickly disappointed him. Too plain or too dull. Other times, he'd get fixated on a girl based on her beauty but these relationships never developed. Luke could never really understand why.

From his brief encounters with girls, Luke had learned some lessons. If he was going to have a life-long loving relationship with a woman she must be perfect, a goddess. Therefore, he must choose wisely. But the search was long and exhausting and he was frequently disappointed. He was fishing in a very small pond and trying to catch a pretty fish. But a few months ago his luck had changed when he laid eyes on 'The One'. Everything he wanted. He picked up his phone from where his father had chucked it on the bed. He gazed at his brown-haired, blue-eyed angel. Forget laying patios, Luke needed to concentrate on how to get this perfect woman into his life.

❖

CHAPTER TWO

Thursday 3rd March 2022

'Oh, shit', Anna swore, as a red light appeared on her vehicle dashboard as she drove on an A road towards Warwick at eleven in the evening. The road was dark, in a semi-rural area, with no street lighting. There wasn't a lot of traffic around at this time.

Anna loved the joy of car ownership and the freedom it gave her to get around. But she was ashamed to admit that she was particularly clueless in terms of what happened under the bonnet of a car and the whole process of keeping a car in operation. Her dad kept an eye on the maintenance of her car and checked tyre wear and tear, tyre pressures, battery connections, spark plugs, oil level, antifreeze and windscreen wash levels. He badgered her into getting the car serviced at the right times. Without her father nearby for advice and guidance, Anna had let things slip, mainly as she couldn't afford the cost of repairs. Now she could feel that the car was seriously losing power, was not accelerating, and, all in all, it seemed as if it would conk out at any moment.

Outside, an earlier light rain had turned heavier and she was struggling to see the road ahead even with the wipers going full pelt. Now a red warning light had come on. In all her father's nagging about car-related matters, most of which went over her head, she remembered one important point. A red light should not be ignored. Trying to keep calm but feeling anxiety bubbling in her stomach, she checked continually in the rear-view mirror for traffic behind her. Terrified that a car would crash into the back of her, on this rainy night, when visibility was reduced by the persistent rain and the darkness of the location.

Taking a bend slowly, before the road straightened, Anna frantically searched ahead for a safe place to pull in. She could barely see as far as the car's headlights and this stretch of road was edged by grass verges that were not suitable to pull on to. Her anxiety levels were rising as the power reduced on the car and she was terrified it would come to a sudden halt. The windscreen wipers were pumping left and right, doing their job, but she was struggling to actually see the road ahead, even when the headlights were on full beam.

Anna leaned forward in her seat in a futile effort to get a better view out of the windscreen. In reality she was now driving on a wing and a prayer, using the centre white line to keep her from veering over into the other lane. Prayer, and a helping hand from God, was what she needed now to help her find a suitable, safe place to pull over. Her friend, Olivia, believed in a 'Parking Angel' to help her locate a parking spot in a busy town. She swore that asking for help from the Angel never failed. Anna now silently begged for the 'Angel in Charge of Laybys' to come to her aid. Perhaps there was an 'Angel for Car Emergencies' that was also on duty. The car was now slowing considerably and no amount of acceleration was making any difference.

There was a car behind, coming up close, and probably frustrated by her slow speed. It would be risky for the driver to try to overtake on this dark road, with minimal visibility, due to persistent spray from the rain. Anna felt guilty that she was holding this driver up but there was absolutely nothing she could do as her car was really no longer under her control. Then, she saw it up ahead. A small layby with a fence to one side and a field beyond the fence. There was an HGV lorry parked half way along the layby with its lights off. Holding her breath, and trying to move the car forward by willpower alone, Anna drove her car into the layby, came to a halt behind the lorry and turned off the engine.

She breathed in deeply to calm her nerves, thankful that her ordeal was over. But was it? It was really late and what could she do in terms of calling a vehicle rescue service? Her membership of a popular motoring organisation had lapsed as she didn't have the money to renew it. She would have to try and locate a breakdown recovery service to assist her, if such a thing was available at this time of night. The alternative was to leave the car in the layby and call a taxi. Reaching over to the floor of the passenger seat, she picked up her bag and retrieved her phone. The rain outside was now starting to ease but as she looked out of the rain-soaked windows, she was surrounded by blackness in an isolated semi-rural area. There were still some cars on the road and their headlights illuminated the gloom for a few seconds before they were gone. She was alone in her car in the layby with a lorry in front of her with the possibly of a driver inside. This thought spooked her so she quickly locked all the car doors.

Anna noted that her phone was down to the tiniest red line indicating that it was out of charge. The phone signal was down to one bar. 'Oh, shit, shit, shit,' Anna screamed in her head. Could this night get any worse? She tried to search for local garages and taxi firms on her phone but there was no signal. It was looking unlikely that she would be able to summon assistance. On this dark, wet night it would be dangerous to try to walk along an A road with only grass verges and no pavements or lighting. There was a real danger that she would be hit by a vehicle. If she remained in the car, it would get cold fairly quickly, and she only had on a dress and a raincoat to keep her warm. Plus, there may be a male driver in the lorry. Anna figured that most lorry drivers were decent men but she still felt as if she was in a vulnerable position.

Perhaps the phone would work if she got outside the car. She fastened the buttons on her raincoat and tightened the belt around her waist. She was already shivering even before she opened the door to step outside. Getting out of the car, she stepped on to tarmac but the area was not well-maintained and was potted with holes. The ground was scattered with leaves left over from the autumnal fall which were now rotted and mulched. The rain had left deep puddles and a slippery surface. Anna concentrated on moving around the car, holding her mobile phone aloft to try to get a signal. It remained weak on the tiny amount of charge left on her phone. A car was approaching and reducing its speed, a possible indication it was going to pull into the layby. Another stranger to worry about.

Anna walked slowly around to the other side of her car, completely focused on her mobile phone, and not where she was walking. Suddenly, her right foot stepped on something round and moveable, and she was lifted off her feet, and hurled forward onto the wet gravelly surface of the layby. She came down hard on her right knee before falling forward and the right side of her forehead smacked onto the hard tarmac. The impact jarred her stomach and she made a loud 'ouch' sound as she fell. Completely winded, and not sure how she was hurt, Anna lay still on the cold, sodden ground, trying to calm her shredded nerves before she made an attempt to stand up. She was vaguely aware of a car door opening and closing nearby but she had no energy to raise her head to investigate. This night had gone from bad to worse and now she was in a nightmarish situation of having hurt herself. Her phone had dropped from her hand and she was unable to summon help. If she had sustained an injury, and was unable to move, what would she do?

⚬—◆—⚬

CHAPTER THREE

As the shock of the fall wore off slightly, Anna placed her hands on the ground to help herself get back on her feet. In the next moment, she could hear the sound of heavy footsteps coming towards her, splashing through the surface water of the layby. A male voice very close by, asked, 'Are you ok? Let me help you up very slowly until we know how hurt you are. I'll put my hands under your arms and gently raise you from the ground.'

Anna looked up slightly from her prone position to glance at the man. He seemed to be young and strong, more than capable of helping her. 'Ok, if you can help I'd be grateful. I think I've banged my knee and my head,' she advised him in a shaky voice. He did as he said. He stood behind her, placed his hands under her arms, and lifted her to an upright position. She couldn't stand fully on both feet, as her right knee was throbbing and she was unable to straighten it.

'Ok, ok. You've grazed your knee. Just stand still a minute while you recover from the shock of the fall,' he ordered, keeping one arm around her waist. As she balanced on one leg, Anna gazed up at the man who had come to her aid. He was now scrutinising her face, as best he could, in these dark, shadowy surroundings. 'You've also bashed your face and there's bleeding from a cut just above your eyebrow. We need to attend to the bleeding. I'll help you to my car where I have a first aid kit.'

Anna tentatively put her hand to the area of her head which was throbbing and saw that her fingers were smeared in blood. 'Oh dear,' she exclaimed, horrified to see the blood. 'T-thanks,' she stuttered due to the ongoing shock and the cold temperature of the rain-soaked air.

The guy was a lot taller than her, and she barely came up to his shoulder, but he held onto her tightly to aid her progress as she hopped over to his car. He opened the passenger door and Anna sat down with her legs outside of the vehicle whilst he went to the boot to retrieve the first aid kit. The kit was a very impressive green rucksack with a white cross and first aid written on it. Her own emergency first aid kit consisted of a packet of paracetamol and a few ageing plasters at the bottom of her handbag. Opening his bag, the first thing he got out was a foil blanket, which he wrapped around her shoulders. 'You're shivering with cold,' he commented. 'The bleeding above your eyebrow has stopped but we'll attend to that first. Given the position of the cut, I need to assist you, are you comfortable with that?' He now squatted down next to her and searched in the bag for the required items.

Anna noted the earnest look on his face. This man was a complete stranger, a male fitter and stronger than her if he wanted to do her harm, but so far he had been exceptionally helpful in coming to her aid. Really, she had no option but to hope she could trust him as she did need help. It was dark, it was cold, her car had broken down and her phone had died. She had injured her knee and banged her head and there was no likelihood of walking home. Despite the foil blanket, Anna's body shook with cold. 'It's ok, go ahead. Have you had any first aid training?'

He nodded, as his eyes met hers. 'Yes, a lot, as I used to be a police officer and they are very keen on training for everything. That said, it's a while since I've had to deploy my skills on a real life person so I hope I'll be gentle with you.' He turned on the overhead passenger light and took hold of Anna's face to inspect the wound. 'It's a small gash very close to your eyebrow, just on the curve of the eye socket. These type of cuts always bleed a lot. I think it can be fixed with a plaster but if you want I can take you to the hospital.'

Anna looked at the wound in the vanity mirror above her seat. 'It doesn't look too bad. I don't really want to go to the hospital as it would be hours of waiting and wasting everyone's time. I'll let you practice your first aid skills on me.'

He used gel to cleanse his hands and then opened a sterile wipe to clean the drying blood that had streaked down the right side of her face. A second wipe was used to clean the wound and she flinched slightly as he did this. He mouthed, 'sorry' but continued to thoroughly cleanse the area around her eyebrow. Anna's face was a mixture of angst and bewilderment when he joked, 'Ok, just about to get the very large hypodermic syringe with a blunt needle to stitch the cut up with.'

Anna laughed lightly. 'It's good that medical staff have a sense of humour when they are going to cause pain.'

He then rooted in the bag, and, to Anna's relief, brought out a small plaster. Re-taking a firm grip on her chin, he ordered, 'Ok, now, keep still or you might end up losing your eyesight as I stick your eyelid down by mistake.'

She kept rigidly still as he applied the plaster, his face very close to hers. When he had finished, and he stood up, she whispered, 'Thanks.'

'Righty oh, let's have a look at your knee,' he then instructed. Anna straightened her right leg as he gazed down at her knee. Though it was still technically winter time, she had gone out earlier without any tights. Now, she was displaying her pale legs to a man she had only met ten minutes ago. There was a large graze on her knee, a mix of drying red blood, and dirt and grit from the tarmac. 'That looks sore and it's impacted with dirt. Do you want to clean it up yourself as I don't want to hurt you?' he asked.

'Yes, ok,' Anna agreed as he picked another sterile wipe out of the first aid bag and handed it to her. Her hands were grubby from the fall so she used this to clean them. She used a second wipe to sanitise the wound on her knee, though she did emit a few 'ooh's' and 'ouch's' as she did this.

'That's looking better. Shall I put a sterile dressing on it?' he enquired, as he continued to gaze at her knee. 'Though I do think that with all this going on I should introduced myself. I'm Nick.'

'I'm Anna. I'd say nice to meet you but perhaps in other circumstances,' she stated, smiling at him.

Very efficiently, Nick applied the dressing to cover the graze, and patted her knee lightly when he'd finished. 'All done. Now we've dealt with the most pressing matters, can I ask what you are actually doing in this layby late at night?'

Despite his kindly assistance, Anna bristled slightly as it felt as if he were reprimanding her for being a female out alone at this late hour. 'I was driving back from a friend's house and my car started to play up and a red warning light came on. I've managed to limp into this layby. Then I find my phone's battery is almost out and there's no signal anyway. I got out of the car with the phone to try to get a signal and that's when I fell over,' her voice cracked as she spoke, as she realised her ordeal was still far from over as she had to deal with her broken down car. 'I'm very grateful for your help. Could I just use your phone to call a breakdown recovery service as I'm not in the AA or RAC? That's if you can get a signal out here.'

He was bending over to zip up the rucksack as Anna said this. Straightening up, he said, 'If you call a recovery service you may be waiting ages and is that advisable, given that you've had a bump to the head. I think it might be better if I give you a lift to where you are going and you can deal with the recovery of the car tomorrow.'

Anna looked perturbed as he said this. 'I can't possibly trouble you any further. I've held you up already. But for the record, I live in Warwick, which isn't too far away.'

'Then that's not a problem as it's the direction I'm going. And it's no trouble though I can understand that you could be nervous getting into a car with a stranger. In that case, you're welcome to use my phone to call a recovery service,' he stated.

Anna felt conflicted. He was right, he was a stranger and all this Mr Nice act could be a way of luring her into his car to take her who knows where. On the other hand, he had been exceptionally kind, and her gut instinct told that he seemed trustworthy. 'Ok, I'll accept your offer of a lift. Oh hell, I dropped my phone when I fell and forgot to pick it up. I'll need to go and find it and get my keys and bag out of the car.' She eased herself up from the passenger seat to walk to her car. Immediately, her grazed knee started to throb and she had difficulty placing her right foot on the ground.

'It might be better if you wait here. I'll go and find your phone, get your bag, and keys, and lock the car for you. Also, you might want to leave a note on the car dashboard stating that the car broke down at eleven p.m. and it will be collected early tomorrow. Leave a contact telephone number. Don't put your name on the note,' he advised. From his car's glove compartment he produced a yellow Post-it note pad and a biro.

Anna took a minute to write the note and handed it to him. Nick went off to find her phone and make her car secure. She sat back down in the passenger seat of his car. Pulling the foil blanket over her legs, she shivered visibly, thinking that she was so chilled to the bone that she may never get warm again. As Nick strode away, through the vanity mirror, she saw the door of the lorry open, and the male driver jump down. The man rushed around the front of the lorry and stood urinating by the fence. He then stood looking at Nick's car as he lit a cigarette. In the next moment, the lorry driver was tapping on the passenger door window. Anna ignored him but the knocking got louder. She eased open the door and looked at the man; mid-forties, medium height, scruffily dressed in shabby jeans and stained sweatshirt.

'You ok, love? he leered, a broad grin revealing yellow-stained teeth. 'I saw you pull up earlier. Looking for a bit of business, were you? If you've finished with him, I'd be happy to pay, you know, particularly as you are proper fit.'

⁂

CHAPTER FOUR

Anna knew she could actually be sick when she realised what this man thought she was. All blood drained from her face and the earlier shaking in her body multiplied exponentially. 'G-go away, you pig. L-leave me alone.'

Luckily, Nick was now back with her bag. He came up to the passenger door to stand next to her potential 'punter'. 'Everything ok, here?' he asked, directing the question to Anna.

She had to breathe deeply to fight back the tears that were threatening to overwhelm her. This night was going to register as one of the worst of her life.

'He's j-just going,' she managed to stutter.

Not knowing what had gone on but sensing Anna's distress, Nick loomed over the lorry driver. 'You'd better make yourself scarce, mate.'

The driver gazed up at Nick, taking in his height and physique. Backing away, the man held his hands up. 'Sorry, love. A simple misunderstanding that's all. No harm done.' As soon he was out of Nick's personal space he scooted back to the safety of his cab.

Nick handed Anna her bag. 'Your keys and phone are in the bag. The phone's got a crack to the screen from when you dropped it, I'm afraid.' Nick closed the passenger door, walked around the car and sat in the driver's seat. 'Let's get out of here. I just need to put your address in the satnav,' he said. Anna gave him her address details and he set the satnav. He started the car, easing it forward slowly out of the layby. 'What was all that about with him, just now?' he asked as he turned to briefly look at her, before concentrating on driving out of the layby, to join the main road.

'H-he thought that I'm a prostitute and that if I'm finished with you, I might like to earn some extra cash with him,' Anna said, trying to make her voice light and jokey to show that it hadn't got to her but it was impossible. All the tension built up over the course of this awful evening was too much and she burst into tears. 'This has been a really shit night.'

'I'm pleased for his sake you didn't tell me that as he was standing next to me or I might have flattened him. Take no notice, he's a moron. It's not worth getting upset,' Nick advised, as he drove his car forward to join the main road. The volume of traffic was now considerably reduced and the rain had stopped but there was still a lot of spray on the road.

Anna was mortified with embarrassment as she tried to stem her crying. She reached in her bag to locate a tissue to blot her tear-stained eyes and her runny nose. 'I'm s-sorry for crying, you must think I'm an idiot. I j-just want to thank you again for all you've done for me including giving me a lift.' The crying helped to relieve the tension in her stomach but made her feel like an utter flake in front of this man.

'Don't apologise for crying, it's probably delayed shock from falling over,' he said, as he glanced kindly at her.

Sitting quietly now, Anna hiccupped occasionally as her crying stopped. The car had warmed up and the icy chill started to leave her body. She stopped shivering and there was actually some feeling coming back into her frozen hands and feet. As more warmth spread through her body she realised that she was sitting on a heated seat. Taking in her surroundings, Anna noted that this was a luxury car with leather trim, interior blue mood lighting, and screens with multi-icon choices not dissimilar to a laptop or the cockpit of a plane. It acutely highlighted the shortcomings of her ageing car now languishing in a rural layby. Nick was a competent driver, negotiating the road expertly, taking account of the darkness of the night and the reduced visibility due to earlier weather conditions. It felt like the car was gliding along, giving a comfortable ride, as if the road was suddenly pothole free. Not like her car which jolted and bounced her over every obstacle on the road.

Having taken account of the car, she sneakily scrutinised the driver. He was very handsome with brown hair, short at the sides, and longer on top. A fine nose, with a slight bump on the bridge, which added interest to his profile. A well-trimmed beard which enhanced the masculinity of his facial features. Anna could not discern his eye colour but she was hoping for blue. He was wearing a dark grey bomber jacket with a light grey crew neck sweater and black jeans.

As the car drove into the urban area of Warwick, there was light and activity away from the dark gloom of the countryside. 'How are you feeling now?' he asked glancing at her. 'At least you've warmed up and there's a bit of colour to your face. You looked quite pale earlier as your face was drained of blood and your lips were blue.'

'Yeah, I'm a little better, thanks. This car certainly has a very efficient heating system compared to mine. I've no idea what's wrong with my car and how much it's going to cost to repair. Plus, I'm not with a vehicle recovery organisation so I'm going to have to contact some random garage to help me recover it and hope they don't rip me off. I suppose I could go back to the layby tomorrow and push it to cut costs,' Anna joked but the whole issue with the car was not making her laugh. Her limit on her credit card was almost reached and a further unexpected expense could max her out. She didn't want to have to ask her dad for help but it may come to that.

'If you do decide to push it, let me know and I'll come and watch,' he teased, turning to smile mischievously at her. 'If you like, I could help with moving the car. A friend of mine owns a garage in Warwick and I could get him to recover the car tomorrow. I've not used him personally but from what I gather from friends his rates are reasonable.'

'That would be very helpful, thanks. This will sound pathetic but my dad always took care of car issues. I wished I'd listened more when he gave me advice. I need to find a garage where I can trust the mechanics to fix the car and not add on unnecessary extras,' Anna stated, seriously wishing that she was back with her dad and his wise counsel.

'How long have you lived away from home?' Nick asked.

'I moved here six months ago to start a new job. It's times like this I miss my family,' Anna explained with a catch in her voice. Tears were threatening to fall again and she swallowed hard to control this. Nick's car was now on her residential street, in a southern area of Warwick. Anna advised Nick that he could park on the parking space at her modern mews house. She turned in her seat to look at him. 'Thank you, Nick, for all your help and bringing me home.' She picked up her handbag off the floor and rooted inside for her door key.

He smiled at her, the corner of his blue eyes crinkling slightly, and she was struck once again how handsome he was. There must be a very lucky girlfriend or wife around somewhere. 'Let's swap phone numbers. With your permission I'll contact my mate, Justin, to move your car. Give me the car key and I'll take it to him tomorrow morning.'

Her gratitude for this man was now off the scale but she really couldn't keep letting him help her. 'No, honestly. Just give me Justin's details and I'll arrange everything in the morning. I really don't want to put you to anymore trouble.'

'It's no trouble. I can arrange it and get the key to him. Without a car, you'll be faffing with taxis and so on,' he now insisted. 'For now, concentrate on getting into your house and recovering from your fall.'

Anna could appreciate the logic of what he was saying. She removed the car key from her keyring and handed it to him. She eased open the passenger door and cautiously got out of the car. Her knee still felt sore and any pressure to stand on her right foot, and straighten her leg, caused her pain. 'Honestly, I know how my granny felt after her knee operation.'

Nick now got out of his seat to assist her to her front door. 'Come on, nana, let me help you.' He held out his left arm and Anna took hold of him to walk the few steps to the front door. She giggled out of embarrassment as she held onto his arm. They arrived at the door and he waited while she put the key in the lock to open the door. 'Thanks again for your help.'

He remained on the doorstep, gazing at her. 'Have you got someone you can phone if you feel unwell during the night? I'm not sure I'm keen to let you in here alone with a head injury.'

Anna shook her head. 'I don't really know anyone that well except work colleagues and I can't call them. I'm sure I'll be ok.'

'Ok, but if you need help you can call me. How are you going to manage getting to work without your car?' he enquired. This may be because he was an ex-cop but he did not seem to hesitate when asking questions.

'It won't be a problem as I can work from home, if necessary. I might even call in sick if I can't shift this throbbing headache. I'll wait and see,' Anna stated, now ready to get into her home and not hover on the doorstep getting cold again.

As she moved further inside to close the door, he retreated back from the doorstep. 'Anyway, goodnight. I'll contact you in the morning about your car.' With that he returned to his vehicle. But she was grateful for his help. In her hour of need, she had certainly been helped by an angel in male form.

⟡

CHAPTER FIVE

Friday 4ᵗʰ March 2022

Anna slept very fitfully that night. Her head was still throbbing due to the knock to her forehead and painkillers weren't doing much to disperse the pain. Many a time when she moved in bed, it hurt her knee, and she flinched, thus waking her up. There was also a dull ache on the side of her right hip bone which she must have banged when she fell forward onto the ground. Injuries aside, worries about the likely cost of the car repair were freaking her out. Trying to pay a mortgage, utility bills, Council tax, and all other bills was stretching her to her financial limit.

When she had purchased this two-bedroom mews property she had been sure that she could cope with all the bills but then unexpected outgoings kept catching her out. A plumber to repair a leak under the sink. A new light fitting in the lounge installed by an electrician. Then there was the cost of socialising with her new work colleagues. She was friendly with Olivia, a Payroll/HR Administrator on a different team, who'd introduced her to the pubs and bars in Warwick. All this cost money, and post lockdown, the cost of drinks and meals out had sky-rocketed. Her salary was reasonable in her job of payroll/HR administrator now that she'd achieved a team leader role but supporting herself financially was much harder than she had anticipated.

Earlier, she had called her boss to say that she was sick due to her ongoing headache caused by the bang to her head. At ten a.m., after attempting to lie-in, she gave up trying and got up. In the shower, she avoided washing her hair as she didn't want to dislodge the plaster covering the cut above her eye. The dressing to her knee was washed off by the shower water and the steam. Examining the graze, it now looked clean but was a mixture of redness and scabbing with a central area of a deeper wound. The shower water had done a good job but now her knee started to throb again. As she dried herself, her whole body still felt stiff and achy. Without her car she would not be going out today. This was perhaps a good option, forcing her to rest and further recuperate.

After re-applying a fresh sterile dressing to her knee, Anna put on a black jersey dress with pink/green pattern. For warmth, she added black tights and a simple black cardigan. She clipped back the top of her shoulder-length, mid-brown hair with a tortoise-shell clip, and left longer strands of hair framing her face. Anna applied a light foundation to her face to give her pale complexion some colour. She coated her eyelashes with black mascara to draw attention away from the greyness under her eyes. The small plaster concealed the cut over her right eyebrow but the area around it was now a smudge of red and purple bruising. She felt a little queasy and light-headed due to the shock of the fall and was not inclined to eat.

Anna made a cup of instant coffee and took it into the living room. The coffee was hot and she sipped it slowly, enjoying the smooth taste and the pleasant aroma which revived her senses. A text pinged on her phone. It was from Nick, her saviour from last night. '**Hi Anna. Hope you are recovering ok. Justin will collect your car from the layby this morning and take it to his garage. He will contact you directly to discuss the repairs. Nick.'**

It was a relief to know that the car was being removed from the layby and not causing a problem. The big worry now was what was going to be the cost of repair. She realised that she may have to contact her father later about borrowing some money. This irked her as she had frequently stressed to her dad that she was capable of managing her finances and paying all her bills.

Dad would insist on covering the bill but she didn't want this as it would call into question her ability to live independently.

Finishing the coffee, Anna got up to take the mug to the kitchen when there was a knock on the door. This was not expected as she really didn't know anyone in the town. Going into the hallway, she saw a tall, shadowy figure through the glass. Living on her own, Anna was reluctant to open her door to unplanned visitors.

Easing open the door, there on the doorstep was Nick. 'Hi,' she stated, staring at him in surprise. He was dressed in a grey wool overcoat worn with black jeans, grey sweater and boots. The coat fitted well, accentuating his broad shoulders and toned build. A navy blue scarf was tied at his neck, giving protection from the chilly, overcast, early March day.

Nick noted that she was a little surprised to see him and stepped back from the doorstep so as not to alarm her. 'Hi. Sorry. I hope I haven't scared you. I just wanted to check you were ok after last night. I was quite worried that you were on your own overnight after receiving a bang to the head. Are you working from home?'

'No, I actually called in sick. I hate doing it but I really couldn't concentrate today as my head's still throbbing,' she explained.

'Did you get my text about your car? Justin's got quite a bit of work booked in to clear for the weekend but he thinks he can have a quick look at yours to see what the problem is. As I said in the text, he'll contact you about the repairs,' Nick said.

'Yes, thanks so much for doing that. I'm relieved my car is being moved this morning. I've worried that the police will thinks it's abandoned and I'll be in more trouble even though I left a note on the dashboard,' Anna stated. 'I should really have got it moved last night but I couldn't think clearly at the time.'

'Well, that's understandable after a bump to the head. I've brought you a little gift of pastries from a local bakery, if you'll accept them. Two almond ones, an all-butter croissant and a pain au chocolat as I didn't know which one you'd like,' he smiled at her, a little sheepishly, trying to ascertain if he was being too forward.

Anna wanted to invite him in for a coffee and to share the croissants but she could hear her dad nagging in her head to be careful around people, particularly men, that she didn't know well. This man had been especially kind and helpful to her last night but he was still a stranger. However, on balance, she sensed she could trust him. 'Would you like to come in for a coffee and you can share them with me?'

He grinned at her, the smile illuminating his handsome features. 'That would be great if I'm not disturbing you.' Anna eased the door open to allow him into the hallway. 'Do you want me to take off my boots?' he enquired, as he gave her the box containing the croissants.

'No, it's ok. Come through.' She led him into a medium-sized living room with oak-laminated flooring, a marble fireplace and French doors leading out onto a patio and small rear garden. Walls were painted with a soft beige colour, and a three-seater cream leather sofa faced a television and flame-effect electric fire.

Colour was added to the room by a blue/grey/green patterned rug and an assortment of deep blue cushions. A small dining table and two chairs were in the corner of the room to the right of the French doors. Anna placed the box of croissants on the coffee table. Feeling nervous in his presence, she stuttered, 'P-please take a seat. I'll make a coffee. It's bog standard instant, I'm afraid. Do you take milk and sugar?'

Nick unbuttoned his overcoat and sat down on the sofa, stretching out his long legs. 'Milk, no sugar, thanks. This is a nice room, very cosy.'

'Won't be a minute,' she muttered, relieved to vacate the room as his presence was very unsettling.

In the kitchen, she waited for the kettle to boil, all the time wondering what she was going to talk to him about. Daftly, she felt as nervous as a teenager on a first date. The kettle boiled and she made the coffees. She took two small plates out of a cupboard and found some paper napkins with a bee design. Taking the two mugs of coffee, plates and napkins into the living room, she placed the mugs on coasters. Anna sat down on the other end of the sofa, leaving a gap in the middle.

'Thanks for the coffee. You must pick the first croissant as they are for you,' he indicated, as he sipped cautiously at the hot coffee.

Anna felt her cheeks redden slightly and she was now pleased that she had applied make-up earlier this morning. Leaning forward, she picked an almond croissant out of the box. 'Thanks. These look delicious.' And she was suddenly hungry.

'My pleasure,' he nodded, and then retrieved an all-butter croissant for himself and bit into it making flaky pieces fall onto his coat before brushing them onto his plate. 'Perhaps I should've brought something less messy,' he said. As he chewed the buttery treat with relish, he asked, 'How's your head and knee?'

Trying now to eat her croissant in a dignified manner, Anna concentrated on biting a small piece and chewing, before responding, 'Not too bad. My knee's still sore when I walk or bend it and my head still hurts. But, all in all, I'll live. Can I ask, how did you know I'd fallen over last night?'

Still munching on his croissant, he replied, 'I pulled over into the layby to have a pee. I noticed you standing by your car, holding your phone in the air, I assumed to try to get a signal. While I was peeing, I heard a thump and you go 'ouch'. When I looked over again, you had disappeared, but you didn't seem to be in your car. Then I saw you face down on the wet tarmac, lying very still, and I was really worried as to how badly you had hurt yourself. It was a nasty tumble and you could've broken a bone. Obviously, I had to help.'

He gazed intensely at her face. Anna looked away and concentrated on eating. 'I'm so glad you did. And knowing what that lorry driver thought I was doing, I'm so grateful it wasn't just me and him. The whole situation was just too awful.'

'Yes, it was. I can't start to think how frightening it must be for a young woman on her own to find herself with car problems late at night. Especially in a semi-rural area with no street lighting and a dead mobile phone. When I worked as a police officer I was called to an incident where a woman was attacked by a 'Good Samaritan' who came to her aid after her car broke down. Being at the site of the incident as forensic evidence was gathered made me appreciate how isolated the place would've been after dark,' Nick explained, but he must have noted the concern on Anna's face, because he added, 'The bastard was caught and sent down for eight years, so that was one less sex offender on the loose.'

Anna sipped her cooling coffee, before commenting, 'It's all very difficult. I was very thankful for your help but I did have concerns about you as well. That sounds awful, doesn't it?'

The smile that was on his face, now slipped. In a firm voice, he said, 'No, absolutely not. You should always be careful in those situations and listen to your gut instincts. You don't know me at all. I could be telling you I'm an ex-cop to fabricate a story and gain your trust.'

'Yes, I suppose so. My dad is always warning me about stranger danger and I have to remind him I am no longer a ten-year-old,' Anna joked.

Nick nodded. 'That's true but then you should heed your father's advice to be cautious around men you don't know.'

Her dad would have cautioned against inviting a stranger into her home so easily. 'Yes, you're right.' She did not know this man but she had been reassured by his kindness, and, partly, because of his handsome looks. Were all predators obvious by their less than perfect features?

Nick now got up from the sofa and brushed a few rogue croissant crumbs off his overcoat onto his plate. 'Anyway, I need to go to do some work. I'm pleased to see you're ok. Is there any further help you want with regards to your car? I could give you a lift to the garage to pick it up when it's ready, if you like.'

'No, I'll be ok about collecting my car. Thanks for all you've done and the croissants,' Anna responded, feeling a little embarrassed about the whole situation.

'Ok, then. I'll leave you to it. You've got my mobile number if you change your mind. Take care,' Nick smiled briefly at her as he headed for the door. 'Here's my business card, just in case.'

After he had left, Anna read the business card:

E-N Security Ltd

Eric Daley – mobile: 07000 000000 Nick Carlton – mobile 07000 000001.

enquiries@e-nsecurity.co.uk

Swift Court, Argon Road, Warwick CV34 5SN

Door Security, Retail Security, Site Security, Mobile Patrols, Manned Security,

Events – public and private. SIA approved.

⚬⚬⚬

CHAPTER SIX

'Hi, babe, I'm glad you're back,' Abbie greeted Nick as he entered the kitchen/dining room of his modern, well-presented, detached home as he walked towards her. She was seated at the kitchen island, tapping her manicured nails on her phone. 'That was good timing as I've just got back from having my nails done. What do you think?' she asked, as she held out her hands for him to inspect her long, acrylic nails in a soft pink varnish with pink glitter tips.

Nick glanced at the proffered nails. 'Lovely,' he commented, not overly interested as all this beauty stuff she was into was beginning to bore him. He liked a woman to take care of her nails, keep them well-manicured and varnished in pretty colours but disliked the long, sharp talon-like ones in garish colours which Abbie favoured. They were not really practical and made her less inclined to help out with jobs around the house in case she 'damaged a nail'.

'Aren't you working today?' Nick asked, frequently bemused as to how she earned a living as a party planner as there was a lot of 'leisure' time for beauty treatments, hair appointments, salon visits and gym sessions.

'I've got to do some work this morning, emails etc for forthcoming events, then that's me done. What's up, babe, you seem a bit grumpy?' Abbie asked, as he went to a cupboard to take out a glass to fill with cold water from a water dispenser in the fridge. 'I thought we could nip into Solihull this afternoon to see if there's a dress I could buy for tonight's dinner party at Eric's. The pink one I was going to wear is ok but I might just check out another one.'

The phrase 'kill me now' ran through Nick's brain. The last thing he fancied doing was to traipse around dress shops on a busy Friday afternoon. Abbie would try on loads of different ones, he would have to give an opinion on each, and then be ignored when she decided on the preferred choice. He would be sat, contemplating how his life had come to this whilst avoiding the stares from snotty shop assistants. After a few hours of mind-numbing tedium they would leave with an expensive dress that he was persuaded to pay for. 'Some of us have actual work to do,' he stated. 'I've got some training sessions on next week and I need to update the training notes and practical sessions in line with SIA guidelines. I'm working in my office to get it done.'

'What's that then?' Abbie asked. 'Trying to prevent some of the bad behaviour of the security staff I see at my parties and events. You want to give them advice on not chatting up the female guests and staff. I'm always being propositioned by the security guys. Some even take women round the back of the premises for a BJ, if they can get away with it. Been there, done that.' Abbie's eyes fixed on Nick as she tried this tactic of trying to shock him.

For a while now, Nick was wondering what he was doing with this woman. She frequently referred to her past in terms of casual hook-ups. At first it didn't bother him as he was only with her for the convenience of easy sex but what should have ended after a few weeks had now dragged on into months. 'If I find out that any of my staff are indulging in such practices they would be out on their backsides before you can say you're fired. And, as I've told you before, I don't want to hear about your sleazy past,' he stated, his voice rising with anger.

'Crikey, Nick, what's rattled your cage?' Abbie asked, taken aback by his response. 'You don't seem to mind taking advantage of all the experience I bring to the bedroom. I don't hear you complaining.'

Ready to close down this annoying conversation about her so-called sexual expertise, Nick said, 'You make yourself sound like some cheap hooker and it's not attractive. I'm off to my office to do my work. Be ready to leave here at six-thirty to go to Eric and Claudia's.'

As Nick went to leave the room, Abbie pouted, sexily, at him. 'Nick, babe, do we have to go? Let's stay in and I'll take away your bad mood. Better than an evening of domestic drivel and smelly kids.'

Feeling his temper rising even further, Nick glared at her. 'Being invited to the home of my friend to have a meal with him and his wife is not domestic drivel, as you rudely put it. And his two gorgeous sons, my godsons, are not smelly kids. If you think that family responsibilities and raising kids is beneath you then this relationship is not going to work, Abbie.'

Nick had been introduced to Abbie by his younger sister, Alyssa, at a night out at a town centre pub. Alyssa had met Abbie through her work in events' management. At first, Abbie had been sassy and flirty. Very confident in all aspects of her life; her looks, her work and her ability to speak her mind on many issues. She was good-looking with shoulder-skimming, wavy blonde hair, hazel eyes, and with a shapely figure accentuated by sexy clothing. Now, he was tiring of her. What he liked as her sassy attitude was now grating on him as it turned into haughtiness and pushiness. She tended to keep a lid on it with him as she sensed he would not tolerate out and out rudeness. But a few times he'd witnessed her out in public being flippant or short-tempered with other people who she deemed were beneath her; waiting staff, shop assistants, one or two of his friends.

Nick was now questioning why he had stayed with her for six months. Call it laziness and access to mutually enjoyable sex. But that incentive was now wearing thin. They did not live together and Nick had resisted her many hints to make their relationship more formal. Abbie talked a lot about how she saw their future together; moving into his house, European city breaks and long haul holidays. Frequent restaurant meals. Ibiza weekends. High cost activities where her financial contribution was minimal. Oh yes, and to cement their living arrangement, they could buy a small dog to become the family 'baby'. Nick liked dogs, preferably large and friendly ones, but a four-legged furry companion would never be a substitute for a child.

Later, they were at the home of Nick's business partner, Eric Daley, a tall, balding, well-built guy of Jamaican heritage, strikingly handsome with friendly eyes and a wide smile. His wife, Claudia, was a beautiful, mixed race woman of Barbadian/white heritage with a curvaceous hour-glass figure. A woman with a thick mass of curly brown hair, melting-chocolate brown eyes and plump lips. But Claudia was more than the physical. She was intelligent, loving and classy, a mother to two young sons, Elijah, seven, and Xavier, four. She was a successful business owner of three jewellery shops. Claudia was currently in the kitchen, finalising dinner whilst Abbie helped. Nick chuckled to himself. Abbie's idea of helping would be refilling her wine glass and avoiding any actual work.

The two boys were now fighting for Nick's attention as each tried to show him their favourite toy. Elijah was shoving a green Lego T-rex towards Nick's face. Younger brother, Xavier, was equally keen to show Nick a brown Velociraptor which had escaped its *'Jurassic Park'* cage.

'Wow, this T-rex has got really big teeth,' Nick stated, as the strong canines locked onto a finger on his right hand, courtesy of Elijah. 'Look, it's bitten my finger off.' Nick held up his hand, ring finger bent down, and out of sight. Elijah giggled and Xavier's large eyes looked alarmed. Xavier then roared at Nick, stabbing the Velociraptor's sharp teeth into Nick's hand. A further finger was then 'disappeared' as the boy's shrieked with laughter. Nick shouted, 'My fingers are back', as he gathered the two young boys in his arms and tickled their tummies. More loud giggles and screams filled the air.

'Ok, ok, boys. That's enough. Uncle Nick doesn't want you two hanging off him all night. Go and play quietly with your toys over there,' Eric ordered, as he pointed at the play area in the lounge/dining room where they were currently sitting.

Nick sipped his bottled beer as he watched the boys start to play with other toys from a large plastic box. 'They're lovely boys, Eric. You are a lucky man. You've got a beautiful family.'

Eric smiled happily. 'Yeah, I know. I sometimes have to pinch myself to count my blessings, particularly when I think what I was like in my early teens. In that gang, dealing drugs, fighting rival gangs, all to live by some macho code of belonging to my tribe. Thank God for a boxing coach who saw potential in me and funnelled my thirst for violence and anti-social behaviour into a more positive direction. It's not all been apples and roses on the way but I'm now where I want to be. My boys will be kept well away from bad influences as long as I have breath in my body.'

'Yeah, Eric, mate, you've definitely got the things that count; a loving wife, great kids, a beautiful home and financial security,' Nick commented, his facial expression rather wistful.

Eric noted this immediately. 'What's up, mate? Your face isn't emanating glowing happiness with your lot. May I remind you that you're thirty soon and should be getting married and having some kids of your own with the lovely Abbie.'

'That isn't ever going to happen. In fact, I've realised that I've just wasted six months of my life with a woman that I shouldn't have wasted two weeks on. We really have nothing in common. Her idea of our future together involves long haul holidays, mini breaks, meals out, and endless shopping, with me being the provider of the necessary cash to finance all this. This so-called relationship is so one-sided and she makes no financial contribution as she's never knowingly paid for anything since we've been together. She barely seems to do any work as a party planner,' Nick paused in his tirade to glug some lager to moisten his throat. 'In her head, I think she feels that she's contributing to the relationship, in terms of her special qualities, her loveliness, female presence and sexual skills. If that's the sum total of what she brings to the table then it would be cheaper if I visited some high-class hookers.' He did whisper the word 'hookers' in case little ears were listening.

Eric looked sympathetically at his friend and business partner, recognising his pain. 'What's brought this to a head? You seemed quite content last time the four of us went out for a meal a few weeks ago. Though I will say that Abbie's attitude to to the waitress was quite embarrassing. No please or thank you. The fuss about her salmon being undercooked. Claudia vowed to never go to a restaurant with her again.'

Nick nodded in agreement. 'I totally get it. She can be rude at restaurants and bars. She says it's because she's in party planning that she expects high standards. Anyway, with my significant birthday looming up, I'm evaluating what I want in life and where I want to be. Abbie doesn't fit these plans of a fulfilling relationship with the right woman and then some kids. Abbie can't stand kids as apparently they smell. She wants a bloody dog, no doubt some small, yappy, finger-nipping furball.'

Eric laughed loudly. 'Tell you what, mate, she has a point about kids being smelly. Wait till you have to change the nappies. So what are you going to do about all this as you're not getting younger?'

Nick laughed slyly. 'Is that so, my friend? One thing's clear, I'll never be as old as you. But I did have a eureka moment this week. I met somebody who made me realise what I'm looking for in a woman. From the very brief time I was with her I noted that she was very beautiful, intelligent, hard-working, determined to be financially independent and support herself, and very likeable. Polite and thankful for being offered help.'

'Blimey, how did you meet this perfect one?' Eric enquired.

Nick outlined the circumstances of meeting with Anna. 'Look, I'm not saying that I see myself with her, though I would be honoured to be. She may be in a long-term relationship. But she was such a contrast to Abbie that I really could quantify that Abbie is everything I don't want.'

Abbie and Claudia came into the room. Abbie sat next to Nick on the sofa and sipped from a glass of white wine. Claudia smiled at Eric. 'I'll take the boys up to bed and when I come down the dinner will be ready. Can you ensure that our guests have got plenty to drink? I know you, Eric, you get stuck into a conversation and forget your duties as a host.'

'Instructions received and understood, my sweet wife,' Eric teased as he got up from his seat. 'I'll get more wine for you ladies and more lager for us boys.' He then addressed his noisy sons. 'Time for bed, kids. Say goodnight to Uncle Nick and Abbie.'

The boys threw the toys they were playing with into a box and rushed over to Nick. 'Night, Uncle Nick,' they chorused as he hugged them and kissed the top of their heads. 'Night, boys,' Nick responded.

Elijah gave Abbie the side-eye, not wishing to engage with her. Xavier a more friendly soul, went over for a hug, but she drew her knees up and leaned back so that physical contact from the four-year-old could be avoided. 'Night, Abbie,' Xavier whispered, his pride hurt by her rejection of him.

As the boys left the room with their mother, and Eric went for the drinks, Nick commented, displeasure with Abbie apparent in his tone of voice, 'You could try a little harder with the boys. Giving them a hug, or at least a smile, wouldn't kill you.'

Abbie gulped down some wine. 'Oh, fuck off, Nick. You know I don't like kids.'

She now glared openly at him as she drained a half glass of wine in a couple of mouthfuls. 'I'm sick of your attitude towards me today. If you are trying to pick a fight then I can promise you one when we get home. So shut the fuck up.'

Nick now countered, 'You can stop drinking that wine like it's water as you get nasty when drunk.'

Eric walked back in with the drinks, a bottle of white wine and two bottled lagers, to an atmosphere so icy that you'd need an ice pick to chip through it.

Later, back at his home, Nick was drinking water in the kitchen to try to rehydrate after too many bottled lagers and post dinner whiskies.

Abbie was sat on a stool at the kitchen island, sipping another glass of wine. As she gazed at her phone, she laughed as she received a text and then responded to it. Her blue, tight, long-sleeved, square-necked mini dress, bought that afternoon, displayed golden thighs. She licked the lipstick off her lips as she concentrated on her phone. 'Yes,' she cheered as she received a second text.

Nick sensed that she was trying to provoke him with this texting, making him jealous that she was in contact with another man. He really couldn't care less.

Abbie's eyes wandered off the phone to look at him. 'I'm in demand tonight. A guy I met last week keeps texting me. We met at that country house venue where I'm organising his fortieth birthday party with a Marvel Comic hero theme. He's loaded. He wants to be Thor with his big hammer and he wants me to be his Jane Foster. I think I've pulled.'

Nick shook his head, trying not to show annoyance. He certainly wasn't jealous, just peeved that she was playing drunken games to wind him up. 'Well, perhaps he'll take you to Asgard and you'll live happily ever after. Anyway, I'm off to bed.'

As he walked past her, Abbie put the phone down, and pulled on his arm to stop his exit from the room. She placed her arms around his waist and cuddled into his chest. 'You've been really off with me today, babe, and I don't really know why. I don't want us to fall out as I really like being with you. I'll come to bed and show you why I'm the only woman you need.'

Fleeting images of another face filled Nick's mind. Wavy mid-brown hair framing a lovely face. Pretty blue eyes, a smattering of freckles, and the most kissable of mouths. Poor Abbie, she was right, he had been off with her today. It had took all his self-control to keep his temper in check with her. Taking Abbie's hands off him and easing out of her embrace, he noted the bewilderment in her eyes.

'Not now,' he said, tersely, as he went to exit the room. The excess alcohol he had consumed would likely keep him awake but he knew that his head would be filled with thoughts of a beautiful woman called Anna.

⚜

CHAPTER SEVEN

Friday 4th March 2022

Luke chomped down on a sausage from the casserole his father had cooked in the slow-cooker from early that morning. 'Great sausage casserole, dad,' Luke stated, dipping crusty white bread into the casserole juices. 'You'll make some woman a good wife one day.'

Jez Milner chuckled. 'Shut up, you cheeky git. In fact, if you want to attract your fantasy woman then she will expect you to know how to cook and clean. You are a lot better at these things than your neanderthal brother but you are still a work in progress. Your bedroom is often in a disgusting state and no fair maiden will be enticed inside if she had to trip over pizza boxes and empty beer cans to get to the bed. Plus, women like a room to smell fresh and fragrant. They do not like the odour of sweaty sock or musty underpants.'

Luke grimaced as his father chuntered on. 'Ok, dad, my room is a mess but I am going to blitz it tomorrow and it will smell as sweet as a bouquet of roses. You are unfair about my culinary skills as I can cook a meal when necessary. I'm so much better than Homer Simpson, here,' Luke joked, staring at his brother, Russ.

'I'd expect a woman to cook for me, particularly if I'm out earning,' Russ said, leaning over to place a further portion of casserole on his plate. 'Men are idiots these days and let women walk all over them.'

'Well, brother, the days are long gone when you could club them over the head and drag them back to your cave,' Luke goaded his brother. 'I would be very willing to look after my beautiful wife.'

Luke quietly ate his meal whilst looking at his brother. They were so different that it was difficult to conclude that they had the same parents. Russ, the eldest, was tall, strong, and facially attractive with dark brown hair, styled short at the sides, and slicked back off his face. There was a hardness to Russ, carved into the sharp planes of his cheekbones, and apparent in his dark, hooded eyes, which when they focused on you were intense and non-smiling. Dark beard stubble also added a ruthless element to his face. He gave off the 'bad boy' vibe which was a magnet for women. Russ was tough and hard working so an asset to the family plastering business. He had the right level of physical fitness and stamina required to ensure that a job was done quickly and efficiently. There could be no slacking once a batch of plaster had been mixed and speedy application was essential. Luke knew that his father viewed Russ as an asset to the business.

But Russ wasn't always the ideal offspring. Russ was self-centred, arrogant and quick to temper which had got him into fights in his youth. He had a chauvinistic attitude towards women who he used and discarded fairly quickly. In his late teens and early twenties he had been involved in criminal activities, drugs, car theft and burglary, which had landed him in jail, for twelve months, for burglary, at the age of twenty-three. This had brought shame to their father but he was now optimistic that his son steered clear of crime. Luke knew that Russ took drugs on a regular basis and dealt them on occasion.

Luke had been reluctantly accepted into the family business but was only useful at mixing the plaster and general labouring. In essence, Luke knew that his father saw him as more of a hinderance than an asset and not suited to the building trade. Luke had not got his brother's powerful physique or stamina. He had not been blessed with good looks like Russ. Luke was of medium height and build, with short, light brown hair, a round podgy face, brown eyes, and a button nose. He was clean shaven as he found it difficult to grow facial hair thus people often thought he was an adolescent and not a twenty-five-year old man.

Realistically, Luke would be more suited to shop or office work but lacked the motivation to put himself into the job market to find a more suitable role. Luke wanted to achieve his dream of writing fantasy novels and getting them published. His dad frequently told him he was away with the fairies. But for now, Luke had to earn money in more mundane ways and his father felt obliged to offer him work. But times were difficult for tradesmen, post-Covid and lockdowns. The costs of raw materials had soared and no business could afford to employ poorly-skilled, unmotivated operatives, and Luke was aware that he was a burden on his father's business. Luke knew that things would soon change. He had found his ideal woman, the muse for his writing, and she would be the inspiration he needed to complete his best-selling fantasy novel. A series of movies would follow. Stand aside *'Game of Thrones'* there was a new kid on the block.

Russ laughed, a smirky smile on his normally hard features. 'Wife, Luke? How are you going to get a wife when you never go out with any women and have never had a proper girlfriend. You live in a fantasy world where you expect the perfect woman to knock on your door. Ain't going to happen, mate. You need to get out there, go on some dating apps. At least you'd get a shag now and then.'

'That's all you seem to do, Russ. It's all casual hook-ups and no commitment with you.' Luke glared at his brother, pointing his knife dangerously in his direction. 'I want more than that. A loving relationship with a beautiful woman.'

'You need to get real,' Russ elaborated, whilst mopping the casserole residue off his plate with a slice of bread. 'You should settle for the average looking ones and be clear that you aren't wanting any long-term relationship. They'll be up for the sex but thinking that they'll change your mind on the relationship thing after a while. But you don't change your mind. Once they start nagging and getting needy, you move on. Anyway, brother, if you want a wife you need to go on dates. Get some action or your dick will shrivel up and drop off as you never use it.'

Luke listened to his brother's take on women and relationships. Due to his good looks, Russ had always been able to attract women. But at thirty-years-old, he had never sustained a relationship of longer than nine months with any woman. He never committed to anyone or fell in love with them. Russ had been deeply hurt by his mother's rejection of him, when he was a boy of ten, and his distrust of females was deeply ingrained into him as ammonites solidified into rock. Russ wanted women but only for sexual gratification and nothing else.

This was not what Luke wanted. He would marry his perfect woman and have children. 'Russ, you are so crude in terms of women. I will strive to achieve my goal of getting the perfect wife.'

Jez sighed, an indication of his weariness at the bickering between the two men. 'The pair of you aggravate me. Luke, you have unrealistic expectations by trying to find a Hollywood beauty and it stops you living a normal life. Russ, you are too detached and unemotional about women. I don't like how you view them as some sort of sex service for your needs. Find a nice girl and settle down. You'll be happier.'

'So, superstud, what are you doing tonight?' Luke asked Russ, sitting back in his chair to rub his stomach after too much food. 'What lucky lady will be experiencing Russ's dubious charms?'

'One I've lined up on Tinder. Meeting at a pub in Barford where she lives then take it from there. Hoping to go back to hers as her kids are with their dad,' Russ explained.

'Go on, then, let's have a look at her dating pic and profile?' Luke pressed, ignoring Russ's scowling expression.

Reluctantly, Russ took out his phone and found, 'Leanne – 28'. A photo showed a smiling young woman with light-brown hair framing an engaging face.

'Profile: Three pros and cons. 1. Pro: Great cook. Con: Best dish baked beans on toast. 2. Pro: Likes to watch sunsets. Con: From pub near canal in Southam. 3. Pro: Fond of a wine or three. Con: Start singing (badly) after two glasses.'

Luke considered the whole profile. 'Nice girl, she looks pleasant. Not the adventurous type. In fact, quite lazy, hence the inability to cook and likes to stay in her local area. Likes a drink but could become rowdy. What made you swipe right, Russ?'

'Sense of humour, easily pleased and grateful for small pleasures,' Russ explained. 'I get sick of the types that are full of grand plans to travel around the world but are never going to achieve it on a hairdresser's wage. They are all going to live their best life and meet a millionaire to enable them to do it. Instead, they meet Kyle at the pub and end up with two kids before they know it. This one's got the kids, got rid of Kyle, and has more realistic expectations. Anyway, I'm off.' Russ vacated the kitchen, leaving the clearing up.

Jez now stood up and stretched his aching back, a result of kneeling to lay the patio yesterday. 'Anyway, you two boys need to both readjust your attitudes to women. I don't want you both living here in twenty years' time. 'I'm off to see Angie. Make sure you do the clearing up. Night son.'

As he started to take the plates to the dishwasher, Luke thought that his father should take his own advice and commit to his woman, Angie, who he'd been in a casual relationship with for years.

⊶⟨⟩⊷

CHAPTER EIGHT

The garage where Anna's car had been taken was on an industrial site in Warwick owned by Justin of JB Car Repairs Ltd. Getting out of the taxi, she saw her car parked in a parking bay outside the garage which she assumed was good news.

That the car had been repaired and was waiting to be collected. The garage was a small size unit, and walking in through the main door she saw two cars, in two bays, being repaired. One car, a white Audi, had its bonnet open as a mechanic leaned in, totally focused on finding and fixing a problem. Anna was hit by the typical garage smell; a mixture of dirty motor oil, petrol, exhaust fumes and engine grease. The powerful aroma hit her nostrils, highlighting to her that she was in an alien environment, which emphasised her distinct lack of knowledge in relation to cars.

Her dad would be berating her now, reminding her that if she was capable of driving a car, she was able to understand how a car engine worked and how to undertake basic repairs. She argued back that if this logic were taken to its obvious conclusion then she would be wise to learn how all gadgets and appliances worked including laptops, washing machines, dishwashers and so on. There wasn't enough time in the world for all this. Dad counterclaimed that the failure of your washing machine was not going to leave you stranded on a layby on a cold, dark night. It was a question of priorities.

Apart from the mechanic working diligently on the car, there was no one else around. Anna walked over to the man to get his attention. 'Hi, I'm here to collect my car from Justin.'

The man, middle-aged and balding, looked up, put down a wrench and wiped his hands. 'Ok. Justin's just in the office working on some invoices. Just go in.'

The mechanic pointed to the office at the end of the garage area. Anna walked to the office where the door was open. The man she assumed to be Justin was sat at an L-shaped desk, staring at a computer screen, with a pile of invoices in front of him. To his left was a printer and a stack of filing trays. Shelving along the wall held a number of lever arch files. Anna knocked lightly on the door. 'Hi, I'm Anna Louden. I've come to collect the VW Polo outside.'

Until this moment, Justin had not looked up from his computer screen. He stopped working to glance at her and then did a double-take as he properly gaze at her which made Anna feel uncomfortable. Penetrating brown eyes scrutinised her face and she could sense he was resisting the urge to run those eyes over her body. His short, layered, platinum blonde hair was on-trend and gelled to within an inch of its life. The word 'vain' popped into Anna's head but then she chided herself for being too judgemental before even speaking to him. Justin stood up to shake her hand. He was tall and muscular as revealed by a black T-shirt showing well-toned arms. 'Wow..er.. I mean, hi, Ms Louden. Anna. Wonderful to meet you.'

'Yes, it's Anna,' she agreed but felt a bit like keeping the formality of Ms Louden. The on-going assessment of her face by his roving eyes made her feel like a car being examined for scratches.

'The car's ready but I was just finishing off the invoice. Please take a seat. Would you like a tea or coffee while I finalise it?' He pointed at a chair to the side of his desk and she had no option but to sit down.

'No drink, thanks. I'll just wait while you complete the invoice,' Anna stated, sitting down on a basic wooden chair hoping that it was grease-free so as not to soil her navy wool coat.

Justin re-settled at his desk. 'You know Nick Carlton do you? We were at school together though I was in the same year as his brother, Ed. Went out with his sister, Alyssa, back in the day. It wouldn't have lasted.'

'All very cryptic,' thinks Anna, hoping not to be given the details of his full dating history as she suspected that it could take a very long time. 'I don't know Nick at all. He just very kindly came to my aid when my car broke down.'

'Well, I think he was very taken with you. Very keen that I should give your car my urgent attention,' Justin teased, a smirk on his good-looking face. 'Bit of advice, though. Be careful. He's going out with Abbie Steele and she's a woman you would not want to cross. Before Nick, she went out with someone I know. When he dumped her for another woman, Abbie posted things on social media about this guy, all of it untrue, but giving him a bad reputation. It nearly got Abbie into trouble with the police.'

Anna sighed, watching Justin as he seemed intent on filling her in on the main branches of his circle of friends and not producing the invoice for her car repairs. 'It won't be a problem for me. I don't know Nick and I don't make a habit of going out with other people's boyfriends. If you could just finalise the invoice.'

Luckily, he did now focus on working on his computer and two copies of the invoice were printed off. He picked up the invoices and gave one copy to Anna. 'As I said on the phone, love, I've had to replace the water pump and the timing belt so the total bill including VAT came to £430. Just to say it could cost you double that at some of those franchise places.'

'Ok, I know the cost of repairing cars isn't cheap. The MOT's due in a couple of months and it should have a service at the same time,' Anna stated, dreading more additional car costs.

'Bring it here, if you like. Do a bit of homework and find out the general costs in the area and you'll find I'm quite competitive,' Justin explained as he shoved his copy of the invoice into a filing tray.

'Yes, I'll do that,' Anna stated, as she rooted in her handbag for her credit card to pay the bill. 'Here's my card.'

Justin laughed which Anna thought a bit rude. She was near to reaching her credit limit but knew she could manage the cost of this car repair without having to ask her father for help. Did she look like someone who couldn't pay their own bills?

'No need for that, love. It's all been taken care of.'

'What do you mean, taken care of? Who's taken care of it?' Anna's mouth opened in utter surprise as she tried to make sense of this.

'Nick Carlton. He phoned up earlier and paid it on his credit card.'

Anna still looked gobsmacked as she tried to make sense of this. 'Nick Carlton. Why would he pay my bill?'

'Are you sleeping with him? If you are, I would suggest you buy a protective vest and helmet if Abbie finds out,' Justin teased but stopped smiling when he noted the shock on Anna's face. 'As I said earlier, I think he likes you. And to be honest, who could blame him. Without being too forward, can I just say you are very beautiful.'

'Oh dear,' Anna exclaimed, ignoring his remark about her looks. 'Can you cancel his transaction and take payment off my card?'

Justin shook his head. 'I can but I'm not going to. Nick said he thought you'd argue and I was not to give in. You should take it up with him directly, if you want. If I was you I'd accept a gift when it's given in good faith. Nick's a decent guy and will not expect anything in return.' Trying to cheer her up, he added, 'It's like that pay it forward thing with the coffees, a nice gesture. You can pay my mortgage for a month if you like.'

'Let's just get back to reality, ok. I'll have to contact Nick directly about paying him back,' she sighed, another hassle she could do without. 'Anyway, thanks for all your help in collecting and fixing my car. Just give me my keys and I'll be on my way.'

'Oh, just to say, as a favour to Nick, I didn't charge you the cost of recovering the car from the layby as it was only a short distance,' Justin grinned, an angelic smile on his face. 'Why not say thank you by letting me buy you a drink sometime, if you are single. But I expect you're too pretty to be single.'

Anna could now find herself getting exasperated by the audacity of both Nick and Justin. 'What is it with you men. I'm quite capable of paying my own way and don't want any favours.' She got up from the uncomfortable wooden chair which had started to make her bottom go numb. Her knee had also gone stiff as it was still healing after her fall last week. 'I'll swerve the offer of a drink, thanks. The keys please?' she stated, annoyance creeping into her voice.

Justin stood up, took the keys off a nearby hook and gave them to her. 'There you go, darling, and the offer of a drink still stands at any time. 'I'll text you,' she heard as she hurried out of the office into the main garage area.

Anna prayed that this wasn't going to be the case but this mechanic was obviously over-confident and cocky so she knew that he probably would. It was a relief to get into her car. Her phone pinged just as she was going to place her handbag on the floor of the passenger side. Taking out the phone, she read the text, **'I need to put some coolant in my body as I'm so hot from meeting you. Justin x'**

CHAPTER NINE

Tuesday 8th March 2022

Anna felt flustered as she drove her car to the commercial premises on Argon Road where Nick Carlton had his company, E-N Security Ltd. She was turning up on spec and she hoped that he would be in so that she could give him the money he had spent on her car repairs. There was no way she was going to phone him as he would likely fob her off and not cancel the credit card transaction. Well, he couldn't refuse an envelope with old-fashioned cash placed on his desk. Having to go to the building society during her lunch break had not improved her day. Trying to find a parking space in the town centre and then joining a lengthy queue wasn't her idea of lunchtime fun.

She'd left work on time for once, struggling with the heavy traffic to get to Nick's workplace, fingers crossed that he'd be in or this would be a wasted journey and she'd have to try again. Also, nagging in her brain, was the foolish thing she'd done earlier today. After a number of cheeky texts from Justin, she had agreed to go for a drink with him tomorrow night. She was very conflicted as to whether she liked him or not. Guessing that he was a bit of a player with women, Anna debated the wisdom of agreeing to the drink. But his texts were funny, and some self-deprecating, which surprised her.

Pulling up at the premises, a low-level brick built building, she parked in a space near to the front entrance. There was an intercom system and she pressed the button for 'E-N Security Ltd'. A female voice responded, 'Nick's in a meeting at the moment. But if you'd like to wait, he will be free in fifteen minutes. I'm Chelsea and I'll come and fetch you.'

Chelsea, a young woman in black jeans and blue jumper, arrived promptly and welcomed Anna with a friendly greeting. Anna was taken to a waiting area by Chelsea's desk and offered refreshments and she said yes to a water. Anna now felt a bit foolish in coming to his place of work. Perhaps she should have phoned him first. But she did not want to give him an opportunity to wriggle out of meeting her. It did not sit well with her that he had paid her car repair bill and she would not rest until he had been reimbursed.

As Anna looked around she could see an open plan office space with some desks occupied, some empty, a total of about thirty desks in all. She could not see Nick Carlton but assumed he had a private office away from the open plan area. After twenty minutes, he was walking towards her. 'Good afternoon, Ms Louden, please follow me.' He was dressed in navy shirt, stone-coloured chinos with mid-brown dress shoes and Anna was again reminded of his masculine attractiveness.

Anna smiled, quite shyly at him, as he led the way through the main office which had large windows to let in maximum light and was made less functional by the presence of plants. Though no Monty Don, Anna recognised a rubber plant, an umbrella plant and spider plants, all large, lush and thriving in cream ceramic pots. Nick's office was separated from the main area by part-frosted glass walls. He opened the door to his office. 'Please take a seat, Ms Louden.' He pointed to one of four chairs around a circular table away from his desk.

Anna sat down in the comfortable chair, and undid her coat, which revealed her knee-length, cobalt blue dress, belted at the waist, and worn with black court shoes. Anna crossed her legs as she settled elegantly in the seat. Nick sat in an adjacent chair and she noted that his eyes did flick over her legs.

'Well, Ms Louden, this is a very pleasant surprise. How can I help you in terms of the security services I offer? Are you in need of a bodyguard?' he said, grinning at her mischievously. 'I think you would be wise to acquire one as you seem to have a propensity for getting into trouble.'

'No, Mr Carlton, I do not require a bodyguard but if a handsome one is available I may change my mind,' Anna teased, going along with the joke.' She reached into her handbag and brought out an envelope containing cash and placed it on the table. 'This is the £430 I owe you for the repair of my car. It was very generous of you to pay my bill but I cannot allow you to do so.' She pushed the envelope towards him.

Nick glanced at the brown envelope. 'Ok, Ms Louden, I appreciate it was too forward of me to pay your bill but I just wanted to do one nice thing for you after you had such a terrible evening.'

Having initially felt annoyed with him for making the payment, she now mellowed towards him, as it was a kind gesture on his part. Anna stated, 'A cup of coffee or a glass of wine would've been more appropriate. In fact, you did buy me those delicious croissants which were lovely.'

'And, how are you now, Ms Louden? Are you recovered from you injuries?'

'Yes, thanks. Please call me Anna. My knee's healing fine. You did a good job with the plaster above my eyebrow, as there's only a tiny scar which will be barely noticeable. Ever thought of being a doctor?' Anna joked.

As he contemplated how to answer, he smiled sneakily. 'A doctor? I don't think I'd have the appropriate bedside manner required as I can be a bit touchy if I see people lounging about in bed for days after major heart surgery. But it might be fun giving injections and ripping off plasters. Does that make me sound like a sadist?'

Anna laughed. 'Yes, it does a bit. Anyway, you have very competent first aid skills. Thanks again for all your help last week.'

'No problem,' Nick commented, giving her a concerned smile. 'I was pleased to help as you were in a bit of a predicament with injuries to your face and knee, no car or mobile phone. Stuck in a rural layby on a dark, rainy night with a dodgy lorry driver.'

The laughter left Anna's face as she recalled what the lorry driver said. 'I still find it really awful that he assumed that I cruised country laybys seeking lorry drivers who may want to pay me for sexual favours. I didn't realise such things happen. I think I've led a sheltered life.'

Nick sighed softly. 'That may be a blessing. I saw too much of the seedy side of life when I was a cop. Anyway, were you satisfied with the car repairs that Justin did?

'Yes, he seems to have done a good job at a fair price,' Anna stated, 'but it's a cost I could've done without. But Justin has been very helpful.'

Nick shook his head. 'He will have been very, very helpful to you. He can't resist a pretty face. He's got a reputation around the town as being a ladies man. My sister, Alyssa, went out with him for a short time. But he likes to keep his options open and started to date another girl at the same time. Alyssa was upset, mainly as her pride was hurt. Justin is a friend but I did call him out at the time for the way he treated my sister.'

'Oh,' Anna said, as her face reddened slightly. Nick immediately picked up on this. 'Don't tell me. He's asked you out on a date?'

Mortally embarrassed, she tried to avoid eye contact with him. 'Yes. He kept texting me to see if I'd go for a drink with him. And foolishly, I've given in. We're going to The Frizzy Lion pub in the town centre for a drink tomorrow night.'

'Well, be careful. Justin comes across as funny and caring but he loses interest in one woman very quickly and is soon onto the next. Justin doesn't get emotionally attached. Just don't fall in love with him,' Nick jested but she did detect a note of hardness in his tone which indicated he wasn't pleased.

'That's unlikely to happen. I'm not looking to fall in love. Just a drink and a laugh. I got the impression that he could be a bit of a player so I sort of know what I'm letting myself in for. Don't buy a wedding hat just yet,' Anna joked to lighten the mood as she sensed a change of atmosphere in the room.

'That's a shame as I have a blue fascinator with feathers that I've been dying to wear,' Nick tried to tease her but there was still a lack of frivolity in his voice.

Anna picked up her bag and got up from her seat. 'Anyway, I'd better not keep you.'

'Thanks for the money. I'm sorry I embarrassed us both with my over-the-top gesture. I'll show you out,' he stated as he opened the office door.

****

As Nick watched Anna Louden exit the office, he was knocked for six at how attractive he found her. Though he had paid for her car repair bill in good faith, as a supportive gesture, he was pleased that she had returned the money as it had given him the opportunity to see her again. With every meeting, his good opinion of her increased. It may be harsh to admit but Abbie would never have declined his offer to pay a repair bill on her car. Abbie never knowingly refused any money offered by him to her. And this was now a major niggle for him. Nick chided himself as he had been weak in being overly generous with Abbie and indulging her by buying clothes, restaurant meals and so on. It wasn't as if Abbie was really grateful for his generosity. It wasn't as if he was overwhelmed by love for her that he used money to keep her tied to him. In reality, he actually knew that he wasn't in love with her and never would be. The whole relationship was founded on an initial explosion of lust which had burnt bright for a few weeks but now like any firework, once the initial flame died, all that was left was scorched paper, all the excitement gone.

Meeting Anna again, in her work attire, he reflected on her beauty; the shoulder-length brown hair that framed her face, blue eyes the colour of cornflowers, enhanced by thick black lashes, and a luscious mouth that he would give anything to kiss. The dress she wore enhanced her body, hinting at perfect breasts, slender waist and overall curvaceous shape. At this moment, he had to remind himself that he was at work, and not allow his mind to wander into flights of fancy where he was making love to the gorgeous Anna Louden.

Nick was also incensed by one other factor. That she was going on a date with Justin Hawley. A serial womaniser. Justin was very poised in the art of seduction, displaying an easy charm, making women laugh with his witty banter, and being superficially thoughtful and caring. Justin's short relationship with Alyssa had started well, drinks in pubs, meals out, country walks and romantic evenings at his flat. For a few weeks, they were a loved-up couple and Nick wondered if Justin really did want a relationship with his sister. It then all went spectacularly downhill. Justin had all the attention span of a fruit fly and was easily distracted by other delicious sweet delicacies. A young, ripe female brought her car in for servicing and Justin was soon offering all sorts of servicing extras. Thinking that he could handle the two relationships, Justin was caught out when a friend of Alyssa's saw him with the other woman in a Warwick pub. The downside of living in a small town. Alyssa confronted him at the garage with a slap to the face and a bawling out. Nick had been tempted to thump him but had let him off with a verbal dressing down.

Now, Justin was going on a date with Anna and this knowledge was a stab to Nick's heart. He didn't want a player like Justin hurting her. Anna was a woman that sensible men wanted. If they were lucky enough to go out with her then they held onto her as there would be many men trying to date her. An idiot like Justin would not see her true value, her diamond quality, her sparkle and vitality. He would dispose of her like all the other temporary adornments he collected. Shit. Since meeting this woman, Nick felt his life had gone off kilter. Anna was a woman he would like to get to know better but at the moment too many obstacles were standing in his way.

CHAPTER TEN

Saturday 14th May 2011

Luke was wetting himself with excitement due to what he had got planned today. His dad was away for the week staying with his brother and sister-in-law in Wales. Russ had been left in charge to look after the house and Luke. Luke had chuckled at this as he was the one who had cared for his feckless, older brother. Luke had done the shopping, cooked a few meals, done the washing and cleaned the house to the best of his ability as a fifteen-year-old kid. When Russ had invited two mates over last weekend to drink, smoke weed and eat pizza, Luke kept his promise to keep out of the way in his bedroom. Unsurprisingly, two girls turned up, Mel and Katie, and Luke kept his fingers in his ears when he heard the noises from Russ's room and he realised that Mel stayed the night. In return for his co-operation, Russ had agreed that Luke could invite a friend over on this particular Saturday.

Thus, Luke's dream girl was due to arrive in thirty minutes. Imogen. The prettiest girl in Year 10 and she was coming to his home. She had glossy, long wavy brown hair, stunning blue-grey eyes, delicate nose and heart-shaped lips. At a stage in life when most adolescents were cursed with spotty skin she had a flawless complexion. But as well as her physical beauty, Imogen was a likeable, intelligent girl, well-mannered and kind to everyone in the class, including Luke. He spent a lot of time at school trying to get near to her. It was the best day ever last week when they were paired together in Biology to investigate photosynthesis. Whilst they sat, heads almost touching, counting oxygen bubbles emerging from pondweed, Luke was close enough to inhale the delicate essence of her coconut hair conditioner. He pestered his dad to buy a similar smelling hair conditioner and would dab some on a tissue at night to remind himself of her scent when he dozed off to sleep. At the time of that closeness in the science lab they had discussed an English homework assignment on John Steinbeck's *'Of Mice and Men'.* Imogen mentioned that she was struggling with the essay and he'd offered to help. She was now coming to Luke's house for this purpose. Russ agreed to stay away for the whole afternoon and early evening.

Luke decided that it should not be all work without refreshments so he had organised some food and drink they could enjoy when taking a break from Steinbeck's tome. Luke was satisfied with his choice of clothes, loose-fit blue checked shirt and blue jeans. Clothes ok, the rest not. His brown hair was longish and floppy, and in need of a restyle. His face was pale and chubby except for a sprinkling of unwelcome acne spots on his forehead and chin. Now, his anxiety levels were high and he was starting to sweat which even a generous squirt of Russ's aftershave was struggling to disguise. A knock on the front door halted Luke's panic.

Luke dashed to the front door, smoothed down his shirt, took a deep breath and opened the door. A vision of teenage beauty was standing before him, dressed in blue denim shorts, white T-shirt, waisted pink jacket and white trainers. In a small purple backpack she carried her school books. Feeling the familiar heat hitting his cheeks, Luke stuttered, 'P-please come in.' He nearly moved in to peck her on the cheek but remembered that this was a school project and not a date.

Imogen smiled brightly at him. 'Thanks for inviting me over. You're so much better at English Lit than me. I can't really say I'm enjoying this novel, it's all a bit unsettling, especially with the death of the puppy. It made me cry, it's so horrible.'

Luke wished that he could've been present when she cried to hold her and dry her tears. 'Yes, I feel the same. At least we're near the end of studying this book.' He led the way into the kitchen/family room. 'Please take a seat at the table. I'll get a drink. What would you like? Cola? Squash? Water? OJ?'

'Cola, please,' she requested, sitting down on a chair and taking the homework and a pencil case out of her backpack.

Luke went to the fridge and removed two cans of cola. He was feeling a tad disappointed that they were jumping into the school work straightaway. But this could be a good thing. Get it out the way and then they could get to know each other better. He placed the can of cola in front of her and sat down opposite her at the table. Picking up the assignment paper, he gazed shyly at Imogen. 'Let's read the passage and then discuss how it adds to our understanding of the relationship between George and Lennie.'

An hour later the work was done and it was time for refreshments. 'All that studying has made me hungry. Would you like some snacks and another drink?'

'Yes, that would be great,' Imogen said, giving him her most beaming smile.

Luke felt that due to his high excitement his heart was missing many beats. Breathing in and out slowly to calm himself, he went to the fridge and got out the snacks he had bought; mini sausage rolls and mini Scotch eggs, all the time hoping she was not vegetarian. A healthy, non-meat option was hummus with carrot and celery sticks. There were also butterfly cakes and Haribo sweets. Luke brought the plates of treats to the table, his face a livid red colour from sweating and embarrassment.

'I love these,' Imogen stated, popping a Haribo fried egg in her mouth.

'What would you like to drink? Another cola or lemonade? There is also a bottle of low-alcohol fizzy wine my dad got for Christmas if you fancy? It's only 5% alcohol so it should be ok,' Luke explained, though in reality he knew very little about alcohol percentages.

Imogen bit her top lip as she thought about what to drink, an endearing action that sent Luke giddy with love for her. 'I suppose I could try the fizzy wine if it's not too strong. I must not get drunk or my dad will go ape.'

Luke brought the bottle and two wine glasses to the table. His hands trembled as he took the foil off the bottle, removed the wire hood and started to push the cork out with his thumbs. This was more difficult than he anticipated and he tried to look manly and not grunt as he did it. Luckily, the cork did pop out and he poured the bubbly liquid into the two glasses. They both sipped their first mouthful, pulling a face as they expected it to be dry, but it was pleasantly sweet.

'Wow,' Imogen said, before licking her delicious mouth. 'This is fruity and I love the bubbles tickling my nose.' She rubbed her cute little nose as Luke stared at her in awe. He knew at this moment he had fallen in love for the first time. They sat for a while consuming the food and drinking the fizz. Imogen seemed to have a liking for hummus, carrot sticks and mini Scotch eggs. Her sugar-rush favourite was the Haribo sweets and he made a mental note to buy her a bag next week. Luke was now getting a sore bum due to sitting on the hard, wooden chair. 'Let's go into the other room as it's cosier,' he suggested.

Luke led the way into the sitting room which had a rustic feel due to exposed ceiling timbers and a stone fireplace incorporating a wood burning stove. Two ageing, cream fabric, two-seater sofas and a Persian-style terracotta rug in front of the fire place, gave the room a cosy vibe.

Imogen wobbled forward, carrying her glass, and flopped on one of the sofas. 'This is comfy,' she said as she tucked her legs under her, very much at home.

Luke followed with the bottle of fizz and his glass and hesitated as to where to sit, next to her or on the other sofa. In the end, a burst of courage made him sit on the sofa with Imogen.

'Want some more of this fizzy stuff?' he asked. She nodded and he filled up her glass.

She turned towards him, hiccupped and giggled. 'I love this f-fizzy wine,' she stuttered, but the word sounded like 'pizzy' and she made herself laugh. 'I am very, very pizzy. Are you pizzy, Luke?'

Luke realised that she had drunk three glasses to his one, mainly as she was his guest and he wanted to be hospitable. It now seemed that she may be getting a little drunk. 'Yes, Imogen, I am a bit pizzy. I am dizzy with the pizzy fizzy.' With that he laughed loudly at his own joke and Imogen doubled over with mirth.

Imogen held out her glass for a further refill and slurped a large mouthful. 'I am in a tizzy being dizzy with the pizzy fizzy.'

Luke, who was a writer after all, had to top this. 'I am bizzy being dizzy and in a tizzy with the pizzy fizzy.' This was too much for him and he convulsed with laughter and he rolled to his right to knock against Imogen.

She laughed hysterically and accidently spat out a small quantity of the drink. Their eyes met and Luke could feel a rush of emotion as he gazed at the large, blue-grey eyes, the colour of a stormy ocean. His eyes then moved to her delicious mouth, moist and inviting from drinking the wine. For a moment, Luke's body was frozen, mesmerised by her beauty. He knew that there was nothing else he'd rather do than kiss her but his adolescent ignorance was holding him back from making a move. He was acutely aware of her inviting mouth but also the closeness of her soft female body. This was sending flames of excitement burning in areas of his own body, most specifically his groin.

Trying to focus, Luke thought, 'what would Russ do?' The answer came in a flash. Russ would get rid of the wine glass in her hand and then edge in for a kiss. Luke placed her glass on a coffee table and leaned over to kiss her mouth. He was tentative at first in case she pushed him away. When she didn't, he tenderly kissed her, enjoying the softness of her mouth and the sweet taste of the wine on her lips. Luke was in heaven. After a few minutes, they paused for breath and Luke studied her face carefully to see how she was reacting. She seemed relaxed and not heading for the door so that was a good sign.

Imogen pulled off the pink jacket. 'Ok, Luke Milner. I am bizzy being dizzy from the kissy-wissy so I need more fizzy pizzy.' She leaned over and filled her glass from the wine bottle and drank it down in one go. 'This is such fun. Have you got any more low-alcohol wine? I t-think we'll be ok if we s-stick to this sort of stuff.'

Luke was now conflicted. He was having the best day a boy could ever have and he did not want it to end. And the low-alcohol wine was making her very happy. He got up and went to a drinks cabinet by the side of the fireplace and peered inside at the bottles of booze collected over the years. There was a bottle of Martini Bianco which he held up. 'We could try this but the alcohol percentage is a bit higher at 15%.'

Imogen eagerly took hold of the bottle, poured the drink into her glass and drank a good few mouthfuls. 'Yum, this is nice. I will soon be drunky as a skunky.' Thinking this hilarious, she rocked with laughter, spilling some of the drink onto the cream carpet. 'Back to the kissy-wissy, Lukey.'

Luke didn't need any encouragement and he was soon back kissing the lips of the most beautiful girl in the world. As his excitement grew, he did a gentle feel of her breast, ready for his hand to be slapped away but it didn't happen. In fact, she seemed to be responding fully to their mutually satisfying encounter. Perhaps this was going to be the day when he could go all the way with a girl. It would make him an equal to Russ who always hinted that he was a master of the art of sex and Luke would never join this secret club.

As Luke's hand eagerly progressed under Imogen's white T-shirt, his breathing was laboured and he squeezed her left breast, above her bra. They were lying side-by-side on the sofa as the kissing heated up.

The door of the room suddenly opened and a cool draft of air filled the room. Luke could hear his father's voice. 'What's going on in here, then?

Reluctantly, Luke withdrew his hand from under Imogen's T-shirt and turned to look at his father. Jez Milner was standing, hands on hips, staring down at his red-faced son and the young woman lying beside him. Sheepishly, Luke pulled himself up to sit on the sofa. 'Hi, dad. This is Imogen from school. We're doing homework.'

'What homework? Biology? How the reproductive system works. Well, son, I'll tell you one outcome can be a baby so I suggest you stop now.'

Further comment from his dad was interrupted by a knock at the front door. Jez went to answer it.

Imogen sat up on sofa, adjusted her T-shirt, and pouted her sexy lips at Luke. 'What a shame. Still, let's have another drinky winky.' She picked up her glass and swigged from it before offering it to Luke, who declined. Jez Milner was soon back followed by a scary looking man who was openly scowling at Luke as he entered the room. Luke realised that this was likely to be Imogen's father, a muscular Jean-Claude Van Damme clone, who grabbed the glass out of his daughter's hand. Hard, intense brown eyes bored into Luke. 'Have you been giving my fifteen-year-old daughter alcohol?'

Luke's head was trembling and his teeth were rattling as he eyed the man's toned biceps displayed by a black T-shirt. 'We've only h-had a low-alcohol fizzy wine.'

The man tugged Imogen onto her feet, and she swayed from side to side, so he had to clasp her around the waist. Imogen giggled nervously. 'It's ok, Daddy, I've only had a lickle drop of the fizzy wizzy wine.' The man then firmly led her to the door, out into the hallway, to the front door. On the outside path, he picked her up and carried her to his car, planting her back on her unsteady feet whilst he opened the car door. Luke and Jez followed, and stood watching the man place his daughter into the passenger seat and then fasten her seat belt.

Luke breathed a sigh of relief. He'd expected a telling off from the man who he guessed would have a short-fuse and a tendency towards violence. Luke thought he might do a little friendly wave to say goodbye to his angel and indicate to her father that there was no hard feelings. The man left the door of the car open which surprised him. He then charged along the driveway towards Luke, an angry snarl on his chiselled face. His head was down, eyes squinting, nostrils flaring and Luke could imagine saliva dripping from his mouth. A raging bull. As he drew closer, Luke's focus moved to the man's right arm as the biceps tightened and his hand fisted. Knowing his intention, Luke scurried behind his father which proved to be a good move for him. But not for Jez Milner who received a hefty punch that landed on his left eye, cutting the area above his eyebrow.

Luke had helpfully brought Imogen's rucksack and pink jacket to give to her father. The man snatched the items out of Luke's hand and then pointed his finger at a cowering Luke. 'Keep away from my daughter, you little prick, or I'll be back.'

━━◅◆▻━━

CHAPTER ELEVEN

Saturday 12th March 2022

Russ Milner sprawled out on Leanne's light grey, faux leather sofa as she went to get him a canned lager. Her semi-detached was a social housing property, north of Warwick, and the other two occupants, her two boys, were currently staying with Leanne's mother overnight to facilitate this date. The lounge was sparsely furnished. A television rested on a grey storage cabinet with one shelf and two cupboards. A wooden coffee table was in front of the sofa, currently cluttered with empty lager cans, an ashtray, cigarettes, a lighter, an empty bottle of white wine and one glass. White plastic boxes full of kid's toys were stacked at the other end of the room next to a small dining table and three plastic chairs. A door led onto a scruffy patio and untidy back garden.

Leanne entered the room with a four-pack of lager and another bottle of wine. She handed Russ another can. 'Here you are.' She opened the new bottle of wine and filled her glass. She then sat down on the sofa, near to, but not touching Russ and she glugged down a few mouthfuls of the wine. 'I need to slow down with this as it's really going to my head.'

'Good,' thought Russ, it will loosen her up a bit as she was coming over as a bit shy. Generally, women he met on his favoured dating site were up for the sex as much as him. For a woman with two kids, Leanne seemed awkward, and was avoiding intimacy with him. Russ really didn't want his time wasted. Their first date at the pub last week had been ok. He was attracted to her, for though she was only passable facially, she did have a sexy little body that was well-displayed in tight jeans and scoop-necked white T-shirt. Glimpses of cleavage down the low-cut top had definitely kept his interest and was the reason for this second date. But this one would have to be worth it. 'So, kids are with your mum. What about the ex having them?'

'It's my weekend to have them. But as you texted about meeting up, Mum said the kids could stay with her. Mum wants me to get back to dating again. After the way my ex, Matt, treated me, she wants me to find a nice fella,' Leanne explained. Russ glimpsed the sorrow on her face as she mentioned her ex-boyfriend and father of the two kids. Apparently, Matt started sleeping with a woman he worked with and they were now shacked up together.

Russ had to suppress a laugh as no mother would view him as a 'nice fella' if they knew the heartless way he treated women. He was willing to see how this thing with Leanne panned out as a short-term arrangement, if things progressed on the physical side. Though he never intended to seek a long-term relationship with anyone, if such a thing happened, it would never be with a woman with children. Acting in the role of stepfather to another man's offspring was something he needed as much as a hole in the head. Mainly, he disliked children and knew that he would not have patience for parenting them. He really couldn't trust himself around kids if they played up, cried, or whined, as he could not guarantee that he could control his temper.

Leanne was curled up on the end of the sofa, away from him. Her brown eyes searched his face as she sipped her wine. 'What about you then? No wife or ex-girlfriend who's broken your heart over the years?'

Russ sighed loudly. This was always the fun bit. He'd tell his 'heartbreak story' and then women saw him as vulnerable and a member of the 'losers in love club'. 'Me, yeah, same as you. Never married. Had a relationship with a girl from school for a few years and I thought we were in it for the long haul. I wanted us to live together, have a couple of kids. Yer know, the usual thing we all want. She worked as a flight attendant, and on the nights away, she was sleeping with one of the pilots. They live in Australia now. Yeah, it was painful at the time. Since then, there have been a few other relationships which fizzled out. So, at thirty-years-old, I'm single and looking for the right woman.'

Leanne's sorrowful expression was reward enough as she bought into the lie of his past heartaches. His two longest relationships had not exceeded nine months and they lasted only because the sex was exceptionally good. After a few months into a relationship, women started to get clingy and look for commitment. Russ always knew when it was time to cut and run.

Russ reckoned the white wine was slipping down nicely into Leanne as her face reddened and body relaxed. She picked up the bottle and topped up her glass. 'This wine's pretty good for a fiver at the cheapo supermarket. Help yourself to the lager?'

Russ's intense eyes scrutinised Leanne. Tonight she looked prettier than last time. She'd applied more make-up, emphasising her brown eyes which were her best feature. This distracted from her fleshy nose and thin lips. The shapely body that he admired was displayed in tight jeans and nipple-skimming black top. He slowly licked his lips, a hungry wolf ready to eat a tasty, delicate morsel.

Russ moved towards Leanne, taking the wine glass out of her hand, and placed it on the coffee table. He pulled her against him for an exploratory snog. The first one. As she gave up her mouth to be claimed by his devouring one, she moaned slightly. Russ used the closeness of the kissing to put his hand on one of her ripe, round breasts and freed it from the restraints of her bra and T-shirt. His mouth paused on her lips and traced a line down to the enticing pink nipple which he sucked greedily whilst she squirmed under his touch.

'This is more like it, Leanne. Us getting to know each other,' Russ commented, pulling her down under him on the sofa. 'You know I liked your dating profile – those three pros and cons.' As she gazed back at him with puzzled eyes, he elaborated, 'I did think about what mine would be, if I wrote in your style. Shall I tell you? Whisper them in your ear. 1. Pro: Great fuck. Con: None. 2. Pro: Well-endowed. Con: None. 3. Pro: You'll beg for more. Con: None.' With that he fully freed her body of her bra and top and resumed the hungry devouring of her delicious breasts. Russ guessed that Leanne was not overly experienced in sex and Moron Matt may have been her only partner. This was going to be a great time for him as he liked to lead the inexperienced sexual traveller into new unexplored territories. 'Ok, babe. Let's have some fun.'

◆

CHAPTER TWELVE

Saturday 12th March 2022

The Frizzy Lion pub near to Warwick castle was rammed with people on a Saturday night. It was a popular drinking place and not one overrun by students; there was a mixed range of age groups and an upmarket vibe. Anna was present with a work colleague, Olivia, and her two friends, Georgie and Kate. Olivia was pretty, with wavy brown hair, but she caught your attention due to her loud and sociable personality. Anna found that Georgie, a sleek-haired brunette, was harder to get along with. Anna sensed that Georgie resented her presence, that she was an interloper into their close-knit gang of three. Kate was blonde, curvy, welcoming to everyone and fun to be around. The levels of noise in the bar were loud. The four women were huddled together into a small circle but it still felt necessary to raise a voice to be heard over the general hubbub.

Due to the difficulty of getting to the bar and being served, the women were drinking white wine and had bought three bottles between them. Two bottles of wine had been consumed quickly and they were now on the third bottle. Olivia was the scarlet lady, in a short, tight, bodycon dress. The more she drank the more her voice went up in volume to high-pitched and squeaky as she told risqué jokes. Georgie, in a silver mini dress, appeared sober and sophisticated, even though she had drunk the same as the rest of them. Kate, in a knee-length purple dress, lacked confidence and concentrated on enjoying the company of her friends. Alcohol made her giggly and more outgoing. Anna, in a dark green, belted, mini dress, was feeling relaxed and happy due to the effect of the wine.

'Well, girls, seen any guys that we could attract over to buy us drinks and chat to?' Olivia asked, scanning her eyes around the immediate area for any rich looking men. 'I'm a bit skint this month due to paying for car insurance and the cost of wine in this place is off the scale. If I go out for the rest of the month, I'm going to drink at home before I come out. I thought of putting a small hipflask of vodka in my bag but I'd be bound to get caught if security do a bag search.'

'I wouldn't dare do that,' Kate stated, 'I'd go bright red and look as guilty as hell.'

Georgie nodded her head towards a group of three men who were glancing over. 'Those three look interested and I'm sure the one in the blue shirt is going to come over in a minute. We keep making eye contact. Leave it to me and they might buy some drinks..'

Anna noted that the man in question was handsome with dark, curly hair and a friendly smile. Having just had a week where she had returned unwanted money to one man she was keen not to be hustling other men for free drinks. Olivia and Georgie had different ideas on this and Kate just fitted in with the general consensus.

Due to the over-crowding in the bar, Anna was constantly jostled as people shifted around. As she moved slightly to let someone pass by with two pints of lager, she accidently bumped into the guy in the blue shirt. 'Sorry,' she stated.

The man smiled broadly at her. 'Do not apologise. It's like a rugby scrum in here but no rugby team has ever had a member as pretty as you. I'm Gavin, by the way.' He was tall, and he stood looking down at her, his eyes carefully taking in the details of her face.

'Yes, hi. I'm Anna. I've never played rugby. Too wimpy, I guess.'

'I played at school but was never a great fan. Though it might be fun to pick you up and run with you to the touch-line,' Gavin jested, moving in closer to her.

'I think you pick up the ball not the other players,' Anna commented, a little perturbed that he was already trying to invade her personal space. His two friends were now in conversation with Olivia, Georgie and Kate. Anna could feel Georgie's hostile laser stare scorching into her as she spoke to this man.

'Can I buy you a drink? he asked, 'Then you can tell me all about yourself. I'm hoping that you are single as you are seriously gorgeous. I come in this pub a lot and I would've remembered you.'

Anna felt herself flushing slightly at the compliments. 'I'm ok for a drink as I'm sharing wine with the girls. I've only recently moved to Warwick so don't really know many people here. I'm here with a girl I work with and her friends. Do you live locally then?'

'Yeah, lived here all my life except for three years at university studying politics. I now work as a journalist for the online edition of a Coventry newspaper which also covers Nuneaton and Warwickshire,' he elaborated, as his eyes continued to focus on her face.

Trying to deflect this gaze, Anna joked, 'Lots of articles on WI jam making and cat up a tree stories, then?'

He laughed. 'You look like a modern woman but have you just time-travelled from the 1950s? Local news has moved on a bit since jam and cats were stories of interest. In fact, I spend a lot of time reporting on crime, drugs, violent assaults and court appearances. Interesting, I know, but depressing as well.'

As their conversation continued there was a commotion to Anna's right, towards the end of the long bar which dominated the room. She could hear 'fuck off' and 'tossers' shouted by a slurry male voice but couldn't actually see what was happening.

Being tall, Gavin had the advantage of seeing what was going on. 'Some argy-bargy between a drunken guy and two of the bouncers. A bit of pushing and shoving as they try to persuade him to leave, I think. I wouldn't argue with those two if I were him, they are well-muscled bruisers.'

'I hate trouble in pubs, I hope they can get rid of him,' Anna stated. Just as she said this, Olivia rushed over to her. 'Watch out, Anna, it's that guy you know, Connor. He's drunk and heading this way.'

Anna now felt panic gnaw in her stomach. When she had first come to the town she had met Connor, all swank and swagger, who chatted her up and persuaded her to go on a few dates. Very big mistake. The man was funny and charming when sober and she quite admired that he oozed confidence. He made her feel special and beautiful at a time when she was feeling lost and lonely. He lifted her spirits. But alcohol brought out his worst side. At one pub he picked a fight with a guy who stared at her for too long, apparently. Another time, he accused her of flirting with a man standing near to her in a bar. Not true. After this, Anna declined further dates and ignored his persistent texts. If she did run into him in a pub, he would badger her for a date. Catching her off guard one night, she agreed to go for a drink in a pub, and he assumed they'd started dating again. This led to him turning up at her house on a Saturday night with drinks and snacks. They had sex for the first time and it was an experience she never wanted to repeat. That was it, absolutely no more contact with Connor.

'Anna, babe,' she heard shouted as he pushed through the crowd, cold brown eyes lasered onto her, an Exocet missile locked on its target. There was no way he was going to achieve the precise and straight trajectory of a missile as he staggered forward, bumping and shoving people, as he moved towards her. 'I've been looking for you, babe.'

Anna felt the hot gaze of every customer in the immediate area now staring at her as they watched the man with cropped brown hair lurching towards her. He came to an abrupt halt in front of her and drunkenly swayed from side to side. Licking his lips, his eyes slowly scanned her face and body. 'You look really hot, Anna, babe.'

'Go away, Connor. I've told you that I don't want anything to do with you.' Anna demanded, in a voice that she hoped was calm but assertive. Luckily, he would definitely hear what she said as it seemed that the whole pub had gone silent and were listening for how this drunken idiot would respond.

Connor seemed oblivious to the staring throng and moved closer to her to put an arm around her waist. 'Don't be like that, babe. Let me buy you a drink and we can get reacquainted. It was s-o-o-o good when we were together last.'

Trying to free herself from the tentacle of his arm clutching her waist, Anna backed away but his grip tightened on her. There were trickles of fear running up and down her spine as she struggled to know how to get rid of him. It was mortifying to be the centre of attention in this unpleasant situation. 'Go away, Connor, and sober up.'

The hopeful, drunken-smile on his face turned instantly to anger. 'Oh, acting like a fucking stuck-up bitch now are you. I don't think so.' Strong fingers grabbed her lower right arm, making her wince.

Gavin now butted in. 'She's said she's not interested, mate. Let her go.' Moving closer to Connor, he squared up to him, determined to intervene.

This did not please Connor. 'Ok, fuckwit, this is between me and her and none of your business, so keep out of it.'

'Ok, ok, folks, stand aside. What's going on here?' Two hefty doormen had now arrived, one tall and bearded, the other a stocky, balding type, a muscular Staffy dog in human form. Staffy's hard facial features were an aggressive scowl, baring his teeth, as he stared at Connor. He weighed up the situation, the grip on Anna's arm, and the fear on her face. 'Right, mate, you need to let this young woman go now while I'm being polite and friendly. Don't make me ask you twice.'

Still holding Anna's arm, Connor's eyes flicked between the two doormen as he considered his options. Reluctantly, he let go of Anna who moved away from him. The two men then stood either side of Connor, not touching him, but their physical presence persuading him not to react violently. Connor surrendered to their authority as he held up his hands in a conciliatory gesture.

'Right you, out,' Staffy ordered as the two doormen started to escort him off the premises. In a final act of defiance he blew a kiss at Anna. 'See you soon, babe.'

As he disappeared, the subdued atmosphere in the area lifted, and people resumed their conversations and their drinking. Anna felt sick and shaken by the whole thing. Olivia gave her a hug and repeated over and over, 'Are you ok?'

Georgie and Kate were now also standing around her and forming a little circle of protection. Kate's pale cheeks were flushed and her voice wobbled as she said, 'OMG, I thought he was going to drag you outside when he grabbed your poor arm. It was all so scary. Thank goodness those two bouncers came over when they did. I've never seen trouble in a pub before.' Kate was a few years younger than the other women and appeared more unworldly and naïve.

'All the wines gone. We need another bottle to give us some Dutch courage,' Olivia stated, draining the last dregs of a bottle into Anna's glass.

Anna gratefully swigged it as her mouth was dry and she hoped the wine would soothe her churning stomach. 'It's my turn to get the drinks. I'll go to the bar.'

'You can't go, you're in shock,' Olivia advised her. 'I'll go.'

'No, Olivia, it's totally fine. I'll go as it's my turn. I'm ok, let's just forget it and pretend it never happened. Same again, girls, another bottle of Sauvignon Blanc?'

Picking up her bag, she slipped through the crowd to get to the bar. It was still busy and she'd have to wait to get served. As she waited, she concentrated on deep breathing to steady her nerves, but she knew it would take a while to get over what just happened. In reality, she just wanted to go home. But if she baled now, Connor would have won, and she wasn't going to let that happen.

A voice nearby roused her from her musings. 'Ms Louden, you must stop following me around or I will take out a restraining order against you.'

Glancing to her left, Nick Carlton was now standing next to her.

❖

CHAPTER THIRTEEN

Anna smiled weakly at Nick not able to summon the necessary energy to laugh at his joke. 'Oh, hi. Yes, it does appear we can't escape each other.'

The middle-aged bartender came over to Anna. 'Yes, love, what can I get you?'

'A bottle of Sauvignon Blanc, please,' she ordered but her voice was croaky and she hoped he could hear above the noisy din.

Nick Carlton grinned. 'Wow, I didn't know you were a serious alcoholic. Is this the first bottle or have there been others, earlier?' A cheeky grin was on his handsome features as he gazed at her.

'For your information, this is number four. And the way I feel at the moment, I could seriously drink it in one go,' Anna said, as the bartender brought the bottle of wine and she presented her card to the payment machine. She really felt drained all of a sudden and in need of a seat.

Nick seemed to note that she was not responding to him with light banter and he asked, 'Are you ok? You seem a bit upset?'

'I'm ok, now.' Anna picked up the bottle of wine to take to her friends.

'Ok, now?' Nick framed this as a question. 'That implies that something has happened, want to tell me about it? Unless you're on a date or something.'

'No, I'm not on a date. I'm with some girlfriends. I'll take this bottle to them and you can buy me a very large glass of Sauvignon Blanc. Thanks.'

After ten minutes, Anna was seated next to Nick, at a table in a quieter part of the pub, a conservatory area with a glass ceiling and plenty of windows. Not all the tables were occupied and she was grateful to sit down to take the pressure off her still trembling legs. Picking up the wine glass, she gulped down two mouthfuls in quick succession. 'Thanks for this. I hope I'm not imposing on your evening.'

'No, it's ok. I'm out for a birthday drink with an old mate from school. There's a number of us and everybody is starting to break into groups, particularly the ones that want to chat up girls.' Nick smiled at her and she could feel his eyes on her, taking in the details of her face and clothes. Often, this type of attention from a man would unsettle her but it never felt that way with him. Even though she didn't really know him, she felt a connection to him. A sense of comfort as he made her feel at ease. That was exactly what she needed right now. 'Anyway, are you going to tell me why you're looking a bit shaky?'

Anna sipped more of the wine. She was not kidding earlier, she could honestly now drink a whole bloody bottle. 'Yes, but don't gaze at me too intently or I think I might cry and you'll think I'm the world's biggest idiot.' Anna outlined the situation concerning Connor, his gripping her arm to try to get her to go with him, and the intervention of the two doormen.

Nick now gently took hold of her right arm and examined it. Her lower right arm was still red and there two faint marks where Connor's nails had marked her skin. 'That looks sore and no wonder you looked upset. I did see a bloke being escorted out by the two heavies. Do you know the man?'

Anna felt herself blushing under her make-up. 'Yes, I do. He's called Connor and I met him in here a few months ago when I first came to Warwick. We went on a few dates and he was good fun, a cheeky charmer type, you know?'

Pulling a puzzled face, Nick laughed, 'Not really. But then I've never dated a man.'

This made her smile. 'Anyway, the cheeky charm quickly disappeared after he'd imbibed large quantities of booze and his inner monster was revealed. He started to become very possessive and would accuse innocent men of staring at me and then pick a fight. After this happened a couple of times, I ignored all his texts and ghosted him. We then met a few weeks later and he's apologetic and begging for a second chance. Being an utter fool, I gave him another chance but again it all went wrong. I haven't seen him again until tonight.' Anna glugged down the wine which was starting to calm her. 'So, that's my sorry tale. I just hope I'll never see him again but it seems impossible to avoid people in this town. Look at us, there's no escaping each other.'

'You're right.' Nick shook his head as he gazed into her eyes. 'What are we going to do with you? You're not safe to be out on your own.' There was kindness in his eyes and she liked that fact that he was teasing her.

Then she remembered that Justin had mentioned a girlfriend so this could only ever be a friendly drink. 'Justin said that you have a girlfriend. Is she out tonight?'

'Yes, she's gone over to Leamington for a curry with my sister and some friends. The males of that town will not be safe with them on the prowl. They're like a pride of hungry lionesses searching for prey, seeking out fresh young blood,' he commented looking pretty relaxed about this.

'Don't you get jealous?' Anna asked but then regretted it as it was a rather loaded personal question. 'Sorry. Ignore me. I shouldn't have asked that, it's none of my business.'

'Don't worry. Do I get jealous? Not really. I'm sure Abbie flirts and wrangles free drinks from men when she's out,' he reflected, whilst finishing his bottled lager. 'Want another drink?'

'That would be great but let me get them this time,' Anna insisted, picking up her bag off the seat.

He placed his hand on hers. 'Ok, Anna Louden. You and me are going to fall out soon over this money situation. I'll go to the bar. A woman, you, gave me a load of cash this week, so technically you are paying.'

Anna was going to object but decided that there were better battles to fight. 'I'll accept another wine and we won't debate who's paying. I only returned to you what you paid for my car repair. So, technically, this is the second drink you've bought me.' As he disappeared off to the bar, Anna took her compact out of her clutch bag and applied some powder to her cheeks and nose. A refresh of her red lipstick was also applied. Plus a quick squirt of perfume on her wrists. Immediately, she chided herself. She was not on a date and this man had a girlfriend.

He returned with the second round of drinks and gave the wine to her. 'Thanks,' she said and tapped her glass against his lager bottle. She drank a large mouthful of the wine, to settle her nerves. Nerves no longer frazzled by her earlier encounter with Connor but with her nearness to this man. The wine was now seriously going to her head and she really must take it steady. After their first meeting when she had been bruised and bloodied, she did not want him to see her in a drunken state.

'I hope you don't mind me asking but how did the date with Justin go?' Nick enquired, a twinkle of amusement in his eyes.

'Ok. We had a laugh but I don't think we've much in common. I hadn't much to say about his favourite topics; Formula 1 racing, Coventry City Football Club and some video game called 'Wreckfest'. The conversation didn't exactly flow at times.'

Anna watched as Nick grinned and then laughed loudly. 'Oh my God. Poor old Justin, having to suffer an evening with a woman who's not into 'Wreckfest' and doesn't know about racing your customised vehicle, defensive driving to avoid collisions and block opponents, or aggressive driving to damage your opponents and get them out of the race. I must send him a 'Get Well Soon Card'.

'You'll be the one needing such a card when you're in a hospital bed eating soup through a straw,' Anna joked, giving him a dagger's look.

He now shook his head. 'Not only are you stalking me but now you are threatening me with violence. I will alert those two doormen to have you escorted out of the pub. You're not as innocent as you look, all big eyes and pretty smile.'

The conversation between them flowed effortlessly. And adding in the pleasure she was getting from the wine, Anna realised that she really enjoyed spending time with this man. They were sitting close to each other, their arms almost touching, and Anna mused as to what it would be like to be held and kissed by him. A subtle waft of his cologne, with notes of bergamot and amber, ignited her senses, taking her to hot desert nights, starry skies, and raunchy kisses in a Bedouin tent on a Moroccan rug. Yikey! Time to pull herself together. Back to the reality of the present where outside was a cold night in an English town at the tail end of winter. Yes, there would be stars visible in the clear night sky but no chance of warmth and passion in a tent outside, only the promise of frostbite.

'Not that innocent' as Britney Spears once said,' Anna teased, noting the amusement on his face.

'Oh, really, Ms Louden. Are you trying to seduce me as well? My mother told me to be on my guard against women like you,' he quipped, but the expression on his face was now serious and his eyes once again surveyed the details of her face. 'I should've listened to my mother. She said all the most dangerous ones come in the most perfect packages. That's you Ms Loudon.' He turned to face her, his intense gaze locked onto her eyes.

Anna believed that they were the only two people in the room, the pub, the universe as they focused on each other. Two people whirling round and round in a vortex which wrapped them in a glowing light outside of which was blackness. She could only concentrate on him, his bewitching blue eyes, and the nearness of his lips which she knew would consume her mouth in a commanding, controlling kiss. His hand touched her chin, drawing her towards him, and she tingled inwardly of the thought of his mouth laying claim to hers. Closing her eyes, she could feel his soft breath on her face.

'Oh, there you are Anna, I've been looking all over for you,' a loud voice interrupted and the magic of the moment vanished in an instant, as fragile as a soap bubble that popped.

Anna quickly drew back from Nick and smiled at Olivia. 'Hi, Olivia. Sorry I should've come over to see what you were doing. What time do you want to get a taxi?'

Olivia avoided Anna's eyes. 'Change of plan. I'm going off with one of the guys, Jamie, for a drink at The Vibe. Georgie and Kate have gone home already. Georgie was pissed as that Gavin didn't seem interested in her. Gavin was asking where you'd gone to and wants your phone number.'

Ignoring this, Anna stated, 'Well, have a good time and I'll see you at work on Monday.

'Are you ok about getting home?' Olivia asked.

'Yeah, I'll be fine. I'll order an Uber.'

'Well, be careful that Connor isn't lurking outside. Wait in here till your cab comes.'

Nick having listened quietly to the conversation, now interrupted. 'She can share a cab with me.'

Olivia now gazed fondly at Nick. 'If my friend isn't going to introduce us, I'll introduce myself. I'm Olivia.'

'I'm Nick, nice to meet you,' he smiled at her.

Anna could see Olivia's interest growing in Nick as her eyes trawled over his face. 'Are you the guy that helped her when her car broke down? Wasn't she the lucky one. If that happened to me I'd be helped by a well-meaning granny in sensible shoes driving a Fiat Panda.'

Anna was now mortified that Nick would think she'd been giving Olivia great detail about his high-class car which was not the case. She'd only mentioned the heated seats as they were so efficient at warming her up after she got cold and wet. Olivia was very money and status-orientated and made no secret that she was going to marry a man with financial stability. Anna commented, 'Yes, I was very lucky as Nick really did help me in my time of need. But then a granny in sensible shoes would've been very welcome. Anyway, don't leave your new friend waiting or he might disappear.'

Later on in the cosy warmth of her bed, Anna tried to sleep but images of Nick Carlton filled her head. His fingers on her chin, drawing her to him for that kiss. She now ached to know what that kiss would've been like. Anna speculated that Nick would be an expert kisser and she felt deflated that she would never find out if this assessment of him was correct. After all, the man had a girlfriend.

⚜

CHAPTER FOURTEEN

Monday 21st March 2022

Luke was doing his thing of lurking around the vegetable and salad aisle of the supermarket, waiting for her, his girl as he thought of her. Studying her pattern of food shopping over a number of months, he noted that she tended to shop on a Monday, a Wednesday, and then on a Friday for the weekend. Her arrival time was generally between five-thirty and six-fifteen. She always headed for the veg area first to purchase healthy vegetables, salad items and fruit. Luke expected nothing less. To protect her goddess-like beauty he did not want to meet her in the biscuit, pies or crisps sections but she did stray into these aisles as well. He'd worked out that her vices were crisps and white wine.

He now lingered in the veg aisle, keeping an eye on the entrance to watch her come into the store. Luke had become an expert 'hoverer' in the area and closely studied the ingredients of salad dressings and stir fry sauces. The store was not too busy for a Monday evening. Then he saw her, pushing a trolley, towards his aisle. As always, she looked stunning and Luke felt that his heart must be wearing out with all the beats it skipped when he saw her. She had on a beige raincoat which was belted at the waist, hinting at a shapely figure, and she had on black, tapered trousers and boots. Her hair was a little dishevelled but it added to her sexiness as it framed her beautiful face. He loved it when she looked flustered, as if she were in a rush, as it gave her cheeks a cute pinkness which accentuated the blueness of her eyes. She stopped at the stir fry section and placed a mixed vegetable bag into her basket.

Tonight's dinner was going to be stir fry with probably chicken and a sauce, a popular choice of hers. Luke mused about cooking a meal for her, eating together at the dining table, and enjoying a crisp white wine with their meal. Two lovers, sharing a life together. Watching as she moved to select the sauce, he noted that the ones on the top shelf were going to be out of her reach. It always made him smile when he thought about how petite and perfect she was. Luke saw her go on to her tiptoes to try to reach a sauce sachet at the back of the shelf. Grabbing his trolley, he turned it and rushed over, before stopping just short of her, a type of manoeuvre that Lewis Hamilton would be proud of. Setting aside the trolley, he was just about to swoop in and say, 'let me' but the words did not leave his lips. A tall male, with designer stubble, got there first. Luke felt his cheeks scorch a fiery red and, to cover his embarrassment, he picked up a couple of bags of beansprouts to examine their freshness. And eavesdrop on the conversation.

The man, with a handsome face and twinkly brown eyes, stared down at her. 'I don't want to be intrusive but do you need help to reach the sachet?'

She blushed slightly, and then laughed nervously, gazing at the lucky man. 'If you don't mind. I'm trying to reach the sweet chilli sauce.'

Luke was intensely annoyed by the man's interference but due to this interaction, he was rewarded to hear her speak for the first time. As expected, she had a warm, sexy voice that sent shivers down his spine. He took out his phone to try to record her and hoped this conversation with the man continued.

The man took down the sachet and handed it to her. 'Sweet chilli, a good choice. Is that your final selection. There are some others up there if you want to change your mind? Teriyaki? Chow Mein? I'm not sure why they're all at the back. Perhaps they've just employed a very tall shelf stacker.'

She laughed at his lame joke. 'Well, it's not a job I shall apply for as it is very frustrating trying to grab items off a top shelf when you are short.'

The man dipped his head as if to say 'glad to be of service'. 'It must be frustrating. However, it is a bonus for me to be tall so that I get to assist very pretty women in supermarkets.'

Luke's favourable opinion of this conversation was now changing. The man was obviously enchanted by her, as he continued to gaze at her, a friendly smile exuding warmth. Luke had to stop himself from making a growling sound, the type of noise a dog may make when seeing off a rival. The way this conversation was going it was likely that the guy was angling to ask her out on a date.

Her cheeks reddened slightly at his comment. 'The chilli sauce is fine, thanks. I must now go and get some chicken.' She placed the sauce in the trolley with the veg and took hold of the trolley handle to move away.

The man was keen to continue with the chat. Luke noted that he was well dressed in a blue suit, white shirt, blue and white polka dot tie, all worn with black leather shoes. Over the suit he wore a grey overcoat. The whole outfit reeked of money and Luke guessed he'd have an expensive car parked outside, an Aston Martin or BMW. It infuriated Luke that this man exuded class and confidence, the type who was generally at ease around beautiful women.

'Before you go, I cannot lose this opportunity to ask for your phone number,' the man said. He was very smooth, with a low, sensual voice that gave him an authoritative air. 'If you are single, and I doubt that you are, I would be honoured to take you out for a drink sometime. I'm Gerard, by the way.'

Luke was pleased that his girl was hesitating. She was not sure of what to do. Luke was sure that a date would not be a good idea. She did not know anything about this man. He could be married with children. A love cheat. A fraudster. A con artist. A smooth operator, expensively dressed, but a dangerous wolf inside the charming exterior. Luke did not want his girl to be hurt. He waited with bated breath for her reply.

'Oh,' she said, and sighed softly, contemplating what to do. She may be tempted as the guy was handsome, well-dressed and friendly. 'I don't know. Maybe grab a coffee, sometime. Discuss which Chinese sauce is best in a stir fry.'

'That conversation would not be over as quickly as you anticipate. I do like to cook and could suggest some sauces you've not heard of, like XO Sauce a Cantonese seafood sauce, or Lao Gan Ma, a mild chilli oil that is a condiment to add to rice and other dishes,' he explained, a slight smugness on his face. 'If I may take your phone number we could arrange that coffee, to suit you.'

Luke wanted to laugh at how pretentious the guy sounded with his knowledge of Chinese sauces. Luke knew that he could only offer up two options in terms of sauce with food, tomato ketchup or brown. Would his girl meet up for a coffee with this man? But he noted that she did give the man her phone number.

Shortly after, Luke was sat in his car, ready to depart the store car park. He was conflicted about the interaction between his girl and the man. He listened to the voice recording of their conversation on his phone and felt a glow of warmth at the knowledge that he could listen to her honeyed voice whenever he wanted. But he could not bear the thought of her going on a date with the man. This could lead to a second date and before long he would be kissing her luscious mouth and making love to her perfect body. The image of this in Luke's mind was a twist of the knife to his gut.

Luke noticed the man getting into a metallic grey BMW, a few rows away. An arrogant, pretentious, flash git. Not good enough for his girl. He'd bore her to death with his waffle about sauces. She needed a fun guy to make her laugh.

Luke did a mental note to scatter a few plasterboard nails around the man's tyres if he saw the car again.

⊷⊶◀◇▶⊷⊶

CHAPTER FIFTEEN

Saturday 9th April 2022

Nick woke up on the morning of his 30th birthday feeling lethargic and not refreshed after a fitful night's sleep. The day ahead was not exactly how he planned to spend this milestone birthday. A number of options would have been preferable; a meal out with family, a city break away for two or a week away at a coastal resort in Europe now that foreign travel was returning to normal after the Covid nightmare. The one thing he couldn't summon enthusiasm for was a party. Yet, a birthday party was happening. The downside of going out with a party planner and having a sister who was an event's organiser. Two different job titles for doing the same thing in his opinion. Two head-strong women who insisted he must celebrate thus all the party essentials were due to arrive in over two hours.

He glanced at the alarm, noting that it was nine-thirty and that Abbie had vacated the bed. In the last few weeks his restlessness regarding his relationship with Abbie was growing. Things about her were irritating him more and more; her selfish streak, her on-going rudeness to people and her desire to spend his money. Last weekend a slanging match ensued when she wanted a spa day at a nearby hotel and he'd refused to pay for it. If sulking were an Olympic sport, Abbie would be a gold medal winner. But sulking did not change his decision and he would not be bullied into giving in. Abbie sensed that he was becoming distant with her and that she was losing him. When not giving him the silent treatment, she was being the sexual temptress to keep him interested. The whole relationship was one big mistake and he vowed to go into this new decade of his life with a clean slate. For the past few weeks he'd evaluated what he wanted to achieve by the age of forty. He intended the security business should continue to grow. It was his personal life which was unsatisfying and stalled. By forty, he hoped to have a wife and at least two kids. The wife would not be Abbie Steele. He had met his ideal woman, a blue-eyed, brown-haired beauty who was also well-educated, intelligent, funny and sexy. Anna Louden. The memory of that near-kiss played in his head at night when he almost laid claim to her perfect mouth. He ached to take her in his arms, hold her, and make wild, passionate love to her forever forward. Cruel as this all seemed, he had to free himself from Abbie, and soon. In the brief time he had known Anna, he knew of three men who wanted her, Connor, Justin and Gavin. There would be others. Once this party was out of the way, he could take action to try to realise his dream of dating Anna. If she'd have him.

As he lay under the duvet, reluctant to leave its warmth, Abbie slipped back into the bedroom and walked towards the bed. 'Ok, honey, are you ready for your special birthday present before you start the day.' Nick studied her as she approached him, dressed in a black camisole which accentuated her soft breasts beneath black lace and highlighted the tops of golden thighs. Black hold-up stockings added a further sexy dynamic to the whole outfit. At other times, this would have been a massive turn-on, but today it would be wrong to indulge in momentary sexual pleasure when in his heart he no longer had any feelings for her.

Abbie did a little pirouette on the carpet and the hem of the camisole spun out displaying more thigh and rounded buttocks. She had applied make-up and waved her hair to heighten her allure. She was holding an unopened bottle of champagne and two flutes. 'Don't say I don't spoil you, babe.' She placed the bottle and glasses on a nearby bedside cabinet. Pulling back the duvet covering Nick, she climbed onto the bottom of the bed and crawled seductively towards him, focusing her gaze on his face.

Stopping at his hips, she started to fondle his crotch with her hand.

Nick was not proud that he was getting aroused but this was an automatic response. 'Ok, Abbie. I'm just off to have a shower. Let's put all this on hold for now.' He removed her hand and got up off the bed.

Lust that was burning hot in Abbie's eyes now turned to anger. 'What's wrong with you, Nick? Most men would die to be in this position. A beautiful woman in sexy lingerie about to fuck you senseless and you walk away. What's this all about as you've been off with me for weeks. Have you got someone else?'

'No, I've haven't. I've just said to put the sexy show on hold as I'm not feeling it,' Nick stated, not wanting to give too much of an explanation in case he lost his temper and told her bluntly the whole relationship was over. Despite his lack of keenness for the party, he didn't want to remember his 30th birthday as a day of fighting with Abbie, ending in her inevitable rage and tears.

Abbie sat on the bed; her eyes as cold as an icy winter blast as she glowered at him. In a sing-song voice, she caustically asked, 'What's up, Nicky? Do you need a little blue pill to boost your performance now that you're an old man?'

Ignoring her taunting tirade, Nick left the bedroom and went into the ensuite bathroom. In the shower, the hot water revitalised his body and washed away his growing annoyance with Abbie. Today, he must concentrate on the party as family and friends were coming with gifts and good wishes. Paint on a smile, play the perfect host. Tomorrow he would take back control of his life.

****

By eight p.m. most of the guests had arrived. His parents, Jeff and Sophia, brother Ed, and sister Alyssa who had entered the house like a tornado bringing noise and chaos. Abbie had refused to speak to Nick for the rest of the day but was cheered by Alyssa's presence as the two women oversaw the party preparations in the kitchen/family room. A colour theme of black and gold had been adopted and two large black banners proclaimed in gold writing 'Nick Carlton 30th Birthday'. Bunches of black and gold balloons were either side of the kitchen island where a buffet was due to be laid out by the caterers. Alyssa's events company had supplied bartenders to keep guests supplied with drinks. In total, about sixty people, family and friends, were gathered for the celebration. Nick was trying to get around, greeting and chatting to everybody, but he was constantly drawn into long conversations by one group or another.

Now in a corner of the kitchen, Nick was chatting to Eric who spotted that he didn't have the look of a man that was really enjoying his own party. The conversation in the room was loud and a playlist of Nick's favourite music had been organised by Alyssa. Currently playing, '*Hey Ya*' by Outkast. Eric addressed his business partner. 'Ok, man. You don't look overly happy at your own party. I know what it is, you think you're past your prime, and it's all downhill from now on. I sympathise, mate, as I felt the same at thirty. What you need is a wife and a couple of kids, no time to worry about old age then.'

Nick sighed loudly. 'Therein lies the problem. Since we last talked the whole situation with Abbie has got worse. I have zero interest in being with her and cannot understand what made me go out with her in the first place.'

Eric grinned lecherously. 'I can see she has a certain attraction. It's on display tonight in that little black, butt-hugging, mini dress she's wearing.'

Nick sighed. 'Yeah, she's breaking her back to ensure that I notice her and flirting with guys to make me jealous. When we're not fighting she's coming over all sexy siren to keep me interested. Well, it's a turn-off and it isn't going to work. I'm tired of it all. But going into my thirties I do want a solid relationship and the possibility of children. I don't want a vacuous life of partying, clubs, spa breaks and holidays, and time spent with a four-legged, furry, child substitute,' Nick vented as he grabbed a bottled lager off a passing waiter.

Nick watched Abbie, standing nearby, talking to a male friend, Noah. She was pretending to laugh at Noah's apparently side-splitting jokes. Once all the party preparation had been done earlier; Abbie started drinking white wine. Flirting openly,now she placed her hands on Noah's chest. He reciprocated by placing a hand on her back. Abbie's face lit up from Noel's touch and her eyes focused on Nick for his reaction. There was none, as he looked away, not taking the bait. She eased away from Noah to come to speak to Nick and Eric. As she approached, Eric said softly, 'She's playing the jealousy card, don't fall for it. I'll leave you to it,' before slipping away to find Claudia, his wife.

Abbie leaned up to kiss Nick's cheek. 'Hi, babe. Honestly, Noah is trying to get off with me. Don't worry, I've only got eyes for you.'

There was nothing that Nick wanted to say about this so he ignored her which didn't impress Abbie. 'I hope you're enjoying your party. I went to a lot of effort to get this organised. You can thank me properly later by giving me the best sex ever.'

'I think Alyssa contributed to organising the party as well,' Nick reminded her. This was another of her irritating traits, claiming the glory for things, whilst putting in minimum effort. He knew that Alyssa had done the lion's share of the work. 'You've both done a good job.' The caterers had now put out the food and Alyssa stopped the music playlist to encourage the guests to eat the buffet.

After all the food had been consumed, a lush birthday cake appeared, covered with soft vanilla and chocolate icing, topped with a gold '30' decoration, and assorted chocolate buttons, Maltesers and Ferro Rocher. A sparkler was lit which fizzed and burned as Abbie gathered everyone around to sing 'Happy Birthday' to Nick. The bartenders were busily giving everyone a glass of champagne. Take That's '*Shine*' stopped abruptly mid song. Abbie stood close to Nick, smiling up at him, and addressed the guests, 'Hi, everyone, thanks for coming and helping Nick celebrate his 30th birthday. We've been together for six months now and it has been an amazing time in my life. I'm hoping that we can continue together on our life journey, just the two of us, visiting amazing places and making special memories. I have truly found the gorgeous man of my dreams.' A few cat-calls were heard from the audience.

Nick really hoped that his face was not showing the revulsion he was feeling right now. He plastered a smile on his face as Abbie gazed lovingly up at him. It all felt so off and for one excruciating heart-stopping moment he thought that she would do something ludicrous and propose to him. That would be the kind of stunt that Abbie would pull. For a moment the room held its collective breath, waiting for some reaction from him. She licked her lips anxiously as he looked at her face.

The guests were now feeling the uncomfortable silence and a chorus of 'kiss, kiss,' started up, led by his brother, Ed. Nick leaned into Abbie and gave her a peck on the cheek. 'Hi everyone. Thank you to Abbie and Alyssa for arranging this party. Thank you all for coming to my thirtieth birthday party to celebrate with me, or commiserate, with me. At this age all doctors and police officers start to look young. Teenagers think you are really old. It's all downhill from here as you leave the fun of your twenties behind but who wants booze, drugs and sex all the time, anyway.' His brother Ed yelled, 'Me, me.' Nick now wanted this over with. 'Ok, folks enjoy the rest of the party and thanks again for coming.'

Abbie raised her glass of champagne. 'A toast to Nick.' 'To Nick,' was the response.

The volume of the music was turned up and disco lighting flashed reds, blues and green colours into the room, transforming the kitchen area into a dance floor. Abbie tried to take Nick's hand to lead him to dance to '*Yeah*' by Usher ft Lil John & Ludacris. 'Come on, babe, shake your booty.' Really not wanting to be near her, Nick resisted. Scowling at him, she started to dance alone, doing sexy hip shakes and bum wiggles to try to impress him. Luckily, she was quickly joined by Aylssa and the two women jiggled and gyrated their bodies like two dancers at a strip club. The next record, Christina Aguilera's '*Dirty*' further incited their raunchy dance moves.

Nick's drink of lager soured in his throat as he witnessed Abbie's desperation. He went over to talk to his brother Ed, and mates, Ethan and Noah. There was a commotion as Justin, joined them, shouting loudly to be heard over the music. 'Happy birthday, bro. Got the pipe and slippers yet?' He nodded at Ed, Ethan and Noah.

'Hi, Justin,' Ed commented, 'Punctual as ever I see. The party started ages ago. We thought you weren't coming.'

'Yeah, went for a drink with my new lady first before we came here,' Justin stated, as he drank from a bottle of lager he'd just acquired. 'Here she is.' He introduced a beautiful brown-haired woman in a bottled green, short-sleeved, fitted mini dress that drew attention to her breasts, slim waist and slender legs. Justin placed a possessive arm around her waist and pulled her to him. 'Everyone, this is Anna.'

⸻◈⸻

CHAPTER SIXTEEN

All males in the group stood straighter and smiled beguiling at Anna. The multi-coloured disco lights swirled around Anna as music blared and nobody spoke.

Justin broke the collective trance. 'Anna, these wankers are Nick, the birthday boy who you've met, his brother, Ed, and friends Ethan and Noah. Anna smiled hello at the group of men, avoiding eye contact with Nick.

'Hi, Anna,' Ed extended his hand to her. 'I've been waiting for this day all my life when we were fated to meet.'

'Hands off, Ed, she's with me,' Justin scowled at him. To Anna he said, 'Watch out for him. I wouldn't trust him with my eighty-year-old granny. Mind you, I don't trust her either.'

Anna ignored this teasing banter as she comprehended that she was at Nick Carlton's birthday party. This was her third date with Justin and he'd asked her to come to a friend's party, and she'd accepted, but was mortified to find out who the birthday boy was. The nearness of him was playing havoc with her senses as he looked gorgeous in button-down navy shirt with dark grey, slim-fit jeans. She was fiercely reminded of that time when they nearly kissed. The memory of that had stayed with her as she frequently imagined how thrilling it may have been. Tonight, she was once again in his company but this time she was with Justin. And in this room would be Nick's girlfriend. Ed started a conversation about a kid from school. 'Do you remember the time he put some of that realistic fake poo on Miss Peabody's chair.....'

Anna pretended to listen when this hilarious school prank story was being recounted, quietly regretting that she was here at this party.

Nick addressed Anna. 'Justin is not looking after you. What would you like to drink?'

'Dry white wine, please,' she responded as Nick grabbed her a glass from a nearby waiter and handed it to her. 'Thanks. Are you enjoying your party?'

He moved away from the small dance area which was occupied by enthusiastic female dancers, including his mother, who were dancing to '*Mercy*' by Duffy. 'Follow me,' he ordered her and went to sit on a stool by the kitchen island, tapping the adjacent stool for her to sit next to him. 'Am I enjoying my party? Yes and no. Yes, as it's great to see family and friends. No, because I'm not really feeling the party vibe if I'm honest.'

'Why, is it because you are leaving the fun twenties behind and becoming old,' she teased. 'Applied for your bus pass? Don't forget to get your seniors discount at Warwick Castle.' Anna smiled as his eyes narrowed and he feigned annoyance.

'What are you implying Ms Louden, that I am now a pensioner? I'm slowing down, my body's wearing out, and I need to find more sedate hobbies? Never. I'm doing a one mile charity stroll next week. My new dentures are at the dentists, smilingly awaiting my arrival. And do not mock my best birthday present, a year's subscription at the bowls club.'

Anna laughed loudly, almost choking on a mouthful of wine she had just drunk. 'So, what are your real plans for the future, do you have any?'

'Yes, to be an advocate for the older generation and deal with cheeky young woman who have very ageist views,' Nick goaded her.

'How do you deal with those young women?' she asked, a quiver of excitement going up and down her spine as she hoped that he might 'deal' with her in a physical way with his strong arms and commanding mouth.

'Well, if my frail body would allow, I would tickle them into submission, and they would be forced to apologise for their ageist jokes about bus passes,' he kidded, as his eyes never left her face.

For Anna, this longing of wanting to be held by him was a tidal wave, building and building, strong and powerful, but never breaking on the shore. He leaned towards her, his eyes locked on hers, and for one heart-stopping moment, she thought he was going to touch her.

As the music continued to play, people danced and sang to favourite songs. Nick used the cover of the noise to say, 'It's been great to see you on my birthday. I'm glad that you came but I can't say I'm chuffed that you're here with Justin. He's a mate but you can do far better than him. Don't let him mess you about.'

Anna blushed, noting the earnestness in his voice. What else was he saying? She kept getting the feeling that he liked her but that couldn't be true as he had a girlfriend. 'I won't. I like Justin, he's funny and a bit silly. But he's also immature, if I'm honest, and there won't be a relationship. I'd like to think we'd just go out as friends now and then.'

'Well, be careful. Justin doesn't see beautiful women as just friends. If you are thinking of a platonic friendship he'll be pushing for more,' Nick commented. 'He does have a bad reputation in this town for not treating women well. I don't want you to get hurt.'

Anna could feel her hackles rising slightly on being given this unasked for advice. But she did have a well-developed habit of picking unsuitable men and getting hurt, both emotionally and physically, so perhaps she should pay attention. Regardless, she wanted to demonstrate that she was capable of making sensible decisions. 'Thanks. I'm hoping to learn from past mistakes. I won't be getting serious with Justin. I'm keeping my options open and going out with a guy called Gavin next week. He's a journalist and seems like a nice guy. We shall see.'

On hearing about Gavin, Anna noted that Nick's face suddenly went from smiley to frowning and for a moment she wondered if he was jealous at the mention of her date. Surely not, this man had a girlfriend. His voice was flat as he said, 'Well, have a good time. Just be careful. I don't think you realise how beautiful you are and will be a target for men, some good, some not so good. Can I add that you look exceptionally lovely tonight.'

This was all getting too intense for Anna. She was more and more drawn to this man in a physical way but she knew he had a girlfriend who he should be concentrating on, not her. Time to find Justin. Getting off the stool, Anna slipped slightly, and to steady herself, her hand ended up on Nick's thigh. Taking her hand away so quickly as if she had scorched it on a burning log, she still felt an electric jolt from the physical contact. 'Sorry. I'd better go and find Justin. Enjoy your party.'

⋯◈⟨◈⟩◈⋯

CHAPTER SEVENTEEN

Abbie stood across the room, standing next to Alyssa, as she topped up her glass from her own personal bottle of white wine. Having drunk a lot, she was slurring her words as she pointed the bottle towards Nick, who was sat on a stool at the kitchen island. 'Who's the f-fucking bitch he's talking to? Have you s-seen her before? Abbie asked Alyssa. 'You know what, Alyssa, I'm f-fucking sick of him at the moment. I've gone to all the trouble of organising this bloody party and he can't be bothered to spend time with me. Now, he's sitting near some bitch, their knees almost touching, as she smiles and simpers at whatever he's saying. Looks f-fucking intimate to me.'

Alyssa grabbed the wine bottle off Abbie and topped up her own glass. 'Yeah, Abs, they do look pretty cosy. Ed said that she's here with Justin. Don't worry, Nick's not the type to play around. He always finishes a relationship before going with someone new.'

'Oh, fuck, Alyssa. That's not giving me any fucking comfort. I seriously think he's going off me as he swerved my attempt to shag him this morning. What man turns down all this loveliness. If it's anything to do with that bitch, I'll kill her,' Abbie's eyebrows dipped, nostrils flared, and she bared her teeth as anger contorted her features. 'I'll get one of those sharp knives out of the rack and stab it through her beating heart until it stops.'

'Jeez, Abbie, cool it will you,' Alyssa chided her friend. 'You're pissed and getting aggressive and that will not impress Nick. Look, she's gone now to find Justin, I assume. You need to go over and talk to him. Have another dance and stop the drinking, ok?'

People had generally stopped dancing except for Ed and Ethan jumping around to Jeff Beck's *'Hi Ho Silver Lining'*. Abbie took her compact out of her clutch bag and quickly powdered her face to disguise faint red blotches and moistened her lips with a high gloss red lipstick. She spritzed a spray of her perfume, a vanilla/rose mix, on her neck and pulled down the front of her mini dress to expose her cleavage. 'Ok, into battle we go.'

'Abs, it's not a battle. You'll only get him mad if you go in all gun's blazing. Sexy and seductive is the best way,' Alyssa reminded her friend. Abbie's features were still exuding an angry look last seen on Mel Gibson as '*Braveheart*' as he fought for Scottish independence against King Edward I of England at the Battle of Stirling Bridge.

Ignoring Alyssa's advice, Abbie stormed up to Nick who was about to vacate the stool. 'Who's that woman you've just been talking to? You looked pretty cosy, I must say.'

Nick looked confused. 'What are you on about, Abbie? She's here with Justin. He and Ed were reminiscing about their school days and she was excluded from the conversation so I got her a drink. That's all.'

Somehow this seemed to placate Abbie, and she stood between Nick's thighs, leaning into kiss him. 'Ok, babe. I thought that might me the case. She looks a bit boring, it won't last long with Justin.'

Pushing her away to avoid physical contact, Nick commented, 'Where do you get that idea from? Actually, she's witty and good fun. Too good for Justin.'

'Yeah, maybe, but I'm not worried about them. It's you and me that counts tonight. Have you enjoyed your party, babe?' Abbie smiled seductively at Nick, her eyes glued onto his. Her fingers trailed upwards along his thigh. 'Poor Justin, that little cow's not going to be the type that keeps him interested. Justin has a reputation for liking sassy, hot women. The ones that get down and dirty. She's too much of a good girl for him and not that sexy.' A cat-like smile touched Abbie's lips as her fingers lingered on Nick's groin. 'All men want a bad girl, don't they, Nicky.'

Nick sprang up from the stool thus halting Abbie's game-playing. When he spoke, the angry tone in his voice shocked Abbie. 'Shut up, Abbie. From what I can see, she's a beautiful, classy woman who is far too good for Justin. Stop bad-mouthing her.'

'Wow, Nick, what's up with you? You starting a fan club for her anytime soon?' Angry hazel eyes bored into Nick's as she staggered slightly due to her intoxication. 'You've been a real shit to me for weeks. You need to up your game or you'll lose the sexiest woman you've ever had. And the best fuck.'

Though her brain was befuddled due to too much alcohol, Abbie hoped that she was making herself clear. What she said was spot on. She had an exquisite face, a curvy, sensual body and her lovemaking skills would make a street girl proud. No other female could offer what she did. For years she had been honing her skills as to what men liked. Learning the art of sexual seduction. Hands that stroked and brought a man to life. A soft, moist mouth used expertly to give a man the ultimate thrill. Now, she had found the man that she wanted above all others and had used all the tricks in her hooker's repertoire to lure him in and keep him interested.

Noting the fury develop on Nick's face, Abbie realised that she had gone too far and started to back track. 'Yeah, sorry, I know that we are sound...'

Before she could comment further, Nick stopped her. 'Ok, Abbie. I don't want to hear any more. I don't want to hear about your so-called sexual prowess. You're drunk and getting aggressive. I suggest that you drink some water and sober up.' He left her standing and went to speak to other party guests.

Abbie grabbed a fresh glass of wine from a passing waiter. '*Survivor*' by Destiny's Child started playing.' That's me, thought Abbie, a survivor. She spotted Justin standing at the edge of the dance area, talking to the woman, with his hand casually around her waist. 'Aw right, Justin, long time no see.' Abbie nodded at the woman. 'I'm Abbie. And so there is no misunderstanding, I'm Nick's girlfriend. You're cute but you're not his type so I suggest you keep away from him.'

Justin's mouth fell open like a stunned fish as he looked at a drunken, swaying, Abbie. 'Ok, Abbie. Anna's here with me and not making a play for Nick. You are making a fool of yourself. Go away and leave us alone.'

Drinking more wine, Abbie turned her full attention to the woman in the green dress. The bitch had a name, Anna. Abbie eyes scanned Anna's face and figure before giving her a look of disgust, the type of distain one has when finding a maggot in a slice of bread. To Anna, she said, directly. 'Look, you. I know your game. Keep away from my Nick or you'll be sorry, ok. Nick's mine.'

Anna backed away from an angry Abbie. 'I haven't got a game, as you call it. I'm here with Justin. I've no designs on Nick.'

Abbie now felt that she was being mocked by this superior little cow. 'Designs eh? Stuck-up bitch. Don't look down your pretty nose at me. As I said, Nick's mine.'

'As I said, I'm here with Justin.' Anna emphasised but Abbie was pleased to note that there was an anguished expression on her just-above-average features. Justin moved closer to his date, ready to step in if things turned physical. 'Ok, Abbie, just cool it. Go and dance.'

'Yeah, right, Justin. I am a fighter and a survivor,' And she started to dance alone to the song, focusing her eyes on the woman, emphasising random words such as 'survivor' and 'make it'. She held up her arms, still holding the glass of wine in her right hand, and swayed from side to side as the wine sloshed about. Suddenly, Abbie upended the remaining half glass of wine down the front of Anna's green dress. Without missing a beat, she sang 'Survivor'.

⸺◈⸺

CHAPTER EIGHTEEN

Nick could hear Justin shout, 'You're a fucking bitch, Abbie. Get away from her.' He dashed over to where Justin, Abbie and Anna were standing in the makeshift dance area of his kitchen/family room. Anna was pulling her dress away from her body in a way that suggested the front of the dress was sodden. 'What's going on here?' Nick asked as his eyes searched the faces of the three people.

Abbie spotting Nick's less than pleased expression, cut in to answer. 'Yeah, a little accident. I was dancing with my glass of wine and I accidentally spilled some on Justin's girlfriend. Whoopsie.'

Justin's pale features were flushed an exotic flamingo pink. 'Accident, you did it on purpose, you bitch. You're still smirking, so don't try and deny it.'

Nick watched as Anna concentrated on keeping the soaked material of the front of her dress away from her body as she avoided eye contact with him. He turned his attention to Abbie who was now cowering under his stern gaze. 'Is that right, Abbie? Have you done this deliberately?'

Abbie swayed slightly, inebriated from all the alcohol. 'N-no. J-just a little accident with the wine in the glass. The wine decided to whoosh out of the glass and down her dress, nothing to do with me.'

Nick addressed Abbie in a loud but controlled voice. 'Enough. Go away from here now and stop drinking.' Abbie visibly flinched at the way he addressed her but this did not placate Nick and he could feel the rising heat of his temper. 'I won't tell you again.'

Noting Nick's furious expression, Abbie registered his level of anger with her. She shook her head slightly to release herself from the grip of some mental fog, knowing that she had pushed him too far. 'Yeah, ok, babe. Sorry.'

Nick's attention was now on Anna. 'Are you ok? Come with me and I'll get you a towel to dry off with.' Nick led the way out of the kitchen, up the stairs and led her into a bedroom. The room was dominated by a large bed with oak headboard, and quality bedding of duvet and pillows in a navy blue/white stripe. An ensuite bathroom led off the room and Nick disappeared in there, before returning with a soft, fluffy white towel. 'Here you are, dry yourself off. There's a hairdryer's in the bathroom if you want a quick blast of hot air. It's not pleasant having to endure wet clothes. I'll leave you to it and come back in a few minutes.'

It was now after eleven p.m., and to be honest, Nick now just wanted this party over and done with. Going over to the bar staff, he instructed them to stop serving drinks so that people would be inclined to start making their way home. His mother, Sophia, a fair-haired, no-nonsense practical type, accosted him. 'Hi, Nick, what's going on? Ed says that Abbie has just thrown wine over Justin's girlfriend. Is that right?'

Nick swept his hand through his hair. 'Yeah, it is. Abbie's had far too much to drink and was jealous that I was talking to this girl, Anna. Abbie's poured wine down the front of her dress. I've taken Anna to my room so she can dry off.'

Sophia shook her head and sighed loudly. 'Oh, dear. I've said a few times to you that I'm not fond of Abbie but at the end of the day I have to accept that she's your choice of girlfriend. But I would seriously question if she is the right one for you. There have been a few instances of her showing herself up at family gatherings particularly after too many drinks.'

His mother was not the first one to comment on Abbie's behaviour. 'Don't worry, mum. I've realised that we are not a match and I've let this relationship go on for too long. It needs to stop,' Nick advised his mum whose sensible opinions he generally respected. His mother had not taken to Abbie but had tried to be welcoming to a young woman who was also Alyssa's friend. 'Can you do me a favour. I've asked the bar staff to stop serving drinks. Can you start encouraging everyone to go home. I've had enough of this party.'

'Ok, son. Will do. I'll go and tell Ed to stop the music after another couple of tunes.' Sophia patted her son's arm before going over to Ed. Despite his annoyance, Nick always smiled when his mother referred to songs as 'tunes'. 'Tune' was a great way to describe Ed Sheeran's *Perfect* not so accurate to describe Rage Against The Machine *'Killing In The Name'*, which Ed played endlessly when they beat X Factor's Joe McElderry to get the Christmas Number 1 in 2009. Nick can still remember his mother shouting at Ed to turn that 'tune' off.

Nick found Justin who was sat at the kitchen island, drinking lagers with Ed.

'Where's Anna?' Justin asked, sipping his beer and looking subdued.

'She's upstairs and I've given her a towel to dry off with,' Nick explained. 'Do you know where her bag is?'

'Yeah, it's that black bag there on the kitchen island, I think,' he answered, pointing to it. 'I could swing for Abbie. It's a pathetic thing to do. She's got a reputation for being a bit psycho. Got a very jealous green streak running through her like a stick of rock. Beware, mate.'

'Yeah, cheers. Duly noted. I'll take Anna the bag and she'll be down shortly. I suggest you take her home and away from Abbie. I don't want any further incidents,' Nick commented.

Nick picked up the bag and Ed jeered. 'Suits you, brother dear. Got your lippy and perfume?'

'Fuck off, Ed,' Nick shot at him before leaving the room. Racing upstairs, Nick knocked at the bedroom door and waited for Anna to invite him in. She was sat on a cream-coloured single chair. 'I've brought your bag. Have you dried off yet?' Nick asked as he gazed at her. It caught in his gut how lovely she was as brown hair cascaded around her face and how her eye make-up enhanced the blueness of her eyes. She caught him looking at her and smiled weakly but it did not disguise the anxiety in her eyes. Nick thought at this moment he could bloody swing for Abbie.

Anna took the bag off Nick and retrieved her perfume, spraying some of it around her neck area, as she joked, 'Better to smell of lotus flowers and peony than sour grape, I think.'

'Anna, I'm really sorry about all this,' Nick commented as he sat on the edge of the bed. 'Drinking alcohol doesn't suit Abbie and can bring out her worst side. Justin said that she threw the wine at you on purpose, do you think that's the case?'

'Justin's right, that was no accident. There was a cold determination in her eyes as she threw the wine at me. I don't know what I've done to upset her,' Anna wondered. 'I suspect my crime was to sit talking to you. Is she the jealous type?'

'Yeah, I'd say so, amongst other things. The relationship, for my part, has been allowed to limp on and I need to sort things out, once and for all.' Nick sighed loudly, feeling weary and annoyed that he'd left things to rumble on when he should've acted more decisively a long time ago. 'I'm not talking out of turn when I say that there have been a lot of examples of inappropriate behaviour and people who's opinions I value are starting to comment. Again, I'm sorry that you got caught in the crossfire.'

Anna got up out of the chair and picked up her bag with the intention of leaving the room. 'It's not your fault. But drinking a lot of alcohol doesn't seem to suit her. It could land her in trouble one day.'

Nick got up off the bed and held the door open for Anna. She stopped as she came to stand by him and he could smell the faint traces of her perfume stimulating his nostrils. Looking up at him, he was mesmerised by the hypnotic blue eyes and plump red lips. It took every ounce of willpower to stop himself from picking her up, carrying her to the bed and kissing the most tantalising mouth he'd ever seen. 'Well, Anna. It was great that you unexpectedly attended my birthday party. Justin's waiting downstairs to take you home.'

A smile touched the corner of the tantalising mouth, as she teased, 'If I am with you and your girlfriend again, I shall bring my waterproof jacket and umbrella. And wellies. Cover all areas.'

Nick laughed. 'Come on. Let's get you back to Justin. If you start to tease me I might put you in the bath for a proper soaking.'

After saying goodbye to his last remaining guests, Nick went into the kitchen area to find that Abbie was seated on a stool at the kitchen island, a large glass of wine in front of her. She was slumped over, head on her arms, as Alyssa sat next to her. His mother, Sophia, placed dirty glasses in the dishwasher and wiped down surfaces with antibacterial spray and a cloth. 'Hi, Nick, darling. Has everyone gone? Your dad's taken granddad home and will be back for me shortly.'

On hearing Nick's name, Abbie lifted her head and tried to focus her eyes on him. Her face was sweaty and any remaining black eyeliner and mascara was now smudged under her eyes. 'Oh, here he is. Been looking after the bloody damsel in distress have you. Miss Green Dress. I hear that she's been in your bedroom whilst you've given her a rub down.'

Sophia stopped the wiping, picked up a glass tumbler, filled it with tap water and took it over to Abbie. 'Here you are, Abbie. Drink this water, it'll sober you up.'

Deliberately ignoring the glass of water, she picked up her wine glass. 'Don't want your water, Nick's mum. Always trying to organise people, tell them what to do.'

'Right, Abbie. That's enough. I told you earlier to stop drinking,' Nick walked over to where she was sat and removed a half-full bottle of wine to place in the fridge. As he did so, the glass tumbler was hurled at him, landing just by his feet where it smashed to pieces. The wine glass followed, sloshing wine over the laminate flooring as it bounced but did not break.

'Stop telling me what to do, you bastard. I've done this amazing party for you, dressed in the sexiest way but you've ignored me all night. More interested in some stupid pixie green whore with Justin. He'll be having a great time tonight with her, it'll be as exciting as shagging a sack of potatoes,' Abbie raged, as she clumsily got down off the kitchen stool. In her heeled shoes, she staggered towards Nick, anger blazing in her eyes. '

'Abbie, I think you need to calm down,' Sophia ordered the drunken woman. To Nick she asked, 'Have you got a dustpan and brush to clear this up before someone gets hurt. She'll cut her feet on this glass in those open-toed shoes.'

Nick was standing, his back to the kitchen worktop, as Abbie progressed in a zig-zag manner towards him, her shoes crunching on pieces of the broken glass. Ignoring her, he said to his mother, 'The dustpan and brush are in the cupboard under the sink.' He could get it himself but a faint trickle of fear was running through him as Abbie's behaviour was getting out of control. He needed to focus on what she might do next. 'Alright, Abbie, you need to go and lie down and sleep off this alcohol before you hurt someone or yourself,' Nick ordered her in a commanding voice.

This now seemed to send Abbie into a sky-rocket soaring level of rage as her face flared a crimson red. 'Will you and your stupid mother stop telling me what to do.'

Alyssa now got down from where she was seated. 'Ok, Abbie, that's enough. Don't speak about my mum like that. Do as Nick says and go into the other room and sleep it off.'

'Fucking hell, are you all deaf and stupid morons? Don't tell me what to do.' Abbie took a couple more steps towards Nick, lurching slightly to his right, as she picked up a sharp-bladed, black-handled knife from a knife rack. 'No one tells me what to do. I'll slice your heads off.' The knife was pointed out in front of her and waved from side to side as she continued to sway and stagger about, almost losing her footing.

Alyssa cried, 'Oh my God, what's going on?' as she paused, hand to her mouth, contemplating the seriousness of her friend's actions.

Sophia stood motionless holding the dustpan and brush, frozen with fear.

As Abbie circled the knife nearer to his body, Nick remained still and calm as she trapped him between the kitchen island and the kitchen cupboards. He was acutely aware that if she lunged at him, and he failed to take her out, then his mother was then within the danger zone. In a calm, but authoritative voice he'd used many times in his police career to try to talk down violent offenders, he stated, 'Ok, Abbie. This is now a serious situation. You need to put the knife down before someone gets hurt.'

Abbie, due to her alcoholic intoxication, thought that this was hilarious. Laughing maniacally, she commented, 'We're in the presence of PC Carlton of the Warwickshire police. I've always fancied a man in uniform. You can get the handcuffs out again.' Laugh. Laugh. 'Note Mrs Carlton, that I said again. Your son likes a bit of bondage play when we're at it in bed. Don't you, Nicky?' Half-closed eyes locked onto Nick's face as she continued to lurch from side to side with the sharp knife before stabbing it randomly towards him.

Nick's body stiffened as he prepared to take action. This situation could not be allowed to continue. There was not a lot of energy as she yielded the knife, no thrusting the blade forward, just a more casual stabbing of it at no specific target. It felt like she was just playing a game to get his attention. But a knife was a lethal weapon, and even if she had no serious intent to harm, the situation could be fatal if she slipped or fell. 'This is your last warning, Abbie. Put the knife down very carefully before you injure someone and you alter the course of your life for ever.'

She now flipped her head from side to side, almost in a trance like state, as the knife was still waved weakly in front of her. 'Nick, Nick. Don't be such a spoil sport. I'm just having a little bit of fun before we go to bed. I can then give you a birthday gift. Whatever you fancy. You can spank my naughty bottom or put the handcuffs on me. Anything you like, Nicky.'

The only thing that Nick now wanted was to get this repugnant woman out of his house and out of his life. Smiling seductively at him, Abbie stepped forward, the knife now pointing straight at him. In a second, Nick had grabbed her right wrist in a powerful, painful grip and twisted it, thus pointing the knife down and away from him. She emitted a high-pitched squeal as pain radiated through her hand and up her arm and she was forced to drop the knife. Nick kicked the knife away, out of her reach, and eased up on the pressure on her wrist. 'Ok, I'll let go if you calm down. Ok?'

Abbie continued to struggle and shriek, trying to escape his grip. 'Ok. ok. Let go, you're fucking hurting me.' Nick let go of her arm and she rubbed her wrist with her left hand. Anger still flashed in her eyes and she brought her right hand up to try to slap his face.

Nick blocked the hit, grabbed her right arm, twisting it around her back and forced her face down over the kitchen worktop. She was impeded from moving by the weight of his body. As her face was welded into the cold kitchen worktop, her cries and screams were muffled. Nick continued to restrain her. 'No more, Abbie. Try one more thing and I will call the police. You'll be arrested for threatening with a weapon in accordance with the Criminal Justice Act 1988. This carries a minimum mandatory sentence of six months' prison and a maximum of four years.'

Any residual attempt to struggle now stopped and he felt her slump. Nick moved off her but continued to hold her down over the worktop. In the next moment, all that could be heard was loud, juddering sobs as Abbie cried, as she continued to lie over the worktop. Nick took his hands off her and moved away. He grabbed a tea towel, picked up the knife, and returned it to the knife block. He instructed his mother. 'Take this out of here to the utility room. Keep the tea towel over the knife to retain her fingerprints on the knife handle. I'm willing to be lenient at this moment but if she kicks off again, I will involve the police.'

A white-faced Alyssa now came over to Nick. 'God, that was awful. Are you ok, Nick?'

Nick felt drained of energy and exhausted as he gazed at his sister's anxious face. 'Yes, I'm fine. She needs to sleep off the alcohol. I'll sleep down here with her in the sitting room to ensure she doesn't try any more stunts,' Nick advised his sister who was shivering from shock. 'Don't worry. This will all be resolved tomorrow.'

❦

CHAPTER NINETEEN

Waking up at eleven a.m., Nick glanced over at Abbie, noting that she was still fast asleep and currently making little whimpering noises as she slept. With Alyssa's assistance, they had brought her into the sitting room, covered the sofa with a bed sheet, covered her with a duvet and arranged towels around the floor area in case she vomited. A washing up bowl was also strategically placed near to her head. Abbie was sleeping in her black dress from the evening before as it would have been too difficult to wrestle it from her almost comatose body. Nick had also slept near to her on the sofa to ensure that she did not cause any more trouble.

Throughout the night Nick lay thinking about Abbie's behaviour at the party. He had been shocked by her excessive drinking, her over-the-top jealousy of Anna and the terrifying situation where she had brandished the knife. It really made him shudder to think that one slip or trip on her part could have caused injury to his mother, his sister, himself and Abbie. But he was resolved now to end this relationship which was bringing no happiness to his life. If last night's incident was anything to go by, it was imperative that he put distance between him and her. He was also stunned at how fast she had targeted Anna and drenched her with the wine. Shuddering slightly, Nick realised that he was grateful that the sharp-bladed knife had not been directed at Anna or the outcome could have been a lot more serious than a mere soaking.

Nick eased back his duvet and sat up on the sofa, rubbing his head with his hands to try to disperse a general mugginess. He'd barely drunk anything last night but he could feel the throb of a headache starting due to lack of sleep. He was certain that he had made the right decision that his relationship with Abbie should end. And end it must, today. For the safety of his family and friends, it was his responsibility to finish with her.

A groan was heard and Abbie emerged from her duvet cocoon, to sit up slightly, and she squinted at Nick as some light shined in through the curtains. Her face was a mess of black eyeliner smudged under her eyes and streaks of black on her cheeks, the result of the heavy crying. Overall, aside from the black make-up grime, her face was pale except for red splodges at her cheeks. She tried to open her right eye whilst shading her face from the light. On noticing Nick, she spoke in a raspy voice whilst looking at him with anxious eyes, 'Hi, Nick. What time is it, babe?'

Nick gazed at her and grimaced. He hated it when she referred to him as babe. The term was generally only used when she was trying to cajole him into something she knew he would be reluctant to do or to make up for doing something he didn't approve of. 'It's just gone eleven. I suggest you take it easy as you consumed a large amount of booze last night and I don't want you spewing up on my sofa.' He tried to hand her a glass of water and a packet of paracetamol. 'Take a couple of these and drink some water.'

Abbie sat up a little and tried to win Nick over with a weak smile. As she moved, a wave of nausea must have hit her and she rushed up off the sofa, out of the room, and hopefully to the toilet in the utility room. After ten minutes, she was back, her face drained of all colour. Appearance wise, she was dishevelled as her black dress was high up her legs, displaying a lot of thigh. The top of the dress was barely holding in her breasts. She smiled slightly when she caught his eyes scanning her legs, presumably thinking that she could pay a penance for her sin with her body and all would be forgiven.

Nick scowled at the sight of her. She was way off the mark if she was thinking that he fancied her. He was finding her utterly repugnant as a man might feel after waking up in bed with a prostitute.

Abbie moved towards him, confident of his interest in her, and sat next to him, her arms encircling his waist. Red-rimmed eyes stared at him. 'You ok, babe? I know I got a bit pissed last night. I can't really remember what I did but I hope I didn't do anything naughty? You know I'm your good girl, right?'

Nick unentangled himself from her grasp and pushed her away. 'Drink the water and take the painkillers. We need to have a chat. I'm going to grab a shower, but I'll be back shortly.'

'Ok, babe. We'll have a little chat but be gentle with me as my head's pounding as if twenty jackhammers are drilling into my skull,' Abbie begged, giving him a beguiling smile. 'Later on when I'm feeling better, I'll give you the little sexual treat you missed out on last night on your birthday.'

Half an hour later, Abbie was still lying on the sofa, covered by a duvet and looking at her phone. Nick re-entered the room and sat down on the sofa, near to Abbie.

She gave him her most winsome smile. Did she really think that her behaviour at the party would not have consequences? 'Hi, babe,' she greeted him. 'I'll go for a shower in a minute and then we can decide what to do for the rest of the day.'

'I think that our plans for the day will become pretty clear when we've had a talk,' Nick clarified. The earlier mugginess in his head had now cleared but an overall weariness was sapping his energy. There was not an iota of regret about ridding himself of Abbie but he was nervous about how she was going to react. 'Right, Abbie. I think it's fair to say that you drank an excessive amount at my party, yesterday. Can you remember what you did?'

Noting his grave expression, and hearing the serious tone of his voice, Abbie's face went from smiley to sombre. 'Oh, yeah. I think I did have too much to drink but it's all a bit of a blank, really. Have I got to make up to you for something?' Dragging the duvet with her, she shuffled over to sit next to him. Trying to place her head on his shoulder, and giving him her best sexy smile, she hoped this would put her on the road to forgiveness. 'I'll give you a BJ if you like, to make amendments.'

Pushing her away from him, Nick moved further along the sofa. 'I think you do remember what happened but are pretending to forget. Let me remind you.' He outlined what had occurred including throwing the wine at Anna and threatening his family with a knife. 'That was a very serious situation as a knife is a deadly weapon and someone could have been injured or killed, including yourself. As I told you last night, and you conveniently don't remember, threatening with a weapon is a criminal offence under the Criminal Justice Act 1988 which carries a minimal custodial sentence of six months up to four years. Do you want to go to prison, Abbie?'

A worried look on her face now morphed into anger. 'Don't be stupid. I won't go to prison. It was just a bit of silly fun to shut you dumb lot up. You and your stupid mother were doing my head in.'

'It wasn't a bit of silly fun, as you call it. I'm telling you now, I was very close to calling the police to have them arrest you,' Nick emphasised, ensuring that she grasped the gravity of the situation.

Abbie's anger was now replaced by a cajoling, little girl, cheesy grin. 'You wouldn't do that to me, Nicky. You love me too much.'

A harsh, rasping laugh left Nick's throat. 'Love. I don't think I've ever said that word to you. In fact, at the moment, I can honestly say that I don't even like you.'

Once again, she edged nearer to him, to try to reach for him and kiss him. Her go to strategy to win him round was sex. 'Look, Nick. I am sorry if I upset you and your mum with my silly antics. I promise to cut down on the drinking.' There was a pleading in her eyes as she registered his displeasure. 'I can see you're angry with me. And I deserve it. But don't finish our relationship because of it. I promise I'll behave in future.'

'I am angry with you Abbie. And disappointed,' Nick emphasised and she shivered as she noted the icy hardness of his stare. 'I can only be with a woman that I respect. Our relationship is over.'

Abbie cowered slightly, a submissive move, as her eyes beseeched him to forgive her. She started to crawl across his lap. 'Nick, I know I have been naughty and deserve punishment. I offer myself to you. Take your anger out on me and you'll feel better and I can repent for my sins.'

Nick gazed in horror at her as she lay across his lap, the shortness of her black dress offering him a view of her ample thighs and the swell of her buttocks. He did give her bottom one hard slap. 'Get up. This is not a game. Don't tempt me because if I did spank your bottom now you would not sit down for a week. Now, I said, get up.' With that, he physically moved her off him and into a sitting position on the sofa. Nick knew he couldn't sit another moment longer next to her and he got up to put distance between them. She looked a mess. Her hair was tangled from her recent sleep, her face streaked with mascara, and she reeked of rancid wine and stale perfume.

'We're over,' he said clearly so there could be no misunderstanding. 'Your outrageous behaviour last night was the last straw. I've put up with your selfish attitude, laziness, greed, and the rude and unpleasant way you treat people for long enough. No amount of chandelier-swinging sexual athletics can offset all that. In fact, while we're on that subject you do overrate yourself. There's too much porn actor and too little real passion, if I'm honest. But last night was it for me. I'm not prepared to put people I love in danger.'

Abbie started to sob. Large, fat tears flowed down, running through the mascara streaks under her eyes and down blotchy cheeks, as she cried and wailed, 'Please, Nick, no. I l-love you. I l-love you.'

This torrent of tears and snot had no effect on Nick whatsoever. He did chide himself for this. How could he have been with this woman and have sex with her but now feel nothing but loathing for her? 'When you've pulled yourself together, you need to get your bag and shoes. I'll drive you home as you are not fit to drive after all the alcohol of last night. After that, we'll arrange for you to collect your car and any of your stuff you have here. Then, I don't want any contact from you again.'

The icy chill in his voice was too much for Abbie. 'Pull yourself together. What am I, a pair of fucking curtains? You're a patronising bastard. Think you're better than me just because you own a business and have a lot of dosh. Well, you're not.' She picked up one of the blue sofa cushions and lobbed it at his head. It missed. 'And, FYI, I take being called a porn actor as a compliment. I'm the best fuck you'll ever have, Nicky.'

'That's enough of the crude talk, Abbie. I'm done with it. Go and get ready to leave,' Nick ordered, his voice quavering with barely controlled anger.

Not making any attempt to move, Abbie rubbed her hands over her eyes to dry the wetness of her tears and swept a hand under her nose to get rid of the snot. She then stared intensely at him. 'I've just thought of something. That girl with Justin, Anna, was she the girl whose car broke down the other week and you got Justin to take it to his garage?' Nick didn't deny it and this seemed to be all the confirmation Abbie needed. 'You know her, don't you? That's why your chat at the kitchen island looked so cosy. I sensed that you knew her. Do you fancy her, is that why you're finishing with me?'

'Yes, I have met her before. She broke down in a layby a few weeks ago and I helped her out. Anna's a lovely woman but as you can clearly see she's going out with Justin,' Nick insisted, not wanting this conversation to continue as it would only rile him further. Two more cushions were launched at his head and he lobbed them away.

Abbie screeched, 'Anna. Lovely. That sums it all up. I could see how you were with her last night, all laughing and joking. If I find out that you've finished with me to go out with her, I shall make it my business to seek her out and destroy her. Do you hear me?'

'Making threats about her is unlikely to win me back, is it? Go and get your stuff as you're leaving now. I'll stop being nice and friendly in a minute,' Nick growled at Abbie, as he moved towards her. Red hot anger was raging in him and he was barely holding back from wanting to strike her. He clenched his fist which Abbie immediately noticed. She now looked genuinely frightened that she'd pushed him too far.

Getting up off the sofa, Abbie was cowered by his physical presence and towering rage. 'Ok, Nick, sorry,' she muttered as she rushed to exit the room to find her belongings.

In the hallway, Nick put on his shoes and jacket, and picked up his car keys, ready to remove Abbie from his life. It felt that he should bring a priest in to perform an exorcism to cleanse the house of her malevolent spirit after she'd gone. Abbie's threats against Anna did make his blood run cold. Abbie's out-of-control behaviour with the knife indicated that Abbie was not a woman to cross.

⚜

CHAPTER TWENTY

After Nick had dropped Abbie off at her apartment, she made it to the sofa, threw herself down and sobbed. And sobbed. There could be no tears left as the crying took hold of her. Loud, wailing noises were only muffled by a cushion. A large hard, cold, solid lump formed and grew in her stomach weighing her down to cause actual physical pain. It was a pain like she had never experienced before. Abbie knew her life had ended. What had she done? She had lost the most perfect man to come into her life. A man she loved beyond life itself and there would never be another compared to him. In terms of looks, he was the most handsome man she had ever seen and she had actually been a little surprised when he'd asked her out on a date. Abbie believed that she was stunning with her blonde hair, hazel eyes and sexy figure. In terms of attractiveness, she rated herself ten out of ten. Let's face it, lots of girls overestimated their physical allure, deluded that they were eights when in fact they were fives. Abbie never had this problem. She could easily attract men, mostly good-looking ones, so it was obvious to rate herself as a ten.

Plus, she had a lot to offer aside from her looks and her body. She was confident and pushy to succeed as a professional woman as a party planner and she used her people and business skills to organise special events for clients. Every man liked a career-orientated, focused woman. She was good at networking, contacting and liaising with the right people to self-promote and win contracts. It was important in business to be ruthless, and determined, to mix in the correct circles where the money and the power were to be found. Helping the rich celebrate those special occasions in their lives, a birthday, an engagement party, a wedding anniversary, a party to celebrate the success of a business venture. Nick upbraided her on occasion about her rudeness to people but for a party to be exceptional the bar staff, caterers, DJ, suppliers of marquees, decorations, balloons, banners, cakes and so on all had to be on top of their game. No place for slacking. Away from work Abbie still expected high standards from staff in bars and restaurants and would not shy away from calling them out for sloppy service. Nick should be proud that she had the guts to point out when good money was paid for shoddy service.

Her confidence also boosted their relationship in other ways as she was sexually experienced and put a lot of effort into delivering him satisfaction in the bedroom. Abbie had many sexual partners and had learnt her craft over the years. She had her own personal kinks that she enjoyed, a strong interest in BDSM, and had brought a lot of variety to Nick's life as she made it clear that she was up for anything. They had indulged in the normal stuff, masks, hand and leg cuffs, some play with riding crops and floggers, and she was sure he'd enjoyed it. There had been pleasure and pain but at times it was still a little too tame for her. A compulsion in her to experience pain at the extreme end of the spectrum was never quite sated. How dare he say that she overrated herself in terms of sexual expertise – that she performed like a porn star and lacked passion. Abbie was passionate, hot-blooded and equal to a man in giving amazing sex. What did the stupid idiot think was lacking? If his greatest desire was to shag the woman in the green dress, what's her name....Anna, he was going to go, in terms of pleasure, from the sweetest, gooiest wickedest, chocolate cake to a dry, bland, beige biscuit.

As her sobbing subsided, Abbie lay on the sofa, her chest shuddering from the physical energy of crying and the resulting hiccups. Nick was going to deeply regret his mistake in finishing with her. She had a great future mapped out for them and she had been determined to move in with him permanently within the next month. They could then start making detailed plans of where they wanted to travel in the world, some long haul trips interspersed with a number of city breaks each year. She'd hinted at taking a trip to Thailand this year as well as visiting Budapest and Copenhagen. A little dog would also be a must have this year, a fluffy bundle of fun, that would make them a proper family. Abbie had her heart set on an adorable little Shih Tzu which she'd name Gigi. Oh yes, that was another thing. Abbie intended that she would press for an engagement and a wedding to happen in a short time. Men like Nick needed to be pinned down, secured, safe away from other hopeful bitches, and marriage was the best way to do this. That would never happen now. Unless.... Abbie forced herself to get up off the sofa and find her mobile phone. Her head was throbbing from the crying and the reawakened hangover. She felt nauseous and hungry at the same time and had a raging thirst. In the hallway, she found her handbag where she had dumped it and retrieved her phone. Going into the kitchen, she filled a glass with tap water and drank it thirstily, also swilling down two paracetamol. She went back into the lounge and sat back on the sofa.

Time to focus on the reasons he had finished with her if her befuddled, alcohol-soaked brain would allow her to think clearly. Nick had berated her on her drunken behaviour and her deliberate act of drenching soppy Anna with the wine. Yes, Abbie could acknowledge that she had drunk too much and behaved badly but women coming onto her man would not be tolerated. They should expect to be challenged. The incident with the knife was not her finest moment but she really had not meant any harm. Nick had totally overreacted and WTF was he thinking when he mentioned calling the police. Typical ex-police officer fuss about nothing.

What else had he said? These words had made their mark in her brain, each one causing a searing pain as if a dagger stabbed into her heart. Selfish attitude? Was he referring to her single-mindedness, a skill she had honed to help her succeed in life? Abbie did look after number one, who didn't? Laziness? It was hard to level this one at her after years of hard graft as a party planner working long and unsocial hours. But over the last six months she had taken her foot off the pedal, happy to relax and enjoy life more at Nick's expense. Hadn't she earned a break? Greed? Abbie liked nice things, clothes, shoes, bags, beauty treatments, meals out and holidays. If Nick, the idiot, was willing to pay, it was not greedy to accept, just realistic. Rudeness? Yeah, she could be unpleasant and exacting to those who deserved it. Nick should be grateful that he was with a strong, independent woman who wouldn't let others take advantage of her. All in all, Abbie did not have the personality flaws he accused her of. Generally, they were assets that made her stand out from the crowd. A she-wolf in a world of sheep.

Picking up her mobile phone, Abbie breathed deeply and thought about the first text she was going to send. Should it be an angry, vitriolic one that started an all-out war? Or should it be a conciliatory one, taking some responsibility for her actions at the party and acknowledging some of what he perceived to be her flaws? Time to tap out the text message.

⚜

CHAPTER TWENTY ONE

Arriving home after dropping Abbie off, Nick lay on his sofa, feeling wrung out and weary. This was not turning out to be a great start to his life as a man in his thirties. He could see clearly now that Abbie was completely crazy and it was a total relief that she was out of his life for good. He seriously could not think why he had got together with her in the first place. After his split with his ex, Helen, he knew that he had wanted a period of freedom with no commitment. He had been with Helen for seven years, and they lived together for five, until their split nine months ago after which he bought his current house.

To establish his security business he worked long hours and at times, to secure lucrative contracts, he'd have to travel and stay overnight in hotels. It dawned on him that when he was away from home, he never missed Helen. Their life together had become dull and routine. She had morphed from a pretty, sexy, fun girlfriend into one that spent all her time on her phone or watching boxsets on streaming channels. Her initial sexiness that had enticed him, of long dark, free-flowing hair, dresses and high-heels, had all but disappeared, replaced by pony-tails, joggers, T-shirts and trainers. Ok, he knew that she couldn't lounge on the sofa in black stilettos but she made no effort on the rare occasion they went out for a meal or a visit to family. The sexual spark had long fizzled out. When he initiated sex, she endured it, but wanted it over as quickly as possible. Nick knew he could never be happy with a life of no sex.

It had all come to a head when he had met the woman. An auburn-haired, green-eyed beauty in an hotel in Cheshire whilst securing contracts to provide security staff to venues in the North West. Nick was sat at a hotel bar, enjoying a couple of whiskies, when the woman had sat next to him on a vacant stool. She wore a tight-fitting green dress, the colour of her eyes. Long glossy hair. Cat-like green eyes enhanced by black mascara on long, but natural, eyelashes. Luscious lips stained by ruby red lipstick. Slender legs made sexier by black heels with diamante straps. They got talking, buying drinks, mild flirting. But then she leaned into him, a hand on his arm, and their eyes locked. He was then in her room. The green dress hit the floor. Black, hold-up stockings blew his mind. The black heels remained on her feet. Nick felt the most powerful surge of lust, a tidal wave washing through him, as he laid her on the bed. His hungry mouth devoured hers. His strong hands squeezed her perfect breasts. As a man, he felt an inner beast unleashed, powering and driving him. He needed to make her yield, place her under his total control. He freed her breasts from the confines of her bra and subjected her nipples to the harsh caress of his mouth as she groaned softly. Moving downwards, his mouth and fingers took control, and she moaned, and writhed from his touch, as he explored the most intimate spot of her sex.

Grabbing his hair, to ensure that his tongue continued to excite her to an exquisite ecstasy, she pleaded with him to take her. But this was Nick's show. He had control and there was more begging to do before he allowed her the joy of release. He flipped her on to her stomach. She strained and arched her hips, enticing him to take her but he continued to hold back until he was ready. He slapped her proffered bum and continued with his hands and mouth to arouse her, and was rewarded with her begging to be taken. His own lust was a wanton, super-charged desire, an unstoppable need to possess her in a primal way. Eventually, as she pleaded for release; he was ready to give her what she desired. Her entered her, and thrust into her, over and over again, as a raw savage power swept through him, until he felt her juddering climax which synced with his own.

That night changed the course of his life. The woman, Vanessa, would never be his. She had a husband and a kid. But Nick knew he must finish with Helen. He could not endure a life with a woman who only offered routine sex and slopped around in jogging bottoms. His explosive sexual power of that night was, in part, due to the stockings and heels.

He swapped the woman called Vanessa for one called Abbie. Surfing on a tide of lust after the encounter with Vanessa, Abbie seemed perfect. She'd easily agreed to come back to his house on the first night and a raunchy sex fest of multiple positions went on all night. It was not quite of the Olympic gold standard of Vanessa but Nick was only focused on frequent, intense encounters. Abbie was up for anything and very soon she was almost permanently residing at his house so they could indulge their craving for each other. His credit card took some hits when she ordered a range of lingerie and sex toys from a well-known retailer. But as quickly as the sexual rocket took flight, it exploded, burned and broke. Nick's eagerness for Abbie's sexual hotness started to fade and the blinkers, bondage style, fell away from his eyes. He was a man who had lost touch with reality for a short while and had swirled in a murky mire of lust and, to a certain extent, depravity. Waking up from it all, he soon grasped who the real Abbie was, self-centred, rude and greedy.

Today, Nick was free of Abbie but he wanted also to be free of the sexual fever that had consumed him for a short period of his life. To be free of the addictive, orgasmic rush of oxytocin that compelled him to engage in frequent sex with a willing Abbie. But ultimately it all became unemotional and cold on his part. It had helped that he had met Anna. She didn't know it but her presence in his life was taking him back to normality. Yes, he yearned to kiss her. Yes, he longed to make love to her. But if this were to happen he wanted it to be without the all-consuming, damaging, lust-surge that could destroy him if he found another Vanessa or Abbie. With the next woman he wanted an emotional connection as well as a physical one. If the woman was Anna, all the better.

A text pinged on his phone. Before even looking at it he guessed it would be from Abbie. He picked up the phone and read the text. '**Nicky, babe. I can fix this. Don't throw it all away including great sex due to a little drunken idiocy on my part. We should talk. Abbie xxx**'

Nick shook his head. Typical Abbie, never took responsibility for her actions. No, darling, it can't be fixed. 'It' was not worth keeping. The 'great sex' was all a hollow sham. A 'little drunken idiocy' was you stumbling around in an inebriated state with a knife in your hand endangering my mother, sister, and myself. There's nothing to talk about. I told you earlier how I felt. Quite clearly. This was what Nick wanted to text but he did not have the inclination or energy. Instead, he texted '**I told you; we are over. There is no going back.**' He pressed send and felt a glimmer of relief.

CHAPTER TWENTY TWO

Thursday 14th April 2022

Getting out of her car at her local supermarket, in the early evening, Anna was in a good mood. The day had been pleasantly warm for mid-April and she had a four day break from work to look forward to. Two public holidays, Good Friday, and Easter Monday, which straddled the Easter weekend. On this Thursday, she was buying something tasty for dinner and then intended to chill with a glass of wine and a good film. On Saturday, she was going for a meal with Gavin so hopefully this weekend would work out fine.

Since last Saturday, Nick's 30th birthday party, Justin had been texting her to meet up again but she was stalling him. Justin was fun, and a bit silly, but she couldn't see the relationship going anywhere. If she were honest, she needed a bit more intellectual depth in a man. Anna recognised that she was no Laura Kuenssberg but she did take an interest in politics and current news events. Justin's interests did not extend further than football, cars, gaming and going to the gym. Also, their relationship was currently at the kissing stage and Anna had no interest in taking things further. Justin was good-looking with a toned body but she felt no real sexual connection with him. Realistically, it was time to call it a day.

Inside the supermarket it was busy as everyone was stocking up for the bank holiday weekend and the weather was forecast as sunny and warm. Anna wandered around the food aisles having put some items into her trolley including semi-skimmed milk, wholemeal bread, a tuna pasta bake, a bagged salad, and a cucumber. There was also the essentials, crisps and two bottles of white wine. Noticing a display of tulips, she decided to give herself a treat as she would not be buying an Easter egg. She stood contemplating what to buy, one individual colour or a mixed bunch. In the end, she decided on a mixed bunch of whites, yellows, purples and oranges. Tulips weren't her favourite spring flower, she preferred daffodils, but the time for those was over and she really wanted the joy of spring flowers to brighten her home. As she went to pick up a bunch, a young man to her right also went to take the same bunch out of the display bucket. 'Oh, sorry,' he said, a bright red flush washing over his pale, round face. 'Please, you go first.'

Anna muttered, 'Thanks' and placed a bunch of tulips in her trolley.

The man then picked up his bunch of tulips and smiled shyly at her. 'I love tulips at Easter time. My mother always used to have some in a vase on Easter Sunday.' His eyes intensely scrutinised Anna's face and she had to glance away from his penetrating gaze.

Anna felt that she ought to respond to this but how. Was he implying that his mother was dead or was it just a casual comment about a mum who would be cooking him a lamb roast dinner on Easter Sunday? 'Yes, they are really beautiful and it's the one time of year I like to buy flowers for my home. They bring the joy of spring indoors after a long, dark winter.'

An expression of happiness lit up his face. 'Gosh, you are so right. After all the endless cold, grim days it's lovely to be reminded that spring and summer are on the horizon.'

Feeling that he was inclined to linger, Anna wanted to get on with her shopping. 'Anyway, have a happy Easter,' she said, turning her trolley to return back to the fruit aisle to buy a melon/strawberry fruit mix she had forgotten earlier. For now, this was all the shopping she needed. Her date with Gavin was going to be at an Italian restaurant where she was really looking forward to having a pizza topped with mushrooms and black olives. Anna decided on a self-service till to pay and she quickly breezed through and walked out of the exit door.

Just as she was heading for her car, a voice calling, 'Miss, Miss,' distracted her. Not sure if the voice was calling her or not, Anna did look around and noted that the guy from earlier was waving at her. Thinking she may have dropped something or that he needed help, Anna stopped.

He rushed up to her, a little out of breath and his face a bright shade of red. Gazing at her intensely, Anna was reminded of a shy teenager who was plucking up the courage to speak to his schoolgirl crush for the first time. But this man was no gauche teenager but a male in his twenties. He managed to splutter out, 'Thanks for stopping.'

Thinking there might be an emergency, Anna asked, 'Are you ok? Can I help you with something?'

'No help required, thanks. I just thought that as it's the Easter weekend, I would love to give an Easter gift to someone. A bunch of lovely, colourful tulips that brighten up our world should be given to someone who also brightens up the world with their beauty. And who better to give them to than the most beautiful girl I have ever seen. You. Please do me the honour of accepting my gift.' He placed the tulips in Anna's trolley next to the other bunch as she reacted with utter shock.

'Er, thank you but I can't accept them. Didn't you say they reminded you of your mother. You should give them to her,' Anna said. She then regretted saying this, because if his mother was dead, she didn't want to add to his grief.

'Don't worry about it. My mother left me and my brother when I was five. It's just that dad recently made a comment about our mother liking tulips at Easter. The tulips should go to someone who deserves them, you,' he stated, smiling kindly at her.

For Anna, this was all starting to get a little strange. 'I already have some tulips so you should take these home,' Anna insisted, as she picked them up out of her trolley and pressed them towards him.

'No, no, please have them. With yours, they will make a spectacular bunch and, anyway, I shall be deeply offended if you do not take my Easter gift. If you refuse, I will go and place them in the nearest bin so no one will admire their radiant beauty. All that time and energy spent on developing from bulb to magnificent flower only for their efforts to be discarded in a smelly, dark bin. The Society for Kindness To Tulips will be holding a candlelight vigil in places as far apart as Norfolk and the Netherlands, if they end up in a bin,' he joked, as he stood away from her.

Anna, though feeling uncomfortable with all this, decided that to accept the tulips was probably easier than to prolong this interaction any longer. 'Ok, ok. I'll accept them to avoid the Tulip Society going to the trouble of organising candlelit vigils. Thank you. I shall enjoy their beauty, a reminder that springtime is here. Anyway, I must go. Happy Easter to you.'

Anna pushed her trolley to her car, bemused by this encounter with the man and his persistence on giving her the tulips. She chuckled to herself. He was an awkward type, who blushed easily, so it must have took a lot of courage to give her the flowers. Though she didn't encourage it, she was used to being hassled by men but it was often the confident types who approached her. This man was the exact opposite, shy and unsure, a harmless soul, and a change from the usual pushy types.

❈

CHAPTER TWENTY THREE

As Luke walked into his home, a beaming smile still touched his lips. He felt like doing a little hop, skip and a jump, such was his joy at this moment. As he went into the kitchen, his father was preparing dinner. Jez Milner frowned slightly as he glanced at his son. 'You look very pleased with yourself, was the supermarket giving away free money?'

Luke couldn't keep the smile off his face. 'No free money but I did get to speak to someone special.'

Jez sighed loudly. 'That'll be a woman, I expect. Anyway, did you get the shopping I wanted including the gravy mix?'

'Yeah, dad, I got it all,' Luke clarified, emptying the shopping bag of milk, bread, butter, and the gravy mix on to the kitchen worktop.'

'Great, son. Lay the table and then go and get your lazy brother. The dinner's ready, I just need to make the gravy.'

The three men were soon seated at the kitchen table, eating a dinner of steak pie, mashed potato, carrots and peas. Jez removed a small piece of gristle from his teeth to put on his plate. 'These pies from the butchers are not as good as they used to be. Less steak and more cow offal. I shall have a word with Brian next time I see him. The prices are going up and the quality is going down. Talking of food, we need to do a list of food for the BBQ tomorrow.'

Luke was now peering closely into the pie to identify any unwelcome pieces of offal. 'The weather forecast is good, warm and sunny. It'll be great to sit out on the new garden furniture on the patio. Russ's girlfriend, Leanne, will impressed. We must make her very welcome and show her that not all Milner men are monosyllabic, moronic misogynists.'

Jez guffawed loudly, ignoring Russ's angry expression. 'Luke, you are very cruel to your brother. Russ has been able to speak in complete sentences since the age of twenty,' he joked. 'Oh, yes, I forgot that she's coming. One of you had better give the bathroom a quick clean after dinner. I can't have a possible future wife of Russ entering out male only bathroom in its normal state.'

Russ looked daggers at the two men. 'Right. Firstly, I can't clean the bathroom as I've got a date with a woman in a pub in town. Second, Leanne is not my girlfriend. Just a friend who's a girl with benefits until I get bored. She invited herself to this BBQ so don't read anything more into it. I've told you, I don't do relationships, weddings or kids. All I'm after is a good time.'

Jez gazed at his oldest son, a sadness in his eyes. 'That, lad, is a depressing statement. That type of life is all well and good when you're young but you're thirty now and should think of settling down with a nice girl. Have some children. I know my marriage failed with your mother but I never regretted having you boys. From what you've said, this Leanne is a good mum to her sons, and could be good for you if you gave her a chance.'

Russ scooped a huge pile of mashed potato and peas onto his fork before eating with relish. He then stabbed the empty fork into the air towards his father, his voice gruff with anger. 'As I've said, Leanne is temporary, a convenience until I've had enough. If I ever felt the need for a relationship, it would be with someone hotter than her. You should look at your own love life, dad. How many years have you been with Angie for your weekly booty call? You were sleeping with her, a married woman, for years before her husband died a few years ago. I thought you'd have made things a bit more permanent with Fergal gone. Angie keeping her options open, eh?'

Luke noted that his father looked a little hurt by this. Jez Milner was now a man in his late fifties who had been deeply wounded when his wife left him for a handsome Turkish waiter over twenty years ago. Jez was an average man, of medium build, who was not ageing well due to a beer belly paunch, receding hairline and flabby red cheeks. It was common knowledge that Angie was not looking for a permanent relationship with her husband gone. She had a reputation in the town for sleeping around which his dad was not aware of. Jez clung onto this casual setup with Angie for fear of being alone.

Jez bristled with indignation. "Shut up, Russ. My relationship with Angie is none of your business. I spend time with Angie, having a drink and watching telly, that's all.' His reddened cheeks glowed brighter and this was not due to the lager he was drinking.

Revelling in his father's discomfort, Russ added, 'Well at least we're getting some which is more than can be said for Luke. You need to get on dating apps if you want to get laid.'

Luke scowled at his brother and failed to concentrate as several rogue peas fell off his fork and onto the floor. 'Not all of us want to get laid with anyone who'll have us. I was speaking to a girl I like in the supermarket today. Who knows, I may invite her to a BBQ one day soon. When I do, you'll all be envious, I can tell you.'

Russ scraped his knife across his plate to consume the remaining gravy. 'Spoke to a girl you like, eh? What did you say, 'Is that till open, love?'

Jez and Russ both laughed as Luke fumed. 'She doesn't work at the supermarket, she's a customer. I think she works in an office as she was wearing a violet dress that made her look smart and professional. She could be an administrator, or an accountant, or a solicitor, who knows. One thing is clear, she is intelligent as well as beautiful.'

'Well, brother, that's you done for as no intelligent and beautiful woman is going to go out with you,' Russ smirked, before laughing loudly.

Luke remembered the details of the conversation with his girl. He wanted to treasure it and relive it in his head when he got into bed. A glorious, private memory. But these two smart-arses were goading him and he blurted out. 'You're wrong. I was chatting to her for a few minutes about how lovely it was that spring had arrived. I persuaded her to accept my gift of a bunch of mixed tulips in the spirit of how the tulips and her beauty both brighten up the world at Easter time. I think she was very happy with them.'

This revelation did silence Russ's laughter momentarily. He supped a mouthful of lager and then started to chuckle. 'Oh my God, how cheesy. Honestly, brother, you were born in the wrong era. I see you in the 1930s, dressed in a smart suit and tie, walking out with your lady, offering her your jacket if she gets cold, holding open doors for her and walking on the pavement nearest to the traffic for her safety.'

Luke shrugged. 'Nothing wrong with any of that if she's worth it and my girl is. You, Russ, are a coarse, beer-swigging, neanderthal only interested in getting your end away. You could do with being infused with a little bit of 1930s courtesy and politeness in terms of how to treat women. Stop being a selfish, arrogant pig.'

'Watch who you're calling a pig, brother,' Russ stated while getting up from his seat, picking up his plate to take it to the dishwasher. The knife slipped slightly and he grabbed hold of it, flashing it near to Luke's nose which made him jerk back in his chair. 'Let me be clear, Luke, this girl, whoever she is, is not yours. Will never be. And if she's as beautiful as you say then there will be a handsome boyfriend who won't take kindly to you giving her flowers.'

Later, lying in bed, Luke gazed longingly at the girl of his dreams on his phone. Today had been amazing. He had got close to her, so close as to be hypnotised by the sheer bewitching beauty of her blue eyes. Close enough to stare in wonder at her perfect mouth, lightly tinted by a rose pink lipstick. What would it be like to kiss those lips? He was impressed by her natural easy laugh, the way she pleasantly engaged in conversation with him, and the kindness she had shown when she thought he needed help.

Physically, he had been inches away from her and he wondered what it would be like to hold her in his arms. He'd been close enough to inhale the scent of her perfume. He thought about where she might have dabbed that perfume this morning, on her pulse points; on her wrists, on her neck, on her cleavage. But he'd made the best discovery of all when he came close to her today. He'd immediately recognised the perfume with its notes of magnolia, peony and lotus flower. The perfume he had already purchased in anticipation of gifting it to the woman he loved. The perfume he had just sprayed on the inside of his left wrist, the scent of which made his heart race and his body tremble. This to Luke, was serendipity, another indication that he and his girl were meant to be together.

⊷⊶≺◈≻⊷⊶

CHAPTER TWENTY FOUR

Thursday 14ᵗʰ April 2022

Back at her house, Anna was putting the shopping in the cupboard, and the fridge, when there was a knock at the front door. On opening the door, Anna was surprised to find Nick Carlton holding an exquisite bouquet of flowers. 'Hello,' was all she could mumble.

'I hope I'm not disturbing you. I just wanted to drop by to see if you're ok after my party last week and to offer these flowers as an apology for Abbie's atrocious behaviour towards you,' he stated. He was dressed casually in a navy, quilted jacket, beige jumper and dark blue jeans. He stood grinning sheepishly at her whilst holding the huge bouquet and the sweet scent of freesias assailed her nostrils. He pressed the bouquet into her hands. 'These are for you.'

'Wow, thanks. You can come in if you like,' Anna stated, feeling her face flushing red at the thought of being in close proximity to him. Why couldn't she act all cool and nonchalant in the way that other women would do?

'Thanks,' he said and Anna opened the door fully to allow him to enter before leading the way to the kitchen. The two bunches of mixed coloured tulips were by the sink. Nick's bouquet of spring flowers was really stunning; pink and purple tulips, white roses, white freesias, pink Limonium and eucalyptus. 'I see someone else has beaten me to it with the gift of flowers,' Nick commented, but it came out more as a question.

Anna glanced at the array of flowers in front of her. 'My only problem is that I may have insufficient vases to accommodate them.' Anna opened a kitchen cupboard and glanced up at the two vases on the top shelf that she wouldn't be able to reach.

Recognising her problem, he laughed. 'Shall I lift you up to get the vases or shall I get them down for you?'

Anna felt he was teasing her about her lack of height. 'I normally get the stepladder out of the shed but if you could get them down that would be helpful.'

Anna stood aside as she watched him take down the two round vases, one smaller one for the tulips and a larger one for the bouquet. In the space of her small kitchen, she was keenly aware of his masculine presence, and she shivered slightly as she speculated what it would be like to be held by him. This man was seriously attractive but out of bounds. She must get a grip. He placed the vases on the oak worktop, and smiled at her, as if he knew the details of her secret thoughts. Her face flushed a brighter pink. To distract herself, and his intensive gaze, she asked, 'Would you like a drink while I just put these in water? Coffee, tea, lager, wine?

'A lager, thanks.' He leaned against the kitchen worktop as Anna took a bottle of lager out of the fridge, removed a bottle opener out of a drawer, and flipped off the bottle top.

'Glass?'

'The bottle's fine,' he indicated as Anna gave him the bottle and he took a quick swig. 'Cheers.'

Anna started on the task of putting the tulips in the smaller, round vase. It was easy as they were all the same length and seemed to fall in a naturally attractive arrangement immediately. Admiring her handiwork, she quipped, 'Well they look good. Let's see if I can be successful with your beautiful bouquet.' She placed water in the second vase, added the cut flower food from the little sachet, and then opened up the wrapping around the bouquet. The flowers and greenery were of nearly equal length and had been artfully arranged by the florist. Once in the vase, they settled into an eye-catching shape. 'They look amazing without any input from me. I'll put your bouquet on the table in the living room, shortly.' She placed the tulips on the window sill over the sink. 'These will cheer me up when I'm washing up. I'm going to have a glass of wine in the garden. Do you want to join me?'

Outside, the garden was a small, rectangular space with a sandstone patio laid across the back of the house which led to a lawned area. Two terracotta pots on the patio displayed daffodils in all their yellow glory. Anna, carrying her glass of wine, escorted him to a patio set of two chairs and round table.

Nick leaned over to tap his bottle against her glass. 'Happy Easter. I love the pots with the host of golden daffodils, to quote Wordsworth. What are your plans for the Easter weekend?'

Anna sipped on the chilled Sauvignon Blanc, appreciating its fresh, intense taste in the mouth. The blueness of the sky, the warm evening, the prospect of four days off work were all lifting her spirits. 'Plans? Tomorrow, I'm doing some jobs around the house. On Saturday, I'm going to an Italian restaurant in the evening. On Sunday, I'm driving back home to see my dad and brother and have lunch with them. On Monday, I'm intending to have a lazy day, perhaps a walk followed by reading a book or watching a film on Netflix. What about you?'

Nick sighed. 'Nothing specific but I will be with the family on Easter Sunday when my mother will be cooking a gigantic leg of lamb with all the trimmings. We will all go home half a stone heavier after eating the roast and then sampling all three of her homemade puddings; bread and butter pudding, a cheesecake, and apple crumble served with options of custard, cream or ice cream. My granddad, Bill, has been known to have all three puddings in a dish and all three of the accompaniments. Custard in the same bowl as cheesecake, it's against the laws of pudding.'

Anna laughed, 'It must make him happy. At his age, he might as well eat what he likes.'

'Yes, you're right but I hope you're not thinking of my granddad as old. It's more that he has an adventurous side. He did abseiling at an outdoor site for the first time last year,' Nick explained, laughing softly as he noted her bemused expression.

'How old is granddad?'

'Eighty-five. For Christmas, my wicked brother, Ed, bought him a zip line experience in North Wales where you enjoy views of Snowdonia going along at 100 mph. Granddad's well up for it. He's the ultimate risk-taker, puddings, abseiling, zip lining, you name it. He's also got a bad boy reputation but that's a story for another day.'

They laughed but then Anna noted that Nick's face was now serious. 'Anna, I want to apologise again for Abbie throwing the wine over you at my party. After that, things went downhill rapidly.' Nick fully explained to Anna, Abbie's drunken behaviour with the knife. 'Basically, she was totally hammered and out of control. I was terrified that my family were going to get seriously hurt. This was the last straw, for me. The next day I ended our relationship and I don't want to see her again.'

'Good grief. What a terrible thing to happen on your birthday,' Anna commented, truly shocked about what he had told her. Anna knew that Abbie had thrown the drink at her deliberately and there had been a maniacal look on her face as she closed in on Anna's personal space. 'I'm sorry, it must be painful if you've gone out together for a while.'

'You know, Anna. It's not painful at all,' Nick explained, a lightness in his tone of voice. 'All week I have felt relieved and freed from a burden I have been carrying with me. We were together for six months and I don't know why as she brought no positives to my life, only negatives. Now, I'm looking forward to an Abbie free future.'

Anna's heart did skip a beat as she realised that he was now a single man. Most likely he would be steering clear of relationships for a while after his experience with the truly awful Abbie. 'I'm going to get another glass of wine. Would you like another lager?'

He didn't seem to have any inclination to leave. 'Yeah, that would be great as long I'm not interfering with your plans. One more lager would be good.'

Anna was soon back with another bottled lager, a further glass of wine, and a bowl of sweet chilli crisps. 'Help yourself to my home-cooked snacks.'

Pinching a few crisps out of the bowl, he crunched on them appreciatively. 'Yes, excellent. Just the right amount of sweet chilli, exactly how do you get the flavour just right?'

'Simples. I just shake the bag and open it,' Anna joked then deeply regretted that she had just said 'simples'. The wine was definitely going to her head.

He laughed, shaking his head in disbelief. 'Good, I'm glad you've owned up to your fake claim of making the crisps. Honesty is the best policy.'

'Always,' Anna agreed.

He shifted slightly on his seat, sitting up straighter as he addressed her, his intense blue eyes focusing on her face, 'When I brought you the flowers, I said that it appears someone else has beaten me to it. I'm going to ask who bought you the tulips?'

Flushing slightly from his scrutiny, Anna joked, 'And I reserve the right not to tell you.'

There was a flicker of sternness in his eyes before he quickly responded to her teasing. 'Why, was it Ryan Gosling and you don't want to make me feel inadequate?'

'No, it wasn't Ryan Gosling but I can wish. It was some guy at the supermarket.' Anna related the story of the man who'd insisted that she take the tulips. 'They weren't a poignant reminder of a mother who had died. The mother had left him when he was five-years-old and didn't deserve tulips. It all started to get a bit odd so I accepted the tulips to get away from him as he was starting to come across as weird.'

'And do we know why the tulips were given to you?' Nick asked, still staring at her face.

The intensity of Nick's gaze, and the reason why the man gave her the tulips, was making Anna blush. 'He said a bunch of tulips brightens the world and should be given to someone who brightens the world with her beauty,' Anna avoided Nick's eyes as she was mortified about relating this to him. 'He wanted to give them to the most beautiful girl he'd ever seen. These were all his words, not mine.'

Seeing that she was embarrassed with this whole conversation, Nick looked away from her to take a handful of the 'home-made' crisps. 'Well, I'd say he was right. You are very beautiful. Do you know this man?'

'No, not at all. I've seen him a couple of times in the supermarket when we're in the same aisle and he always smiles at me. He seems harmless enough. One of those young men that are quite awkward with women, I think. After today, I shall have to ensure that I avoid him. I don't want any more surprise gifts,' Anna sighed, loudly. 'And I don't want to give him the chance to ask me out on a date but I do think he's too shy to do that.'

'Good,' Nick stated. 'I have to say Anna Louden you do seem to have acquired a number of male admirers and I've only known you a short while. Let's see, there's Justin, a Gavin that's interested in you, Connor who accosted you in the pub, and now Tulip Man.' He leaned forward slightly in his chair, his eyes locked on hers. 'Ok, cards on the table. I came here with the flowers to make up for what Abbie did. But, I also came to ask you to go on a date with me. Would you like to spend the day with me on Easter Monday? We could go for a walk and then go for a meal in a pub, what do you think?'

Anna hesitated. There was nothing she'd like more than to spend time with Nick Carlton but she was a little frightened at the same time. It was fine with the others. In her mind, Justin was just for casual dates with no commitment. Something that was fizzling out already and there had been no fizz there to start with. She would have no further contact with Connor and, frankly, the man scared her. Too much like Alistair. Tulip Man was not relevant. The only one she quite liked was Gavin and she was looking forward to their meal tomorrow.

Nick was different and she knew that she had a strong liking for him already. Her last, and most serious relationship with Alistair, had been difficult, and at the end, violent. Alistair was the reason she'd started a new job, and a new life, in a new town. Yes, she would like to go on a date with Nick but she would have to fight hard to stop her feelings for him overwhelming her and thus laying herself open to being hurt all over again. One date would be ok, though? 'Yes, I'd love to go out with you on Easter Monday. Where shall we go?'

'I thought a twenty mile trek in the Peak District would be doable. Have you got hiking boots? I've got some trekking poles so I can poke you in the bottom with the pointy end if you fall behind. What do you think?' He smiled slyly as he waited for her response.

Anna gritted her teeth at this suggestion, hoping he was joking. 'Yes, I have got hiking boots but I'm not sure about a 'trek'. Are you being serious?'

Laughing loudly now at her mortified expression, Nick clarified, 'It'll be a normal walk, no boots needed. I'll pick you up at twelve, if that's ok?'

CHAPTER TWENTY FIVE

Friday 15th April 2022

The sunny afternoon of clear blue skies and warm temperature marked the end of winter and the time for the first BBQ of the year. The Milner home was a detached property, originally a farm house, situated south of Warwick. It was in a pleasant spot located away from other houses with fields to the rear. April was the month of growth and renewal in nature after the harsh winter months; trees were in leaf, fresh and green, birds were nesting, and it was a good time to be alive. A group of five people were all seated around the new patio table, drinking and talking, after consuming a BBQ meat-feast of steak, spicy chili chicken thighs, burgers and sausages.

As his father babbled on about Boris Johnson and lockdown parties at Downing Street, Russ sipped a cool lager, whilst his woman friend, Leanne, chatted to his father's woman friend, Angie. 'Woman friend', this description made Russ chuckle as he never regarded women as friends. If he were in a casual relationship with a woman, then they were not two people of equal status. Russ was in charge and the female would be subservient to him. He dictated what went on. This is why he had stayed with Leanne for longer than he intended. Though average, looks-wise, she liked a laugh and when he was at her place she did his bidding by providing food and drinks. This was when her two boys, aged seven and five, were with their dad. Russ was never going to meet the kids. From how she described them, they were typical of boys that age, arguing, scrapping, misbehaving and determined to get mum's attention. All this would wind Russ up, as he had no patience with brats and the chaos they brought to a person's life. For now, Leanne was good for sex-on-demand and never complained.

Russ's eyes drifted over to Angie. He assessed her critically as she sat laughing with Leanne. A woman with a mass of brown curls and watchful green eyes that were always scouring for opportunities to enrich herself, be it through money or sex. Brown curls and witchy eyes suggested a soft, feminine beauty. But her body was more masculine, a lean frame, toned arms, small breasts, slender hips. Angie had a reputation for casual hook-ups. Due to her diverse means of making a living, selling veg, repairing cars and flogging antiques, Angie came into contact with a lot of men. If she fancied someone she was not shy of making that known to them so many a brief encounter was achieved in her van, her garden shed and occasionally in her bed. Russ felt a bit sorry for his old man who seemed to think that he was exclusively with Angie when she had sampled the wares of a good proportion of the men in the town.

Jez got up out of his chair. 'Ok, folks, I'll go and get more drinks, seen as my lazy sons aren't offering. Wine for you girls?

Leanne had lost her initial shyness and was telling Angie about her kids. 'Leo, seven and Isaac, five. They get spoilt at their dads, lax bedtimes, too much sugar, frequent fighting, and then I have to calm them down when they come home. They are a right handful.'

Russ gave her a dismissive look. 'What did you expect? You've got two kids. If you found it hard work with the first one, why have a second? Bloody daft. If I had kids they would know exactly who's in charge and get a whack if they stepped out of line.'

A pinkness flared in Leanne's cheeks. 'I would never smack my boys; I don't know how any parent can do that.'

'This is why I steer clear of long-term commitment, no wife or kids,' Russ stated, noting that Leanne was staring at him, disbelievingly. Was she harbouring ideas that they were in a relationship? If so, it was good to remind her frequently that this would never be the case.

Luke, who had been concentrating on his phone, now addressed his brother. 'Honestly, Russ, you are not being fair to Leanne. But I bet you have her attending to your every need when you are at her house.' Then to Leanne, Luke said, 'When Russ says that he doesn't do commitment, believe him. Don't waste your valuable time trying to make him into a caring boyfriend, and loving stepdad, as it won't work. You're a nice girl, go find a man that appreciates you.'

Though Luke was exactly right in what he had just said, this now irritated Russ. He had a nice little thing going on with Leanne and he didn't want Luke messing it up. Russ would decide when things needed to end. 'Luke, keep your fucking nose out of my business or I'll knock it off.'

Jez returned with a tray of drinks, a bottle of white wine, bottled lagers and a bottle of whisky and three glass tumblers. Jez was wise to his sons' interactions over the years and knew when trouble was about to start. There had been many occasions when Luke had been battered by Russ. 'Russ, stop the swearing and leave your brother alone. Everyone, help yourselves to a drink.'

Russ took hold of the whisky bottle, and a glass, and poured himself a generous amount of the golden liquid. Drinking a large mouthful, he wiped his hand across his mouth, and addressed Leanne. 'We're good for now, babe. Take no notice of Luke.' To Luke, he said, 'For someone very good at giving out advice on relationships, I note that you are the only one here without a woman. Even our old dad has got pulling power.'

Pouring herself a large glass of wine, Angie drank thirstily. 'Stop being mean, Russ. I'm sure Luke will find a girlfriend when the time is right.'

Russ laughed loudly, the alcoholic rush of the whisky making him antagonistic. 'Luke's got a girlfriend, a fantasy woman he's in love with. As I keep telling him, you can't get your leg over a fantasy.'

'Shut up, Russ. She's not a fantasy. She's real and I hope to be going out with her one day soon. We had a proper chat at the supermarket yesterday. She's perfect; beautiful, intelligent, funny and kind. You'll be jealous when you meet her, I can tell you,' Luke insisted, as he placed his phone on the patio table.

Immediately, Russ snatched up the phone and fought off Luke's attempt to take it off him. 'Have you got any photos of this goddess that you keep talking about.' Russ started to scroll through recent photos in the phone's album and found some from yesterday. At the supermarket. A young woman standing at her car to place her shopping in the car boot. It was a photo of her from the back, taken by Luke standing a distance away. Russ noted that she was slim, with mid-brown, wavy hair to just below her shoulders. Luke had then moved closer to the woman to take more photos. One was of her reaching up to close the car boot. She had a shapely figure, displayed in a knee-length violet dress, which highlighted a slender waist and curvy bottom. She had moment's anxiety as her empty trolley tried to escape downhill before she stopped it. As she chased the trolley, images of how the hem of the violet dress swirled and flared around her lovely legs were captured by Luke in a number of photos, one shot at a time. Having seen the back view of this woman, Russ was eager to get a glimpse of her face. He wasn't disappointed. A heart-shaped face with well-defined cheekbones, blue eyes, a perfect up-turned nose, and natural, plump lips. Exploring further in the phone's photo album, Russ found hundreds of photos of the woman over a number of months, from autumn through winter, into spring. All the photos captured her incomparable beauty. Russ had to hand it to Luke, his fantasy female was a real stunner.

'Give my phone back to me now, Russ,' Luke insisted, reaching over to take it off his brother but the phone was kept out of his reach.

Russ took his time, enjoying winding his brother up but also gazing at the hot babe.

Jez, Angie and Leanne all looked at Russ with interest, as Jez asked, 'Who's he got photos of, some famous actress or pop singer? I can't give you any names as I don't really know much about current films or music artists.'

Russ laughed. 'Well, if this one is famous she likes to do her shopping at the local supermarket. In terms of beauty she is truly gorgeous but would never go out with the likes of our Luke.'

Luke now picked up his phone where Russ had placed it on the table. 'Keep out of my business, Russ. And for your information, I've had a couple of pretty girlfriends in the past, Imogen and Naomi. I'm not too bad looking and a girl once asked if I was in a boy band.'

'Jeez, brother. Don't you know the golden rule of boy bands. Always have one ugly member to make the others look more handsome. Poor Luke, that girl was just feeling sorry for you,' Russ sneered as Luke's face went puce.

Jez supped his whisky and chuckled loudly. 'Oh, yes. Imogen and Naomi weren't really girlfriends, were they?. Those two were memorable for all the wrong reasons. I got battered by Imogen's dad when you gave his fifteen-year-old daughter alcohol. Naomi was the girl at the library you were infatuated with. That resulted in a criminal conviction for stalking and a community order. These aren't the greatest testaments to love.'

Everyone laughed loudly as Luke looked upset. 'Well, we'll see. I might have the last laugh yet.'

The warmth of the sun was now fading and it was getting cool. Jez, Angie and Leanne took their drinks indoors but left the whisky bottle. Russ lingered, refilling his glass with whisky and taking a large mouthful. The whisky was hitting the spot but it was making him restless. He wasn't rushing to be with Leanne though they would be sharing a bed later. 'That woman on your phone is a hot babe. I might ditch Leanne and seek her out.'

Luke sneered. 'My girl would not want a lazy idiot like you. I would take care of my girl.

'That's where you go wrong, brother. You just need to find a woman who likes caring for a man. Give them a lot of the old love stick in return. Women will never admit it but they like a man who's in charge and knows what he wants. Too many men are wimps these days and let women walk all over them. Women then lose respect for the pathetic pricks.'

Luke wrinkled his nose as if he had discovered a bad smell. 'I would treasure my girl as she deserves.'

Russ roared with laughter. 'You are such a soppy git. If want to stand any chance with your fantasy woman then you need to wise up, grow a pair of balls and make her beg to be with you. Don't be a simp, be an alpha male. An Edward Rochester, a Rhett Butler, a James Bond, masculine, arrogant, sexually intense, commanding. These are the men women want.'

Luke sneered at his brother. 'Edward Rochester? Jane Eyre. When did you ever read a book, brother? Which one are you? Moody, troubled Rochester? Charming yet cynical Butler? Alpha male, loner, and dangerous Bond? Misogynistic, lazy, arrogant, sexually promiscuous Russ Milner. They should write a novel with you as the main protagonist. There's a dark side to you which will one day be revealed when we find out where all the bodies are buried. In fact, I'll write a book, 'My Brother Russ, Serial Killer'.

Russ leaned over in his chair and grabbed Luke in a head lock. Russ was in a mood to indulge in a little violence right now. 'No need to worry about writing that book. But you will be the first person to disappear if I go on my killing spree.' Russ squeezed his arm around his brother's neck, applying pressure, as Luke squirmed and squealed to get free. As Russ released him, he said, 'You're safe for now. But you have got me interested in your fantasy girl.'

Luke gasped for air and rubbed his neck as Russ let him go. 'Keep away from her. You've got plenty of women to go after.'

Russ patted Luke's anxious face. 'Yeah, you're right, brother. I've already had the two women in this house.' Luke turned to stare, open-mouthed, at Russ. Russ relished the look of shock and surprise as Luke realised what he'd said.

'W-what? The two women? Does that mean you've slept with Angie? Oh my God,' Luke stuttered, all earlier colour draining from his face. 'How could you do that to dad?'

There was a hardness to Russ's face and an icy coldness in his eyes as he spoke, 'The old man shouldn't send me on errands to her house. It didn't take us long to get down to it. Ask dad about the mole on her left buttock.'

Later, as Leanne lay beside him asleep in his bed, Russ was finding it hard to sleep due to a mixture of too many whiskies and overindulging in the BBQ food. He had instigated sex with Leanne, and the initial high of the orgasm, and the release of hormones had not brought his usual post-coitus sleepiness. Gazing at a sleeping Leanne, mouth open and making little snorty noises, was not endearing her to him. Plus, she was decidedly average in terms of sex. When he was in a relationship for a few months, he liked to be with an adventurous woman who would go on a journey with him. Leanne was currently stuck at the start of that journey about to take a train to Margate with a pack of cheese sandwiches. Boring and dull.

Another reason for his lack of sleep was that the image of Luke's fantasy girl kept popping into his head. When he had shagged Leanne, her average features were replaced by those of a beautiful girl with wavy brown hair and a kiss-perfect mouth. He thought of all the things he would do to that seductive body. A wicked smile formed on Russ's handsome face. Life was generally mundane and boring and he yearned for some excitement. He set himself the challenge of meeting Luke's fantasy woman. And he would make it his mission to get to know her intimately.

•••••◄❖►•••••

CHAPTER TWENTY SIX

Saturday 16th April 2022

Nick spent the morning of the Saturday of Easter weekend putting Abbie's clothes and other belongings into black plastic sacks for her to collect later this afternoon. He did not want to see her but she had persisted in texting him over the last week with a range of texts on a spectrum from extreme begging to issuing threats. **'I miss you, babe. Please let's get back together. I will change and improve. You'll love the new Abbie xxx'** was one cringy texted he'd received recently.

Others were vitriolic. **'I tend to make people pay for making a fool of me. Watch out Carlton family.'** And about Anna. **'If you're stupid enough to go out with that insipid cow then more fool you.'** In line with Abbie's deranged thinking, she'd concluded that his finishing with her was to do with a liking he had for Anna. This was true but Abbie had no evidence to support this claim. Once Abbie had collected her belongings today he would never have any contact with her again.

As it was a warm spring day, Nick sat in his garden, drinking a cold lager, and waiting for Abbie to arrive. The thought of spending a day with Anna on Monday was lifting his spirits. He needed this to counteract the negativity brought into his life by another encounter with Abbie. It had been great to see Anna on Thursday when he had taken her the flowers and liked the way she was appreciative of his gift. Very quickly he knew where to draw the line in terms of making gestures to her. The payment of her garage bill had been a miscalculation on his part. But it was difficult to stop himself wanting to do things to please her as it did give him pleasure. Nick knew that there were other men vying for Anna's attention. She had not explained who the meal was with this evening but her lack of clarity led Nick to believe it was a date with a man. Then there was the male who had given her the tulips. Anna described him as shy but he had been bold in presenting her with the tulips. One to watch. For now, Nick would play it cool. One thing was clear to Nick, he was determined to get to know Anna Louden and he would not be put off by the presence of other men in her life.

At just after three p.m. Abbie arrived. As Nick opened the door, she did not remain on the doorstep waiting to be invited inside but pushed forward to enter the hallway. Nick had to stifle a laugh when he looked at her. She had put in maximum effort to impress. This was Saturday night out Abbie in a blue, tight-fitting, mini dress worn with four inch black heels. Immaculately waved blonde hair. Perfect makeup of well-defined eyes with false eyelashes entering the house ahead of her. Vibrant, glossy red lips. A fog of hairspray and perfume surrounded her which made Nick cough.

Abbie paused in the hallway and leaned up to kiss Nick on the cheek. 'Hi, Nicky, babe. Great to see you,' she whispered in a Marilyn Monroe breathy voice as Nick swerved her embrace. 'I'd love a coffee, if you're making one.'

Nick looked at her peevishly. 'I'm not. I've put all your stuff into black sacks which I can get now and then you can be on your way.'

Abbie made her way into the kitchen, uninvited, and sat down on a chair at the dining table. 'It won't hurt to have a little chat. See if we can't put things right. A glass of wine would be nice while we talk.'

Resigning himself to hear what she had to say, Nick sat on a chair opposite her. 'There will be no wine, Abbie. That is one of the reasons we are no longer together. You drink too much, never know when to stop, and it makes you very rude and unpleasant.'

'Jeez, Nick, that's blunt. I know I went a bit over the top at your party but normally I'm a good laugh after a few drinks.

Everyone says so. Your sis, Alyssa, loves me when I'm in party animal mood. Plus you know how frisky a few wines makes me,' Abbie winked at him. 'You never used to say no even if I was hammered, as I recall.'

Nick gazed at her in disbelief. She really had no self-awareness of how ridiculous she was looking and sounding right now. 'Ok, Abbie. I'll repeat what I told you after my birthday party. Your drunken behaviour was unacceptable. Throwing the wine over Anna. Waving a knife around was downright dangerous and could have caused serious injury to my family. And like I keep stressing, you committed a criminal offence.'

Abbie did manage to look contrite as he said this. 'Ok, ok. Yes, I will accept that I was out of order but don't let it ruin what we had. I really want to be with you, Nick, and I promise that I will change. I think you called me selfish but it's not that, I'm single-minded to get what I want. I accept I have let my work slide a bit over the last few months but I will work harder from now on. I will pay my way more and stop accepting money from you. But if this was a problem you should have said something. I know I can be a bit rude to people at times but it comes with my job. I won't compromise on expecting high standards. I'm a strong, independent woman.' This was all emphasised with a little girl poutiness of her red lips and a sweep of the large, bats-wing eyelashes.

Nick sighed loudly and shook his head. 'Yes, you do go on about being strong and independent, a career woman, but you were ready to give it up when the offer of a free ride came along. But I was the fool that willingly paid for you all the time, so I can't lay all the blame on you. And, I like to pay for a woman who appreciates it but I won't be taken for a mug. Anyway, that's all over now. What's done is done.'

This seemed to give Abbie a bit of hope and she smiled softly. 'Yes, it's done. We can start again. As I said, I'll work harder, pay my way, especially if I move in permanently. And I promise to discuss with you more about how our relationship progresses, forget the expensive holidays, and focus more on the important things. No silly dogs. Perhaps a baby would be nice.'

Nick shook his head in utter disbelief. 'A baby. You don't like children. Smelly, howling brats is how I think you once described them. I do want children in my life, very much, in the future but I'm sorry Abbie, that will not be with you. Anyway, there's no point in prolonging this discussion. I've made it clear; we are finished and there's no going back.'

Abbie placed her hands over her face and started to sob. 'Please, Nick, I can change. I can. I love you so much.'

The coldness he now felt in his heart did shock Nick. How could he spend six months of his life with a woman, have frequent sex with her, and feel nothing at all for her pain at this moment. It made him heartless, and cruel, but there was nothing he could do. It would be a mistake to reach out to her now as she would misconstrue his intentions and it would be much crueller to give her the hope of a reconciliation. Instead, he got off the chair, ripped a piece of paper towel off a roll and gave it to her. She ignored the paper towel and wept loudly, taking long shuddering breaths. Tears streaked down her face, smudging her eyeliner and mascara, smearing her foundation, leaving her face red and blotchy. Through raspy breaths, she stuttered, 'P-please N-nick, g-give me another c-chance. I w-will change.'

A tiny flicker of sympathy did touch Nick's heart. 'I know you're upset now. But it will be for the best in the long run and you'll meet someone who shares your goals. There'll be holidays and silly dogs. Just not with me.'

She ran the back of her hand under her nose a couple of times and sniffed loudly. 'Here we go, patronising bastard. I can actually get any man I want so I don't really need you. You'll be with some drippy thing like that Anna who'll give you vanilla sex and pop out pretty babies. Don't come running to me when she gets fat, and frumpy, and stops delivering. You need a woman like me to give you the variety you like.' Abbie locked eyes with Nick, giving him an angry scowl.

Nick was getting irate. Abbie's references to how Anna was somehow inferior in terms of her sexual abilities were nauseating. Abbie really believed she was the high priestess of the sex act, the ultimate fuck. No other women could match her expertise. It was really pissing him off. He had not had any physical contact with Anna but he ached to kiss her luscious lips and to feel her soft, sensuous body close to his. Abbie could offer a ten hour marathon of sexual delights but it would no way entice him to spend one more minute with her.

Having more than enough of this bullshit, Nick said in an angry voice. 'Right, I've packed your stuff. We'll go upstairs and you can quickly check around to see if I've missed anything. Then I want you gone. Now.'

Abbie noting the change in him and the curtness in his voice, reluctantly got up from her chair and followed him upstairs. In his bedroom, she looked in the black sacks to see what was there before doing a search of all drawers for any other items. She went to the wardrobes and checked all the hangers for items of clothing. Finding a white shirt, she placed it into one of the black sacks. Something caught her eye and she fell to her knees. Out of the sack, she brought out a red camisole, buried her face in its silky folds, and started to cry again. 'Y-you used to l-love me in this when I wore it with my hooker shoes.' From the sack she pulled out a riding crop. 'Wow, remember this, Nicky. You used to lash it across my bum and it left those red marks. It was such fun. We can do it again.' A loud sob was the prelude to another bout of crying.

Nick looked at her pityingly. 'Get up. We're over. I don't want to hear anymore. Have some dignity.' He picked up two of the black sacks. 'I'll take these to your car. We had some good times, let's remember those.'

When the car was loaded and Abbie finally drove away, Nick breathed a long sigh of relief. On reflection, during recent months, with Vanessa, and then with Abbie, he had been bewitched by a sexual magic spell. Now, he hoped he was free of its power and potency and he wanted to be cleansed of its poison in his body and soul.

CHAPTER TWENTY SEVEN

Monday 18th April 2022

Anna stood in her bedroom, trying to decide what to wear on this date with Nick. The weather was cooler today than over the Easter weekend and so she opted for blue slim-fit jeans rather than a dress. Plus, the jeans would be more practical if they were going for a walk and she would be wearing trainers. She wore the jeans with a long-sleeved cream blouse with blue floral pattern that was floaty and feminine. A lightly padded navy jacket would be protection from any dip in temperature.

It was now eleven forty-five and he was due to arrive in fifteen minutes. The level of nerves she was experiencing in anticipation of this date was as if a swarm of butterflies were fluttering and flapping in her tummy. Her skin was clammy, her mouth was dry, but she couldn't afford to drink too much coffee or tea to relieve her parched mouth as she would then need the toilet and would be embarrassed to request a loo stop at the start of their outing. She was aiming for perfectly applied make-up but this was not happening. The light foundation blotched on her sweaty skin and would not coat evenly. Both black eyeliner and mascara had to reapplied as she smudged them under her lower lashes. All the result of having trembling hands. She was hungry but the toast from earlier had stuck in her dry throat and she gave up trying to eat after a few bites. She had not had the same levels of anxiety for her date with Gavin. The date at the Italian restaurant had gone smoothly, she had eaten delicious pizza, drank Sauvignon Blanc, laughed at his silly jokes and debated topical issues. Why was she so nervous about this date with Nick Carlton? Before she could answer her own question, there was a knock at the door. He was here.

She opened the front door and Nick grinned at her, looking devilishly handsome in black jeans, light grey crew-neck jumper and dark grey jacket. 'Ready?' he asked.

'Yes,' she replied picking up her handbag and a pair of black, high-heeled shoes.

He laughed at her as he noted the shoes in her hand. 'Are we going dancing later? I should have put my tux in the car.'

Anna now felt a bit of an idiot with these spare shoes but tried to conceal her embarrassment by frowning at him. 'I thought I'd wear these at the pub but that now seems a bit daft.'

Thinking that he'd upset her, Nick gave her an encouraging smile. 'Don't take any notice of my teasing, you'll get used to it. Just tell me to behave if it becomes too much. My mother often comments that I need to be a bit more sensitive at times as not everyone finds me hilariously funny. I think I'm very sensitive and she gets confused between me and Ed. Ed's two years younger than me and as far as I am concerned he's emotionally stunted at the early teen stage. Put the shoes in the car and you can decide later whether to change into them or not. My preference would be that you do wear them as I like a woman in heels.'

Anna locked her front door and followed him to his car. He held the passenger door open which she found really charming. Once again, she noted the luxury of the car as the warmth of the heated-seat embraced her body. He got into the driver's seat and glanced at her. 'Ok, ready to go.'

'Go where, is the million dollar question,' Anna commented, as she waited for him to start the car.

'Right, Ms Louden. Relax, let's have some music and enjoy the ride. I'm not telling you where we're going but I'm sure you'll like it,' he grinned as he started the engine and pulled away from the kerb to join the traffic. 'What music do you like?'

'I like a mix of genres; I'm not hooked on one type of thing. Heart Radio would be good,' Anna suggested, glancing to see his reaction. If he were a heavy metal fan or a hip hop lover, he didn't flinch at her middle-of-the-road choice. Immediately, Ellie Goulding's *'Love Me Like You Do'* was playing, pouring smoothly and perfectly out of a number of speakers, filling all corners of the car with this seductive song. Anna remembered this song from the movie *'Fifty Shades of Grey'* and images entered her head of Anastasia Steele being tutored by handsome billionaire, Christian Grey in his red room of pain. Though they were driving on an A road out of Warwick, Anna felt she was in a cocoon of sound, warmth and comfort in this luxurious car being driven by a man as exotic and mysterious to her at this moment as Christian Grey himself. She shut her eyes to allow the words of the song to seduce her, closing out the world so that only the song, and the images of the film, where evoked.

As the song ended, Anna opened her eyes. Nick glanced at her and commented, 'I see that you enjoyed that song. Next time, I'll collect you in my helicopter.'

Anna gave him a look that said, 'oh yeah' and said, 'Is that so, Mr Grey? Will you be taking me to your red room as well?' Immediately, she regretted saying this. What would he think, that she was some sort of submissive who wanted to be dominated, tied up and whipped?

The car slowed to stop at a red light and he turned to face her. 'I haven't got a red room, sadly, but I can accommodate any of your interests, if that's what you'd like,' he said with an earnest tone to his voice so that Anna didn't know if he was joking or not. As the lights changed, and the car moved forward, Anna again wondered about this man. Her newly found status as a single woman after a long-term relationship left her vulnerable in terms of how to negotiate the world of dating and sexual relationships. She certainly didn't want to sleep with lots of men but she was finding that their expectations were high that sex would be on the agenda very quickly. She had made the mistake of sleeping with Connor after only a few dates and that experience had traumatised her. She had been shocked to find out what some men thought was acceptable on a first time of intimate contact. Justin was pushing for more than prolonged kissing and she really would not go further with him. Gavin had kissed her goodbye, just before she had got out of a taxi drawing up to her home. A pleasant kiss but nothing more. Instinctively, she knew that Nick would be sexually competent, a good lover, but that made her afraid that she would disappoint him. He'd hinted that the one thing that had kept him with Abbie was the sex. Anna knew that she was no wild, ultra-confident Abbie but then wild had ultimately led to dangerous.

After forty five minutes, they arrived just outside Bourton-on-the-Water, a pretty Cotswolds village. As they walked from the car, they followed signs for the public footpath, the Windrush Way. Walking along pavement, then a narrow path, past splendid houses and high walls built from Cotswold stone, they came to a footpath alongside the River Windrush. Having picked a bank holiday for this walk, there were people around but it was not too overcrowded. The weather was cool, but it was a bright day, and signs of spring were everywhere as greenery was returning to dispel the drabness of winter. The narrowness of the path meant that Anna walked ahead of Nick, so conversation was limited. Anna stopped at a wider part of the path to admire the wild yellow daffodils, with their trumpet-shaped, egg-yolk yellow centres and pale yellow petals, resplendent on a bank across the river.

'Daffodils look so pretty in their natural habitat,' Anna observed, as Nick stood next to her. 'They provide a lovely splash of colour to the outdoors after the long, drab winter.' Nick's eyes scanned her face and she felt a bit shy, suddenly. Would he think her as overly soppy? She turned her eyes away from his intense gaze. 'Don't worry I'm not going to come over all Poet Laureate on you.'

He grinned at her, lines wrinkling at the corner of his eyes with amusement. 'Please do. In fact, I'll google the poem by William Wordsworth, '*I Wandered Lonely as a Cloud*'. He found the famous poem and read aloud the four verses while Anna luxuriated in the deep, husky tone of his voice, '*And then my heart with pleasure fills, And dances with the daffodils.*'

'It's a beautiful poem and as joyous as the daffodils it describes,' Anna added, before resuming her walk along the footpath. The narrowness of the path continued but to the right a barb-wire fence opened up to a large field, giving the area a more spacious feel. She stopped by the water's edge to gaze at two mallard ducks as they searched for food in the water. One was a drake, with a glossy green head, a white ring around its neck and a chestnut-brown body. The mottled brown female looked dull by comparison. 'It seems unfair that the male is more attractive than the female,' Anna observed.

Nick gazed down at her. 'It is much the same with humans where the females are plain and the males are gorgeous specimens. Look at us two,' he stated, pointing a finger at her and then at himself.

Anna smiled at his smug expression. 'Oh really. I think human females are the exception to the rule as we are generally lovely. And some males near to me are very dull and drab in terms of their looks.'

'Well, is that so, miss,' he berated her, playfully. 'I should put you in the water for your cheek.' In an instance, he lifted her off her feet, took a stride to the river's edge and held her over the water.

Anna looked down anxiously at what she knew would be cold water and he teased her more by lifting her up and down in the air. 'Put me down,' she ordered, in a low, but firm voice, as she wrapped her arms around his neck . She was trying not to shriek as an elderly couple were walking towards them and she didn't want to attract attention to herself.

'I will put you down when you apologise for calling me dull and drab. I am mortally wounded by your cruel words,' he teased, putting on a sad face. He then dipped her down in his arms which made her squeal loudly.

Anna's face went white as she felt that he was going to let go of her. 'Ok, ok. Nick Charlton, you are the most handsome peacock in the bird kingdom.'

'That's more like it. You have avoided a soaking,' he stated, as he gently placed her back on her feet.

Anna punched him lightly on his upper arm. 'I will have a job bringing you into line.'

As the elderly couple came close, the man commented, 'That's it young man, show her who's boss.'

'Absolutely, sir,' Nick agreed, grinning at Anna.

The man's wife then said to her husband. 'Remember when you used to do that to me.'

The man replied, 'Yes, dear. But now I have to be careful of putting my back out.'

The older lady looked wistfully at Anna. 'Enjoy your time with your handsome boyfriend, dear. They soon get old and grouchy.'

Anna had to admit that she had gone all goose-bumpy after Nick's pretending to chuck her into the river. This was not due to the proximity of the cold water but the proximity of this self-assured man with an unpredictable streak.

CHAPTER TWENTY EIGHT

Monday 18th April 2022

Sitting at a table in a Warwick pub, Nick was drinking a pint of lager-zero and was reflecting on how he had enjoyed a perfect day with Anna. As it was a bank holiday the pub was full but it did not have too many tables crammed together, thus, the noise of people's conversations did not impinge on your enjoyment. There was a general cosy ambience. When Anna returned from the pub's restroom, Nick noticed that she'd refreshed her make-up and reapplied a glossy, red lipstick. Her hair fell gently around her shoulders. As she smiled at him, he was again hit by her stunning beauty. But it wasn't just that he liked about her. The day had been fun, a low-key walk in a pretty village on a pleasant spring day. They'd enjoyed refreshments of coffee and cake in a small, traditionally English, café. Anna was quick-witted, funny, and fun to be with. It had been a truly relaxing, enjoyable time. His mind drifted, unintentionally, to Abbie. Today would not have been her idea of a good time as it did not involve designer shops and expensive lunches. 'Well, Anna, have you enjoyed your day, so far?,' he enquired, as he scrutinised her lovely face.

Anna sipped her chilled white wine. 'Yes, it's been wonderful. I've been to Bourton-on-the-Water before but it was years ago and it's been great to visit again. It's often the case that we travel the world but fail to fully explore our own doorstep.'

Nick realised that though they had met a few times now, he didn't know anything about her personal life. 'Actually, Anna,' he commented, 'I don't really know anything about you. Where is home?'

Placing her wine glass down on the table, she stated, 'I'm from Tewkesbury. A pretty market town but due to its location where the River Avon meets the River Severn it's vulnerable to flooding. My dad still lives there. He's a qualified mechanical engineer and is a senior manager at a local engineering company. I have an older brother, Dan, who lives in Gloucester with his current girlfriend. I say current, as they do have a habit of changing frequently. He's ex-army and now works as a self-employed electrician. I studied 'A' Levels, went to University of Gloucestershire and did a Business and Management degree. I lived in Gloucester for five years, first as a student, and then afterwards.' She paused to drink a little more of the wine and to take a breath before continuing. 'In terms of my personal life, I was in a relationship for five years which ended badly during lockdown last year, in spring 2021. I moved back in with dad, temporarily. But then I felt I needed a new start so I applied for my current job as a Payroll/HR Administrator – Team Leader for NPX Payroll Solutions Ltd, Warwick. I bought a property here and moved in just over six months ago.' She rolled her eyes at him. 'Payroll work, eh? The excitement never ends.'

Further conversation was temporarily halted by the male waiter bringing their starters. The waiter was blonde, with a buzz-cut hair style, and a cheeky confidence which radiated off him. He was also making it clear that he liked Anna as he stared at her and ignored Nick. The waiter placed Anna's starter of Devon crabcakes with chili lemon mayo in front of her with a flourish. Nick half expected him to wink at her such was the guy's cockiness. 'There you go, sw...' He did stop short of saying 'sweetheart' as he caught Nick's less than pleased expression. Nick recognised that this could be his life going forward if he got together with Anna. Having to growl and scowl at all male chancers and admirers.

Nick grudgingly thanked the waiter for his starter of crispy calamari with Cajun mayo. He would never normally be off with serving staff as this used to irritate him when Abbie did it. But Anna had perfect manners and the male waiter melted when receiving a 'thank you' smile from her pretty lips. Nick stabbed his fork into the crispy battered squid and dipped it into the mayo and ate it with enjoyment, before stating, 'So, a business and management degree, very versatile in terms of employment, I would think. Call me immensely intuitive but I'm getting the impression that working on payroll deadlines is not your dream career. What did you want to do with that degree?'

Anna cut into a crabcake, dipped a portion into the chili lemon mayo, popped it into her mouth and chewed. 'My degree? I suppose I imagined a job in publishing, journalism or HR,' Anna explained. 'This starter is lovely. How's your calamari? I've never tried squid as people say it's quite rubbery.'

Nick cut a battered squid ring in half, dipped it in the Cajun mayo and pushed his plate towards her. 'There you go, try that.'

Anna forked the squid, placed the morsel in her mouth and chewed, whilst pulling a face as Nick laughed. After swallowing, she stated, 'It's nice with the crispy batter and Cajun spice but it is like chewing a rubbery plimsoll. I'll pass.'

'Good,' Nick grinned at her. 'As you won't be swooping in to eat all mine. You mentioned your last relationship was for five years, what age did you get together with this guy?' Anna now looked a little subdued, making Nick regret asking this question. He quickly added, 'Sorry, for prying. Don't feel obliged to answer.'

Anna finished her starter and picked up her wine glass. 'It's ok. I was nineteen and working at a coffee bar in Gloucester. Alistair was a newly qualified solicitor and five years older than me. He was brought up in a very wealthy family in the Cotswolds, went to a top public school, got a law degree at Bristol, and then did three years to qualify as a solicitor. He worked at the family firm, established by his grandfather. His mother was from a banking family. The family bought him an apartment in Gloucester and after six months together, I moved in with him.

Let's just say that over time a cocaine habit and an enthusiasm for on-line gambling changed the loving man I first met into an unpredictable, aggressive boyfriend. The pressures of lockdown just added to his problems and so we split. I moved here partly to get away from him.' As she finished speaking, her eyes filled with tears.

Noticing her distress, Nick reached over and held her hand. 'Hey, sorry, I don't want to upset you if there is something that's too difficult to talk about.'

'It is difficult and not something to talk about in a public place.' There was a catch in her voice as she said this and Nick guessed that there was perhaps a traumatic ending to the relationship. 'I came to Warwick with the intention of meeting new people. But it's difficult as I don't know many people here. Olivia at work has been great and I go out with her and her two friends, Kate and Georgie. Kate's lovely but it's trickier with Georgie as I don't think she's keen on me.'

'Probably as she sees you as competition in terms of potential boyfriends, I guess,' Nick suggested. 'I can see her point. If I was a woman, I wouldn't want you around getting all the attention from the men.'

Anna looked shocked at this comment which Nick now deeply regretted. 'I can assure you that I do not actively seek the attention of men. I'm not some outrageous man-stealing, flirt.'

Nick was taken aback by the vehemence of her response. 'I know you aren't. What I think is that a lot of men would be interested in you based on the fact that you are very pretty. Our waiter tonight is very taken with you.'

Once again, her eyes started to water. 'Well, the male attention thing can get tiring after a bit. Alistair was always jealous if other men tried to speak to me and accused me of encouraging them which I didn't. Connor started acting in the same possessive way after a few dates. One, I can't control what other people decide to do. Two, I don't do anything to encourage them.'

Nick took hold of her hand again, covered it with his own, and stroked his thumb across the top of her hand as a gesture of comfort. 'If a man has a very beautiful girlfriend, he has to learn to deal with the circling male vultures in a grown-up way. Having said that, our waiter will get one of my death stares if he tries to call you sweetheart again. I didn't have a problem with Abbie. She was very attractive but her rude manner could scare off a serial killer. She also had a jealous side to her if a woman spoke to me. We must make a pact to keep away from possessive people.'

Later, lying in bed, running over the memories of his day with Anna, Nick felt peaceful and happy. When he had dropped her home, he'd got out of the car to walk her to her door. He'd stood on the driveway, and she on the step, facing each other. He had wrestled with the idea of whether to kiss her or not. In the end, he drew her into him, almost lifting her off her feet because of their height difference. It had been sensational to hold her in his arms, clasping her tightly around her waist, to bring her face close to his. Gazing into those lovely blue eyes, he'd whispered, 'I've wanted to kiss you for so long.'

The pleasure of kissing her perfect, wine-sweet mouth for the first time was as wonderful as he'd imagined it to be. He kissed her softly at first, tentatively, so as not to scare her but it was all he could do to hold back from possessing her mouth completely with a demanding kiss. A surge of passion swept his body but he had to control it. No lustful, clothes-ripping antics this time. This woman was more precious than a hundred Vanessa's and a thousand Abbie's. Nick wanted Anna Louden but in a way that wasn't just a frantic coupling with no emotional connection. If he were lucky enough to be with Anna, then he intended to make love to her with his body, mind and soul.

Nick ended their first kiss, though his body screamed for it to continue. Anna looked conflicted, as if she too did not want things to end, and they both seemed to be struggling with what should happen next. Nick loosened his grip on her and smiled cheekily, telling her that this perfect kiss was a great way to end a lovely day. That he'd be in touch. And he would be in touch, as there was no way he was going to let this woman slip through his fingers.

⊶◈⊷

CHAPTER TWENTY NINE

Tuesday 19th April 2022

Anna sat at her work desk, staring at her computer screen, failing to concentrate on the final payroll inputs she was going to make that day. Images of her perfect day out with Nick filled her head, affecting her work, and her employer would be entitled to reprimand her for her lack of attention to what she was paid to do. It had been magical to be kissed by him but the kiss itself had disappointed her a little. She'd expected a more forceful, possession of her mouth, and his more tentative approach had been a surprise. Perhaps he hadn't enjoyed their day out and had kissed her out of politeness. He said he'd be in touch but was this just a casual remark to keep her happy before he could escape her company for good? This was making sense as of now, late Tuesday afternoon, there had been no contact. Then, just as she was preparing to leave work, she received a text. '**Hi. Really enjoyed our day together yesterday. Are you available to meet on Saturday? N x**'

On reading the text she did feel giddy with excitement that he had got in touch as promised. Olivia, sitting nearby at her work desk, noticed the beaming smile on Anna's face. 'Someone looks happy. Have you received a message from a certain hot guy?'

'Yes,' Anna stated and read the text aloud. 'He wants to meet on Saturday. That would work as I'm out on Friday for an important person's birthday celebration at the Frizzy Lion'.

'And that my friend is the right answer. The important person is me. Don't forget Gavin will be there on Friday,' Olivia reminded her.

'Yeah, I know. This could all get a bit tricky as I like Gavin but I really like Nick,' Anna said, whilst sighing loudly. 'Shall I text Nick to say that I am available on Saturday or will that appear too keen?'

Olivia now moved to sit on the corner of Anna's desk. 'Ok. Auntie Liv says that you should tell him that you enjoyed your date. And you are available on Saturday. Don't miss this chance as he's a real hottie and seemingly well off. Charge for Auntie Liv's dating advice, one bottle of white wine on her birthday.'

'Olivia, you know I'm not interested in his money. In fact that puts me off him a bit. As he was so generous in paying for the meal on Monday, I was wondering about inviting him to my house for a meal. Would that be a bit too forward as we don't know each other well?' Anna pondered, as she half-concentrated on tidying up payroll reports on her desk.

Olivia was now fully thinking through Anna's suggestion. 'Right. Good idea about the dinner as long as you can cook. No ready meals from M & S. But it will be a more intimate situation in your home, what with food and wine. Be aware, if he wants something sweet and tasty for dessert, that may be you. You know what I'm saying.'

Anna acknowledged that her friend could be right. Did she want to have sex with Nick Carlton if the situation developed? Anna sighed again. 'I know what you're saying. He is very attractive but it does seem too early as I feel I should get to know him better first. But I think I will invite Nick for a meal on Saturday.'

Olivia jumped down off Anna's desk to pick up her bag. 'Go for it, girl. Right, I'm off. See you tomorrow, babe.'

Taking account of Olivia's advice, Anna texted, '**Hi. I had a great time too. I am available on Saturday. Would you like to come to my house for a meal? A x**'. After she'd sent the text, Anna panicked that it was a bit too soon to invite him to her house. But too late, the text was now pinging through cell towers to Nick's phone so no time to regret her actions.

Within minutes, he had texted a response. **'I would love to come for dinner at your house. Can you cook? N x'**

Anna was already experiencing a touch of nerves as she contemplated being alone with him on Saturday evening and also of deciding what to cook. **'I may do my signature dish, oeufs brouillés dessus griller,'** she texted.

Immediately, he responded. **'Scrambled eggs on toast. What time shall I arrive for this culinary feast?'**

'Seven pm ok? I may even attempt something a little more complicated. Just wait and see.'

'Seven pm is fine. Looking forward to it. See you then. N x'

Half an hour later, parking her car at her local supermarket, Anna flipped between feelings of happiness and nervousness as she thought about Saturday evening with Nick. Standing at the supermarket entrance with her trolley, she was partly blocking people's way as she contemplated what she was going to cook for Nick on Saturday. As someone muttered, 'Excuse me' she refocused on the groceries she required for the next few days. She headed to the fruit and veg section to buy vegetables, egg noodles and a sweet and sour sauce to make a stir fry dish.

In the meat aisle, a man came to stand next to her, and they both scrutinised the uncooked chicken thighs. The man was tall, dark-haired, dressed in a red polo shirt, and faded blue jeans, worn with scuffed work boots. Initially, he was standing a foot apart from her but then he edged sideways until he bumped into her.

'Oops, sorry, love,' he said, as intense brown eyes closely examined her face. 'I get carried away when I'm looking at a bird's nice, firm thighs,' he grinned, possibly waiting to see how she would respond to his smutty remark.

Anna's response was to ignore him. She grabbed a two pack of chicken breast fillets and pushed her trolley away from him and towards the dairy aisle to get milk and yoghurts. She placed a two pint bottle of semi-skimmed milk in her trolley, just as the man caught up with her.

'Hello, again, sweetheart,' he stated, his muscular presence imposing on her personal space. 'I see you've got some plump breasts, I mean, chicken breasts in your trolley. Making a stir fry are you? You can cook for me whenever you like.' This man was now making her feel uncomfortable with his sleazy comments and lack of personal boundaries. He had strong facial features, hooded eyes, chiselled cheekbones, prominent straight nose, all of which gave him the unsettling persona of a movie villain. The word that sprang to mind was menacing.

Anna hated these sort of confrontations with men which happened to her from time to time. The sleazy ones. Ignoring them was technically the best option but this often provoked them. Anna made an off-the-cuff comment. 'You wouldn't want to sample my cooking, I can burn water,' and moved up the aisle to the yoghurts section. Not looking back, hoping that the man had gone, she picked up a four-pack of Greek yoghurt.

As she placed the yoghurts in her trolley, he was once again standing next to her, boxing her in between his body and another customer. He edged close to her, all broad shoulders and toned arms, a physical barrier restricting her movement. 'Don't keep running away from me, sweetheart. Do you know that you are off-the-scale beautiful? I'd like to get to know you.'

The supermarket was busy with people doing their after work shopping but Anna suddenly felt completely alone with this intimidating individual. Anger was now flooding through her. 'Move out of my way, now, or I will make a fuss, and alert the shop's security staff.'

He continued to stare at her, challenging her, with a small smirky smile on his lips. 'I like a feisty woman. Are you a hell-cat in the bedroom because I shall enjoy taming you,' he joked, before he stood aside to let her pass. 'Bye for now, sweetheart. I'm sure we'll meet again.'

All this had now unsettled Anna and she decided to cut short her shopping and head for the tills, to make a quick exit from the store. She watched as the man went to one of the self-checkout tills so Anna went to a staffed checkout, despite there being a longish queue. Anna concentrated on placing her groceries on the checkout belt. The customer in front of her was an elderly lady buying an assorted selection of tinned cat food for her cat. After every item was scanned by the female cashier, the woman spoke to the cashier before slowly putting the individual tin in the trolley. Anna tried not to feel annoyed with elderly people but today she wished the woman would stop chatting and load her trolley any time before the summer solstice.

'Hi, we must stop meeting like this,' a cheery male voice behind said.

Anna froze, praying that it would not be the sleazy man but realistically she knew it couldn't be as he was paying for his shopping at another checkout. Slowly, Anna turned and standing behind her was Tulip Man, a beaming smile on his podgy features. Inwardly, Anna groaned. 'Oh, hello,' was her less than enthusiastic welcome. She was truly sick of men today except for Nick.

Tulip Man gazed intensely at her with wide-eyed adoration. Anna felt she knew what it would be like to be a famous pop star being worshipped by a love-sick fan. 'Did you have a good bank holiday weekend? The weather's been good,' he commented. 'It's changed now and it's a bit drizzly out there at the moment. My hair always frizzes when I get it damp and my brother loves to call me Albert Einstein. Sadly, I don't have his intellectual genius.'

Anna feared that she would now be trapped in conversation with him whilst cat-lady continued loading her trolley at a snail-like pace. But she couldn't be rude after his gift of the tulips which were now starting to wilt. She nodded, 'I get what you mean. My hair finds its natural curl if it gets damp.'

Tulip Man's face adopted a blissful look. 'Oh, gosh. I can just imagine you with the softest brown curls framing your stunning face.'

Anna was now silently begging the customer ahead to hurry up. But cat-lady was handing over a number of money off coupons for the tins of cat food, as she informed the cashier, 'These save me a bob or two I can tell you. Professor Purrington is very fussy in his eating habits.'

Tulip Man chuckled when he heard the cat's name and he whispered to Anna, 'Some of these cat owners are nuts as they have the most ridiculous names for their feline friends. If I had a cat I'd call it Genghis Khan but then it would probably go out and slaughter all the bird population in the local area.'

Though not wanting to encourage conversation with him, Anna did smile at this. 'Just hope that Genghis is a strong, healthy tomcat and not a nervous wimp or the name might not fit.'

Luckily, before any further conversation, the cashier was scanning Anna's shopping and she concentrated on bagging it and paying by Visa card. She pushed her trolley quickly to the exit and went outside the store. It was raining lightly, so she paused under the store's canopy to find an umbrella in her bag. As she did so, she looked to her right and was alarmed to see the sleazy male from earlier standing further along under the canopy. As they made eye contact, he made no pretence of looking away, and then nodded to her, before giving her a toothy grin. The grin didn't really convey friendliness; it was more a parody of a smile which was unsettling. The grin of the protagonist in the film *'Joker'*, a little maniacal and insane. Then, unbelievably, he took out his mobile phone, pointed it in her direction and blatantly took a number of photos of her. He then made a thumbs up sign, as if she'd agreed to the photos. Turning abruptly, he then headed off.

Anna put up her umbrella and pushed her trolley in the direction of her car. She had not bought all the items of shopping she needed but her priority was to escape this store and the unwelcome attention of two strangers.

CHAPTER THIRTY

Luke got to Russ's metallic grey VW Golf 2.0, ahead of Russ, and hoped his brother would hurry up as the drizzly rain was threatening to get heavier. But the rain couldn't dampen Luke's spirits. Luke was fizzing with excitement after this most recent conversation with his chosen girl. Today she was in a knee-length, A-Line olive green dress, with long sleeves, and a silver zipper which ended between her breasts. The jersey material of the dress clung to her shapely figure accentuating her feminine curves. Luke knew that he had picked the ultimate female as his muse for his fantasy writings. He couldn't wait to get home to write a chapter about his goddess/princess, the daughter of an all-powerful king, in a magical world where she was the focus of rival lords fighting to possess her and secure their lands with those of her mighty father.

Luke's happiness was tinged by Russ's sudden interest in his chosen girl. Since the BBQ, Russ had been questioning him about his girl. Commenting that she was 'freaking hot' and 'a sexy babe', and that he wanted to get to know her. Luke initially tried to ignore him. It was often difficult to tell with Russ whether he was being serious. But today, after they had finished work, Russ had insisted on coming shopping to the supermarket and he was clear that they would shop separately once they were there. This could only mean that Russ was going to check out his girl.

Russ suddenly rushed up and opened the car door. 'Hurry up and get in, Luke. I've just seen the girl get in her car, a silver Polo, and if we hurry up I can follow her and find out where she lives.' Russ started the engine and backed sharply out of the parking space causing an approaching car to pap their horn. Russ gave the driver the finger. 'Tosser', he shouted.

Luke always felt his heart pounding whenever Russ was driving as he was an 'angry' driver which involved a lot of speeding, risky manoeuvres, sudden breaking and cursing. To catch up with the girl, he had to do a quick left then right to exit the car park. To keep up with her and to join the main traffic, he bolted forward almost colliding with a transit van. The van driver, another 'angry' gave Russ a two finger salute. The girl headed towards the Heathcote district and Russ kept tight on her tail and after a few short miles she pulled off Othello Avenue to one of the adjoining roads. She pulled onto a driveway of a small, modern terraced property. The road was clear of traffic and Luke expected Russ to come to a halt close to her house but, instead, he drove past, went into a side road, did a U-turn back on to the road where the girl lived. He came back up the road on the other side. Then did a typical Russ, came to a jerky stop in a place where they had a good view of her car and her front door.

In a few seconds she was out of the car, opening the boot and taking out her shopping bag. Two sets of intense male eyes gazed openly as she stood on tiptoes to lower the boot door. Luke sighed wistfully as he watched. 'See, she needs a taller man to help her out. That could be me. I'd be her willing slave.'

Russ laughed at his brother's puppy dog expression. 'You are a wuss. She'll not want a willing slave but a strong male figure to guide her. Feminine women like her will be your willing slave if you train them right.' Russ grinned slyly at Luke. 'I had a quick chat with her at the supermarket, brother. Up close she is truly beautiful. Good choice, man. Sexy, kissable mouth. Great tits in that clingy green dress and I really had to use all my self-control to stop myself pulling down the zipper at the front of the dress. Lovely bum and legs as well.'

Luke stared over at his older brother. Women found Russ to be hot and handsome with his hard, chiselled features, dark, broody, brown eyes, moody expression and hard, muscular body. Sounding like a five-year-old trying to cling on to his favourite toy, Luke stated, 'Leave her alone, Russ. You'll only shag her then dump her. I am looking for a long-term relationship not a casual fling.'

Russ pursed his lips. 'You've got absolutely no chance with her, bro. She's bound to have a fit boyfriend who'll scare off any male predators.'

'I've seen her quite a few times in that supermarket and she's always been alone,' Luke commented. 'She tends to buy enough fresh food for one person, for a couple of days. I guess she lives here on her own. But there are bound to be men who are interested in her. We won't be the only two.' Luke was now trying to fathom out what Russ was up to. 'Anyway, I found this girl, not you. You are going out with Leanne if you haven't forgotten.'

Russ shrugged his shoulders. 'I am not going out with Leanne. We're just having a casual thing. I'd drop her like a hot stone in a minute to get near that hot babe. I did speak to this girl. She wasn't overly impressed with the Russ Milner banter. In fact she was a bit standoffish, TBH. Not a problem. I told her that she's a little hell-cat that I'd enjoy taming.'

Luke leaned forward with his head in his hands. 'Oh for fuck's sake, Russ. You are an arrogant idiot at times. Not all woman like dominant, alpha males who tell them what to do. Some women like a more intellectual, cultured man with a sense of humour. I don't want you messing things up for me with this girl.'

Laughing hysterically, Russ shook his head. 'Women want soppy men, do they? Who can get virtually any woman into bed, eh, brother? Me. Who probably has never shagged a woman in his whole life? You.'

Luke was fuming inwardly that Russ now had the capacity to crush all his hopes and dreams involving this girl. But it was a real bonus to know where she lived. His next plan was to find out where she liked to socialise, hopefully a local pub or bar, and then organise an opportunity to 'bump into her'.

'Now we know where she lives, we can keep an eye on her. See where she hangs out and who with. I intend to ask her out,' Russ insisted.

Luke could not believe the stupidity of his brother at times. 'She's an independent woman with a good job, her own car, who rents or owns a property. What have you got to offer her? You live with your dad and your brother. You earn an average wage as a plasterer. You're a commitment phobe. She doesn't need anything from you.'

This did not overly please Russ who never liked to be reminded of his shortcomings. 'Maybe, but her life's probably a boring routine of work, eat and sleep. I can bring some excitement to it and great sex.'

'I'm sure there's a lot of men that can bring excitement and great sex as well as offer her financial security, and perhaps marriage and children,' Luke explained, also realising that his own chances of being with her were not exactly high.

Russ glanced over at the property. 'That's a nice place to get my feet under the table. Perhaps I've been doing things all wrong all these years. Grafting to earn a bit to spend on booze, drugs and women. I should've picked a pretty one with a bit of money and got myself comfortable. Yeah, this could all work to my advantage.'

Initially, Luke thought that Russ was playing him by trying to compete for the woman he liked. A silly Russ game and he would soon get bored. Now, it appeared that Russ was seeing potential in getting to know his girl. Luke had learned long ago to never underestimate his brother if he set his mind to something. Russ could be ruthless and dangerous if thwarted in achieving his goals.

⸺⋆◇⋆⸺

CHAPTER THIRTY ONE

Friday 22nd April 2022

Friday night and Anna was back at the Frizzy Lion to celebrate Olivia's twenty-sixth birthday. As money was tight for Olivia, she had planned a night in the pub with a few friends, hoping that everyone would buy her drinks. Olivia had now been dating Jamie for a few weeks and was relying on him to fill in any gaps if the flow of drinks dried up. Once again the place was heaving, people jostling for space as they were crammed in close together, all trying to hold conversations in groups, which was often impossible because of the noisy din of voices. Anna was in a group with Olivia, Jamie, Georgie, Kate and a few people from their work's payroll teams. Gavin was also present and though Anna had not firmed this up as an exclusive date with him, she got the impression that he believed they were together. He had kissed her lightly on the mouth when she arrived, kept close to her the whole time and occasionally placed an arm around her waist when they were pushed by other people. At any other time in her life Anna may have liked to get to know Gavin better. But this was not the time, as her mind was consumed with thoughts of Nick after their day out together.

Olivia was in her element, displaying a large pink badge with 'Birthday Girl' written on it. A steady supply of drinks had passed her way and she was now at the 'tipsy' stage of alcohol intoxication. Usually at this stage, shy people become more confident and outgoing. Olivia, normally loud and sociable, was now the focus of attention, a one woman comedy act performing to her friends. 'God created childbirth to give women the chance to experience what it's like for a guy to catch a cold,' Olivia stated, a large glass of white wine in her hand which she slurped between jokes. 'Why do some women prefer doggy style. They hate to see a man having a good time.'

Anna stood next to Gavin, laughing at her friend's jokes. Olivia looked super sexy in a mid-blue mini dress that accentuated her petite figure. She had started out the evening with immaculate make-up but her cheeks were now a rosy glow after too much booze.

Gavin now leaned in closer to Anna. 'Well, Olivia's having a good time. And considering she's normally quite loud, the alcohol is taking her decibel levels up a notch to that of high-pitch cackle.'

Anna nodded. 'Yeah, she is quite loud but she is fun to be around. She's been a good friend to me since I moved to Warwick.'

'I think Jamie likes her. It's worked out well really. He met Olivia and I met you. You look sensational tonight and I can see quite a lot of men staring at you,' he added, grinning broadly. 'I'm pleased that you are with me.'

Anna flinched at this. She hoped he wasn't starting to make assumptions about them being a couple or things would get awkward. To escape him, she said, 'It's my turn to go to the bar.'

Trying to get close to the bar in this packed pub was near on impossible. Eventually, she managed to squeeze into a small space next to the bar counter to wait to be served. Immediately, another male eased in beside her. The man was tall, muscular with dark brown hair, and jostled her, as if he were being pushed by someone to his left. 'Oh, sorry, sweetheart,' he stated, as intense brown eyes swarmed all over her face, before he gave her a friendly nod. 'Why, hello, again. It's the beautiful girl from the supermarket with the lovely breasts. Chicken, I mean. Remember me, babe?'

Anna did remember him, sadly, the sleazy man. But to deflate his ego she said, 'No, not really.'

A bartender now intervened to ask Anna what drink she wanted. 'A bottle of Sauvignon Blanc, please,' she requested, 'I'm ok for glasses.' As the bartender brought her the bottle, she presented her card for payment and the transaction ended.

The man now placed his order for a pint of lager, then said to Anna. 'Don't go. I'll just pay for this drink and then we can have a little chat. I want to get to know the most beautiful woman in this pub tonight.' His hooded dark eyes continued to scrutinise her face and her body. It was like being in the presence of a gecko as it licked its lips and she was the cricket about to be devoured.

Anna decided that the best option was to move back to her friends before he completed his purchase. The scrum of the crowd was hard to penetrate but she shoved her way through. Before she got to her destination, a hand was on her right arm which slowed her progress.

'Hey, wait,' he ordered, 'I just want a chat. I'm assuming you're sharing that bottle of wine with friends but get your glass and have a drink with me.' He let go of her arm and closed the personal space between them. The predator eyes hypnotised her own and for a heart-stopping moment she thought his hand was about to touch her face. 'It would be great to get to know each other. I will rein in my immediate urge to kiss you, for now.'

Eager to get away, Anna didn't want to give him the satisfaction of seeing her unnerved by his indecent proposal of a kiss, so she responded, nonchalantly, 'You'll have to form an orderly queue. Have a good evening.' Anna smiled at the guy as she moved away but his expression went to one of annoyance instantly. A flash of anger in his eyes indicated that he didn't like being made a fool of. Anna's smile faded as she knew this expression, it meant 'don't mess with me.'

Head down, eyes forward, Anna pushed through the remaining pubgoers to get to Olivia, grasping the bottle of wine tightly in front of her as if a protective weapon to fight any foes. She resumed her place next to Olivia and the others. They were all circling Olivia, encouraging her to drink a number of tequila shots, one after the other. 'Drink, drink,' Georgie was shouting as Olivia downed two shots in quick succession.

Anna watched as Olivia staggered slightly and went to sit on a bar stool by a high table before sliding off towards the floor. Jamie stopped her fall and balanced her back on her feet. Anna noted that Olivia was becoming uncoordinated as she wobbled on her heels and clung onto Jamie's arm. Anna then said, 'She's had enough and we don't want her to get ill.'

Anna placed the bottle of wine on the high table and Georgie quickly grabbed it to replenish her glass. Taking a large gulp of wine, Georgie scowled at Anna. 'Who made you queen? Stop being a party pooper. It's her birthday and girls just wanna have fun.'

'Well, it'll be no fun if she ends up in hospital attached to an IV drip,' Anna stated which seemed to inflame Georgie even more.

'Are you a fucking nurse, then?' Georgie retorted, glaring openly at Anna.

'Actually, Georgie, Anna's got a point,' Kate added, 'I think she probably needs to go home.' This was said as Olivia started to slip down to the floor again as Jamie had loosened his hold on her. Her legs folded under her and her body flopped as if she'd been drained of all energy. A cheesy grin on her face melted away and her eyes closed. Jamie just managed to stop her falling onto the sticky pub floor.

Jamie called over to Gavin for assistance. 'Gav, mate, I'll need a hand to get her in a taxi.'

Anna picked up Olivia's black jacket, bag, and a number of gift bags containing birthday presents. 'I'll bring these as you take her outside.'

The pub had thinned out from earlier and there was more space to guide a limp Olivia through the pub customers. A lot of people stared, and a few laughed, as they saw the intoxicated young woman being carried out of the pub. The outer pub door opened and a group of people allowed Olivia to be taken outside by her two helpers, followed by bag carrier, Anna.

The men smiled at her and she recognised, Justin, followed by Nick, and Nick's brother, Ed. Justin grinned at her, leaning in to give her a peck on the cheek. 'Hi, Anna. It's my lucky night, seeing you.'

Anna noted that from the unsmiling look on Nick's face that this didn't please him but his irritation was directed at Justin and not her. Nick stated, 'Justin, I think Anna needs to follow her friend to get her home as quick as possible, judging by the state of her.'

Anna nodded 'hi' to Nick who rewarded her with a smile. 'Yes, she's been downing birthday drinks, wines and shots, and suddenly her legs stopped working.'

Jamie hailed a black cab which pulled up by the kerb. Jamie slid along the back seat and Gavin assisted Olivia to get in next to Jamie. Anna placed Olivia's belongings on the seat next to her. As Jamie struggled to fasten Olivia's seat belt, she opened her eyes, squinted at Anna, then pointed, 'It's Anna. Love you, babe.'

'Bye, Olivia, go home and sleep it off. I'll call you tomorrow,' Anna stated as she closed the cab door and the taxi gently pulled away to join the traffic. Gavin placed his arm around Anna's waist to guide her back into the pub. 'Come on, let's get inside as it's bloody cold out here.'

Anna noticed that Nick was standing by the door. Was he waiting to speak to her? She could feel Nick's eyes boring into her as she was rushed to the door by Gavin. Anna now felt sick herself, not through excessive alcohol consumption, but by Nick seeing her embraced by Gavin. Shit, oh, shit, oh, shit! Anna disentangled herself from Gavin and stopped in front of Nick. To Gavin she said, 'I'll be in shortly.' She shivered slightly in her black mini dress as the cool night air contrasted with the steamy heat of the pub. 'Hi, Nick, I'm surprised to see you here.'

'Evidently,' he said, a sardonic tone to his voice. 'I see that your friend's a little the worse for wear. Celebrating her birthday?'

Anna squirmed a little from Nick's annoyed expression. Trying to lighten the mood, she quipped, 'What gave it away, the 'Birthday Girl' badge? Yes, it's Olivia's birthday.'

Her semi-sarcastic tone didn't help as he gave her a stern look. 'And who's that guy with you?'

'Oh, him, that's Gavin, a friend of Olivia's boyfriend, Jamie. He's a friend.'

'Yes, he seems very friendly,' Nick stated, in a non-friendly tone, as he gazed at her face.

Anna gauged that Nick was annoyed with her being with Gavin but was trying not to make a direct comment. Subconsciously, she rubbed at her arms, partly due to the cold evening and partly as a mechanism to deflect from his scrutiny.

'You're getting cold,' he said, his tone of voice softening and he opened the door to allow her inside. As they entered the rowdy, warm atmosphere of the pub, he took hold of her arm. 'I'm looking forward to tomorrow to discover what culinary delights you will be cooking,' he joked. 'Just to say that I generally like most foods so don't get hung up on the cooking bit. It's the company that I'm looking forward to.'

Anna felt relieved in a way, as she was no Nigella Lawson. 'Thanks, but I do find cooking for people all a bit stressy.'

'Do you want me to bring dessert?' Nick asked moving away slightly from the doorway as they were impeding other customers from exiting or entering the pub though Anna remained in the way, facing Nick.

A tall man walked by and Anna immediately recognised the sleazy man who had spoken to her earlier. Again, his dark, haunting eyes fixed on her as he made his way to the exit. The outer pub door opened and a couple entered the room, separating Anna and Nick. As they all jostled for space, the sleazy man grabbed her lower left arm and muttered, 'Stuck-up bitch' under his breath. Anna flinched inwardly as she glimpsed a cruel coldness at the heart of this man. As the couple passed by, he let her go, and gave her a slight push, causing her to stumble into Nick whose arms went around her in a protective manner. Anna laughed nervously and said 'sorry' to Nick who smiled but kept her in his embrace.

'I knew you'd fall for me eventually, Ms Louden,' Nick joked. 'Perhaps we can go somewhere else more private if you want to make a pass at me.'

Feeling embarrassed, Anna tried to break away from Nick. 'This place gets so crowded at times there's no room to move.' He persisted with keeping his arms around her and she liked being held by him. A smile on his face indicated that he was enjoying it a bit too much. But the smile faded when he noticed that she was not looking too happy.

'What's up, you look a bit upset, are you ok?' Nick asked.

'Yes, eh,' Anna stuttered. 'That guy who just walked by, he wanted to buy me a drink earlier. He can't cope with rejection and just made an unpleasant comment.'

Nick still kept a firm hold on her and placed his hand on her chin. 'Honestly, Anna Louden, you do seem to bring out the wrong side of some people. What shall I do with you?'

Reluctantly, Anna pulled away. What could she say, he probably had a point. Plus she didn't want him to keep seeing her as some sort of idiot that kept attracting trouble. 'I honestly don't know. Find me a desert island to live on. Anyway, I should go back to Georgie, Kate and people from work. See you tomorrow.'

As she walked back into the bar to find her friends, Anna reflected on what Nick just said. Since her move to this town she did seem to be antagonising people without meaning to. Connor. Abbie. The sleazy man. At times, Anna longed for an invisibility cloak so that people would leave her alone.

CHAPTER THIRTY TWO

Saturday 23ʳᵈ April 2022

As seven p.m. approached, Anna wondered if she could feign an illness, sudden onset sickness bug or severe influenza, to allow her to cancel the evening. As her anxiety levels rose, she concentrated on doing breathing exercises but they didn't help. These were abandoned for a small, medicinal glass of white wine. This worked but her inclination to drink a second small glass had to be curbed or she would end up reeking of booze and in danger of burning the meal. After a lot of reading recipes online, Anna decided on honey and garlic chicken with parmesan-roasted potatoes and French beans.

Her other stress-inducing anxiety was due to deciding what to wear. After wasting time delving into the depths of her wardrobe like an explorer fighting their way through thick Amazonian rainforest, she pulled out a dress that was suitable. It was navy with cream spots, with a V-neck and long sleeves, which fitted at her waist and a frill hemline skimmed her knees, adding femininity to her look. She had taken time to style her hair to fall in gentle waves and carefully applied her make-up.

With fifteen minutes to his arrival, the chicken and potatoes were in the oven and the French beans ready to be microwaved. Anna sat on the sofa trying to be calm so as not to get sweaty and red-cheeked from the cooking and her nerves. But the wine glass trembled in her hand as her nerves got the better of her. Part of the problem was that she knew she liked this man but she worried that she was too unworldly and inexperienced for him. By his own account, his relationship with Abbie was based on passionate sex. Anna had lost confidence in herself as a sexual woman and a man liked Nick Carlton could have any sexually proficient woman he wanted. Her sex life with Alistair had been good in the initial lust filled stage. As time went on, he wanted regular sex but Anna had become disillusioned with his selfish 'wham, bang,' attitude and had switched off mentally when doing the physical act. This didn't overly bother Alistair most of the time, as he was content with their frequent, brisk couplings to satisfy his needs. On occasion, her lack of enthusiasm riled him and things could become unpleasant. Then, her one encounter with Connor had shocked her. Anna now believed that there was something wrong with her approach to sex and men were punishing her for her failings.

A sharp knock on the front door pushed these negative thoughts out of her head, to concentrate on enjoying this evening with Nick. Anna took a deep breath before opening the front door. Nick Carlton stood on her doorstep, dressed in dark grey jeans, white shirt and black jacket, holding a jute shopping bag. The epitome of male perfection. 'Hi, please come in.' Anna muttered but now she felt self-conscious as he entered her hallway, his tall presence dominating the small space.

He leaned over, giving her a quick peck on the cheek, and she shivered slightly at the rough touch of his beard stubble on her skin. 'Hi, thanks for inviting me, Anna,' he said as his intense blue eyes looked at her.

Anna hung his jacket on the coat rack in the hallway and led him into the kitchen. He placed the shopping bag on the kitchen work top and brought out two bottles of white wine, four bottled lagers, two desserts, and a box of assorted chocolate truffles. 'I've brought two desserts; tiramisu, and lemon and mascarpone cheesecake, as I didn't know what you'd like. The chocolates are a thank you for preparing the meal.'

After sorting out a bottled lager for him, Anna led the way into the living room and offered him a seat on the leather sofa. Still feeling shy, Anna put distance between them by sitting on a single armchair. She picked up her wine, with a hand now shaking like a leaf in a hurricane, and drank a large mouthful, in a bid to hide her inability to speak.

Nick seemed to be immediately at ease. 'Have you spoken to your friend today to check that she's still alive?'

'Yeah, I rang her earlier. She managed to get home ok without incident but is today recovering from the hangover from hell. Vowed to give up alcohol forever, apparently,' Anna joked. 'I doubt that will be the case. Forever will last as long as next weekend.'

Nick nodded. 'I do try to swerve excess drinking now. I don't like to waste the next day feeling nauseous and with a throbbing head.'

The addition of more wine was now making Anna more mellow and less tongue-tied. 'Yes, it's not so easy to recover from heavy drinking when you get older, I'm told,' she stated before quickly realising that he might take this as a dig at his age.

He straightened in his seat and honed in on her, a devilment in his twinkly blue eyes. 'Was that a general comment, Ms Louden, or were you having a pop at me now I'm the ancient age of thirty?'

Liking that he was challenging her, Anna responded, 'Well, I expect that as you are getting on in years, you should do things in moderation. You know, go easy on alcohol, gentle exercise, eating soft foods, that sort of thing.'

A look of feigned annoyance came her way. 'It's a good job for you that my elderly knees keep giving out or I might have to come over there and sort you out.'

Anna laughed, beginning to feel relaxed despite wondering what 'sort you out' meant. 'Please have a sweet chilli crisp as long as they don't damage your dentures. I need to go and check the food in the oven.'

He leaned over to take a crisp out of a bowl on the coffee table. 'Yes, I would escape my presence if I was you after all your impudent comments.'

The meal turned out a success and Nick complimented her on the succulent, honeyed chicken and the crispy potatoes. Each chose their preferred dessert, lemon cheesecake for Anna and tiramisu for Nick. Anna then started to clear the table and Nick immediately got up to help her. At the kitchen sink, he ran the hot tap to fill the washing-up bowl and squirted in a lemon washing-up liquid. He rolled up the sleeves on his white shirt which was an action in of itself that made Anna's heart go bumpety-bump. Once the bowl was full of hot, frothy liquid he picked up a brush and set to washing the dinner plates. Anna was going to say she would do it later but it was already too late as the first clean plate landed in the sink drainer. Instead, she picked up the tea towel and dried the wet plate. 'Thanks for doing the washing up but you don't have to. I could do it later.'

He placed a serving bowl into the hot water and washed it with gusto. 'No, I must do my share after you prepared that great meal. I was very impressed. I know it may be remiss of me to say this but Abbie could never find her way around a kitchen. I can barely remember her cooking a meal when we were together. As she never permanently moved into my house, I think she always saw herself as an honoured guest.' He started to wash the individual cutlery items before rinsing them under the hot tap.

Anna stood by his side, happily drying the washed items. It sort of felt good, a partnership, a team. 'Well, I suppose in this day and age a lot of women resist doing any sort of domestic chores in case it's expected of them on a regular basis.'

Nick nodded and looked at Anna. 'Yes, I think that was Abbie's thinking. But if no one cooked or cleaned, everyone would starve surrounded by their own filth. You can take this feminism stuff too far, in my opinion.'

'Well,' Anna chuckled. 'It's taken years for women to escape being shackled to the kitchen sink and we aren't going back.' She finished drying the knives and placed them in a drawer.

'Is that so, Emmeline Pankhurst,' he teased, as a bubble of soapy froth landed on Anna's nose. Anna sneezed softly and rubbed it away. Other frothy bubbles quickly took their place followed by two flicks of warm water.

Anna realised that he was trying to soak her and shouted, 'Stop it.' This had no effect as more frothy foam landed on her. Another method of retaliation was required and Anna flicked the tea towel at him, aiming for his bottom. The high velocity of the flying tea towel was meant to hit its target with the desired sting but ended up as a small slap on his well-defined buttock. No pain delivered. Nevertheless, he stopped washing a fork to face his adversary.

Anna stood still, noting the gleeful look in his eyes as he moved towards her. She started to giggle as he closed the space between them, ready to defend herself with her weapon of choice, the soggy tea towel.

'Well, Anna, I believe that war has been declared and you have made the first attack by trying to hit my bum. Very bad mistake, I think,' he teased with a light tone of voice but there was a steely look in his blue eyes.

Glimpsing his broad shoulders and his toned biceps, well-defined by the white shirt, and noting his weapon of choice, the washing-up brush in his right hand, Anna decided her best option was to flee the room. In seconds, she was in his grasp, pulled off her feet, and leant over so that a light slap of the brush landed on her bum. 'Ouch,' she squealed, but this was a pretence on her part as it didn't hurt, just made her laugh.

He held her firmly, still leaning her forward, with feet off the ground, as he asked, 'Ok, are you ready to put down your weapon, the tea towel, or do I have to deliver another blow. First rule of war, do not weaken if you have the enemy within your grasp.'

Anna did weakly try to flay the tea towel around to inflict some damage but it was limp and ineffective. This did not deter him from giving her bottom a second, stingier slap with the washing-up brush. 'Are you ready to surrender, now?' he asked, as Anna giggled.

'Yes, yes, see the white tea towel is now a white flag of surrender. Please stop,' she cried, trying to catch her breath from laughing so much.

Nick flipped her back onto her feet as she dropped the tea towel onto the floor but his arms were still around her waist as his eyes examined her flushed face. 'Ok, Ms Louden, I accept your plea to surrender. But we will go about negotiating the peace treaty, in a few minutes, when we have finished washing-up. There will be consequences for your actions in starting this war, I can assure you.' He winked at her as he finished washing the remaining dishes and passed them to Anna.

All the excitement of their tussle was now playing havoc with Anna's insides. There was no denying the strength of him as he held her in his arms and her senses were on overload as she revelled in the proximity of him. The well-fitting white shirt outlined the structure of his muscular body. The touch of his hands on her as he manoeuvred her around was causing her to shiver in anticipation of what the 'consequences' would be. The low, masculine, growl of his voice implied that the 'consequences' would have a sexual connotation. The citrusy, musky smell of his cologne was tantalising her nostrils and taking her mind to thoughts of naked passion. She longed for his mouth to cover hers in an all-consuming kiss. Anna vowed that she was not ready to sleep with this man yet. It was too early but after this 'battle' her traitorous body was ignoring what her rational mind wanted to do.

Calming down, Anna resumed her place in the living room on the single armchair as Nick once again sat on the sofa. She felt hot and bothered, her cheeks were flushed, and she sipped at her now tepid white wine to try to ease her jangling nerves.

He laser-locked his eyes onto hers. Anna shivered; it was time to pay the piper. 'Ok, Ms Louden, I must request that you come over here so that we can discuss the terms of your surrender after I won 'the tea towel war'. Over here, please. And note that I am being very polite to my enemy,' he mocked, his eyes never leaving her face.

Anna was enjoying the fun but was truly a little worried about going to sit with him. They were not about to jointly complete a crossword. 'I was going to say, make me, but I think that may be unwise.'

'Very unwise. I may have to go and get the washing-up brush if I get a tone of dissent,' he joked, but there was a resolute look on his face which meant that she should comply with his request.

Slowly, Anna got up from her chair and sat down on the sofa next to Nick. He immediately pulled her towards him and she slipped across the leather sofa into his arms. Her waist was encircled in a powerful grip, drawing her against the hard frame of his chest, as tender blue eyes looked into her own. Their mouths were so close and she could feel his soft breath on her as his eyes scanned her worried face. A large smile touched his lips and eyes. 'In terms of the peace treaty, I accept your apology in the tea towel war. I propose that we skip the usual handshake which is customary on these occasions and seal the deal with a kiss. This won't be something that catches on generally as I can't see Emmanuel Macron and Boris Johnson kissing any day soon though both of them might be pre-disposed to do so.'

Though still mesmerised by the closeness of him, Anna managed to stutter, 'ap-p-ologise for the tea towel war. You'll find that you initiated the hostilities with the soap froth attack.

But in the spirit of entente cordiale I will agree to a ceasefire and a kiss would be a suitable way to put the war behind us.'

Their mouths were now only inches apart, as Nick gave her a wry smile as his right arm encircled her waist. 'Still not quite ready to accept defeat, I note, Ms Louden. How very brave you are,' he goaded her as his left hand gently clasped her chin. 'But, enough, a truce has been declared, and I the victor claim my prize.' At this, he drew her mouth towards his and kissed her. Once he felt her willing mouth yielding to his, she was subjected to a hot, steamy assault which left her breathless with a growing ache in her tummy. After they stopped to draw breath, Nick's eyes caressed her face taking in her sculptured cheekbones, well-defined eyebrows, bluey blue eyes and perfect mouth. 'Anna Louden, I don't think you realise how truly beautiful you are. I feel privileged to be here with you right now, about to kiss your enchanting mouth for a second time.'

Anna blushed from his scrutiny and his compliments, but did feel there was sincerity in what he said. They were now lying on the sofa, as he leaned over her, and she was acutely aware of the hard masculinity of his body. Tracing his thumb along her lips, he lowered his mouth back down on hers to explore and probe with passionate fervour. She was clasped fully against him as he pulled her body into his, his right hand cupping her buttocks to lock her hips against his groin. His hand then explored upwards to knead her breast before edging downwards to caress her waist and the curve of her bottom. All the time continuing with the expert assault of his mouth on hers. Anna's mind was overwhelmed by a tingling in her breasts and an aching softness in her belly. A liquid heat melting between her legs that would evolve to become an all-consuming hot, throbbing desire that needed to be sated. Anna knew that she was one hundred percent wantonly responding to his caress and there would be no stopping this until its inevitable end. 'Anna, sweetheart,' he whispered, 'I hope you want this as much as I do.'

This sweet fusion of growing lust and raging desire was suddenly interrupted by a knocking at the front door. Nick swore softly, stating, 'ignore it'. Anna backed away from him. 'It's probably Ben from next door collecting a parcel that came earlier. I won't be a moment.'

CHAPTER THIRTY THREE

Anna was floating on air as she walked towards the front door. Perhaps she should have listened to Nick and ignored the knock at the door. By ending their passionate encounter before its inevitable conclusion, her body felt cheated and unfulfilled, a hollow emptiness of yearning. If they resumed their embrace shortly would it still reach the earlier promise of satisfaction. Her mind was flooded by all these worries as she opened the front door expecting to find her middle-aged, friendly neighbour, Ben, on the doorstep. Instead, on opening the door she gasped in alarm. This was not Ben with curly, brown hair and a goofy smile but a lecherously grinning Connor Peterson.

On seeing who it was, Anna tried to close the door but Connor pushed on it with his hand to keep it open. 'Ok, babe, don't be like that. I came round for a little friendly chat, that's all. See if we can take up where we left off. It was really good last time, wasn't it?' White teeth flashed at her as part of a leery grin which was meant to entice her to allow him inside the house. He swayed a little as he stood on the doorstep. Was this an indication that he was drunk or had he been snorting his drug of choice, cocaine? On their one and only sexual encounter together, she believed he had snorted the drug before he slept with her. The drug made him overconfident and pushy, sexually charged, which had resulted in the incident which had alarmed her.

'Connor, I'm not interested in taking up where we left off. I have no interest in being with you again, ever,' Anna stated firmly. His hand shoved the door hard and Anna jumped backwards to prevent being hit by it. Connor walked into the hallway and closed the door behind him.

'Babe, babe, I don't think you're getting it. I just want us to have a little chat and see if we can fix things between us,' Connor cajoled as he pressed slowly forward and Anna backed away from him.

The presence of this obnoxious man in her home was freaking Anna out but she wanted to get rid of him quietly and quickly without Nick finding out. Nick might misunderstand what was going on and think that she had invited Connor here. And she also had the issue of Gavin to resolve who Nick had seen her with last night. Nick might conclude that she had a whole army of men that she was multiple dating. In the case of Connor there was a diary failure and two men had arrived on the same day. Anna addressed Connor in a low but determined voice. 'There's nothing to fix. Get out of my house before I call the police.'

The leery jollity in his brown eyes now disappeared, replaced by a hard, granite expression. 'Shut the fuck up about the police. You won't call the cops. I'll go when I'm good and ready.' He was still moving towards her as Anna hurried into the kitchen where she knew she would find her mobile phone.

Anna could hear the Spice Girls 'Wannabe' coming from the television in the living room. This would drown out her voice and that of Connor as she persuaded him to leave. Nick would assume she was talking to her male neighbour. Connor still followed her into the kitchen, determined, but not in a rush, as if he were stalking his prey but was not ready to pounce. Anna went over to near the hob where she could see her phone. Connor flicked his cold brown eyes at the phone and then at her. 'Don't pick that up or I'll smash it out of your hand.'

Before she could get to the phone, Connor moved swiftly towards her and trapped her in a corner between the sink and the hob. He loomed over her, a smile of satisfaction on his smarmy lips. She pressed hard into the corner to try to escape his touch. His piercing, hunter eyes swept her face and body, and she was the prey, waiting wide-eyed and frightened, as the wolf licked its lips ready to devour her. Whisky-soured breath fanned her face and his right hand whipped out to clasp her chin with bony fingers. Anna winced. He was unsteady on his feet and swayed from side to side. He was on edge, agitated, and Anna believed that he had once again used cocaine to get him into this state of sexual excitement. Anna felt a rising panic. Connor under the influence of this drug was unpredictable and capable of inflicting pain.

'Listen up,' he snarled, 'there's unfinished business between us and tonight you pay what you owe me.' Crushing his fingers into her flesh, he held her face in a vice-like grip. Greedy eyes swept over her once again. 'Don't fight, bitch, or you'll regret it.'

Anna shoved at his chest with all her strength but it was like trying to push open a steel door. 'Let go of me,' Anna demanded, still keeping her voice low so as not to alert Nick though at this moment she could really do with his help.

Connor slammed his mouth on hers, jarring her jaw, and his left hand behind her head ensured that she could not break free. His right hand whipped onto her breast, pinching and pulling, so that she jerked in pain. 'So good, babe,' he murmured, as he briefly paused the kiss. 'We'll put your pretty mouth to another good use in a minute.'

Anna's upper body was shackled by his tight grip and her confinement in the corner. She wanted to gag as his mouth scorched and slurped over her own. The whisky he had drunk put an acidic, rancid taste in her mouth. The comment he just made froze her blood as it became clear what he wanted to do. 'Get off, get off,' she tried to say but her voice was muffled by his persistent mouth on her own. Anna brought up her right leg and slammed her knee into his groin. It was enough of a thump for him to pause his violation of her mouth.

'Bitch,' he moaned, as his body crumpled, and a red hot rage burned in his eyes. 'You'll pay.' His right hand slammed hard across the left side of her face. A follow-up blow sent shards of pain vibrating through her left cheekbone. Anna screamed.

※

CHAPTER THIRTY FOUR

Three songs into watching '*Top of the Pops, The Biggest Hits 1996*' and having endured the Spice Girls singing '*Wannabe*', Nick was wondering where Anna had got to. He could hear murmurs of conversation and assumed that the neighbour, Ben, was lingering for a good old chat. Then, a scream ripped through his mellow, lager-fuelled trance of watching Peter Andre babble on about his '*Mysterious Girl*'. The scream was a high-pitched sound of a female in trouble.

Nick leapt up from the sofa and dashed into the hallway but there was no sign of Anna or her neighbour. The front door was closed. Nick was positive that the scream came from inside the house. He sprinted into the kitchen and couldn't quite make sense of the sight in front of his eyes. Anna pinned in the far corner of the room, by the sink, by a man with his back to Nick. A look of sheer terror was on Anna's face and she stroked the left side of her face which indicated that she may have been hit. No time now to find out what had happened as Nick's first priority was to get this man away from Anna. Placing his left arm around the man's throat, Nick pulled him backwards whilst delivering a powerful punch to his ribs. The male wrestled to escape Nick's grip but he could not get free of his control. 'Get off me, you fucker,' he screamed at Nick.

The man flayed around with his arms in an attempt to strike Nick but this was not bringing results. All the time, Nick was managing to overpower the man with the intention of pushing him down on the floor. The male was of slim build, and of medium height, so slighter and shorter than Nick. The guy squealed and squirmed but he couldn't break free of Nick's hold on him. In his police career, Nick had frequently been confronted by smaller men who often liked the challenge of squaring up to a tall, muscular cop. He had learnt over the years not to underestimate these men, as for all their smaller physique they often packed a lot of energy into a small frame, and were ferocious fighters. Like Jack Russell dogs, they could be tenacious scrappers. 'Fuck off,' the man screamed over and over.

Anna was still in the corner, slumped slightly, as she was unable to escape with this fight in front of her. Nick kept a strong grip on the man, then gave him a swift punch to his back to further subdue him, before pushing him, face down, onto the floor. 'Get down on the floor,' Nick bellowed.

To Anna, Nick asked, 'Who is this, Anna? What's going on?'

Visibly shaking, Anna responded, her voice croaky. 'He's Connor Peterson. We went out a few times. He's just barged his way in saying he wanted to take up where we left off. I told him to go or I'd call the p-police.' Anna faltered, then took a deep breath. 'He starts kissing and groping me. Then, he's slapped my face, twice.'

Peterson was still struggling to break free, but Nick restrained the man's arms behind his back and placed a knee on his back to prevent him getting up. 'Connor Peterson. I am Nick Carlton and I am making a citizen's arrest on suspicion of sexual assault and common assault on this woman, Anna Louden. To ensure her safety, I am restraining you until the police arrive.' He then addressed Anna. 'Get out of here and call the police, Anna.'

Anna stared at him, obviously in shock, and blinked rapidly, but failed to respond to his command. The man on the floor was struggling to get up but for the moment he was under Nick's control. Nick wanted Anna out of the danger zone in case his hold on the man broke. Nick's voice was now loud and commanding to bring her out of her trance. 'Anna, get out of there and call the police.'

Anna failed to move and remained staring at Nick and Peterson. 'I s-should s- stay and help you,' she said, trembling visibly.

Nick's patience was truly running out. 'Anna. You'll help me by moving out of the way so I know you're not going to be hurt. Do as I ask, NOW. Call the cops.'

She finally did as instructed and went into the hallway where he could hear her calling 999. Suddenly, the man ran out of energy, stopped struggling, and slumped, face down, onto the floor. Not fooled by this, Nick did not relax his hold on the man's hands and renewed the pressure of his knee into the man's back. Nick had to crush his urge to batter the man senseless after his attack on Anna. Having called the police, she reappeared at the kitchen door. 'The police are on their way.'

This seemed to revitalise the man who wanted to take his one last opportunity to escape. Trying to get onto his knees to free his body of Nick's weight, he pushed upwards and rolled slightly, to de-stabilise Nick's hold on him, but he failed to make an impact. Nick had him clamped down and unable to move, though his mouth was open and he shouted a string of profanities of what he wanted to do to Nick.

To Anna, Nick ordered, 'Go and get a chair from the other room and we'll make our guest more comfortable while we wait for the police.'

Anna carried in the chair and Nick dragged the man to his feet and plonked him down on the chair. Nick positioned himself close to Peterson to prevent him bolting for the door. 'I am detaining you until the police arrive. Don't try to get away as I will stop you. And to be clear, I am an ex-police officer and I have been trained in restraint techniques.'

Peterson openly scowled at Nick. 'I've committed no crime, you tosser. I just came round to see my ex-girlfriend. Thought I'd have another go as she is pretty tasty. But the little bitch turned me down.'

Nick grabbed the back of Peterson's neck and dug his fingers into the bones at the two sides of his neck. The man howled in pain and Nick snarled at him, 'Shut your filthy mouth or I'll break your neck. One more disrespectful word out of you and I'll send your teeth so far down your throat you'll need the help of a surgeon to remove them from your stomach.'

Nick was now aware of a blue flashing light penetrating into the kitchen and Anna went to let the police in. Nick could hear her speaking to the police before she escorted two male officers into the kitchen. The taller, older police officer stated, 'I am PC Bright and this is PC Rossiter. 'I need to let you all know I am recording at the moment', and he pointed to his body-worn camera. PC Bright looked at Nick, and said, 'I am assuming you are Nick Carlton.'

'Yes, Nicholas Carlton,' Nick confirmed.

PC Bright then gazed at the man seated on the chair. 'Can I confirm that you are Connor Peterson?'

Peterson took this as an opportunity to stand up. 'Yes, I am. I'm pleased to see you. This tosser has overpowered me and beaten me up. You should arrest him.'

'Mr Peterson, I suggest you retake your seat whilst I get a clearer picture of what's going on here,' PC Bright instructed Peterson. Peterson resisted for a moment but then noted the less than friendly expression on the police officer's face. 'I'm going to ask Ms Louden to clarify what happened for the benefit of us all.'

Anna took a deep breath. 'I am Anna Louden and I live here. This man is Connor Peterson. I went out with him a few times a few months ago. He turned up here, tonight, uninvited, and barged his way in. He wanted us to get back together. I've made it very clear that will never happen. I tried to get rid of him without alerting Nick, Mr Carlton. I went in the kitchen to get my mobile phone to call you. Connor followed me, pinned me in a corner, and started kissing me forcefully and touching my breast. I told him clearly to get off me but he didn't so I kneed him in the groin. He then slapped me twice across the face, hard. I screamed and Nick came in and pulled him off me. Nick got him under control and told him he was doing a citizen's arrest. Then we waited for you.'

Connor Peterson quickly tried to give his side of the story. 'I came round to see Anna, my ex-girlfriend, to try to get back with her. We were kissing when this maniac appeared, dragged me off her, punched me twice and then grappled me down on the floor. He's a nutter – you want to arrest him.'

Ignoring Peterson, PC Bright then turned his attention to Nick. 'Ok, Mr Carlton can you tell me what happened.'

Nick responded, 'I was in the living room when I heard Anna scream. I came into the kitchen to find Anna pinned in the corner of the kitchen by this man. Anna looked terrified and she was stroking the left side of her face which indicated to me that she may have been hit. My first priority was to get him away from Anna and ensure her safety.' Nick then described his actions in dragging Peterson off Anna and how he restrained him. 'I served as a police officer for a number of years and I have been trained in restraint techniques. I also explained to Mr Peterson that I was making a citizen's arrest and my reasons for doing so.'

'Ok, thank you, Mr Carlton,' PC Bright stated, and addressed a scowling Connor Peterson. 'Stand up and turn around.' He took a pair of handcuffs off his belt and handcuffed Peterson's hands together behind his back. 'Connor Peterson, I am arresting you on suspicion of sexual assault and assault by beating to Anna Louden. You do not have to say anything. But, it may harm your defence if you do not mention when questioned something which you later rely on in court. Anything you do say may be given in evidence.' PC Bright then advised his colleague. 'Take him into the hallway.'

PC Bright moved closer to Anna and scrutinised her face. 'I can see there is a redness and some bruising to the left side of your face. Do you need medical treatment?'

Anna placed an exploratory hand on her left cheekbone. 'No, I think I'm ok. It feels tender and stings a lot but it should be ok. I will seek medical advice if it gets worse.'

PC Bright continued to scrutinise her face. 'Do I have your permission to take photos of this injury, Ms Louden?' Anna gave her agreement and her injuries were recorded by PC Bright, who then stated, 'Mr Peterson will be taken to the police station for further questioning and we will be in contact with both of you regarding your statements.'

.'Thank you,' Anna stuttered as she watched Peterson being led away. Her face was deathly white, except for the area of redness on her face where she had been slapped. Nick could see that she was totally exhausted and upset by the whole incident. Going up to Anna, Nick placed his arm around her shoulders and then he felt her crumple against him, sobbing against his chest.

CHAPTER THIRTY FIVE

Luke arrived in Anna's street just after eight p.m. and parked close enough to her property to be able observe if she left the house or if there were any visitors. He would have liked to have arrived earlier but his father had been late preparing dinner and so his proposed schedule for surveillance had been thrown off kilter. Luke decided to do his observation from the back seat of the car and had a blanket to cover himself if people walked by. Luckily, this was a street that didn't get a lot of pedestrians but an observant neighbour may report him to police if they saw him lurking. Luke noted that her car was on the driveway and a light was on inside her house, perhaps indicating that she was in residence. A night in watching the television. Luke's imagination lingered on cuddling up on the sofa with his beloved. He had now started to refer to her as his beloved, not his girl, as he felt there was a strong connection between them after their recent encounters. His mind flipped to the two of them snuggled up, watching a romcom, and drinking wine together. His fingers caressing her soft, silky, gently waved hair. The delicate smell of her perfume assailing his nostrils, the one he adored, with its notes of magnolia, lotus flowers and peonies. He would tentatively seek to capture her sensual lips with his own as they both lost interest in the movie. Luke sighed, happily imagining their loving embrace.

The bubble of this fantasy quickly burst as just after nineten; a car pulled up nearby and a male got out, who walked purposely up to his beloved's front door. The man was young, with cropped dark hair, and was of medium height and slim build. He knocked on the door and waited. Luke immediately took a dislike to the man. There was an agitation to him as he paced from foot to foot. The type who was used to getting what he wanted, when he wanted it, and who did not like to be kept waiting. Luke could feel his temper rise as the cocky male waited for his beloved to open the door. He did not want to think about this man alone with his beloved as he perceived that his intentions were not good.

After a couple of minutes, the front door was opened by his beloved and Luke's heart lurched when he glimpsed her. She was wearing a fitted dress, of a dark colour with lighter spots, which flared to her knee. Wow. She looked feminine and beautiful in the pretty dress as her brown hair fell gently to her shoulders. Initially, her face was composed as she greeted her visitor, possibly expecting it to be someone she knew. On fully recognising the caller, her facial expression changed to one of alarm and she went to close the door. The male was quick, putting his hand on the door to keep it open. The man spoke to her, swaying again from side to side in a hyped-up state, which Luke wondered was due to having imbibed drink or drugs. The man's words did not incline his beloved to open the door and admit him. When she spoke, Luke guessed it was to tell her unwanted visitor to go away. The man was not going to be deterred and this time he pushed the door inwards, more powerfully, and his beloved had to step back hastily to avoid being hit by the door. The male strode into the hallway and closed the front door.

'Oh my God, oh my God,' Luke kept saying over and over again. He knew without a shadow of a doubt that his beloved was in danger from this man but what could he do? Luke was not brave like many men and was always cautious to avoid trouble. Russ was the alpha male of the family and would use his fists without hesitation if the situation warranted it. But Russ was not here. Luke felt his breathing getting shallow and he struggled to draw oxygen into his lungs. He could not get images out of his mind of his beloved being alone with this potentially violent, unwanted visitor. Should he call the police? But they would want to question him about what he was doing near to his beloved's residence. He could make an anonymous phone call but weren't all phone numbers recorded when answered by the call operator? His mobile phone number would be traced.

Luke kept the car window down and listened for any noises coming out of the property. He could hear traffic on nearby roads, the drone of a plane overhead, but no other sounds. Thinking of leaving the car to peer in through a window at the front of the terraced property crossed his mind but what would he do if he saw that she was being attacked or worse. Russ always joked that Luke couldn't knock the skin off a rice pudding. Perhaps it would all be ok. As the effects of the drugs or drink wore off, the man would mellow and his beloved would no longer be in danger. But thoughts of this sent Luke's imagination hurtling in another direction where the dark-haired, wiry male was removing her dress and her underwear to lay claim to her sensuous body.

Luke's mind was crippled by all sorts of thoughts swirling around in his brain; his beloved in danger from the man, his beloved having sex with the man, willingly or unwillingly. His overall perception was that the man was trouble but Luke was unable to decide what to do. He thought about calling Russ and they could both storm the house and ensure her safety. But Russ was staying at Leanne's tonight and would not want to be interrupted in his love fest with the obliging, single mother.

Troubled by the arrival of the unpleasant male visitor at his beloved's house, Luke could only wait and watch from the car to see what developed. There was a dip in the evening temperature as Luke observed the property and he pulled the blanket around him to keep warm. He was determined to stay longer to ensure that he was satisfied that she was ok.

Then, just coming up to ten p.m., Luke had the fright of his life as a police car with blue flashing lights pulled up behind his car. Fucking hell. Perhaps a nosy neighbour had spotted him and reported him for what, stalking? Luke slowly crouched down as low as possible, pulling the blanket over himself, all the time trying not to draw any attention to himself. He heard the double slam of doors on the police car, and inhaled deeply, ready for the police to try to open his car door or tap on the window. He held his breath for as long as possible as beads of sweat formed on his upper lip. Tensing his body so as not to move, he almost forgot to breathe, such was his fear of being spotted by the police. Eventually, he exhaled to stay alive, but even this action added to his rising panic as the cops may notice even the tiniest of movements. Thankfully, the heavy footsteps of the police officers faded as they passed by his car. The next sound a trembling Luke heard was a loud knocking on a door. He decided to risk peeking to find out what was going on and was shocked to see two tall male police officers on the doorstep of his beloved. Fear squeezed at Luke's heart as he realised that something must have happened to her at the hands of that man. Was she injured? After a minute, the front door was opened by his beloved, and Luke exhaled loudly, a great sigh of relief, when he glimpsed her. He scrutinised her intently, not bothering if anyone could see him in his car. She seemed to be in one piece, uninjured, and not upset or crying, but she looked petite and vulnerable as she spoked to the two police officers. She invited the police officers inside the house and the front door was closed.

Luke's mind was in overdrive now. What had gone on in that house? The police had been called but there was no sign of an ambulance. He ruled out a fire as there were no fire engines and he could not smell or see any smoke. Having assured himself that his beloved was no longer in danger, Luke resigned himself to waiting until the police left the property to see if this would give a hint as to what had gone on.

At around eleven p.m., with Luke getting chillier in the cold car, the front door of the property opened, and one police officer escorted the uninvited male visitor out of the property. Mr Cocky was now handcuffed and his earlier state of agitation had gone. He was scowling but subdued as a police officer assisted him to sit in the car. A few minutes the later, the second police officer got into the police car and it was driven off.

Rushing out of the back seat of his car, Luke hurried into the driver's seat with the intention of following the police car to the police station to continue to try to piece together the puzzle of the night's events. Luke hoped to be able to park up close to the police station and keep it under observation. As his beloved seemed to be ok there appeared to be no immediate evidence of a serious crime, thus Luke was hopeful that the man would be released at some point. Luke now planned to keep the man under surveillance until he found out where he lived.

⸻◆⸻

CHAPTER THIRTY SIX

Anna wondered if her legs would hold up as Nick guided her into the living room and helped her to sit on the sofa. She leant forward and covered her face with her hands, as heavy tears streaked down her cheeks, smudging carefully applied eye make-up. Her body racked with sobs, as she gulped for air, and she attempted to wipe the wetness off her face with her hand. Nick sat next to her and pulled her into him, strong arms encircling her as she cried, saturating the front of his white shirt. Nick said nothing but stroked her back in a soothing action as the torrent of tears continued.

'It's ok, Anna. He's gone now. You're safe now,' he muttered, his own voice choked as he witnessed her despair.

Anna shivered violently both from the coolness of the night and from the shock of the attack. It was all too awful. A man had come uninvited into her home, had sexually assaulted her, and had hit her in the face. If Nick had not been present, she could not bear to think about what would have happened. Managing to voice a few shaky words between sobs, Anna said, 'I'm s-so glad you were h-here .. sob, hic...'thanks f-for'...hic...'your h-help.' Another tidal wave of crying now halted her speech as her mind tried to process the horror of it all.

'Let it all out, sweetheart,' Nick encouraged her as he held her juddering body tightly in his arms. 'It took a lot of will power on my part not to batter the tosser's ugly face so that his own mother wouldn't recognise him.'

As her crying subsided slightly, Anna looked up at Nick, noting the angry expression on his face. She stated, 'I was v-very impressed'...hic...'w-with how you p-pulled him away f-from'.....sob....'m-me and r-restrained h-him. All that p-police t-training'....hic.'

Nick shrugged. 'Yeah, it was a combination of my police training with the addition of a bucket load of rage that he felt entitled to come into your home and behave like that towards you. It's a pity that society does not let us deal with idiots like that in the way they deserve without involving the criminal justice system. But we will wait and see what the police and courts do with him.'

Still hiccupping slightly but mainly having stopped crying, Anna asked, 'w-what do you t-think would be the likely outcome in terms of the courts?'

'Very difficult to predict from my experience,' Nick explained, handing Anna her glass of wine for her to sip to quash her hiccups. 'For the sexual assault and assault by battery, he could get a custodial sentence but knowing how the law never favours the victim, I'd be very surprised if this happened. If you're lucky, maybe some sort of community order or fine. Don't worry about all that now. He's gone and that's what counts.'

Anna sipped at the sour, now tepid wine, but it was helping to calm her frayed nerves. She still felt shaky but having Nick present was helping her to relax a little. She was very worried how she'd feel once Nick left and she was in her home alone. Connor Peterson may have been taken away in a police car for now but in a very short time, a number of hours, realistically, he would be out of custody, pending further investigation. Was he likely to return? She would have to look at further security measures to protect herself but this would all be further costs she could do without.

Moving off the sofa, Anna eased away from Nick to go and repair some of the damage to her face ravaged by crying. 'I'll go and get more wine as this is lukewarm and not pleasant. Would you like another drink?'

Nick stated, 'Lager, thanks,' as Anna left the room.

Sitting on a stool at her dressing table in her bedroom, Anna stared at her face. There was a redness and swelling to the left side of her face due to being slapped. Under her left eye there was a deep red marking where his fingers had imprinted and she expected this to turn a red/purple colour over the next few days. The black eyeliner and mascara she had applied earlier was smudged under her eyes, dragged downwards by her tears. Her nose was a particularly unattractive shade of pink. All in all, she looked a damp, blotchy, snotty mess. She had started the evening nervous but excited and everything had progressed well. The highlight had been the joy of losing herself in the sexual madness of being in Nick's arms and on the way to making love. Now, all that had been destroyed and the moment would not be recaptured tonight. Anna repaired some of the damage to her face by removing smudges of eyeliner and mascara and ridding her face of the red blotches with face powder. Then she hurried down the stairs, took the bottle of wine and a bottled lager out of the fridge, and returned to Nick who was watching '*Match of the Day*'.

Having refilled her glass with wine, Anna sat close to Nick but not touching him. Nick closely scrutinised her face, placing a gentle finger near her left eye, where her make-up camouflage was failing to hide the soreness of the assault. 'That's looking sore, sweetheart.' He gently placed his lips on her mouth but the kiss was one of kindness not lust. 'I've been thinking. Would you like me to stay here tonight, on the sofa or in your spare room, as you might be a bit shaky after what's happened?

Sipping the wine now to ease the on-going inner trembling in her belly, Anna stated, 'I would be grateful but I don't want to put you out. I'm so sorry that all of this has spoiled our evening.'

Nick now drew her against him, kissing her lips lightly, his eyes gently caressing her face. 'Yes, it was a great evening until your unwanted guest showed up. But I am hoping we will have other opportunities to resume where we left off earlier as I cannot tell you how much I was enjoying it.' He gave her a leery smile but Anna knew there would be no follow through and she did not want it. 'Right, let's relax and watch this film, *'At Any Price'* with Dennis Quaid and Zac Efron. According to the blurb Dean (Efron) wants to escape working on the family farm owned by dad (Quaid) to do car racing. Sounds ok, what do you think?'

Anna knew she couldn't really concentrate on any film as her head was beginning to pound after her ordeal. 'Fine by me.' But just to be here, with Nick, as they snuggled on the sofa was all she wanted at the moment. It would be wise to stop drinking the wine so as not to compound the headache but the wine was helping to neutralise the fear in her gut. She made herself sip the wine and concentrate on the film but only ten minutes in, her eyes were getting sleepy and she knew that she was not going to stay awake through a film about a feuding father and son with themes of farming and car racing.

⁕⁕⁕

CHAPTER THIRTY SEVEN

Anna woke next morning with a thumping headache, a soreness to her face, and a vague hangover from too many wines which resulted in nausea and tiredness. She was on the sofa, covered by a duvet, still wearing yesterday's dress. The light streaming through the delicate, ivory voile curtains that covered the French doors made her squint and she felt hot from being restricted by the confines of her dress and the weight of the duvet. She was alone. On a chair, a sleeping bag and a pillow were piled together, where presumably Nick had slept on the floor until he escaped from the house of the flaky woman. Who could blame him?

Anna flung the restrictive duvet aside and stretched slowly, trying to pump some energy into her tired limbs and lethargic brain. She needed to get up, to go for a wee, and then have an invigorating shower to wake her up but all she could do was lie still, her head on a pillow, and stare at the ceiling. A sharp pain stabbed her in the gut as she realised that she would never see Nick again. There was also a major feeling of disappointment that he had not woken her to say goodbye. Instead, he had slipped quietly out of the house, obviously wanting to be away without having to make feeble excuses such as 'great to have met you', 'things to do' or the worse one 'see you around'. Anna hadn't viewed him as cowardly but then after all the hassle she had brought to his door who could blame him for making his exit. In fact, Abbie yielding a knife might be a better alternative than Anna Louden who attracted trouble like iron filings to a magnet. The thought of not seeing him again actually made her want to cry but she had shed a river of tears last night and this would be why he had decided to do a flit. A woman with a tear-stained, blotchy red face was not an ideal prospect as a future girlfriend.

Nick Carlton could definitely have his pick of any women and had recently dumped one who had become a liability. The next lucky lady to share his life would have to be fun, sexy and not disaster-prone like herself.

Deciding to stop maudlin and drag herself up off the sofa, Anna wearily went up the stairs into the bathroom. After relieving her bladder, she stared in the mirror at her face. A vivid red mark remained on her left cheek with an intense red/purple area under her eye. When she touched this area gently with her finger, it felt sore and she flinched slightly. Peeling off her clothes, Anna climbed into the shower to try to refresh her jaded body. The steaming hot water and her favourite citrusy lemon shower gel revived her but the water did sting her bruised face.

After Connor Peterson had been arrested last night, Anna hoped there would be no further contact with him. But there was a doubt in her mind, a niggling, persistent tiny parasitic worm in her brain, alerting her to the idea that Peterson may have gone for now but would he stay away for good? After drying herself, she dressed in blue, skinny jeans and white V-necked jumper. A light application of make-up took away some of the redness on her face and made her look less like a fighter post-boxing match.

Downstairs, Anna drank a hot, instant coffee whilst watching television to catch up on the news. A knock on the front door made her flinch. Please, do not let it be Connor Peterson.

Opening the door cautiously, she was relieved to find it was Nick. 'Come in,' she stated. 'I was scared to open the door. I'm glad it's you. Would you like a coffee?'

'Good morning,' he greeted her as he entered her hallway. Holding up a bag from a well-known electrical retailer, he stated, 'This will help to take the worry off your face every time you have to answer the door. I've got you a Ring Video Doorbell so you can check who's at the door. I've also brought croissants and a cinnamon bun, so a coffee would be great.'

Anna went into the kitchen to make the coffees and Nick went into the living room. She was soon joining him with two mugs of steaming coffee and two plates for the pastries. They each selected a pastry of choice and Anna nibbled on her cinnamon bun, sitting next to Nick on the sofa. He carefully read the instructions for installing the video doorbell. 'This all looks straightforward,' he commented.

Anna blew on the hot coffee, before sipping it cautiously. 'I might have to pay you what I owe you at the end of the month, if that's ok. My credit card will have a nervous breakdown if I put anymore payments on it,' she joked.

Nick sipped on his coffee, whilst giving her a peevish look. 'I don't want any payment for this. Just for once accept that this is not a gift but a necessary device to ensure your safety when you are here, alone. I don't want you opening the door to anyone until you know exactly who is at your front door.'

Blushing with embarrassment, Anna had to concede that she definitely needed this doorbell to help re-establish her sense of security after last night's incident. 'Ok, thank you. I will gladly accept the doorbell. It is very thoughtful of you to think of it. I could take you out for a drink sometime to say thank you.'

Nick nodded and smiled. 'Yeah, that would be great. Now, let me get on and fit this thing or do you want to do it? I know women are very capable of doing this kind of thing these days. The installation instructions recommend an electric drill and a hammer which I've brought in the car as I didn't know if you'd have them.'

Anna laughed. 'No, I haven't as my dad helps with any repairs. Dad has shown me how to do DIY stuff but I'm not great at attempting things on my own. Perhaps we can put the doorbell up together?'

'I was hoping you were going to show me what to do,' Nick teased and Anna laughed. 'There are many men these days who do not know the difference between a screw and a nail. I'm ok at this sort of thing. My granddad's a carpenter and I used to love helping him when I was a kid.'

Outside, when he had accounted for all the equipment needed, Nick set to work installing the doorbell with Anna's help. They worked efficiently as a team to attach the mounting bracket to the brickwork and Anna was in charge of drilling the holes for the rawl plugs and screws. He made her wear safety glasses to do this but they were not really her best look in terms of flattering fashion accessories. After a short while the doorbell had been installed, the appropriate app downloaded, and the doorbell connected to the WIFI network. Nick went outside be a visitor to ensure that everything was working. He rang the doorbell and was immediately contacted by Anna from her mobile. 'Hi. I'm Nick. I've come to visit a beautiful woman that lives here.'

Anna grinned as she saw his mischievous face looming large into the doorbell camera. 'Sorry, I don't know you. I'm expecting a visit from a handsome security expert.'

There was a bemused expression on Nick's face. 'Handsome security expert, eh?

Anna smiled. 'I'll let you in till he gets here. Would you like another coffee?'

At that moment, Anna's phone rang. It was PC Bright who informed her that Connor Peterson had been released on bail pending further investigation. Though Anna expected this, it did re-ignited her fears that Peterson may re-appear at her house. The police officer requested that she come to the police station to finalise a written statement. A few minutes later, Nick's phone rang and it was PC Bright also requesting his attendance at the police station to complete his written statement.

Three hours later, Anna returned home from the police station in Nick's car. As he pulled up outside her house, Nick gazed at her face. 'Listen, Anna, I want you to be vigilant and do not open the door to people you don't know. Always check your phone to see who is at the door, ok? I've got to go to do some prep work for a meeting tomorrow but if you need me I can be around as quickly as possible. Ok?'

Anna noted the concern in his eyes. 'Yes, thanks, but I will be ok. Thanks again for the video doorbell. I really appreciate it.'

Nick placed his thumb on her chin, restricting her movement as he claimed her mouth in an explorative kiss. 'I'm really busy this week but I'm free on Saturday if you want to get together. It's another bank holiday weekend and I could do a BBQ if the weather's ok. What do you think? I'd really like us to spend some uninterrupted time together.'

What did she think? Anna thought that this would be brilliant, amazing, off-the-scale exciting but could not reveal all this to him as she wanted to appear interested but not too eager. 'Yes, I'd like that very much.'

CHAPTER THIRTY EIGHT

Sunday 24ᵗʰ April 2022

Russ was lying on his bed, trying to recover from the drink and drug excesses of his Saturday night with Leanne. Luke was sitting on Russ's office chair at the computer desk, swinging from side to side, and banging the desk as he excitedly related a story from the previous night. Russ was reminded of when Luke was a kid and he loved to read stories about pirates and dragons out loud with an animated look on his face and in a high-pitched voice. To Russ, Luke was still that young boy, excited by fantastical tales and daring adventures, except now the stories were a little more grown-up as Luke's imaginary world included beautiful women he would never have.

'Ok, Luke, cut the fuck out of banging that chair. It's not doing my low-grade headache any good. I had a heavy night last night and I really need a kip,' Russ moaned, sprawled out on his bed in grubby, faded blue jeans and grey polo shirt.

Russ's head was propped up on pillows, as he digested what Luke said. 'So, this wanker went to her house, forced his way in, and then after a while the cops arrived. After about an hour the wanker was taken out of the house in cuffs and driven to the police station. You waited at the cop shop till he was released, he got a taxi to the woman's house to get his car, and then you followed him to where he lives.'

'Yeah, that's it,' Luke confirmed, his face red and sweaty with rage. 'That arrogant idiot has done something to my beloved so that the cops had to be called. She looked physically ok when she opened the door to the cops but perhaps he did something where no injuries were on show. I will kill him if he's hurt her.'

Russ smiled as he regarded his brother's upset face and the way he now referred to the woman as 'his beloved'. Luke was always a soppy sap where women were concerned. He could never grasp the concept of having casual sex without any emotional attachment. Luke would always equate sex with love, and then fantasise about one particular woman, generally a singer or an actress. He'd had a massive crush on actress/ singer Selena Gomez and Russ always expected Luke to migrate to Hollywood to meet his petite, brown-haired, brown-eyed bewitching idol. This time, the female of his desires was real, of human flesh, lived close by, and Luke was able to get close to her. Hanging around the supermarket to catch a glimpse of her and make conversation with her. Sitting outside her house in his car to find out where she went and who with. Luke's obsession with this woman was growing exponentially and in terms of the law could be classed as stalking.

In terms of this woman, Russ was still blown away by her beauty and really wanted to get with her. It was by sheer luck that he had seen her in the Frizzy Lion on Friday night, a pub he sometimes went in to pick up women. It was a popular town centre pub, a place to pick up the town's hottest babes. But Russ was furious that this particular hot babe had rejected his offer of a drink and a chat. Stuck-up madam. In the future, when they did get together, she would be reminded of her misbehaviour and made to pay.

Russ raised his head more to directly address Luke. 'I don't think this wanker's going to be trembling with fear knowing that you are coming for him, bro. But I agree that he's stepped out of line. And you know the address where he lives?'

Luke stared at Russ's cold, flinty eyes. 'I know where he lives. What you thinking, Russ?'

'I'm thinking that we could pay the wanker a visit. The cops don't come out for no reason,' stated Russ. 'It could play to our advantage as we could find out who she is. I've not doled out a beating for a while to some deserving tosspot, so it would be fun. Violence is a good way to get rid of pent-up energy.'

Russ noted that his brother visibly shook as he said this. Luke was not able to dole out physical pain to another human being but he could stand by and enjoy it inflicted by someone else. At secondary school when a Year 9 boy kept picking on Luke, Russ had waited after school and taken the kid to a secluded area of a nearby park. The boy had received a thumping from Russ, punches to his ribs and back. Luke had spurred Russ on, jumping up and down with excitement, as a final punch flew to the boy's nose and red blood spurted outwards and down his chin. Luke now clapped his hands together, eagerly. 'Oh yes, Russ, let's get him. I can't bear the thought of him hurting my beloved. He must pay.'

Russ nodded, getting aroused by the thought of indulging in a bit of physical violence. When he eventually got together with this woman, he would tell her about the action he had taken for her. He would expect her to show gratitude, with her mouth and her body, for what he had done. 'Ok, you'll have to do the grunt work by watching his house to find out where he goes in the evenings. To find out where we can nab him. I'm not seeing Leanne next weekend as she's got the brats. Dad's away at the weekend with Angie so we can bring the wanker here and take him in the garage for a thrashing.'

⚊⚌⟨⟩⚌⚊

CHAPTER THIRTY NINE

By Thursday, Anna had recovered from her ordeal with Connor Peterson but a gripey knot of fear in her stomach remained, particularly if someone rang her newly installed doorbell. This had only happened once and it was a delivery driver from Amazon with another parcel for her neighbour, Ben. Anna informed the driver to leave the parcel on her doorstep which she retrieved once he had driven away. She was grateful to Nick for this thoughtful present of the video doorbell and she decided to get him a small gift as a thank you.

Thus, Anna was pushing a trolley around the supermarket, not really knowing what to buy. She couldn't afford a lot of money and discounted a lot of items immediately. Aftershave, generally too expensive. Men's toiletries weren't an option as she didn't know what he liked and as a gift it felt too intimate. Biscuits were more suitable for your grandad. Chocolates were more female than male. In the end she settled for a bottle of Jack Daniel's Tennessee Whiskey which cost more than she would have liked. She also added a bottle of white wine to her trolley as her contribution to Saturday night's BBQ.

The thought of the BBQ had been a major distraction to her all week. At work she often drifted off into a daydream of them sharing good food and wine on a warm evening in the garden before going inside as the night air cooled. What would happen then was seriously making her jittery and excited all at the same time. And a little bit scared, if she were honest. The assault by Peterson had affected her more than she cared to admit. The soreness and bruising to her face was now receding but the area around her left eye and cheek were still bruised and tender to the touch. The attack resurrected painful memories of her final day with Alistair. She was ready for a sexual relationship with

Nick but she didn't want her past traumatic experiences with men to spoil things. This all added to her worry that she would not meet Nick's expectations after sexy siren, Abbie.

In the food aisle, Anna told herself to stop worrying about imaginary problems, and finish her shopping. She let go of her trolley to reach up for a mixed salad to go with the cheese and mushroom omelette she was planning for dinner. Unfortunately, as Anna turned to place the mixed salad in the trolley, she noticed that it had been pushed forward and was about to collide with a customer. Anna grabbed her trolley, muttering 'sorry, sorry' as it lightly bumped into a man with his back to her. The man turned, and smiled broadly, when he saw her. It was Tulip Man who she was encountering quite frequently in this supermarket. Anna stuttered, 'S-sorry again.'

'Oh, hello', Tulip Man beamed at her. 'Is your trolley trying to chat up my trolley? We do seem to keep bumping into each other on a regular basis. Perhaps the fates are trying to bring us together.' The eager expression on his face faded, and his cheeks went a rosy pink, as he realised the boldness of his statement.

Anna cringed inwardly but tried to keep a pleasant smile on her face so as not to upset him. She couldn't fully ascertain how old Tulip Man was, putting him in his early twenties, but he had a gaucheness about him that made him seem younger. 'I don't think it's the fates but people who bash into other people's trolleys.'

'Well,' he commented, 'I don't mind who or what are involved in our meeting, it's lovely to see you again. I think you're like me, live alone, and don't plan ahead with our shopping and so we're always in the supermarket buying just for the next day or two. I know that's what I do.'

Glancing in his trolley, Anna noted two large sliced loaves of white bread, two large pizzas, two packs of smoked bacon and a dozen large eggs. Quite a quantity of food for a person living alone and who shops frequently. There was a definite mismatch between what he was saying and what he was buying.

Tulip Man noticed her gazing into his trolley and seemed to guess what she was thinking. 'I'm going to stay with my dad tonight and over the weekend and I'm taking some supplies to keep us going. He moans if I come empty-handed. I've got all the male essentials, pizza, white bread, bacon and eggs. Just off to get the pork pies, crisps and beer and then we'll be in blokey heaven,' he laughed, as he stared at her. 'Anyway, I can see you're my sort of girl if you like Jack Daniels.'

'It's not for me but a small gift for someone who did me a favour,' Anna informed him but now wanted to end the conversation, finish her shopping and go home. She started to feel uncomfortable under his persistent gaze as he always stared intently at her.

Tulip Man now lingered, in no hurry to move on. There was a large grin on his round face as if he was the perpetual cheeky chappie, full of fun, but Anna was beginning to think that his presence was becoming quite creepy. 'I'm glad your trolley bumped into me. I wonder if you'd like to come out for a drink with me sometime. That's assuming you haven't got a boyfriend,' he then paused, blushing profusely. 'Oh, sorry. A beautiful woman like you is bound to have a boyfriend. Why wouldn't you, every man in the world would want to take you out. I'm an idiot.....' The gabbling stopped as he scrutinised Anna's face for her reaction.

What to say? There was no way she would go for a drink with him but she did not want to upset him either. It often took courage for men to ask women out and she didn't want to bruise his ego even though he was starting to get on her nerves. 'Oh, thanks for the invite and it's nice of you to ask. But I am seeing someone at the moment.' She smiled at him to try to take the sting out of her rejection.

'Boyfriend,' he babbled, as the grin faded and his mouth fell open like a goldfish out of water. 'I hope he treats you well or he'll have me to answer to. Trouble is, pretty women can sometimes get the wrong attention from bad men. The ones that think they're entitled to ownership of a beautiful woman.'

Anna couldn't understand what he was on about. Plus they were preventing other customers getting access to the salads. A large lady in a blue mac wedged herself between Anna's trolley and Tulip Man. She harrumphed loudly as she elbowed her way forward to pick up a potato salad. Anna could hear her muttering, 'shift' under her breath.

Tulip Man giggled as the woman stalked away with her food item. 'I wouldn't want to argue with her. Probably scrum half for a local rugby team.'

Despite wanting to get away from him, Anna laughed. 'Yes, you're probably right but we should take the hint and move out of people's way. Nice to speak to you again. Enjoy the pizzas and your blokey time with your dad.'

****

Luke sat in his car, slammed his hand hard on the steering wheel a number of times, enjoying the pain, a punishment for the fool he'd made of himself. 'Shit, shit, shit.' Luke had blown his life apart by asking her to go for a drink and being rejected. All his dreams shattered like a million panes of glass.

From when he had first spotted her a few months ago, Luke had lived in a different world, a world of happiness and hope, where he could exist without the loneliness and boredom of his normal life. Life at home with his father and brother. A job as a plasterer which was physically exacting, monotonous, and, often uncomfortable when he got wet and cold in his dirty clothes, particularly during the winter months. A job of low pay and no opportunities to lift himself out of his mundane existence.

Luke was witty and clever and his ultimate dream was to write fantasy stories of heroes, villains, monsters and dragons, castles and far off lands. But not children's stories, these would be for adults with enough violence, blood, gore and sex to make them exciting. He was working on a *'Game of Thrones'* type trilogy and he had now incorporated his ideal woman into the story, his beloved, a living, breathing, brown-haired, blue-eyed stunning beauty who would forever be immortalised in print. He had named her. Astraea. A Greek goddess. A celestial virgin representing innocence, purity and justice. A goddess who will return to Earth one day bringing with her the return of a Utopian Golden Age. Luke had neglected his writing recently in his pursuit of Astraea but once she became his he would create magnificent tales with his beloved as his inspiration, his muse. He imagined her, lying naked on his bed after they had consummated their marriage. After he had learned the skills of making love, he would incorporate his new experiences into his stories to add lust and passion to titillate the reader. But now he had blown it. The dream of possessing her was gone. Luke was destroyed. But from his deep despair, came another emotion. Rage.

Rage. A fiery, flaming, red hot rage. Luke banged the steering wheel a few more times to inflict further punishment on himself for his stupidity. But someone else was going to endure pain to satisfy Luke's need for vengeance. The wanker who had messed with his beloved. Luke had been keeping a close watch on the man. He was a regular at a local pub, near to where he lived, which he went to most nights. Well, on Saturday night, he had a nice surprise waiting for him.

⟶⋯⋘❰❬◆❭❱⋙⋯⟵

CHAPTER FORTY

Saturday 30ᵗʰ April 2022

As Anna drove onto the driveway of Nick's house she was once again impressed by the large, modern detached property with double garage. Her car looked old and out of place on the extensive, paved driveway. As the weather had been dry but cool all day, Nick had texted that the BBQ was cancelled and it would be a takeaway instead. She had planned to wear jeans and blouse to the BBQ but now swapped those for a blue, A-line, knee-length dress worn with black, slingback shoes. Anna picked up her bags, took a deep breath to steady her nerves, and got out of the car.

As expected he had a video doorbell and she waited nervously for the door to open. He was quickly at the door and her stomach flipped when she saw him as he smiled widely at her. He was dressed in blue jeans, dark blue zip jumper over light grey shirt which accentuated the blueness of his eyes. 'Hi, come in,' he stated. As she entered the hallway it was an awkward moment for her as she didn't know if she should just say hello, go in for a hug, or attempt a friendly kiss. The problem was solved when Nick pecked her on the cheek. 'You look amazing.'

Anna followed him into the spacious kitchen with views out onto the well-maintained garden. She placed a shopping bag on the kitchen island and took out a bottle of Jack Daniels and a bottle of white wine. 'I've bought you the whiskey as a thank you for buying me the doorbell.'

Nick picked up the whiskey. 'Thanks, JD is one of my favourite drinks. Glass of wine?' he asked.

Nick got the drinks, wine for Anna and lager for himself, and led the way into the sitting room. The room had a stylish but cosy feel with a fireplace with log burner, two mid-grey sofas, and a single navy armchair, grey walls and carpet. A grey/navy rug and a mix of cushions in greys, silvers and navy added richness to the room. Anna sat on the three-seater sofa and Nick sat next to her, leaving a gap between them. He grinned at her with a smug expression on his face. 'Please note, because you offered a selection of homemade snacks at your house, I have made some very superior ones of my own.' He pointed to three bowls on a nearby coffee table. 'Nacho cheese tortilla crisps, red pepper pitta chips, and sea salt and sherry crisps. Help yourself.'

Anna took a sea salt and sherry crisp from the bowl and bit into it. 'Excellent. I expect that you extracted the salt from the seas off the UK coast? she teased.

Nick nodded. 'Of course. And the sherry is obviously from barrels in my cellar.'

'Well, they are exceptionally good and make my meagre offerings look pitiful,' Anna laughed as she noted that he was lapping up her fulsome praise. 'In that case I am a little disappointed that we will not be sampling further examples of your cooking skills this evening as the BBQ is cancelled.'

'Yeah, it's a shame the weather is too cold. You will have to wait another time to try my tasty BBQ food. I suggest that I order a takeaway now as it will take a while to come on a busy Saturday night. What would you like? Chinese, Thai or Indian?' Thai was their preferred option and an order at a local takeaway/delivery place made.

Sitting back on the sofa, Nick was totally relaxed. Anna sat forward, feeling nervous even though she was happy to be here. Nick leaned towards her and gazed at her. 'How is your face after last Saturday's assault?'

Her make-up concealed the now fading bruises. 'Its fine, still a little bit tender and the bruises are a sickly yellow/green. I heard from PC Bright this week that Peterson has been charged with sexual assault and assault by beating. He has been released on bail with the proviso that he should have no contact with me, thank goodness. According to PC Bright, the charges are either-way offences that could be dealt with in either a Magistrate's Court or Crown Court. I must say that PC Bright has been very helpful and will be in contact as things progress.' Anna sighed and sipped her wine.', 'I just hope Connor does abide by the terms of his bail and doesn't try to contact me.'

Nick agreed. 'Let's hope so.' Nick's phone rang, and he whispered 'sorry' to Anna as he answered it. Anna sipped her wine and listened to the one-sided conversation. She detected annoyance in Nick's voice as he said, 'No, Ed, you and Ethan can't come round as I am busy.' Nick listened to Ed as he droned on, not pausing for breath, obviously recounting some important news as Nick rolled his eyes. Nick then stated, 'Ok, Ed, I don't really want to hear about what Abbie is getting up to as she is nothing to do with me.' Ed rambled on further whilst Nick sighed, before firmly saying, 'Ed, I need to go. I'm sure you and Ethan will survive if you can locate the kitchen and find something to cook or order a takeaway. Bye.' He ended the call.

Nick groaned. 'That was my brother Ed trying to invite himself and his dopey friend Ethan round for a takeaway. I blame my mother for molly-coddling him too much as he can't survive without her.'

Shortly the takeaway was delivered and Anna and Nick enjoyed starters of Thai spring rolls and grilled jumbo prawns with sweet chilli sauce. They were now sharing mains; Ped Pad Khing – stir fried roast duck, Gaeng Dang – red chicken curry, Neau Laou Dang – stir fried beef with red wine sauce and veg. Anna was relishing the whole thing, alone with Nick, eating wonderful food and now drinking a smooth Chablis. She paused in munching a mangetout to ask Nick. 'I heard you mention Abbie. What was that about?'

Nick shook his head. 'Don't give me indigestion by talking about her. She was in the Frizzy Lion last night with Alyssa, Justin, Ed and a few others. Drunk and making a show of herself, as usual. She was begging Ed to ask me to take her back, so he was passing this on. She then accosted some guy and was all over him, laughing hysterically, loud snogging etc. Truly embarrassing.'

Anna sipped on her wine. 'Are you tempted to go back to her?'

Nick laughed loudly. 'No bloody way. She was always a bit wild when she was with me, you know, over-the-top drinking and attention seeking, but this behaviour is becoming out of control. She's heading for trouble.'

'I think I feel a bit sorry for her. She's obviously hurting,' Anna commented, as she spooned beef stir fry on to her plate.

Nick gazed at her kindly. 'Well, don't. I'm glad she's out of my life. Though I keep getting text messages and Instagram updates. The texts swing between two extremes. One end is on the lines of wanting to put my balls in a boiling broth. The other extreme is begging to be taken back so she can blow my socks off with her hooker tricks. On Instagram it's photos of her with different men, draped all over them, living her best life. It's all bullshit.'

'Why don't you just delete her from your phone?' Anna asked, wondering why he still allowed this woman to contact him. For all his protestations, did he still miss the sexual side of their relationship?

Anna could feel Nick's eyes on her, a puzzled expression on his face before he commented, 'I decided that it was better to allow her access to me by text so I could keep track of her lunacy. I don't reply to any of the texts, I just ignore them. She'll meet someone new eventually and it should all stop.'

They had now finished the takeaway and drunk the delicious Chablis. Nick got up to clear the table, picked up the empty foil cartons, plates and cutlery and walked over to the dishwasher. Anna helped by throwing the soiled paper napkins in the bin. As he loaded the dishwasher, she teased, 'At least this time I'm not going to be covered in soap froth and assaulted with a washing-up brush.'

Closing the dishwasher door, he eyed her closely. 'So, Ms Louden, you think you're safe today, do you?'

Anna giggled nervously as he took her arm and pulled her towards him. She was then lifted onto the worktop and he positioned himself between her legs. Her dress rose upwards, exposing pale thighs, and she shivered slightly, due to her vulnerability but also at the fact that it was turning her on.

His strong arms circled her back, drawing her into him, as he scrutinised her bemused face. 'Well, Ms Louden, I think I have been too lenient with you so far. I am now going to kiss that delectable mouth of yours.'

Before Anna could speak, her mouth was consumed by his, in a kiss so passionate, that a swarm of butterflies fluttered in her tummy. His left hand gripped her chin, to ensure that there was no escape and she gave herself up to the delight of his mouth scouring hers as she moaned softly. His right hand crept gently along her exposed left thigh, stroking and massaging with his fingers, as Anna trembled at his touch.

Nick paused in the intense kissing but still clasped her chin. Lustful blue eyes surveyed her own. 'Well, Anna, I think we should take this to the bedroom.'

'Yes,' Anna whispered, as her heart skipped a beat. This was the moment she had been waiting for and worrying about since meeting this off-the-scale sexy man. An image of Abbie flicked, momentarily, in her brain before it was gone. Would she be a match for the blonde seductress?

Nick grabbed her hand and led her to his bedroom. Arriving at the bed, he picked her up, placed her down on her back and then lay over her. All the time his eyes did not leave hers as they searched every inch of her face. In a hot, whispered breath, he said, 'It's corny but I want to engrave every beautiful inch of your perfect face onto my memory, sweet Anna.' His fingers caressed her right eyebrow where she had sustained a cut on the first day they met. 'There's a tiny scar there, but that tiny flaw, just adds to your perfection.' His hand cupped her chin as his mouth reclaimed hers, more forcefully this time, and Anna leaned up to receive him. His probing lips and tongue searched her eager mouth and the coarseness of his beard stubbled made her quiver with the masculine feel of him.

Nick pulled her into him and held her securely whilst all the time tormenting her eager mouth. Anna thought she would expire from the longing within her that he was arousing. Pausing from her mouth, he pushed her dress upwards, and helped her out of it to reveal white bra and panties. His lips trailed downwards, licking her ear lobes, along her throat, to the swell of her cleavage. Eager fingers undid her bra to release her soft breasts and he squeezed them greedily, before devouring her nipples with his mouth. Groaning softly, he murmured, 'So beautiful, Anna.'

Anna stroked his hair, not wanting him to stop his delicious exploration of her nipples as ripples of excitement flowed through her body. Moving her hand downwards, she felt the power in his back and shoulder muscles as she touched him. But she wanted him to lead her in this sexual adventure, he, the master, and she, the willing pupil, and thus it was.

On it went, this exquisite caressing of her mouth and breasts, as she groaned softly. Anna's body was craving the conclusion to this but her mind was focusing on each single sensation to prolong the beautiful ecstasy of it all. Her hand moved downwards to his groin to explore his aroused state. Quickly, she assisted him to pull his jumper and shirt over his head to reveal muscular shoulders, toned arms and abs and she was awed at the sheer masculine perfection of him, his power and strength. He removed the rest of his clothes and was soon laying over her again, to arouse her nipples with a flicking of his tongue which made her shudder with excitement. The white panties were soon freed from her body and his exploring mouth found her most sensitive area between her legs. This hot caress made her squirm and moan, driving her longing off-the-scale. This was a masterclass in how to make love to a woman. As her moans increased, he moved back up her body, to assail her willing mouth. Then his eyes locked onto hers. 'I've wanted to make love to you for a very long time,' he murmured as his mouth nuzzled her ear.

Anna was lost in the bittersweet agony of it all as every touch of his mouth and fingers on all parts of her body sky-rocketed her arousal. She moaned softly, saying, 'Nick, Nick' and pulled his hair as his hot, moist mouth tormented her clitoris until she felt that she could no longer contain her need for release. Moving now back up her body, his eyes locked on hers, as she begged 'please' as he entered her and she gasped at the sheer size and potency of him. He thrust into her, gently at first and then more powerfully as he was encouraged by her reaction. Anna moaned and was lost in the sweet agony of the lust that was taking over her body. She had never felt so alive as this beautiful man made love to her. Anna felt her body falling, swirling, melting into a quivering, liquid state. Anna could hold off no longer and a sexual explosion tore through her body and she quivered beneath him, as he came in her.

Nick collapsed onto her, kissing and caressing her mouth, as he lovingly searched her face with his eyes. 'Was that ok, sweetheart?'

They gently drew apart, sated, and spent of all energy. Feeling happy and tearful at the same time, Anna was now wrapped in his arms as he held onto her. Looking at him, shyly now, Anna replied, 'Yes, it was amazing. Thank you for restoring my faith in men and how wonderful sex can be. I've had some shitty times in the recent past. You're a great guy, Nick Carlton.'

He gave a cheeky smile to acknowledge her words. 'At your service, Ms Louden. If you want me to repeat that all over again any time soon, I'm sure I can oblige.'

Suddenly, it was all too much for Anna and she started to cry. Loud, body juddering sobs, as Nick gazed at her, concern etched on his face. 'Anna, sweetheart, what's the matter? I thought that was good,' he stated.

'S-sorry, Nick,' Anna stuttered, trying to hide her wet face and her embarrassment from him. She wanted to speak but continued to cry as he held her in his arms. Eventually the crying abated. 'It was truly amazing, Nick. But it's churned up all the emotions from my most recent bad experiences with Connor and Alistair. Going with Connor was a massive mistake. He was dominating and rough, so that I felt like a ragdoll being thrown about before he gripped his hands powerfully around my throat. It scared me after Alistair. I'd lost confidence in ever feeling secure in a sexual situation until now. Thank you for that. And I've completely ruined the moment.'

Nick brushed his fingers under her eyes to wipe away the tears. 'It might help if you tell me what happened with Alistair.'

⁂

CHAPTER FORTY ONE

Friday 21st May 2021

Sat around the dining table, covered in empty plates, bowls and bottles, Anna watched as Alistair and Sebastian, joked and jeered about life in lockdown. Alistair was the most animated Anna had seen him for a long while, really having a good time fuelled by food and copious amounts of alcohol, red wine and now whiskies. Two private school friends, now grown men, one a solicitor, the other a MP, responsible citizens but when they were together, the inner school boy prankster soon emerged. Alistair was well on the way to getting paralytic and everything Seb said was hysterically funny. Seb continued with his story. 'Yeah, I was sat at my desk discussing a constituents question with a government minister. I had a white shirt on top and my Calvin Klein's at the bottom, plus socks.'

Alistair guffawed loudly. 'I can top that. I was in a Zoom call with a client discussing a conveyancing issue last week. I had no clothes on below the waist. The pretty blonde I was talking to had no idea that my dick was at the meeting too.'

Anna scrutinised Alistair whilst sipping her white wine. Living with him over the lockdown periods of the last year had been difficult. A handsome, fit rugby-playing man had become lazy and podgy during the confinements of lockdowns. Working from home did not suit him as he found it hard to self-motivate outside of the office. He missed the camaraderie of colleagues. Bad habits which were kept in check during normal working hours were indulged more frequently at home. An alcoholic drink with the lunchtime sandwich. A snort of coke mid-afternoon. A gambling habit that helped with the boredom and isolation of lockdowns. The drinking and drugs exacerbated his anxieties and flared his temper so that Anna was walking on eggshells a lot of the time. Both of them were confined to their apartment, working sort of normal hours, and getting irritated at the sight of each other. Small things would cause Alistair's temper to flare and verbally take things out on her. An alcoholic binge would knock him out on the sofa overnight and then he would fail to get up on time to deal with his conveyancing workload. He was lucky that the main partners in the law firm that employed him were his father and uncle.

Portia, Seb's girlfriend, also present, was blonde and skinny, a part-time model, and another product of a private education. Anna found her superior and haughty which in turn made any kind of conversation difficult. She also had a crush on Alistair which she did not try to conceal and blatantly flirted with him on any occasion. Tonight, after not seeing him in ages, her large green eyes were glued to his as she jiggled her breasts at him. Breasts that were not very well confined in a strappy, blue mini dress. Having drunk one bottle of white wine, she was well into her second. 'I think we should liven this up a bit folks with a line or two. What do ya say?'

Portia took out of her clutch a number of small plastic bags of cocaine. To Anna, she said, 'Clear the table will ya. We'll do the lines and play a game of Truth or Dare. Portia's rules. You can choose truth or dare but you must answer truthfully and do the dare you are given. If you fail to do the dare you must do a vodka shot. Let's make it a little raunchy shall we,' she said, biting her lower lip as she looked at Alistair.

All, but Anna, snorted the cocaine, and sat drinking more booze as the effects of the drug took hold and they became giggly and animated. The four then sat in a circle on the carpet, Anna, Seb, Portia and Alistair. To pick player one, a bottle was spun and Portia won. She spun the bottle again which stopped at Alistair who was asked, truth or dare. He opted for truth.

Portia grinned, a sneaky smile on her lips. 'Where's the weirdest place you've had sex and who with?'

Alistair sighed loudly, thinking through the answer as Anna squirmed. 'Erm, in the toilet of a public facilities in Gloucester with a girl from school. Can't remember her name.' He spun the bottle which pointed at Anna. 'Truth or dare.'

'Truth', she responded.

Alistair knocked back a mouthful of whisky and leered at her. 'Ok, my adorable honey bun. I ask this with hopeful curiosity, would you consider doing a threesome and who would the lucky two participants be?'

Portia guffawed. 'That's as likely to happen as me finding the Loch Ness monster.'

Anna smiled sweetly at Portia, a woman who considered herself to be the most out-there party animal. 'Yes, I would. The two participants? Chris Hemsworth and Henry Cavill.'

Looking a bit disgruntled, Alistair stated, 'Honestly, babe, I thought you'd include me.'

The bottle was spun and pointed at Portia, who opted for dare. Anna gave the challenge. 'Find a suitable song on your phone and do a sexy dance for us.'

Portia nodded with enthusiasm. 'Great one. Give me a minute.' *'Señorita' by* Shawn Mendes & Camila Cabello started to play. Portia got up, and danced in the centre of the group, swaying her hips, and turning circles as the skimpy blue dress flashed her thighs. She dragged Alistair to his feet, placed her hands around his neck, wiggling in his arms, as she mouthed words from the song stressing 'lips' and 'tongue'. Alistair moved his hands up and down her body, as Seb drank beer, enjoying the floorshow. Portia enjoyed catching Anna's eye to gauge her reaction to her sexy tease.

When the song finished, Portia spun the bottle which pointed to Seb, who picked 'dare'.

Swigging from a bottle of wine, Portia giggled. 'Take a dick pic and send it to a female MP.'

Seb spluttered, splashing the carpet with beer. 'For fuck's sake, Portia, I can't do that as I'll get arrested and lose my parliamentary seat. No seat equals no money, you dumb cow. I'll do it, but only send it to you.'

Portia still thought this hilarious and squealed as Seb picked up his phone, unzipped his trousers, and delved into his boxer shorts to take the pic. A ping indicated the photo was received by her phone. She looked at the photo and held the phone aloft. 'Here it is, Seb's best friend. And, mine too.'

Anna chose not to look. She hoped that if Seb and Portia split in the future, he didn't live to regret sending his girlfriend a photo of his manhood.

Seb spun the bottle which pointed at Alistair. Alistair chose 'truth'.

Seb gazed at an inebriated, but smiley Alistair, who had Portia leaning her head on his shoulder. 'Ok, best buddy. I know most of your darkest secrets from when we met at school all those years ago. A lot of the naughty stuff. But for the sake of the game, tell us the worst thing you've ever done?'

'Yeah, best buddy,' Alistair joked, 'There's been a lot of bad stuff we've done together in our youth. Nicking stuff from shops near the school till the shop owner reported us to the Head. Smoking too much weed. Done a lot of hook-ups with women I didn't even like.' Glancing at Anna, he added, 'Before you my beautiful girl. Ok, the worst thing. Doing it with Harry Cameron's girlfriend that time at the music festival before he got to. Lost a good pal because of it.'

Seb somehow found this really funny and fell about laughing. 'H's girlfriend. She was that rake thin girl with gappy teeth. Gee, mate, you must've been out of it.'

Alistair then started to laugh, to the point of hysteria. 'Yeah, real crap at it she was, too. I did H a favour by road testing her and she failed the test.'

This evening was now getting to Anna. The men were all still high from the cocaine, getting hammered, and acting stupid. Anna glared at Alistair. 'God, Alistair. She probably thought the same about you. You can rev the engine but can't go the distance.'

His laughter abruptly stopped as Alistair scowled at Anna. 'Is that so? We'll talk about that later.'

This was said with a venomous tone to his voice as he glared at her and Anna shivered. The consequence of too much booze, too many drugs, and the boredom of lockdowns had changed Alistair into a man she no longer recognised and, if she were honest, didn't want to be with. There had been a lot of verbal flare-ups with him during their enforced confinements and she was the focus of his anger, blamed for Covid-19, the government's decisions and feeling trapped in a career he didn't really enjoy just because of family expectations.

The tense atmosphere was broken by Portia spinning the bottle. It pointed at Seb who opted for dare.

Portia licked her lips before outlining the dare. 'Ok, Seb, pick someone here, including Alistair, that you've always wanted to kiss and kiss them passionately for one minute.'

Anna guessed that Portia was hoping that Seb would kiss Alistair, just for the joke. Instead, Seb swigged out of a bottle of vodka before launching himself at her. 'Thanks, Portia. I've wanted to do this for a long time,' Seb stated as Anna toppled onto the carpet as Seb lay over her, took hold of her face, and scoured her mouth with his own. His rough beard scratched her chin and she felt like she was being hovered up by a vacuum cleaner, prohibiting her from speaking. Portia was urging Seb to give it his all. Deciding that one minute would be over soon, Anna went along with it though it wasn't a great experience. Seb seemed lost in a trance as his mouth devoured hers and his breathing was getting laboured as he started to become aroused. His right hand explored downwards, along her neck, towards her breast but Anna deflected the hand away.

'Stop now, Seb, or I'll clobber you,' Alistair's deep voice ordered, harshly.

Seb stopped immediately and rolled off Anna. 'Sorry, mate. It's only a bit of fun, just part of the game. No harm done.'

The party vibe in the room had now died, a stone-cold death. Alistair got up off the floor, picked up a bottle of whisky off the table, went to a sofa and sprawled out. He then started to drink from the bottle, ignoring everyone, an unreadable expression on his face.

Anna glanced at Seb's shocked face and Portia's bemused expression. It was gone midnight and Anna knew that Alistair was going to get slaughtered with the purpose of passing out. Time to encourage the visitors to leave.

An hour later, after they'd got a cab home, Anna cleared up and loaded the dishwasher, leaving Alistair still brooding on the sofa. She went back to the living area to tell him she was going to bed.

He dropped the empty whisky bottle onto the floor and took her hand, pulling her down next to him on the sofa. Cold eyes stared at her. 'I can rev the engine but can't go the distance. But you liked Seb slobbering all over you, didn't you?'

Anna edged away from him on the sofa with the intention of getting up as this drunken questioning would not be pleasant. His hand clamped her wrist to halt her departure. 'No, I didn't enjoy kissing Seb. It's like being sucked by a Dyson. Don't sweat it.'

Hard fingers grabbed her chin as his angry eyes glued onto hers. 'I've always had to put up with men coming on to you, haven't I? You're too bloody beautiful with your blue eyes, perfect features and flowing hair. Who knew that could actually be a problem I have to put up with all the time?'

The sour vapours of his whisky breath and the ominous words he was speaking were making Anna nauseous and fearful. 'I only went along with the kissing as it was part of the game, that's all. So as not appear a killjoy.'

Alistair's angry face was so close to hers that spittle landed on her face. 'Yeah, well, he's always had the hots for you and saw his chance. My best mate.' Alistair tapped her face with his right hand. 'He's the main one to blame and I might just smash him next time I see him. But you are always the one they make a play for.'

Anna could feel her temper rising. 'Alistair. We were playing a stupid game with only four people and Portia did that stupid dare. I don't think he meant any harm and there wasn't a lot of choice as to who to kiss. It was no big deal.'

'Yeah, Anna. But you're missing the point. If there had been twenty women in the room, he'd have still picked you. All men want you, Anna.' Alistair's eyes closely examined her face. 'It's got to stop.'

'I'm not seeking attention from men. In fact, it gets really boring and exhausting,' Anna stressed, an earnestness in her voice.

'Yeah, it's bloody exhausting for me. Being the chump with the woman that gets all the attention from the male gaze.' There was an animalistic snarl to his expression. 'I think now that lockdowns are over, you will have to change. Stop encouraging them. Let's have a little reset now to stop this happening in the future.'

Anna felt the side of her face tapped again before a major hammer blow slammed her left cheek. After a number of repeat hits, blackness overwhelmed her.

****

Saturday 30th April 2022

As Anna related her experience with Alistair, she cried softly as Nick held her.

'How badly hurt were you, sweetheart?' he gently asked.

'He beat me up quite badly and I sustained a black eye, bruising to the face and many punches to my ribs. Leaving me in a sobbing, bloody mess he got another whisky bottle out of the cabinet and slopped off out of the room. I lay on the sofa, crying, and shaking, scared to move as I didn't know the full extent of my injuries. I just hurt all over. After a bit, I found my phone and called my dad. Luckily, the distance between his home and Gloucester isn't much and he was with me in thirty minutes.' Anna shivered as she recalled her ordeal. 'I managed to open the door and will never forget the look on my dad's face as he laid eyes on me. I just collapsed against him, relieved to be safe. My brother, Dan, arrived shortly after and found Alistair conked out on the bed, stinking of whisky, which had poured out from the newly opened bottle. Dan dragged him out of the bed, down the stairs, to look at me. Dan was raging and landed punches to Alistair's shocked face, though dad managed to pull him off before he killed him. I sustained a broken rib, two bruised ribs and the injuries to my face. Needless to say, I didn't see Alistair again. He pleaded guilty to ABH and got twenty-six weeks custodial sentence.'

Nick felt a rage, equal to brother Dan's, surge through him. 'I'm glad your brother battered the bastard. I'd have done the same. I'm so sorry, Anna, my darling.'

CHAPTER FORTY TWO

Saturday 30th April 2022

Luke was sat in the pub drinking a pint of lager very slowly as he watched from a corner table as the 'wanker' entered the pub. The man was casually dressed in faded black jeans, blue T-shirt and black jacket. He walked up to the bar with the swagger that Luke had noticed the previous Saturday and stood between two customers as they waited to be served. The pub itself was an old-fashioned establishment, with fake beams, cream walls, brown patterned carpet and a lot of dark wood-stained tables and chairs. It had a large interior so there was a lot of available seating and on this Saturday evening it was half full of customers, noisy with conversation but there were comfortable spaces between groups of people. The man bought a pint of lager and went to chat with another male who was sat at a nearby table. The man's mate was a short guy, skinny, with glasses and smiled nervously at the man as he sat down. The power dynamic here was clear, the man was doing the nerdy guy a favour by talking to him.

Luke was drinking on his own. This made him nervous. He wasn't a natural pub goer and only felt comfortable in pubs if he was with Russ or his father. He couldn't strike up random conversations with strangers and chat to them about blokey topics such as football, work, more sport. Generally, he got on better with women and could relate to them more easily. Tonight, he had to blend in and look at ease. Carefully, trying not to be caught, he took a sneaky photo of the wanker, and sent it to Russ who was currently waiting in his car parked at the rear of the pub. Luke texted, **'W in the black jacket.'** Luke was to watch the man and text Russ if he vacated the bar to go to the toilet. The plan was that in the toilets Russ would offer drugs to the man. Luke was certain that the man was wired last Saturday based on his erratic behaviour at his beloved's house. The thought of her, his blue-eyed, brown-haired beauty, made Luke focus on the objective of Russ delivering a good hiding to the man.

Luke observed the man and the nerdy guy. The man dominated the conversation, as the geek nodded and smiled. The man downed his pint fairly quickly and indicated to his mate that he should go to the bar. The nerd had at least half a pint of lager remaining in his pint glass but was on his feet and off to the bar at speed. The nerd was soon back with two pints of lager and placed them on the table. Luke noted that the wanker did not speak or nod his head to acknowledge receiving his drink. This man was really sinking lower in Luke's estimation as he was a drug-taker, an abuser of women, and a rude individual with no manners. In some respects, a lot like his brother, Russ. This realisation made Luke chuckle.

After a few more minutes, two young women went to stand near to their table. To Luke, the women were obvious types, overdone make-up, false eyelashes, pouty lips, short skirts, low-cut tops and high heels. Two identikit clones, except that one was blonde and the other a red-head. The man seemed to favour the blonde and he winked at her as she caught his eye. Luke guessed that this was the type of woman he would normally associate with, flashy, loud, and up for a quick hook-up later. This further enraged Luke as this arrogant toss-pot had dared to engage with his beautiful Astraea when he should limit himself to this type of low-rent female. Ignoring his nerdy mate, the man joined the two women, initially flirting with both of them before focusing on the blonde. Luke watched, with a sourness in his belly, as the peacock preened and posed, making the woman laugh at his jokes. After about fifteen minutes, he made a move on the blonde and placed his arm around her waist. The red-head looked peeved and sat down with the nerdy male who smiled sheepishly at her but failed to speak. Luke finished his lager, and grew more irritated, as he observed this player use his dubious charms to draw in the blonde. Blondie giggled, and wiggled her generous bum, as the man's hand slipped down to pinch it and she feigned a look of surprise on her face. Luke cringed at this ugly display between two unclassy show-offs. The man then whispered in her ear as she cackled loudly. He then went to exit the bar and Luke hastily texted Russ. **'W going to bog. I'll come to the car.'**

****

Russ had checked out the toilets earlier. They were in an add-on block at the rear of the pub and the gents had three cubicles. He got out of the car quickly and walked over to the rear entrance of the pub and into the gent's toilet. He was wearing dark jeans, a black hoodie top and black baseball cap. All the cubicles were empty, their doors open, so he hurried into the first one, closed the door and had a quick slash. Sitting in the car on a cold night played havoc with his bladder. He heard the outer door of the toilets open and close and hoped this would be the man coming inside. Listening as a further door closed, he figured that the man had gone into a cubicle, and then waited to hear the sound of a stream of urine hitting the toilet bowl. The male then gave a cough, there was the faint sound of a zip fastening and the toilet being flushed. Russ quickly flushed the toilet as well, to time his emergence from his cubicle at the same time. The man emerging from the cubicle was the one in the photo that Luke had sent. Russ wasn't a great one for washing his hands after a piss but at the sink he did turn on the tap and briefly flicked his hands in the water. He grabbed a paper towel to dry his hands and lobbed the towel at the bin. It missed. The wanker did wash his hands and admired himself in the mirror.

Russ whispered to the man. 'You're Wayne, aren't yer? I've got some blow if you're interested.' Russ had the baseball cap pulled low and the hoodie hood over the top to try to hide his face.

The man glanced at Russ before turning back to look in the mirror. 'Got the wrong guy, mate, I ain't Wayne. But I might be tempted to buy a snort or two. Just met a fit bird in the bar and I think she's up for a quickie. A bit of blow gives it an extra kick.'

Russ mumbled. 'Sorry, mate, mistook yer for someone else. I could shove you a bit, seen as you're interested.' Russ pretended to fumble in his jean pocket. 'I've got none on me now as I've done a bit of good trade tonight. Got some in the car, do yer wanna meet me in the car park in five minutes.'

The man nodded his head, enthusiastically. 'Yeah, great. You go out and I'll follow in a minute or so. Should give my little sex party a real boost.'

Russ went outside the pub and texted Luke. **'I'm coming to car now. W on his way.'** Earlier Russ had scanned the pub car park for security cameras and there didn't seem to be any. All good. The car park was fairly empty of cars, just a few dotted about, and Russ went over to his car to await his customer. After a few minutes the man emerged from the pub's rear door and looked around for his supplier. Russ held up a hand to indicate his presence in the car park. Possibly in anticipation of the double delights he was shortly going to experience, a drug high and sex, the man straightened his body, lifted his head high, and did an exaggerated walk, swinging his shoulder's from side to side. In Russ's head he could hear The Bee Gees singing '*Staying Alive*' as the John Travolta character, 'Tony Manero' swaggered along a NY city street in leather jacket and flared trousers. Russ suppressed his urge to laugh. This strutting poser was not going to know pleasure tonight, only pain. As the man got nearer to Russ's car, both men scanned the area for prying eyes but there was no one around. Russ held tightly onto the wrench he had in his hoodie pocket.

The man approached Russ at the car's boot. 'Alright, mate, what yer got?'

'Got some blow, do you want a couple of bags?' Russ asked as he lifted the car boot to reach for a plastic bag in the otherwise empty boot.

'Give me three. Two for me and one for her, if she's up for it. Better get a shift on or she might have gone and I'll have to find another willing tart,' the man smirked, giving Russ a 'you know what women are like' kind of look. 'I never have much trouble in copping off with them though. They all like a piece of my pipe.'

Encouraging the bragging banter to distract the man, Russ said. 'Yeah, I'm the same with the tarts, they can't get enough.' As the man moved closer to him, Russ rapidly scanned the car park, then swung his right hand holding the wrench, at the base of the man's neck. The man let out a 'oomph' noise, his knees buckled under him and Russ toppled him forward into the car boot. From the plastic bag he took out a roll of duct tape, tore off a strip and fastened it over the man's mouth before he had time to realise his predicament and start shouting. A hessian sack was placed over his head to disorientate him and stop him viewing his kidnapper. Russ used a cable tie to secure the man's arms behind his back and taped around his ankles. Russ slammed the car boot shut, walked to the passenger seat of the car and got in, just as Luke sat in the driver's seat. 'Right, we've got him. Drive,' Russ ordered Luke.

CHAPTER FORTY THREE

Driving the journey to his home, Luke tried to avoid main roads where there were likely to be ANPR cameras though they were travelling in a vehicle with cloned plates so lessening the chances of being caught. All courtesy of the dodgy network of people that Russ knew through his drug taking habit and past criminal activities. Not having really taken part in an actual crime before, Luke's hands were shaking as he held onto the steering wheel to drive the car. Due to the excitement, and adrenaline rush, Luke could feel his heart pounding in his chest, his breathing was fast and he felt he wasn't drawing oxygen into his lungs. His cheeks were bright red and beads of sweat were forming on his brow, threatening to drop into his eyes and make driving impossible. To make matters worse, their captive in the boot was kicking and groaning, and these noises could be heard more loudly when the car had to slow for bends in the road, roundabouts and traffic lights. Luke feared that if a car behind got close enough perhaps they would be alerted to the passenger in the boot. All this was affecting Luke's concentration and a collision almost happened when the car in front stopped suddenly at a junction and Luke nearly slammed into it.

'For fuck's sake, Luke, calm down, breathe normally and drive carefully. If the cops clock you driving erratically they'll pull you over and we'll both be fucked,' Russ ordered. 'When I decided to go along with this crazy scheme I forgot that you haven't got the bottle to carry it out. I thought I was starring in *'The Fast and the Furious'* but it seems like I'm in *'Dumb and Dumber'*.

'Shut up, Russ, and let me concentrate,' Luke shouted and wiped his forehead to disperse the sweat. 'I'm just getting my head around the fact that I've committed a criminal offence which could land me in jail. Yikes.' Luckily, they were now driving along the country lane of their home, just outside the village of Sherbourne south of Warwick. Luke pulled the car onto the drive of their detached property and pulled up in front of a large garage/workshop. Luke parked tight up to the garage, and when the car lights were turned off, the area was dark with no discernible light due to the rural location.

Their passenger was now screeching and banging from inside the boot, making the car rock. Russ put on a balaclava and gloves and instructed Luke to do the same. 'Get the door open so I can bring him inside quickly. I don't want anyone to hear him squealing.' In actuality, the property was once part of a small farm so had no immediate neighbours either side and fields at the rear. It was unlikely that anyone would hear the frightened cries of their guest.

Luke opened the garage door as quietly as possible but winced as a loud squeak emitted from unoiled hinges. Every noise seemed to be several thousand decibels higher than in the daytime when the sound of distant traffic gave off an ongoing drone which muffled other sounds. Russ opened the boot, ripped the duct tape from around the scumbag's ankles, dragged him out, and placed him on his feet.

Russ whispered, in a deep, menacing voice, 'Don't make any noise or I'll whack you with this wrench until you're fucking dead, ok'? He pushed the man forward into the garage where the only illumination was from a single light bulb dangling from the ceiling. The man struggled, and grunted, to rid himself of Russ's hand on his right arm as he was pushed forward into the workshop. At one side the work transit van was parked. Further along the tools and equipment for the plastering trade were stored in a disorganised manner, boxes with trowels, cleaning brushes, mortar boards and mixing buckets. Larger equipment included step ladders and wooden planks. To the side of the equipment there were bags of plaster and a number of sheets of plasterboard. A smell of damp plaster permeated the air.

To prepare for their visitor, the brothers had cleared an area of the floor and covered it with black plastic sheeting from a roll. Just in case of spillage. A black chair with steel frame was available for the comfort of the guest. Russ roughly pushed the man onto the chair and he moaned and wriggled to get up. 'Fasten cable ties around his ankles and the chair legs,' Russ ordered Luke.

With shaky hands, Luke knelt and grabbed the scumbag's right leg. The man kicked out but Russ kept him pinned down on the chair which made it harder for him to struggle. After a couple of failed attempts, Luke's temper rose, he gripped the man's right ankle and secured him to the chair leg with the cable tie. With one leg secure, Luke repeated the process with the man's left leg. Having started out feeling nervous and fearful, Luke was starting to enjoy his participation in controlling the man, remembering that he was doing all this for his beautiful Astraea. The man struggled to release himself from Russ's hold but he was unlikely to escape with a chair attached to his backside. Russ's patience was running out and he gave the man a hard whack across the head with his fisted gloved hand. 'Keep still and settle down.' Russ nodded at Luke to get a nearby roll of duct tape. 'Secure that round him,' he instructed.

The man made a futile attempt to avoid the duct tape but it was soon wrapped around his upper body and the chair several times. His head slumped forward as the fight went out of him. Russ removed the sack from over his head, the man blinked, then looked around frantically, taking in his surroundings before focusing on the two men. Russ picked up a baseball bat which he tapped in his left hand. The man's eyes grew wide and fearful as he noticed the weapon and the menace of it near to his head and body. The man mumbled something but the words were muffled by the duct tape across his mouth.

Russ stepped in front of him. 'Ok, listen up. I'm going to take the duct tape off your mouth. If you shout or scream, I'll whack you with the bat, ok? But you'd be wasting your time as there's no one near enough to hear, anyway.' Russ pulled the duct tape off the man's mouth and he did scream, in pain. Russ kept his promise and banged the bat into the man's right upper arm. The man exhaled loudly, as the pain jarred his body, but the only other sound he made was a 'oomph' noise.

The man directed his eyes between Russ and Luke, trying to identify them. 'Who are you? What do you want with me? I do a bit of drugs but I don't owe nothing to no one.'

Russ stood directly in front of the man, legs apart, the baseball bat held in his right hand and gloved fingers gripped the handle. Luke was to his left side, dressed in black jeans and sweatshirt, feeling sweaty faced due to the confinement of the balaclava. But his initial fear was replaced by excitement due to the violence meted out to the man.

'Shut up. It will go like this. We will ask the questions and you will give the answers, capeesh?' Russ instructed, the baseball bat tapping in his left hand. 'Play smart or if we think you're not telling the truth, you'll get a whack, ok?'

The man nodded, his eyes firmly on the baseball bat. For a man who earlier on had the swagger of a boy band member walking on stage at a pop concert, he was now subdued and fearful. 'Yeah, ok.'

'Last Saturday, you went to the home of a young woman we like and you upset her. As she is a classy lady she would only tell us a bit of what happened so we want to hear it from you. What you say will depend on how much we batter you,' Russ stated, smacking the good old bat into his hand to emphasis his words.

The man's eyes flicked again between the two men. 'Oh, God, are you Anna's brothers? I didn't do anything serious. We'd been out before in the past and then split up. Then we got back together for a few dates and then we fu....' he paused, 'we hooked-up. But it was all consensual, you understand?'

Luke could have done a little jig on the spot but forced himself to keep still and quiet. Anna. Anna. His beloved had a name, it was Anna. All names had meanings, he would look it up when he got home.

Russ spoke, a sneery tone to his voice. 'Hooked-up. Sounds like you're a wanker who uses women to me.' Before the man could deny this, Russ moved to the man's right hand side and swung the bat hard so that it connected with his stomach. The man immediately hunched forward as the impact of the blow hit him but he was restricted in his movements by the duct tape. Russ continued, 'We've got the background story. But you need to tell us what happened on Saturday night.'

Still hurting from the blow, the man's voice was shaky as he spoke, 'I c-called around to s-see her as I wanted us to get back together. S-she let me in and s-she was pleased to see me. W-w were getting down to it again....when the police turned up unexpected like. They were looking to fit me up for drug dealing and my flat mate told them where to find me.' His voice stopped trembling as he got into the story, 'interrupted our loved-up evening, they did.'

Russ addressed Luke. 'What do you think, is he telling the truth?'

Luke stepped forward in front of the man. This was his moment to defend his beloved Anna. He stood up straight, to minimise the shaking in his legs. He inhaled deeply, to compose himself to speak in an authoritative voice and not in a squeaky, timorous way. 'Anna told us that she didn't let you in. You forced your way in. She didn't want you there and it was not a 'loved-up' evening, as you call it. Your drug story is a load of bull. She called the cops on you because you misbehaved but she wouldn't tell us what you did. Better start telling the truth before we batter you some more.' A trickle of excitement went along Luke's spine as he said 'batter'. This would all add spice to his writing as he now knew the power of threatening baddies with physical violence. He looked at Russ. 'Give me the bat.'

Luke took the bat off his brother. It felt good in his hand, a solid wooden weight which was already doing damage to their guest. He walked slowly and calmly behind the chair to which the man was secured. Luke assessed the target area.

A strong swing of the bat could land on the man's higher back and shoulders. It was good to distribute the beating around his body. Drawing back his right arm, he landed a hefty blow to the man's back. The man let out a loud, 'whump' and the chair moved forward slightly. Luke's hand holding the bat was shaking but not out of fear but with raw, primal excitement. This was truly a great moment for Luke. His entry into manhood and away from being the weak simp his brother despised. 'Ok, you, let's have the truth now.'

'Ok, ok,' the man groaned, his head hanging down as the pain permeated his shoulders and back, winding him as his breathing grew raspy. 'Ok. I went to her house with the intention of getting back with her. She's a really fit bird and I did want to fu..' pause for breath to give himself thinking time...'hook-up again but she wasn't interested. I got mad at her and forced my way in. She rushed to the kitchen to get her phone and said she'd call the cops. I decided that she'd change her mind if we got closer so I kissed her, yer know, and touched her breast to get her in the mood. Well, she's not in the mood as it happens and she kicks me in the balls. This got me madder and I slapped her a bit.' The man stopped sharing his story and looked at his two captors.

Luke was still holding the weapon but not ready to yield it again. Yet. Though he was horrified that this piece of scum had hurt his beloved, Anna, he sensed that this was now the real version of events. 'What happened next?'

Seeing that another attack was not imminent, the man hastened on with the story. 'She screamed. And didn't I get the fucking shock of my life when some boyfriend dashes in from the other room and pulls me off her, overpowers me, gets me down on the floor. He tells me he's making a citizen's arrest. I'm struggling to get up and I can't get him off me. He tells Anna to call the cops. Then I'm forced to sit on a chair till the cops arrive. The guy must be ex-cop or army as he was on me real quick. I'm normally a good fighter but this guy's the next level.'

Luke was pleased that this man had come to the aid of his beloved when this pile of dog shit had hurt her. But it also raised the possibility that her rescuer was also her boyfriend, the one she mentioned the other day. 'Right, douchebag, I think we've heard the real story. It doesn't paint you in the best light, does it? Assaulting a young woman that we are very fond of. A question before we deal with you. Where did you meet her?'

'I met her in the Frizzy Lion in the town centre. I was knocked out the first time I saw her by how beautiful she is,' the man stated, a wishful tone to his voice.

'Too good for you, mate,' Russ commented, 'you need to stick to the town skanks in future.' He looked at Luke. 'Give me the bat.'

Russ went behind the chair and gave the man a final blow to the shoulders with the bat. After groaning loudly, the man's head fell forward, and his body slumped as if he had no more energy to hold himself up. Dropping the bat, Russ's fist flew into the man's face, catching his mouth, and splitting his lip so that blood oozed down his chin. A second punch landed just under the man's left eye and he grunted due to the impact. 'Nice talking to you, mate. Time to go.'

Luke was hugely satisfied with the punches to the man's face. Hits to his body with the bat were all well and good but there was no visual evidence of the blows. The sight of the blood, seeping slowly down the man's chin, was proof that a beating can inflict actual bodily damage. The red mark made by his brother's fist on the man's cheekbone, and under his eye, would result in livid red, blue and purple bruising over the next few days. Wonderful colours that Luke would transcribe in his latest fantasy story as the perpetrator of an attack on his Astraea got the battering he rightly deserved from the hero, Xandros. As in all good stories, justice had been served. Luke's stories were morality tales, all about righting wrongs. The good survived and the evil paid for their sins.

There was one black cloud on the horizon. Was the man that had come to Anna's aid, her boyfriend? A fit, alpha male. Men like this always went for beautiful women and, Anna, his Astraea, was the most beautiful of all. This man would be an obstacle in Luke's way of getting to his beloved.

Back in the car to drop their guest back near his hostelry, Luke was now experiencing the low after the extreme high. The reality of having just committed a major crime which could result in a long prison sentence was now disturbing him. Luke feared the police and was terrified of coming to their attention again, after an encounter with them years ago. The police interview, the Magistrate's Court and the conviction for stalking. The punishment, a low level Community Order involving forty hours of unpaid work and an exclusion requirement to stay away from Naomi's home.

⸺◈⸺

CHAPTER FORTY FOUR

February 2018

Luke sat in the police interview room, shaking like a jelly, being interviewed with reference to allegations of stalking. He was seated next to the duty solicitor, Deirdre Lawson, a woman in her fifties who looked flustered as if she had run to the police station after being chased by a dog. She did not fill Luke with confidence. Sat opposite Luke was Detective Sergeant Neil Williams, a hard-nosed individual in his thirties who had an unrelenting gaze which made Luke more jittery. A Detective Constable Sabita Chopra, sat next to the DS, who seemed softer and more human.

Luke was finding it hard to comprehend why he was here as he was not a stalker. He was not some creepy weirdo that pursued young women, making them feel uncomfortable, whilst hinting at sexual acts he wanted to do to them. Didn't they realise that Luke's actions were from a place of loving kindness and he would never, ever, hurt a girl that he cared for. This had all gone wrong. Naomi had misunderstood his intentions. If only they would let him speak to her he could clear things up immediately.

Naomi was a young Library Assistant at his local library where he sourced fantasy and sci-fi novels, the inspiration for his writing. Naomi was cute with shoulder-length brown hair in a choppy style, who dressed in boho chic, floaty, floral dresses, boots and multiple beaded bracelets. She was always helpful to Luke, ordering books from other libraries for him and notifying him of any new books that might interest him. He'd got into a habit of visiting every Saturday, to borrow new books and to use the libraries computer to explore his interests in Greek mythology, Egyptology, science fiction and so on. He could do this at home, on his laptop, but he liked the library with its many visitors and the presence of beautiful Naomi. In fact, his dreams were now being realised as she'd had coffee with him on a couple of occasions when they discussed their love for the *'Dune'* novels by Frank Herbert. He texted Naomi with interesting snippets he found in books, movies or online. Occasionally, he would buy her small gifts, a *'Dune'* birthday card and a Shai-Hulud bookmark.

Luke was lost in his musings when DS Williams broke his trance. 'Luke, do you drive a grey VW Golf registration 'AB16CDF?

Luke nodded, then added, 'Yes.'

DS: Where were you on Tuesday evening, 9th January from six p.m. until midnight?

Luke's face flushed. The Solicitor had discussed the 'no comment' option with Luke but he couldn't see the point of this. He had not done anything wrong except for offering friendship to Naomi. Luke glanced at the Solicitor who pursed her lips, was that a sign he should speak or not? He had been brought up by his father to tell the truth, so he stated, 'I was at home for most of the evening with my father and brother.'

DS: 'What time did you get home?'

Luke answered, 'About seven p.m.

DS: 'Did you remain home for the rest of the evening?'

Luke: 'Yes.'

The DS, giving Luke his laser stare, asked, 'What did you do between six p.m. before getting home about seven p.m.?

Luke swallowed nervously. 'I went to Sainsbury's on Craterlake Drive and bought a four pack of lager and some crisps.'

DS: 'Did you stop off anywhere between leaving Sainsburys and getting home?'

A red flush travelled up Luke's neck to his face. 'I did stop at Laketon Close to make sure that Naomi, Ms Barrymore, had got home safely.'

DS Williams arched an eyebrow. 'Why would you do that?'

Luke stuttered, 'Well, she is my friend and I don't like to think of her getting out of her car on a poorly lit street in the dark.'

DS: Did you get out of your car on this occasion and speak to Ms Barrymore?'

Luke: 'Yes, I stood by her gate and said 'hello'.

DS: 'What did Ms Barrymore say to you?'

Luke: 'She, er, she...' he stuttered. 'She asked me what I was doing at her home. I explained that I wanted to make sure she got home safely.'

DS: 'What did Ms Barrymore say to that?'

Luke avoided the eyes of the intimidating DS Williams. 'She said that she was shocked that I knew where she lived and had no right to come to her home. I never intended to shock her as I want to take care of her.'

DS: What happened next?'

Luke blushed again. 'She told me not to come to her home again or she would call the police. Then she rushed into her house.'

DS: 'When did you next see Ms Barrymore after this?'

Luke: 'The following Saturday at the library. She helped me to get a book I'd reserved on alien life forms.'

DS: This was Saturday, 13th January, is this correct?'

Luke: 'I suppose so.'

DS: 'What was the conversation between you and Ms Barrymore on that occasion?'

Luke: 'I asked if the book was in. She said yes and went to get it. After she gave me the book I asked her if she was free to have coffee after her shift finished at four p.m.'

DS: 'What was her reply?

Luke: 'That she didn't want a coffee with me. She said she was going straight home after the library closed at four p.m.'

DS: 'What time did you leave the library and where did you go afterwards?'

Luke's stomach was churning and he wiped his clammy hands on his jeans before he spoke. 'I...I...er..I drove to Ms Barrymore's home and waited for her to return.'

DS: 'Why did you do that?'

Luke: 'She seemed very distant with me at the library and I wanted to reconnect with her.'

DS: 'Did you speak to Ms Barrymore?'

Luke: Yes, I got out of my car as she parked on her road. I approached her as she walked to her gate. I stood between her and the gate so that we could talk. I said that I would really like it if we could go out for coffee again.'

DS: 'What did Ms Barrymore say?'

Luke: 'She said to get out of the way and went to go past me. I went to take hold of her arm to stop her leaving. I just wanted to talk and I have to say she was being a bit rude.' Luke bristled when he recalled that sweet Naomi was treating him with such contempt after all his kindness to her.

DS: 'How did Ms Barrymore react when you tried to hold her arm?'

Luke could now feel his temper flare. 'The silly girl shouted 'go away'. A dog walker nearby told me to leave her alone. He was a big chap, very tall and burly, so I quickly dashed to my car.' Luke took a deep breath. 'But it was all a misunderstanding. I just wanted a chat.'

DS: What were you doing on Tuesday, 16th January between six p.m. and seven p.m.?

Luke realised that when he answered this, the cold-eyed detective would not understand his motives for trying to contact

Naomi again. 'I parked outside Ms Barrymore's house until she got home from work. I wanted to clear up the misunderstanding from the other day. I just wanted to be friends again.'

DS: 'What happened when Ms Barrymore arrived home?'

Luke: 'I was waiting by her gate and when she saw me, she took her phone out of her bag. She said that she was going to call the police. I begged her not to. I told her that I would never harm her and that I loved her. I called her by her name, Naiad.'

DS: 'How did Ms Barrymore respond to this?'

Luke swallowed nervously. 'I think I upset her as she pushed me out of the way and fled into her house. I waited to see if she would calm down and come out but she didn't so I drove home.'

DS: 'The name you called her, Naiad, what does it mean?' The detective gave Luke the sort of disgusted look he would have if he found dog muck on the sole of his shoe.

Luke: 'Naiad. She is the heroine in one of my fantasy stories. A beautiful girl with an other-worldly, ethereal quality like a water nymph in Greek mythology. A naiad.'

DS Williams paused in his questioning and studied Luke carefully. It was the level of scrutiny a scientist might use when examining a new strain of influenza virus with an electron microscope. Luke shivered.

DS: 'We now need to discuss some of the emails and text messages that you have been sending Ms Barrymore since 16th January to her work email and to her mobile phone.'

Luke was sinking into despair as this interview went on. All this could have been resolved amicably if only Naomi would have co-operated. Why were they calling this stalking? Luke was just a nice guy who befriended beautiful girls to immortalise them in his writings. That's all.

CHAPTER FORTY FIVE

Monday 9th May 2022

Anna was still on a high after an amazing weekend with Nick and special memories of making love with him, a couple of times, filled her mind. As she'd left to go home on late Sunday afternoon, he told her that he had a busy week ahead. He would be working on the Spring Bank Holiday Monday to finalise some contracts for new clients in the North West. In fact, business in this area was thriving and the company were interested in securing a new premises in the Manchester area. Mid-week he was going to assess suitable premises and would be staying in hotels for a number of nights. On Saturday, he and his business partner, Eric, were going to dinner in Birmingham, to meet with a TV company producer to discuss providing professional security services for TV and film sets. All this work meant that Anna would not be seeing him. She was disappointed but realised that he couldn't run a successful business if he didn't put in the work.

But then little doubts would plague her. Did he want to see her again or was he just trying to put distance between them after getting what he wanted sexually? After his sizzling sexual adventures with the confident Abbie had she disappointed him? Nick Carlton was such an attractive man that he could have any woman he wanted, did he really want her?

When she'd arrived home on the Sunday, she received a visit from a DC Vernon with regard to a sustained and violent attack on Connor Peterson. Anna was questioned as to where she was on Saturday evening from eight-thirty onwards and into Sunday morning. DC Vernon indicated that the assault was directly linked to her as the attacker or attackers (the DC did not clarify the number) referred to her as the reason for the attack. The assailant was very focused on her relationship with Peterson and the harm he had caused her. This freaked Anna out. Did she have some sort of vigilante punishing people who upset her? If this were the case, her Superman should take off his cape and leave her alone. Anna informed DC Vernon that at the time of Peterson's attack she was with Nick. Nick rang her later to tell her that he was questioned by DC Vernon about the attack on Peterson. Nick confirmed to the DC that he had been with Anna and showed the officer recordings from his home camera to clarify that he had not left his house since Anna arrived on Saturday evening until her departure on Sunday afternoon.

All this did sour what had been a wonderful weekend. And her doubts continued as to whether Nick did want to see her again. She was encouraged to receive a text on Monday morning that read, **'Hi. Just to say that I really enjoyed our special time together over the weekend. N xxx.'**

Anna liked the way he referred to their 'special' time. But the text did not try to firm up a further date in the near future. Was the text a polite way of saying goodbye? Anna wrestled for hours afterwards trying to think of a suitable reply. She was sure her productivity at work was taking a nose dive as she couldn't concentrate on inputting overtime claims and correcting salary mistakes. After consulting her dating expert, Olivia, she replied to his text. **'It was a special time. I really enjoyed it too. A xxx.'** Olivia assured her that this was perfect, letting him know she had enjoyed herself but not coming over as needy. Allowing him to make the next move in the game of dating chess.

There were a few more texts from Nick over the week, mainly updates on his work. On Friday, he'd texted, **'I'm losing my mind looking at business premises in Manchester area. Spending hours with estate agent Keith, a David Brent deluded type who thinks he's the world's best sales person. Couldn't sell a sausage to a hungry dog. N xxx'** Anna replied.

'**Ha ha. Keep strong. If your dinner goes well tomorrow you may soon be mixing with famous TV people. A xxx.**'

Nick responded. '**Great. A load of pretentious prats. Catch up soon. N xxx**'

Now at work on the Monday, Anna was in panic mode about the vague comment in the text about 'catch up soon' and spoke to her dating consultant. 'It's all so general. Do you think he wants to see me again? Should I text that I'm available at the weekend?'

Olivia paused from typing on her keyboard and wagged a manicured-nailed finger in the air. 'No, no, no. Text something back about hoping he has a good week and leave it at that. Keep it neutral. If you say you've got plans at the weekend, he may think you're not interested. But if you suggest meeting up, it may come across as needy. We don't do needy, ok. Girl power, we don't need a man to have a good time.'

Anna swung from side to side on her office chair. 'Ok, don't be too keen but don't be too aloof. This dating tight-rope walking is very tricky.'

'Right,' Olivia turned her chair to face Anna. 'As I said, just send something friendly or jokey about having a good week and leave it at that. See how he responds.'

Taking all this into account, Anna texted, '**It would be good to catch up. A xxx**'

Later that afternoon, as Anna was just preparing to leave work, a text pinged in her phone. Anna hoped it was Nick but it was from an unknown number. '**Have seen you around town. You are really beautiful. Think of you a lot. Xan xx**' Anna had to read this a couple of times to take it in. Who could have sent this? What sort of weird name was Xan?

Olivia picked up her bag and then got up from her computer chair. 'Right, I'm off home. I'm going to have a long hot bath as my back's aching, eat a ready meal and then watch a dark psycho drama on telly. You ok, you look a little pale?'

Not wanting to mention the text, Anna nods. 'Yeah, fine, thanks. Tired after the weekend that's all. Enjoy your psycho drama but have sweet dreams. See you tomorrow.'

Back home, after a meal of mac and cheese with salad, Anna thought she'd watch *'The Pembrokeshire Murders'* a dramatisation of two unsolved murder cases of the 1980s. After watching the first two episodes, Anna made a tea, when her phone rang. She was ecstatic to see that it was Nick. Her stomach flipped when she heard his sexy voice.

'I know it's a bit late but can I drop by to see you?' he asked.

It was a bit late, nine-thirty, but she really wanted to see him. Thinking of how her dating expert would handle this, she said, nonchalantly, 'Yes, that would be great.' It was work tomorrow so she couldn't afford to have a late night. There was no way that he was going to stay over but a part of her longed for that very thing.

The phrase 'don't panic' kept running through her head as she panicked. She raced up the stairs to her bedroom, checked her make-up, brushed her hair and spritzed her neck and wrists with a delicate floral perfume. She was in her work dress, a knee-length jersey dress in blue/black abstract print, which was practical and comfortable for work. Her panic mode was now making her cheeks glow pink and her heart beat faster.

Fifteen minutes later she was at the door to let him in, breathing in deeply to calm her jittery nerves. She opened the door to be blown away by how handsome he was dressed in black jeans, cream crew-neck jumper and brown jacket. Anna knew she could fall in love with this man but was it safe to do so? 'Hi,' she said shyly. 'This is a nice surprise.'

Within seconds, his arms were around her waist as he kissed her. As the kiss ended, he searched her face for her reaction, and smiled as she blushed slightly with surprise and pleasure. 'Hi, Anna. I wanted to see how you are.'

As she was released from his hold, Anna responded, in a shaky voice, 'I'm fine, thanks. Would you like a drink – lager, wine, coffee, water?'

'Lager would be good, thanks.' Nick went into the sitting room as Anna got the drinks. She handed him a bottled lager, and then sat next to him on the sofa, holding her glass of white wine. 'Thanks,' he said, supping the lager. 'Did you have a good weekend?'

Anna updated him on her weekend spent with her family in Tewkesbury. 'I had to tell them about what Connor Peterson did to me and the subsequent attack on Peterson by person or persons who knew me. Typically, Dan, my brother, was all for murdering Peterson and dad still thinks I'm a ten-year-old who should live at home.' She laughed but it was all so tiring. 'Have you heard anymore from DC Vermont?'

Nick shook his head. 'I'm not expecting to. They've no evidence linking me to the assault and I've proved where I was on the Saturday evening. The same goes for you. But I'm concerned with the link between you, Peterson and the attacker.'

As Anna could not make any sense of this, she found the whole thing unsettling. 'Yes, so am I. It's weird. I don't know why someone would attack Peterson on my behalf. Let's hope the whole thing's over with. But I did get an odd text today.'

An inquisitive frown furrowed Nick's brow as he gazed at her. 'An odd text. Let's see?'

Anna picked up her phone and showed the text to Nick. 'I've tried to search the phone number through Reverse Phone Lookup but I can't find anything. I'm going to ignore it but it's a little bit concerning after the attack on Connor.' Anna shivered and rubbed her arms to generate heat in her body.

Nick took out his own phone and took some minutes looking for the phone number on various other sites. 'Nothing's coming up. My guess is that it's a burner phone, one that can be used for basic calls and texts, whilst the phone owner remains anonymous. A phone bought in a shop paid for by cash. The bigger question here is, who sent this text? It could just be a random text, meant for someone else. Or some scammer sending texts to numerous people to see if anyone bites. Flattery to draw someone in for what, financial gain, sexual purposes? But I don't like the wording. 'Have seen you around town'. 'Think you are really beautiful'. 'Think of you a lot'. It all sounds personal and targeted at you, Anna.'

Anna gulped. 'Oh, shit. What if the sender of this text is also Peterson's attacker? A violent person who knows who I am. Should I reply and ask who they are?' Anna picked up her wine and drank a large mouthful.

'If this is a burner phone then they'll want to stay anonymous and won't tell you who they are. I wouldn't reply as it will only feed into whatever fantasy is playing in their head and their need for control. Just ignore it,' he advised, seeing her worried face and he kissed her lightly on the forehead to try to reassure her.

'I can easily block the number on my phone. That should stop it immediately,' Anna stated, picking up her mobile.

Before she could progress any further, Nick took the phone off her. 'I suggest that you don't do that. From my cop experience, blocking the individual could antagonise them if they want to contact you and then can't. They may find some other way of making contact in person. This is only one text; it could be a random mistake, let's see what happens. Don't delete any texts. Importantly, don't respond.'

'This is now freaking me out,' she stated, thinking who the hell could this be. 'Who is this Xan? It must be a nickname or made up name.'

'Yeah, most definitely. It will have some significance to the sender,' Nick now held her closely, rubbing her back to provide comfort and to put colour back into her bloodless face.

Anna was determined to not let all this unnerve her. 'He's not going to win by frightening me. Let's change the subject. How was your dinner with the TV producer? Are you going to be providing security services to a TV production company?'

Nick's eyes sparkled mischievously. 'Yeah, there could be a contract in it. Offering our security services to protect the cast, crews, equipment and sets from unauthorised access, theft and vandalism. I'll be a bodyguard to Michelle Keegan before you know it.'

'Michelle Keegan?' Anna nodded knowingly. 'Can I apply to be Rege´-Jean Page's Personal Assistant?'

Nick raised an eyebrow. 'The guy in Bridgerton, the Duke of Hastings. My mother, sister and aunties all love him. You like a handsome Duke, do you Miss Loudon? As I recall, all the females in my family were talking about the lustful goings on between him and the beautiful Daphne. I'm blushing just referring to it.'

Anna spluttered on her wine. 'Blushing? You wouldn't know how to blush, Mr Carlton, as you are very self-assured, in a good way.'

A devilment was now apparent in his blue eyes. 'Yes, Miss Louden, I am like the Duke, very confident when dealing with the vagaries of the fairer sex.'

Trying to stifle a giggle, Anna feigned indignation. 'Vagaries of the fairer sex. You sound like a Duke of the nineteenth century who regards women as fluffy, silly creatures who need a man to guide them.'

'But they do, don't they, Miss Louden? He winked at her as she punched him lightly with her hand. In the next moment, she was drawn into him, as his mouth sought hers.

⚜

CHAPTER FORTY SIX

Monday 9ᵗʰ May 2022

It was coming up to midnight as Nick lay in bed, remembering the pleasure of being with Anna, and the difficulty of having to steel himself to leave her soft and yielding body to come home. In an ideal world, he could stay with her forever as he explored every inch of her perfect body. But in practical terms, they both had work tomorrow and Nick had a high workload in the week ahead, the main part of which was finalising the contract with the TV production company and putting plans in place to providing security services at an agreed future date.

Nick smiled to himself when he recalled the few times he had now made love to Anna. And he really did think of it as making love and not an exercise in sexual acrobatics which it could be with Abbie. He knew that Anna had gotten pleasure from it but at her core he sensed a vulnerability to her that gave her a shyness which he found very appealing. Nick acknowledged that Anna had been physically hurt by the awful Alistair but there were also mental scars. From more that she divulged, the man had been selfish and uncaring in his attitude to sex which left her doubting her abilities and undermined her confidence. Nick guessed that Anna compared herself in terms of sexual performance to Abbie and if he wasn't careful she may decide that she wasn't competent enough and withdraw from their relationship.

It was true that his relationship with Abbie was founded on a frenzy of frequent sex. By their second encounter, Abbie had explored with him most of the sexual positions and was single-minded in seeking satisfaction. All good. Women were certainly entitled to enjoy sex as much as men but it did often feeling that he was taking part in a sexual sparring competition and not in an intimate liaison. Abbie had been extraordinarily obsessed with sex and gifted herself the award of Olympic gold champion in bestowing her favours on men. But she also used it to manipulate him and as a diversionary tactic to cover bad behaviour. Nick knew this would never happen with Anna.

Anna was truly a fantastic woman with many qualities that he found enticing, her beauty, her intelligence, her work ethic, her sense of humour and the fact that she laughed at his corny jokes. In physical terms she was female perfection. A luscious mouth that he could devour endlessly. A sensual body with rounded breasts and rose bud nipples that his greedy tongue could tease until eternity. A curved bottom that his hands could not tire of squeezing, caressing and giving a playful slap. Because she was petite in size, it sent his testosterone levels soaring when he was able to move and lift her effortlessly to enhance their sexual pleasure. It felt to him that she wanted him to guide and control, to help her overcome her fears, and rebuild her shattered confidence. At this stage, Nick knew that Anna was not the sex expert that Abbie was with her bag of hooker tricks. But, Anna had engaged with him fully and the orgasmic high he'd achieved each time had been completely sating for his body and mind. He wanted to be her teacher, open her up to new experiences, but wanted to ensure it was not sex by numbers but sex with love. And, already he knew that he had been bewitched by this beautiful siren and a powerful love for her was already crushing his heart.

It was also the flaws that Anna didn't have which also attracted him and in terms of these he could not help but compare her to Abbie. Abbie's way of putting herself first, and not caring for others, had become quite obvious to Nick over their six months together. A lot of the time Abbie had stayed at his house as a guest. Expecting him to cook, order a takeaway, or take her to a restaurant and expect him to pay. Leaving her stuff around the place for him or the cleaner to tidy up. No cleaning the bathroom or kitchen if she used it. Her greed in allowing him to pay for meals, clothes, days out, salon treatments and holidays without any real thank you. For all this, Nick was really angry with himself that he'd allowed this to happen and he vowed never to be taken advantage of by a woman again. Then there was Abbie's work ethic or lack of it. Initially, she'd boasted about her success in her party planning business but there had been very little indication of hard work and dedication to continue this success over the time he'd known her. The thing she did excel at was having an inflated sense of her own worth and that others were inferior to her if they didn't come up to her exacting standards. Hence her general rudeness to people.

With Anna, he already found it refreshing to be with a woman that did not want to take all the time. It was hard to convince her to let him pay for a meal or buy her a drink as she always insisted in trying to pay her way. She worked hard at a job that she really didn't love but persisted as she was determined to buy her own property, pay bills and live within her means. He'd loved it when she'd cooked him that meal and they'd messed around when doing the washing up. She was funny, with a good sense of humour, but she also liked a discussion on more serious issues and they'd had a few debates on politics where they could be on different sides. All in all, Nick knew that he was enjoying having Anna Louden in his life and wanted that to continue.

As far as he could tell, there was only one downside to being with Anna. Due to her beauty, she did attract a lot of attention from men, though he already knew she didn't seek it out. On the few times they had been together in public, he noted that men watched her and engaged with her if possible. At the pub, after their visit to Bourton-on-the-Water, Nick felt that he was in danger of flattening the waiter who was openly flirting with her as he took their orders. But in actuality, this could become a serious matter. Nick knew that he would have to consider his approach to persistent males who came on to her without reacting jealously or blaming her for encouraging the men. The Connor Peterson incident was a good example of how men wanted her and could get nasty if they were rebuffed. This was going to be challenging if he developed a relationship with Anna Louden.

Nick's mind wandered to the physical assault on Connor Peterson. The police had been clear that the perpetrator or perpetrators of the attack had referenced Anna. Who the hell was responsible and what did it mean for Anna going forward? In terms of his professional experience as an ex-police officer and now a security specialist, it did set off alarm bells that this behaviour was bizarre and obsessive. There was also the text from the individual calling themselves Xan. Was this related to the Peterson attack? Something weird was going on and Nick's spidey senses told him that this was not the end of whatever this was. And it scared him.

⚜

CHAPTER FORTY SEVEN

Saturday 14th May 2022

Nick was relieved to leave the Chinese restaurant in the centre of Warwick where he'd celebrated his sister's twenty-sixth birthday. The meal had been booked by his mother, attendance was compulsory, and a group of family and Alyssa's friends had gathered. The girls, Alyssa, their cousin Claire, and two others, arrived late after visiting a local cocktail bar prior to coming to the restaurant and were loud and giddy after imbibing too much alcohol. Alyssa was the centre of attention in a figure-hugging emerald green dress and was holding two gold balloons with 'Birthday Girl' written on them.

Nick's heart sank when he saw that one of the friends was Abbie, dressed to kill, in a vibrant red, tight-fitting, mini dress. Her make-up was literally eye catching, smoky grey eyeshadow, black eyeliner, black mascara on long eyelashes, and glossy red lipstick on her lips. At the restaurant, she was tipsy, and determined to make Nick jealous by boasting about all the male attention she was getting. She then told a story of a recent party she'd organised for a famous actor in the Cotswolds. After drinking more wine, she detailed her antics at the party including snorting coke with a member of the band hired for the occasion. Everyone erupted with laughter when Granddad Bill commented, 'Can't stand that coke stuff, myself. It's sickly sweet crap and gives me indigestion. Give me a good honest pint of beer any day.' But Nick bristled with anger about Abbie's inappropriate behaviour as he didn't want to hear her nonsense at his sister's birthday meal.

Now, Alyssa, Claire, Abbie and friend, Jasmine, were moving on to the Frizzy Lion. They departed the restaurant, a noisy flock of parakeets, all fluffing their hair and sticking out their breasts as they went off to find a mate. Nick was annoyed that they were going to the Frizzy Lion, as he knew that Anna would be in there and he wanted to see her. With Abbie around, and probably keeping a beady eye on him, this would be difficult. Ten minutes later, Nick and Ed strolled up to the entrance of the pub where Abbie was standing, smoking a cigarette. As the men approached, Abbie's eyes locked onto Nick's. 'Nick, can we have a chat?'

Nick asked Ed to go inside. To Abbie, he asked, 'What do you want?'

'That's not very friendly, Nick. We were really good together once. Remember the amazing times we had in bed,' she said, giving him a sexy pout and running her fingers through her hair. 'We could have that hot sex again, if you like.'

On this mild, clear evening the smoke from the cigarette swirled around, drifting into Nick's face which further irked him. 'From what you were saying earlier, it seems as if you've found enough replacements for me in that department. You're obviously having all your needs met.'

Anger flashed on her face momentarily but was then replaced by a sorrowful look. 'Yes, maybe so. But they are all forgettable nobodies.' She dragged on the cigarette, inhaling deeply, and then gazed at him with pleading eyes. 'I'm going to be honest here. I'm opening myself up to you, Nick. I would really like us to get back together.'

Nick could see genuine pain in her eyes and he felt pity for her. 'I'm sorry, Abbie. I do appreciate that you may be hurting. But it is over between us and there will be no going back. There are plenty of good guys out there, I'm sure you'll find one.'

She extinguished the cigarette in a wall-mounted bin and moved in closer to Nick, a red-painted finger nail touching his blue shirt. 'They're not you, Nick. Please re-consider.'

His sympathy for her now evaporated and he swatted her hand away. 'I'm not re-considering. Let me be clear. We are over. Now move so that I can enter the pub.' Nick strode forward, pushing open the door and entered the packed pub, and was hit by the moist, warm heat of the many bodies. A mix of perfumes, alcoholic drinks and body odour assailed his nostrils. The noise levels were high, of shrieks, the tinkly sounds of female merriment, the low belly laughs of males and the overall drone of conversation. Moving slowly through the scrum of bodies, Nick looked for Ed who he eventually spotted speaking to Alyssa, Claire and Jasmine. Joining the group, Nick thanked Ed for a bottle of lager.

Nick's eyes scanned the pub room for the one person he was interested in finding. Anna. He noticed Anna's friend from work, Olivia, close by, standing with a balding guy, who was likely to be her boyfriend. Next to the couple were two young women and a tall, good-looking man who was talking to Anna. Nick guessed that this could be Gavin, the journalist, that she'd been on at least one date with. The guy leaned into her, occasionally placing his arm around her waist to speak privately to her in this noisy pub. Nick's heart lurched, and annoyance flared in him, as Anna laughed at something the man said. She was wearing a deep blue, long-sleeved, dress which flattered her figure. Her hair was styled as tousled waves to her shoulders and her make-up was all sultry eyes and moist red lips. She was seriously beautiful and his stomach did a double flip.

Anna knew that he was at a family meal this evening so she was not expecting to see him. Was she keeping her options open dating Gavin as well as going out with him? The man's possessive, and frequent, hold on Anna suggested that this embrace was more than a casual hug. This whole scenario was not pleasing Nick at all. Nick drank his lager, half listening to the chatter between Ed, Alyssa and Claire, whilst concentrating his attention on Anna and Gavin.

'Hi, I'm Jasmine,' Alyssa's friend introduced herself to Nick. Coming out of his semi-trance, Nick glanced at the young woman in front of him, a tall brunette. 'I work with Alyssa. You're her brother, Nick, aren't you?'

Nick absent-mindedly addressed the woman. 'Yes, I'm Nick.'

'Alyssa said that you own a security company. Do you provide bodyguard services? Have you met any famous people? Jasmine asked, her eyes flashing with excitement.

Nick joked, 'I once sat next to Mel B on the London tube, does that count?'

'I can outdo you then. I served a drink to that actor who played Bilbo Baggins in '*The Hobbit*' at an events do. He said thanks,' Jasmine confided, a cheeky grin on her face.

'Memorable,' Nick commented sardonically. Jasmine seemed a pleasant woman but he really wanted to concentrate his attention on Anna. At this moment, Abbie joined him and Jasmine, a bottle of white wine in one hand and a glass in the other. A third of the wine from the bottle had already been drunk. She swayed a little as she spoke to Jasmine. 'Hi, Jaz, this is my ex, Nick. Keep your hands off he's mine.'

A shocked Jasmine took a step back from Abbie, perturbed by her comment. 'Abbie, babe, we were just talking about famous people we have met. That's all.'

This seemed to placate Abbie. She took a drink of the wine in the glass, which was filled too full, and in danger of spilling onto the floor in Abbie's unsteady hand. Abbie grinned and moved closer to Jasmine, as if to tell her a secret. 'You see this man. We had a great thing going before he dumped me. But he'll want me back as he'll be missing all this.' Abbie wobbled, then wiggled her sexy body, trying to draw Nick's attention to the clingy red dress.

Nick flinched at Abbie's cringy behaviour. 'I think you'd better slow down on the drinking as you've had enough.' To Jasmine, he said, 'Nice to meet you but excuse me as there's someone I want to speak to.' Having noted that Gavin was no longer speaking to Anna, Nick made his way towards her through the scrum of bodies.

As he approached Anna, he saw the surprise on her face. 'Aren't you at a family meal?' she asked.

Nick resisted the strong urge to kiss her. 'I was but the older family members have gone home and the younger ones are in here.'

Anna smiled but Nick thought she seemed nervous about his sudden appearance. 'I didn't expect to see you.'

'Evidently,' he commented which could come across as a bit snarky due to the presence of Gavin. Anna looked at him curiously, not knowing what he was implying. He wanted to be direct with her whilst trying not to show annoyance at her being with another man. This was hard as waves of jealousy were washing through him. 'I've just seen you talking to someone. I hope I'm not interrupting anything?'

Her mouth dropped open slightly. 'Oh, er, that's Gavin. He's a friend as far as I'm concerned. He's a journalist and he was just telling me about reporting on a man who got stuck in a toddler swing in a local park.'

Unable to rein in a tendency for sarcasm, Nick commented, 'Obviously, he's at the cutting edge of journalism.' But he regretted saying it as Anna gave him a reproachful look. Nick watched as top journalist, Robert Peston, aka, Gavin, returned to join Anna and went to place his arm around her waist. Noting Nick's presence and not-so-friendly demeanour, Gavin quickly withdrew his arm.

Gavin muttered, 'Er, hello.'

Evilly, enjoying the fact that the man was sweating slightly and squirming, Nick nodded at him. 'Yeah, hi. I'm Nick, a friend of Anna's.'

'Yes, er, I'm Gavin, also a friend.' He laughed nervously. 'This must be the annual meeting of the friends of Anna club.'

Anna looked anxiously between the two men. 'Well, suffice to say, it's a small select club and we all get on well.'

Nick was generally waying up the situation and considering how to get rid of Robert Peston when the bubble of awkwardness was burst by Abbie joining them.

'Well, what have we here?' Abbie shouted as she barged into the group to stand between Gavin and Nick. She poured some more of the wine from the bottle into the glass. She staggered slightly but her eyes locked onto Anna. 'Oh, it's the pretty little thing from your birthday party. The boring little bitch. Want another drink of white wine from my glass? Don't spill it down your front this time, darling.' She paused to drink a mouthful of the wine from the too full glass and spilled some on the floor.

Abbie addressed Gavin. 'Hi, I'm Abbie. Are you here with this?' She gave Anna the kind of look of disgust one might give to a mangy old dog. Her voice was loud and people in the vicinity were listening in as conversation stopped. Pointing at Anna, a nasty expression on her face, she sneered. 'She's was wearing a green dress when she stole my boyfriend. I drenched her dress last time but I might soak her hair and soppy face this time.'

Nick really had to fight to control the volume of his voice as he spoke to Abbie. His inclination was to roar like a lion, knock the bottle and glass out of her hands, and send her flying across the room but he didn't. 'Abbie. This keeps happening. Once again you are threatening to throw wine over Anna which is assault. I am telling you to get away from her. I will stop you if you try to hurt her.'

The people in the area stared, wide-eyed, at Nick and Abbie. He placed himself between Abbie and Anna, and watched Abbie's face intently, to try to anticipate what she would do next. Abbie's eyes blazed with fury, tearing into his own, before she tried to go round him to get to her target. Nick squared his shoulders and loomed over her, to call her bluff. Defiance radiated off Abbie. 'Fucking get out of my way, fuckwit. You won't like her so much when she's dripping wine onto the carpet from her stupid face and she smells like a vat of sour grapes.'

The people in the area gave a collective groan. Luckily, Alyssa was now making her way through the gathered throng of pub customers. 'Abbie, don't be silly. Move away from Anna and come with me now. Don't do something stupid you'll regret. Nick will call the police.'

Abbie's face crumpled as she heard Alyssa's voice and her shoulders slumped as the fight went out of her. Alyssa took the bottle of wine off Abbie and gently steered her away from Nick and Anna. She whispered 'sorry' to her brother.

As the tension in the room dispersed and conversations re-started, Nick assessed the impact this had on Anna. She was visibly shaken and her face was pale under her makeup. He took hold of her hand. 'Come on, Anna. Let's get out of here.'

⌁⌁◆⌁⌁

CHAPTER FORTY EIGHT

Russ smiled as he watched his brother's face, after the drama of a few moments ago ended. Luke was standing, mesmerised, as he'd seen the drunken woman in the red dress come up to the woman, Anna, that Luke referred to as 'his beloved' and caused a scene. The brothers had managed to find a space in the Frizzy Lion close enough to observe Anna but they took advantage of the crush of bodies to avoid her seeing them. They'd agreed they didn't want Anna recognising either of them. Luke was quite giddy with excitement when he had spotted her earlier, looking exceptionally lovely. Luke was soon in a blissful trance, describing a future chapter in his current fantasy novel, with Anna as the beautiful protagonist in the story. Anna looked stunning in a blue dress which accentuated her perfect figure.

'You see, Russ, in my story, my goddess, Astraea, is wearing a tight-fit blue dress which displays perfect breasts and arching buttocks. Her hair falls in beautiful waves to her shoulders, her sapphire-blue eyes sparkle, and her ruby-red, perfect pout lips are ready for kissing. She is bathed in a warm, golden light as she walks the great hall, to the cheers of the crowd. Awaiting her are two men, two chiselled-jawed, muscular god-like warriors of different tribes who will fight, physically, with fists, flails and daggers until one is dead. The victor, Xandros, will win the hand of the most beautiful Astraea and lay claim to her glorious naked body.' Luke explained, his eyes exuding a joyous happiness as he was lost in his fantasy world.

All this imagery was playing havoc with Russ's dick. 'Ok, Luke. Quit with the storytelling.' But Russ agreed that this woman, Anna, was beautiful and the blue dress was a real turn-on as it displayed her gorgeous body.

As Russ drank his pint of lager, and Luke his gin and tonic, they kept a watchful eye on Anna as she mingled with a group of people, including a tall male. The brothers discussed whether this was the man who had rescued Anna from the wanker they had beaten up a fortnight ago.

Luke gave Russ a puzzled look. 'Yeah, he's the boyfriend, I suppose, but I'm a bit disappointed to be honest. I was hoping for a more toned, muscular man that I could put in my story as a love rival. This guy with Anna's nice looking but he's way too average and underwhelming to make his debut in my book.'

Russ sniggered. 'He'll never know that he was a gnat's cock away from fame and fortune.'

They'd watched as the man draped his arm around Anna's waist, pulling her close to him, as they chatted in the noisy pub. Russ nodded. 'I've got to agree, he's very disappointing for a woman like her. She needs a dominant man to take care of her and see off the chancers that will be sniffing around. That tosser isn't up to the job. But to be honest, brother, that guy there, for all his lack of endearing qualities, has much more chance than you.'

Russ noted Luke's face go its usual shade of red as he was angered that he might not achieve a date with Anna. Luke scowled at Russ. 'Shut up. I'm just enjoying following her around at the moment and being in her orbit. And we are chatting more at the supermarket. Things are developing nicely.'

'Well, I want a crack at her as well and I'm not standing back while you dither,' Russ stated, a determination to succeed apparent in his steely, brown eyes.

The brothers watched as the man with Anna disappeared and another man took his place. On seeing this man, Luke choked on his G & T. 'Yikes, look at that guy. He's super fit, as in a tall, very good-looking, superhero sort of way. Thor. Captain America. Wolverine.' Luke fanned his face with his hand. 'Perhaps I'm gay as I've gone all quivery at seeing him.'

Russ carefully assessed the new arrival. 'This guy obviously knows her and she looks relaxed with him. This could be the man that overpowered the wanker. He kind of looks the part. You do not stand any chance of going out with her if he's around.'

Luke's bottom lip stuck out. The way it used to do when he was denied extra sweets as a kid and was about to cry. 'Oh dear. But then faint heart never won fair lady. Women don't just go for good looks and toned arms; they like a guy who's funny, kind and caring, and that's me.'

Russ noted that the other man had returned to join Anna and the fit guy. Russ took a large swig of lager then laughed loudly. 'Brother, she's now with two men who are better looking and more physically blessed than you. I don't think funny, kind and caring are going to cut it. You're '*The King of Wishful Thinking*' as Go West once sang. Russ softly hummed the tune as Luke started to sulk and go all mardy on him. Five-years-old, again. Just as Russ was about to call Luke a fucking baby, a female in a tight-fitting red dress joined Anna and the two men.

Russ ran his eyes up and down the woman, clocking her flowing blonde hair, full-on make-up, red talons, and a dress that drew all male eyes to cleavage and thighs. She was carrying a glass and a wine bottle and staggered slightly as she joined the group. A female who liked to get slaughtered and then be up for a good time. Russ's favourite type that he looked for in pubs. From the way she approached the group, it was apparent that she knew the fit guy but her angry focus was on Anna. Her voice was loud and shrieky but due to the general noise level, Russ struggled to hear what she was saying but he caught a few words, 'Nick. Pretty little thing. Boring little bitch.'

Luke was practically wetting himself with pent-up emotion. 'OMG, Russ, what's going on? A red witch has entered the room and has evil intent towards my beloved, I think.'

Sighing loudly, Russ hissed. 'Shut up, idiot. Let's try to listen. This is getting interesting. The red witch thinks she has a claim on the fit guy.' The woman addressed the other man and Russ tried to focus on what she was saying. 'I'm Abbie' ....muffled sound..."stole'....'boyfriend.'

Luke's was fanning his face which was sweaty and red. 'The red witch says our Anna stole her boyfriend.' The woman's voice grew louder, stopping the conversations of the people standing nearby, as they now listened clearly to the whole thing. The woman ranted on. 'I drenched her dress last time but I might soak her hair and soppy face this time.'

Luke exclaimed loudly. 'Oh no', then turned quickly in case Anna gazed over and recognised him.

Russ watched the anger flare on the fit guy's face and listened as he spoke. 'Abbie. This keeps happening. Once again you are threatening to throw wine over Anna which is assault. I am telling you to get away from her. I will stop you if you try to hurt her.' This man's voice was controlled, but assertive, and then he placed himself between the drunken woman and Anna. This Abbie was now almost hysterical and trying to get to Anna. Russ could tell that the man was disciplining himself not to physically react to the woman but sensed that he yearned to do so. Russ knew he wouldn't be as controlled in this situation and would deliver a hard slap to her floozy face.

Luke's cheeks were puce with a mix of fury and anxiety as he witnessed what was going on. 'I'd kill the red witch if it were me,' he whispered in a breathy voice. 'I hope the man decks her.'

In the next moment, another female intervened, took the bottle off the woman and led her away. The tension dispersed and the people in the area resumed their conversations. The fit guy, firmly took hold of Anna's hand and guided her out of the pub.

'Gosh,' Luke sighed as his eyes followed Anna. Her blue dress seductively hugging her curvy bottom and hinting at perfect thighs as the hem of the garment swirled around her legs. 'My poor Astraea. First there was the wanker. Is Anna cursed by her unique beauty to be used by those that feel entitled to have ownership of her? Now this drunken harridan. Is Anna cursed as she is held responsible for enticing men away from lesser women? Is she to be continually punished for her crime of beauty?'

Russ ignored Luke's poetic ramblings and his eyes followed the woman in red being led away by her friend. She didn't linger long as she was refused the wine bottle so she stropped over to the bar. Russ knew his chance had come to have some fun. 'Luke, I'm going to the bar to get to know the red witch. Find out if she's up for a bit of action at her place. I'll see you whenever.'

Luke sighed. 'Ok. But find out what the deal is with her, Anna and the fit guy,' Luke urged Russ. 'Don't forget you are seeing Leanne on a regular basis.'

Russ was not interested in further chat. 'Leanne's not important. My goal, now, is to hook-up with our little red-dressed harlot who I guess is up for anything.'

At the bar, Russ positioned himself next to the red witch. Her anger was still radiating off her body, and having ordered a large glass of white wine, she was wrestling with her black clutch bag to take out her payment card. 'Where the fuck is it?' she muttered as the bartender tapped his finger on the bar impatiently.

'I'll pay for that and get me a pint of lager,' Russ told the bartender. He then smiled down at her face which was blotchy from the heat in the bar and her temper tantrum. 'It's ok, darling. I saw that you got a bit worked up earlier with that woman in the blue dress and the guy. They shouldn't be upsetting a beautiful woman like you.' Russ knew this comment would have the desired effect and the woman's eyes, heavily ringed with black eyeliner and mascara, focused on him.

'Too bloody right....' She nodded in agreement but paused in conversation while Russ paid for the two drinks and picked up his pint. 'Thanks for the drink.'

'Why don't we go and find a table and you can tell me about what went on. I'm a good listener,' Russ stated, as he walked to the quieter conservatory area of the pub and they sat at an empty table.

The woman plonked down in a chair, gulped a couple of mouthfuls of wine, and gazed at Russ. Russ was pleased with the proximity as he could inspect her more closely. Yes, she was good-looking in an over-the-top kind of way. Good boobs, shapely ass and strong thighs as well displayed by the short dress. Blonde hair which wasn't natural, make-up as his granny used to say 'caked on', with false eyelashes to enhance her eyes. An unnatural plumpness to her lips which indicated fillers. By the age of fifty, the beauty will have gone. A body filled out by age and unhealthy habits. A desperate attempt to hold onto youth with Botox and fillers. The fit guy had dodged a bullet by getting rid of this one.

She rummaged in her bag for a lip gloss and smeared it over her lips then pouted. 'Yeah, that tramp, the one in the blue dress, has got her claws into my boyfriend. He met the skank a few months ago when her car broke down and he helped her out. I could sense for a while that he was drawing away from me and then at his 30th birthday party the skank arrived with someone else. Like a greyhound out of a trap, he soon raced over to talk to her. I got a little bit drunk...' she paused to drink the wine....'and threw my wine over her.' The woman looked at Russ to gauge his reaction but he was not giving much away for now. 'Not my finest hour, I know. Fucking stupid, actually, as he dumped me the next day. He said that finishing with me had nothing to do with her. But tonight she's here and he's talking to her. Then when I get annoyed, it's me that's in the wrong and he's defending her. Fucking, fuck.'

Russ nearly laughed out loud as she summed up how her relationship with this guy had failed. The guy had a very, very lucky escape. Open this woman up and there would be the word 'trouble' running through her like a stick of rock. A few words flicked through his brain to describe her. Selfish. Entitled. Delusional. Cold.

Russ deliberately ran his eyes over her face, to linger on her mouth. Yeah, he wanted to kiss it and he knew she would be good at all things oral. Her eyes held his own as she licked her lips. This was going to be a good game. Both players believed that they were in control but time would tell who would be the victor.

'Come on, let's go back to mine. I'm dying for a smoke, more drink, a line of coke and a shag, not necessarily in that order. What do you say?' she asked, draining the glass of the wine and picking up her bag.

'I'd say great idea. I'm John. Let's go.'

CHAPTER FORTY NINE

Thirty minutes later Russ was in her apartment, a modern one, in Leamington Spa. He was sat on a sage green, three-seater sofa in the living room which was tastefully decorated and furnished. He guessed that the woman was worth a few bob to afford this property even if she had a large mortgage. In the taxi, she'd mentioned that she lived alone and Russ thought this was a nice little set up for a single woman. The woman brought in bottles of white wine, tequila and Scotch whisky which she placed on a nearby coffee table. She then returned with two tumbler glasses, two shot glasses, and salt and limes to go with the tequila. There was also four small plastic baggies of cocaine, a knife and pieces of drinking straw.

'Ok, party time. Let's do shots,' she stated whilst kneeling by the coffee table to pour two tequila shots, one of which she handed to him, as he sat down on the rug near to her. They both licked the area of their right hand between the thumb and index finger, added salt to the damp saliva patch and licked it off, downed the shot and then sucked the lime wedge. Russ winced as the sharp lime touched his tongue. 'Go again,' she said and they repeated the ritual.

'Just drink anything ya want. There's beer in the fridge if you can be arsed to get it,' the woman instructed, sitting crossed legged on the rug and facing Russ. 'I'm going continue on the wine,' and she poured enough to fill the glass tumbler. As Russ lent over and filled a glass with whisky, she chinked his glass. 'Cheers.'

As the effects of the shots hit him, Russ felt mellow and relaxed, as he drank the whisky. Due to sitting cross-legged, the woman's short red dress rose up to reveal firm thighs and a flash of black thong. Not ready to make a move, he revelled in the nearness and smell of her, a hint of sweat and the underlying essence of her perfume which was sexy and enticing. There was nothing subtle about this woman.

'Ok, Let's do a line, shall we, John?' She licked her lips, and he knew it was a deliberate attempt to draw his attention to her mouth. The woman tipped the contents of one of the bags onto the coffee table, chopped it finely with a knife, and then prepared two lines of coke. Each of them took a straw and sniffed the coke proficiently into a nostril, before sniffing and wiping their nose. Russ felt the sting in his nose and a numbness in his forehead as he waited for the drug to kick in.

The woman scrutinised his face with her feline eyes. 'Yer know what, I don't think you're called John. It's a bit of an old gezza name for a young guy. But I like the intrigue of it all. We'll have a night of wild fun, two strangers, and then move on tomorrow never knowing anything about each other.

'So, darling, you were upset earlier that your boyfriend's left you for the woman in the blue dress,' Russ grinned, a twinkle in his eye as he now wanted to ignite the hot fiery temper he had glimpsed earlier. 'I can see why you'd be upset as she looked pretty hot in that blue dress and has a bum that I'd like to get my hands on.'

Light the fuse on the firework and watch the rocket launch. 'Fucking hot. She's about as hot as a damp tea towel. You men are fools.' Her hazel eyes were fully on him now as she shuffled on the floor, making her breasts wiggle to draw his eyes to them. 'My breasts and butt are super sexy, wait till you get to grips with these. Anyway, John, I've not told you my name yet.'

Russ gave her a sardonic smile. 'I could guess as I think you are a naughty girl and will have all the skills of a hooker when we get going. Let's make up a hooker name and call you that, shall we?'

For a moment her confident persona slipped slightly and he saw a tiny flicker of hurt in her eyes. 'Hooker, eh? You know

John, you are very perceptive as I did do a little bit of escort work about seven years ago when I couldn't pay the rent on just the wages of my bar job. It turned out quite lucrative. I'm not telling you my name because if times get hard I might go back to it.'

Feeling the drug flooding his system, Russ drained the glass of whisky to add to the high. Crawling over to her, Russ pushed her down on her back and ran his hand under her red dress along a golden thigh. 'I think Scarlett or Roxanne would work. Let's go for Roxy, shall we? Now then, Roxy, let's imagine you're still a hooker and I'm a paying customer. I like a bit of slap and tickle, if you know what I mean, so let's get to work on that sexy butt of yours and make it as hot as you like, eh?'

CHAPTER FIFTY

Saturday 14th May 2022

Anna was still a little shaken as she followed Nick into his home, as her mind processed the latest incident in the pub with Nick's ex-girlfriend, Abbie. If this type of situation kept happening to her, assaults by Connor Peterson and Abbie, she was thinking that life on a tropical island, alone, would be a preferred option. It was also going to get embarrassing frequenting the Frizzy Lion pub as people may start to associate her with causing trouble by attracting weirdo people.

Nick said, 'Go in the sitting room and I'll get the drinks. What would you like?'

'I know that alcohol is never the answer but could I have a very large glass of white wine to calm my nerves, please?' Anna requested.

Nick was soon back with the drinks and sat next to Anna on the sofa. He gazed intently at Anna before pulling her against him, his left arm around her in a comforting embrace. 'Anna, I'm so sorry that you keep having to put up with Abbie's abysmal drunken behaviour and her threatening you. If it happens again, and it had better not, I will report her to the police. She's getting seriously out of control and it worries me what she's capable of. If she has to explain her behaviour to the police, it may give her the short, sharp shock she needs. I should have reported her on my birthday when she threw the wine at you and then threatened my family with that knife. Once again, I'm sorry for what happened tonight.'

Anna was troubled by Abbie's drunken rant and fearful of what she intended to do. A drink in the face was unpleasant and humiliating but she couldn't guarantee Abbie would stop at that. 'I can't pretend that she didn't scare me in the pub. She's very unstable and unpredictable. Has she got a history of erratic behaviour or violence?'

Nick shrugged his shoulders. 'Not that I'm aware of. I didn't know her for long but she has a number of terrible personality traits that don't give an impression of a decent human being. I met her through Alyssa who had only known her a short while. I didn't really meet her friends or family except her mother and stepdad who seemed ok. There's a brother who doesn't seem to have a legal way of earning money. She does have bunny-boiler tendencies in terms of extreme jealousy, excessive drinking and out-of-control behaviour. I think I really lost my marbles when I took up with her. I bitterly regret it mainly as you are the target of her wrath. I'm so sorry, sweetheart.'

Anna felt him drawing her closer in a protective circle as he kissed her forehead. 'Don't worry, Nick. I don't blame you for her actions but I just hope she stays away from me from now on.' Anna sipped at her wine, feeling the tension from the encounter with Abbie drain out of her body as the wine helped her relax. Nick's closeness offered safety and security. She put down the glass and then leaned up to kiss him and he welcomed her mouth, laid claim to it, as he consumed it with passion and fire. Anna thought that she would die of a bliss-related heart attack at the touch of his mouth on hers.

When he broke off from the kiss, he scanned her face, his blue eyes flashing with anger. 'You know, Anna, I'm still so furious with her right now that I could put my hands around her throat and literally squeeze the life out of her for threatening you. That makes me as bad as her, doesn't it?'

Stroking his face, Anna softly kissed him again. 'Let's forget about her. I suppose I am the victor as you are here with me and not with her.'

'Yes, Ms Louden, and there is nowhere else I would rather be right now. Let's go upstairs so that I can hold you close and make love to you all night long?'

****

When Anna woke next morning, sunlight filtered into the room, and she lay still under the duvet so as not to wake Nick. This gave her time to reflect on their night together. Last night was another amazing sexual experience for her, with a man she truly connected with, and she believed, he with her. All her senses were aroused. The sound of his low, baritone voice as he extolled her beauty when he whispered in her ear. The sight of his deep blue eyes as they gazed into her own as his mouth came down to claim hers. The taste of him in her mouth, the hint of beer from his last drink. His smell of the male cologne he favoured. The feel of his toned back and strong buttocks reinforced in her mind the power of his masculinity. His touch, the exquisite touch, of his hands on her eager body ramped her pleasure levels higher. Her body had tingled, and trembled, been taken to a place of mind-blowing pleasure as she felt he literally worshipped her with his hands and mouth, before taking her with controlled, powerful thrusts to orgasmic heaven. It was an almost out-of-body experience where her mind was released from the temporal world and she was transported to another state, a nirvana, due to the sexual energy he ignited. Now, once again, she felt a shyness, for though the experience was an all-consuming bliss for her, she could not measure what his assessment of it all had been. Her mind was fleetingly filled with images of a sexually precocious Abbie boasting that sex with her had been the ultimate experience and boring Anna could not compete.

Blinking to chase away these images, Anna turned towards him, her eyes secretly searching across his broad shoulders, well-developed triceps, toned back muscles and down to the swell of his taut buttocks. Suddenly, he turned over, as if he knew she was assessing him and grinned cheekily at her. 'Morning, beautiful. Have I caught you lusting after my body, you hussy?'

Anna tried to smile innocently at him but her face gave her away. She blushed, a fuchsia shade of pink, and her cheeks burned. 'No, n-not really,' she stuttered.

'Judging by the flush on your face, I think you were,' he teased as he leaned over to kiss her softly. 'Ms Louden, it is a Sunday morning, when all godly people go to church and naughty little sinners must be punished. What punishment would be appropriate for the sin of lust, I wonder?'

'Well, Mr Carlton, I can see that there is a lustful glint in your eye at the moment, so if I have sinned, then you are about to do so as well,' Anna joked, in between the eager attention his mouth was giving hers.

Pausing in kissing her, Nick's eyes focused on her own. 'Yes, you have a point, you are leading me on the road to temptation. It is a further reason to administer a punishment, forthwith.' He pulled her against him slightly, so that she was lying on him and his hand swatted her bottom.

As Anna reacted with a 'ouch' and then laughed, Nick's phone rang. He reached to the bedside cabinet to answer it. 'Hi, Eric.....'what am I doing. I am thinking about smacking female bottoms...' he grinned as he looked at Anna's horrified face as she waited to hear what he was going to say.....'as I'm watching a volleyball game on the telly. Yes, mate, I know I need to get a girlfriend.....what can I do for you?' Nick listened as Eric spoke. Then he responded, 'yeah, of course, no problem. I had got plans but nothing that can't be altered. What time do you want me to come over?' Eric spoke and Nick replied, 'no problem, I'll be at yours at one p.m. Bye.'

Anna now felt hurt but tried not to show it. They had made plans to go for a drive in the Cotswolds and have a pub lunch but this arrangement had been abandoned in favour of helping Eric. 'I can get a taxi back to my house if you've got other arrangements,' she said, trying to hide the disappointment in her voice. But she was definitely miffed that he could change their plans so quickly without consulting her.

Nick must have noticed a flicker of sadness on her face before she managed to compose her features. 'Hey, Anna, let me explain what that was all about. I'm not casting you aside for a better option and I wouldn't do that to you. But an emergency has come up with my friend, and business partner, Eric. His wife's grandmother has been taken to hospital and he wants me to look after his two sons, this afternoon. I couldn't refuse. So, Anna, how do you fancy a visit to Warwick Castle?'

⸻◆⸻

CHAPTER FIFTY ONE

Sunday 15th May 2022

Russ was lying on his bed, bottled lager to hand, watching *'Commando: Britain's Ocean Warriors'* as Luke entered the room and slumped down on a chair next to a computer desk. Luke was desperate to know what had happened between Russ and the Red Witch. Russ barely managed more than two words whilst eating his roast lamb dinner, ignoring Luke and their father's attempts at conversation.

'What's this you're watching, Russ? Luke asked, catching sight of military men in rigid inflatable boats, the kind of macho stuff Russ liked.

'It's about a specialist commando unit on a vessel in the Gulf preparing to board an Arab sailing boat that they suspect has a supply of illegal drugs,' Russ commented, his face having lost the tiredness of earlier and he was looking animated and interested. 'I wish I'd joined the military when I was younger. Doing this sort of thing would be seriously exciting.'

Luke sighed loudly. 'Two issues with that Russ. One, if you are part of the authorities stopping the supply of illegal drugs into the UK, that will seriously impair your drug taking habits. Two, as a buyer and user of drugs, you are perpetuating the whole drug problem. Actually, that sort of career would have suited you. All that high adrenaline risk-taking and running around with guns and you would've been on the right side of the law. Instead you're wasting your life on loose women, booze and getting high.'

'Shut up. You've not done so well with your life, have you? All your dreams of writing fantasy novels and producing films have come to nowt. We're both stuck at home with dad doing plastering for a living,' Russ stated, angrily.

'Ok, Russ, I didn't come in here to fight. I want to know how you got on with that Abbie woman last night. Did you find out what was going on with her and Anna?'

Russ sipped his lager and straightened up slightly in the bed. 'Yeah, well, this Abbie is as mad as hell that Anna stole her boyfriend, Nick. She's pretty pissed about the loss of this Nick who she swears is the love of her life. From the bits I could cobble together from her drunken ramblings, I think this Nick was tiring of her before Anna came along. She said the guy has a lot of dosh and was paying for everything including clothes, meals, holidays, the full nine yards. I asked her what she brought to the table and she said it was her looks and her sexual prowess, 'my boobs and booty are outta this world', is how she put it. Seriously, brother, these women today have shit for brains. Every damn one of them have the same bits, tits and ass, and they all think they're owed something because of it. They think we should be grateful for letting us having access to all this and that they're so special. None are particularly special, just one of many. One things for sure, this Nick guy did well when he dumped Abbie for Anna, who's a lot classier.'

'Blimey, Russ, I'm not aware that you knew what a classy woman is,' Luke chuckled but he was careful not to catch his brother's eye. 'You normally go for the easy Abbie types.'

Russ's eyes honed in on Luke as a smirk crossed his lips. 'There is a reason for that. The Abbie types are into sex, booze and drugs. They know how to have a good time. They're into role play and sexual adventure. I called her Roxy after she admitted to being a hooker when she was younger. Roxy knew how to turn a trick or two and I got to indulge some of my favourite kinks. For free, brother. Anyway, Abbie's real name, as revealed on her credit card, is Abigail Steele.'

'Did she say anything else about Anna?' Luke wanted to know.

'After we were done with the sex, she continued to drink heavily. She looked really wasted with straggly hair, smudged make-up and a bright red face,' Russ commented. 'Abbie is truly pissed off with Nick for abandoning her and the object of her fury is Anna. She rambled on about how nobody makes a fool of her and she'll get her revenge. She's definitely psycho.'

Luke gulped as a trickle of icy fear went down his spine. 'Did she elaborate on how she is going to get her revenge?

'No, but I sensed that she was not going to let it go and move on.' Russ commented. 'Anyway, I might see her again as I had a great time last night.'

'She'd better keep away from my beloved or she might meet the same fate as the wanker.' Luke growled; his voice flecked with anger.

'We'll see,' Russ stated, as he yawned loudly, obviously all the exertions of last night's love-in catching up with him. 'Anyway, I'm going to watch the end of this commando thing and then get some kip. But just so you know, this hook-up with Abbie doesn't mean I'm forgetting Anna.'

CHAPTER FIFTY TWO

Monday 16ᵗʰ May 2022

Anna was distracted from her work as Olivia kept turning towards her on her chair and eyeing her suspiciously. 'Ok, Anna, spill. You've had a massive smile on your face all morning and appear to be floating on cloud nine. I'm guessing that you've had a great Saturday night with Nick after he dragged you out of the Frizzy Lion and away from his psycho ex. I know he's your boyfriend, and I'm with Jamie, but your Nick is seriously hot. I bet you got a first class servicing in the bedroom, didn't you girl?'

Anna glanced around, hoping that none of their colleagues were listening in to this conversation. 'Olivia, please shut up. Yes, I did have a great time on Saturday night, after the showdown with Abbie. And yesterday, I went with Nick and his two godsons to Warwick Castle. It was great fun.'

If she were honest, she had been worried about spending time with the boys as she had no experience of being with young children. The boys, Elijah, seven, and Xavier, four, were super cute with curly brown hair and large brown eyes. Super cute but very tiring. They zoomed from one activity to another at top speed. They were impressed by The Kingmaker Experience where the Earl of Warwick, Richard Neville, of the House of Lancaster, and supporter of placing Henry VI on the throne, was preparing for the Battle of Barnet on Sunday, 14 April 1471. Elijah was dazzled by all the weaponry, particularly the swords. Xavier held his nose when his olfactory nerves were subjected to medieval smells of vegetables, fish, beer, sweet smells of roses and lavender, and animal smells of manure. He made people laugh as he ran around shouting, 'Poo, poo.' Next was ice cream eating before moving on to the Horrible Histories Maze. At the end of the visit, they did not escape the gift shop without Nick's credit card taking a hit for knight tabards and plastic swords.

Anna had been very impressed with Uncle Nick and his parenting abilities. The boys adored him and kept vying for his attention. He settled squabbles quickly and dried up tears when Xavier's ice cream dropped from its cone. Anna was surprised at how much fun could be had with young children but it was very energy sapping.

During this work afternoon, her happiness bubble from spending time with Nick burst, when she received another weird text from Xan. **'Hi. Beautiful one. Still thinking about you. Be careful as there are those that wish to harm you. Stay alert and stay safe. Xan xxx.** Was the sender someone at work? She glanced around from her desk at her work colleagues in the immediate area. Everyone was concentrating on their work. No one was holding a mobile phone.

Gazing around again, she did note one of the senior managers, Jack Buckner, walking along the office corridor and he caught her eye and smiled at her as he went past. He had his mobile phone in his hand. Anna sensed that this man found her attractive. In team meetings his intense gazed focused on her which Olivia frequently teased her about. He also made odd comments about her work which could be interpreted in two-ways. A few weeks ago, she was called into his office, and he said, 'Anna, every company needs your beautiful assets to make it shine.' This was said after a particular glowing report from one of her clients. This could have been purely about her employee attributes but it didn't feel like that. As he spoke, his cool blue eyes swept her face and breasts, and she felt strongly that he fancied her. There had been a couple of times when he had stood extremely close to her, gazing down at her chest, and she sensed that he really wanted to touch her. It was creepy behaviour but it would be difficult to prove as sexual harassment at an employment tribunal. Now, having just received another text from Xan, she wondered if it could be from her boss?

After work, in the supermarket, Anna bumped into her supermarket 'friend', Tulip Man. They were now speaking on a regular basis and she had to admit he was quite witty and self-deprecating. They had chatted briefly about what they did at the weekend and she mentioned her visit to Warwick Castle. 'I wonder what it would've been like to live in such a place particularly in Victorian times,' Anna pondered.

Tulip Man said that he had worked at the Castle for a short time, years ago, and loved all of its history particularly the knights, battles and swords. But he also liked the Victorian High Society experience relating to June 1898 when the then Prince of Wales (who became King Edward VII) attended for a Royal Weekend Party. Tulip Man commented, 'You would have been one of the beautiful high society ladies invited to such an event, adorned in a lovely gown, and bedecked with jewels from wealthy suitors. I would be a lowly servant bringing the wine and Windsor soup. And being so overwhelmed by your beauty I would spill the soup over you, be soundly thrashed by the butler, and then dismissed by the Earl and Countess of Warwick.' They had both laughed at this and she admitted that he had a witty sense of humour. But she did wish that he wouldn't focus on her beauty all the time as it became a little embarrassing.

That evening, there was a text from Nick. '**Hi, it's your Monday night pest. Can I pop over for an hour now if I'm not disturbing you? I have a proposal to put to you (not a marriage one). N xxx**' This was followed by the LOL emoji.

Anna replied. '**Phew, that's a relief. I'm allergic to wedding cake. Yes, please pop round if you want. A xxx**'.

Nick was now sat on her sofa, drinking water as he was swerving alcohol for a few days of booze detox. 'I've got four days of training ahead for some new employees so I need to stay focused.' He smiled leeringly at her as he pulled her against him. 'Just to let you know, I'm not giving up all my vices.'

Anna smiled at him, noting the lustful look in his blue eyes. As well as lager, he had turned down her offer of crisps. She was sat with a glass of white wine and was nibbling on lightly salted crisps from a small packet. 'That's good. I couldn't go out with a celibate, tee-total, calorie-obsessed puritan.'

'Rest assured, Ms Louden, the one thing I will never be is celibate,' Nick stated, as he kissed her mouth. 'You taste of salty crisps so I might as well have one if I'm going to kiss you.' He dipped his hand in the packet, popped a crisp in his mouth and crunched on it. 'What are your plans for the weekend?'

'I've been invited to a BBQ at Olivia's boyfriend's house on Saturday, and a few of our friends will be there,' Anna advised Nick. He pulled a face at hearing this news.

'Ok,' he pursed his lips to show disapproval. 'Who's going to be there?'

Anna squirmed slightly as she knew he wanted to know if Gavin would be attending. 'I'm not sure. Olivia, obviously, Jamie, Georgie, Kate, Gavin and other people I don't know.'

'Gavin, eh? Can I trust you two together?' Nick joked; his eyes firmly fixed on hers as he awaited her response.

This did rile Anna, as she and Nick were only at the start of getting to know each other. 'Gavin is a friend and someone I get on with. But if you want you could send one of your security team to chaperone me.'

'Ok, Ms Louden, I am detecting a smidgen of sarcasm in your tone.' Nick's eyes scanned her face. 'I hope we are not going to have our first falling out.'

'We won't fall out, Nick, as long as you don't start to get jealous when I am with friends. I'm only going to a BBQ and Gavin will be there. That's it,' Anna stated, annoyance apparent in her voice.

'Ok, I will say no more about the BBQ. But you do realise that I like you a lot, don't you?' Nick held her chin whilst he brought his mouth down on hers. 'I will try my best not to show jealousy but I can't pretend it's going to be easy as many men are attracted to you. But I hope as we get to know each other better, it will work itself out. Anyway, I don't want us to fall out as I am going to outline the proposal I mentioned earlier. I will be a bit restricted in taking holiday from work in the summer as Eric is taking the family to Jamaica for three weeks in the school holidays. Therefore, I wondered if you'd like to come away with me for a few days or a week, at the beginning of June. That will avoid the school's half term week which includes the Platinum Jubilee Bank Holiday when all the UK will be flying all over the place. We can discuss where we'd like to go. What do you think?'

Anna was a little speechless. It was a lovely idea but was it too early for them to be going on holiday together? And financially it would be another unexpected expenditure which she really couldn't afford. 'Holiday? Yes, a short break could be fun. What had you in mind, somewhere in Europe? I couldn't afford to go any further afield.'

'Yes, a city break or beach holiday in Europe, it's up to you. Somewhere that suits your budget. I generally do five-star hotels and first class travel but I am prepared to slum it, if necessary,' he teased.

Anna knew he was joking but underlying the joke she guessed that he probably could afford a better quality holiday than what she normally managed. 'Ok, shall we both come up with some options and go from there. I've always wanted to go to Prague for a city break. Or visit Croatia. What about you?'

'They're both great suggestions. I've always fancied Budapest or Vienna. But I don't mind. It would just be great to go with you,' Nick stated as he stroked her face and hair whilst gazing into her eyes.

'Yes, a break would be great away from psycho ex's and fruit loop ex-girlfriend of current male friend. Oh, and weirdo senders of texts called Xan.' Anna watched as Nick's amused expression changed to one of concern.

'You've had a further text from the Xan person? When? What does it say?' Show me your phone.' This was said abruptly as he sat upright on the sofa.

Anna leaned over and picked up her phone from the coffee table. She found the text and gave the phone to Nick for him to read. 'It arrived this afternoon at work. I scanned my eyes around my work colleagues to see if anyone was on their mobiles at the time. The only person in the vicinity with a phone in his hand was my boss, Jack Buckner, and, if I'm honest, I do find him kind of creepy as a manager. But I don't think it would be him. The texts aren't really threatening in themselves but they do spook me out. I don't like the inference that there are those that wish to harm me. Freaking hell.' Anna took a sip of wine to calm her nerves.

Nick sighed. 'As you say, they are not really threatening but do imply that someone is watching you. Don't delete the texts but I still don't recommend that you respond to them. This would encourage them. Have you any idea who it could be?'

'The only person I can think of who might play games is Connor Peterson but he's been warned to keep from contacting me. If I get any more I might just mention the texts to the police to find out if it's him. For now I'm going to forget it,' Anna stated, drinking more wine before putting the glass down.

Nick now held on to her, starting to kiss her again. As he paused from sensually exploring her mouth, he stated, a twinkle of amusement in his eyes. 'Just want to clarify one thing. When you referred to a fruit loop ex-girlfriend of current male friend, I assume you were talking about Abbie.' He was now gazing into her eyes as his fingers caressed her cheekbones and lips, and she knew that he was dying to kiss her again. 'I think, miss, I could take exception to being referred to as a current male friend. Current implies as of now but may not be in the future. That I will be upgraded for a new model like buying a new car. Male friend is a very loose term and could include a boy you played kiss chase with at primary school or a guy you beat at chess club. Very generic. I do not consider myself a 'male friend', Anna, I think at the very least the words 'most amazing lover' is the description you are looking for.'

Anna lightly tapped his gloating face. 'Oh really. I shall be the judge of that. Current male friend is a fine description for now.'

'You're going to regret that comment now, Ms Louden, as I subject your body to my exceptional sexual techniques. The word 'superstud' will be uttered from your trembling lips as you beg me to take you,' he laughed.

CHAPTER FIFTY THREE

Saturday 18th June 2022

Anna would remember this as the most fantastic holiday of her life. This was the sixth day of her holiday with Nick in Dubrovnik, Croatia, and she was still awestruck at the beauty of the place. The weather had been amazing, sunny days with only passing cloud, temperatures in the high-twenties centigrade. There was no dramatic drop in the evening so it was pleasant and warm to walk around. They'd emersed themselves in the delights of the city over the last four days. Day one was spent exploring the well-preserved and extensive ancient walls which surround the Old Town and offered panoramic views of the city, the beautiful terracotta roof tops and the aquamarine waters of the Adriatic Sea. Day two was a guided kayaking tour in early evening around the medieval walls and across the water to Lokrum island to sit on a beach to watch the sunset. Day three was a guided walking tour of the Old Town to discover the history of churches, monasteries and so on. Yesterday was a boat trip to Lokrum island for walking, swimming in natural pools, and spotting peacocks.

Nick was a massive fan of '*Game of Thrones*' and the city of Qarth was filmed on Lokrum island. Today, Nick was like a dog with two tails as they returned from a '*Game of Thrones*' guided tour of the Old Town where he had seen famous landmarks from the series including Kings Landing, The Red Keep, Blackwater Bay, and the House of Undying. Nick had teased her cruelly when he discovered she had not watched the 'greatest series ever made' in his opinion.

Now, on Saturday evening, they were seated in the most beautiful, Michelin Guide restaurant, Nautika, at a table on the terrace with views of Fort Lovrijenac. As the natural light faded, the sea was a deep blue with a slight purple haze on the horizon. They finished their delicious starters, shrimp risotto for Anna. Tortellini with mushroom, cheese and truffle flakes for Nick.

'Anyway, it was amazing to see where Cersei made her naked walk of shame through the Old Town as the crowd booed and threw rubbish and excrement at her till she was bruised and bloodied....' Nick was enthusiastically relating to Anna as she sipped her excellent chilled Croatian Malvazija white wine. Her eyes glazed over.

'This is perfect, Nick, the restaurant, the setting, the views of the sea, the dry white wine and the yummy starters. Thank you for booking it. But, can we now have a conversation about something other than '*Game of Thrones*'. You are beginning to make Justin and his love of '*Wreckfest*' sound appealing,' she stated, as he pursed his lips at her to feign annoyance.

'OK, I submit. But I cannot truly believe that you do not want to hear more about the warring families – Targaryens, Baratheons, Starks and Lannisters. Did I mention that Cersei is a Lannister?' he grinned as he noted her eye-rolling and loud sighing. 'Right, let's talk about our holiday. Have you enjoyed it, Anna? I think we have got along really well. I've only noted one or two annoying habits.'

Anna now spluttered out the wine she was currently drinking. 'Annoying habits?' She suddenly looked a little miffed which he immediately picked up on.

He leaned over and took hold of her hand. 'Don't look too worried, I'm only teasing you. But you do have a habit of leaving your shoes in places where anyone could fall over. They were right by the bathroom door today. I obviously foiled your dastardly plan to bump me off so that you can run off with the waiter that fawns all over you at breakfast.'

'Oh dear. I need to try harder with my dastardly plan if that's the case and then I could be with Ivanko the whole time.

He did suggest the other day that I should push you out of the kayak and then batter you with the paddle as you try to get back in. He was very disappointed to see you at breakfast the next day,' Anna goaded Nick as he clutched his throat while pretending to drown. 'You said one or two annoying habits, what else was there before I start on yours?' Anna paused the conversation as their main courses were brought to the table. Sea bass fillet with quinoa, zucchini and olive oil for her. Beef Charolais fillet for Nick with puree and celery chips, baby corn, beetroot and mushroom sauce. 'Wow, this looks amazing.'

They ate quietly for a few minutes until Nick stated, 'Habit number two. Don't worry it's the one all women have. Spending ages in the bathroom, doing what I don't know.'

Chewing a mouthful of the sea bass and zucchini, Anna flashed her eyes at him. 'Wouldn't you like to know, mere mortal male. It's a secret only females know and will never share. All I will say is that it involves magic lotions and balms to keep us looking youthful and lovely.'

'Well, they definitely work as you look especially beautiful tonight, if that's even possible,' he commented, his eyes scrutinising her face. Due to the warmth of the evening, Anna was wearing a spaghetti strap, teal coloured, flared dress which showed off her newly acquired golden tan. The dress was accessorised by white, heeled sandals and a white evening bag. 'What do you want to do after this meal – go for a walk around the town or go back to the hotel?

Anna gazed at him. 'I think we should go back to our room, open that bottle of Croatian sparkling wine, light some candles and see what happens,' she suggested.

'See what happens?' he stated, his eyes twinkling with amusement. 'Have you got something in mind? We could finish that word search puzzle I was doing earlier? Though there are some words I could suggest that won't be found in that puzzle.' He was now giving her that look which meant I'm thinking about making love. This man was so sexy, and Anna couldn't still believe her luck that he'd asked her to go on holiday with him. He was dressed in blue trousers and white shirt, sleeves rolled up, displaying a golden tan that he had acquired this week. The tan emphasised the blueness of his eyes. He teased her a lot about waiters and bar staff ogling her but she was aware that many pretty women eyed him. She was really happy with this relationship but wanted to hold back from giving her heart away. This may all be temporary. If he tired of her, she didn't want her fragile heart to be broken.

'What words won't be in that puzzle?' she enquired, an impishness in her eyes.

'Let me see,' he stated, his shoe gently stroking the inside of her leg. 'Mouth, kissing, nipples, squeezing, buttocks, large, penis. These are a few not normally found in those word search puzzles.'

Drinking the last of her wine, Anna giggled. 'I think 'large' is a word of common usage in some of them.'

'Yes, but in Nick's puzzle 'Find the Dick' the word 'large' is frequently included when referring to Nick's dick,' he stated, as Anna laughed loudly.

****

Back in the hotel room, Nick lay on the bed, white shirt undone, looking at his mobile phone. He glanced at Anna as she placed her white sandals in the wardrobe.

'Look, I've put my shoes away so there's no chance of you tripping over them. Perhaps you should go to Specsavers when we are back in the UK to get your eyesight tested,' Anna suggested.

'It's good enough that I can see a cheeky madam when there's one in front of me,' he replied, 'be very careful or you'll be in trouble.'

'Whatever,' she retorted, taking an item out of the wardrobe. 'I'll be back in a minute. Could you light the candles and open the wine.'

'Yes, boss,' Nick saluted her as she disappeared off to the bathroom. Obeying orders, Nick lit the three votive candles they had bought in one of the many shops in the Old Town, and the gentle scents of honeysuckle, rose and jasmine, drifted into the room. He opened the sparkling wine, the cork making a loud pop, and he captured the frothy liquid in two ubiquitous glass tumblers found in all hotel rooms. Sitting up, back on the bed, he had a drink of the Croatian sparkling wine which was delicious, a balance of acidity and sweetness.

Nick felt utterly relaxed and happy. All the tensions of his issues with Abbie had faded away as he moved forward into a new phase of his life. This week, spent with Anna, had been wonderful; she was great company, easy going, funny and bloody sexy. Too bloody sexy. He couldn't get enough of her. The sex was perfect, a mixture of thrilling and sensual, which left him contented after the event. The intense sexual couplings with Abbie were gone and for that he was grateful. The differences between Abbie and Anna were stark. Abbie only engaged with her body, believing that this was enough to draw him in. Nick realised now that it was all superficial, a false intense high before an unemotional low. Anna was a little shy around him sexually but he found that cute and endearing. But she gave her body fully and willingly and the emotional connection between them was amazing.

Anna stepped back into the room and stood in front of the bed. Nick nearly toppled to the floor. 'Holy shit,' was all he could say. She was dressed in a red babydoll outfit with a deep V-neck which perfectly displayed her rounded breasts. The see-through fabric then swirled downwards to display golden thighs. Her wavy brown hair flowed around her lovely face. Grey eyeshadow and black mascara highlighted her blue eyes and a red lipstick moistened her sensuous lips.

'I thought I'd give you a little gift to say thanks for a perfect week together,' she whispered, as she pirouetted to show him the whole outfit. The delicate fabric flowed around her body and rose over the swell of her curved buttocks. Her beautiful blue eyes connected with his. 'I'm yours,' she whispered.

Having momentarily lost the power of speech, Nick stared as he took in every inch of her as she twirled to show off her sensual body. His body was turbo-charged and he was already throbbing with anticipation of what lay ahead. In a low, gravelly voice, he commanded, 'Come over here, Anna.'

She got onto the bed and crawled towards him. His eyes were enthralled by the deep valley of her cleavage as the globes of her breasts swayed from side to side. He watched, their eyes still locked, as she came to sit on him. Nick ran his hands through her hair, before stroking the back of her neck, and then drew her towards him to kiss her luscious mouth. He had to temper his desire, hold it down, as he consumed her mouth. He savoured every moment of the kiss, the moist softness of her lips, and the faint taste of mint. As he pulled away, he muttered, 'Don't move, Anna, I want to drink in every detail of you at this moment, not a mortal woman but a creation of the gods.' His breath was laboured as his fingers lightly touched along her lips, her neck, her cleavage to hold and squeeze her breasts with his fingers. 'Beautiful, sweetheart,' he moaned.

'Lie across me,' he demanded, his voice low and raspy. She did as instructed, lying over his lap, and he gazed at the swell of her buttocks, round and firm, teasing him through the red gossamer fabric. It felt as if the lustful surge in him was vibrating every part of his body and his hand shook as he ran it over the silky curves of her bottom. 'You know what I want to do?'

'Do it,' she said in a throaty voice.

Nick raised the satiny material to expose her pale bottom, a contrast to the golden tan of the rest of her. He moved her forward, which raised her buttocks higher and then brought his hand down one, two, three, four times, and she flinched and went 'ooph' each time. He didn't want to injure her but he wanted it to be real, to hurt, so that the pain and pleasure would be linked. At the end of the four slaps she moaned softly as he rubbed her reddened flesh. His eager hands were exploring all the area, the rise of her buttocks, the cleft between, and the area between her thighs. As he massaged and stroked her, he could feel her response as her body twitched and her moans intensified. '

Enjoying this, aren't you, my little minx?' he asked, and was rewarded by a deep moan as fingers explored under the thong she was wearing. Two more slaps landed on her rosy red bum. 'Ouch, ouch'. His own sexual tension was off the scale and he wanted to take her now. After quickly stripping off his clothes, he lay back down on the bed. Anna straddled his hips and guided herself onto him, sensually sliding back and forth. Eagerly, he released her breasts from the confinement of the babydoll outfit and teased and tweaked her erect nipples until her moaning was off the scale. It was thrilling to watch her exquisite body moving over him. As the tsunami of lust built in him; he flipped her on to her back. The floral notes of her usual perfume assailed his nostrils as did the slight detection of musk from her body. The sensuality of the babydoll material as it slipped over her curves, further inflamed his senses, as his fingers moved from the feel of satin to soft skin. Nick could hold off no longer. This was the time, as the tsunami of lust rushed through him, he moved inside her, with continuous, controlled thrusts, as he was overwhelmed by the feminine softness of her. She yielded and groaned under the power of his masculine force until she spasmed uncontrollably at the point of her climax. He growled as he came in her until he was spent.

Afterwards, when they had drunk the Croatian sparkling wine, they were snuggling together as Nick stroked her hair and gazed into her eyes. 'That was amazing, darling. That sexy outfit really blew my mind. I hope it will make more appearances in the future,' he stated, an eager expression on his face.

Anna kissed him softly. 'We'll see. But such things cannot be for the every day or they become too familiar and boring. You wouldn't want to eat ice cream for breakfast, dinner and tea, would you?'

'No, but perhaps once a month would be lovely,' he teased, giving her a look which a puppy might do when hoping for a doggie treat. 'Anyway, suffice to say that you pulled out all the stops with that. It will be fun to find new ways to bring excitement to our lovemaking. Perhaps a little role play, me, the sexy cop, arresting you, the naughty shoplifter, sort of thing.'

Anna laughed. 'Yeah, maybe. As long as you don't go too bossy on me. I'm sure there'll be handcuffs involved, won't there?'

Nick kissed her forehead. 'Oh yes, indeedy.' But he then got serious. 'Just to say that doing these things together with you has been amazing. Abbie always boasted that we had the 'best sex ever' to quote her. Yeah, at the beginning it was good but there was no real connection for me.' He gazed into the most beautiful eyes he'd ever seen. 'Sometimes, Anna, sweetheart, I think you compare yourself sexually to Abbie and you think you are inferior. Never think that. What you and me have right now is a million times more fulfilling.'

Nick knew that he had fallen in love with Anna Louden but it was perhaps still too early to tell her how he felt. She seemed vulnerable after bad experiences in her past and possibly wary of commitment at the moment. For now, it was just important to have her in his life.

CHAPTER FIFTY FOUR

Saturday 18ᵗʰ June 2022

'Shit. Fuck. Shit,' Abbie screamed as she threw two cushions across the room from her position on the sofa. The first cushion skimmed over the glass coffee table to land on the dark-oak flooring. The second connected with a cream candle which fell over, rolled, and clattered, onto the floor. Abbie was sitting cross-legged on the sofa, next to Russ, looking at her mobile phone.

'What's up with you now, crazy psycho?' Russ asked, drinking from a bottle of lager.

A look of pure, undiluted anger distorted Abbie's features. 'I'll tell you what's wrong. My ex, Nick, is on holiday in Dubrovnik with the dopey, drippy cow he dumped me for. He's been sending some photos to his family and his sister has sent them to me. Get me a sick bucket so I can throw up.' Abbie picked up her wine glass from the table and drank thirstily, determined to get pissed to take away the perpetual ache in her stomach every time she saw his face, reminding her of what she had lost. The ache intensified when the photos showed him laughing with the simpering bitch, his arm protectively around her waist or shoulders. Did she need a bodyguard?

On the first day of their holiday, the she-bitch was wearing a pretty yellow/red floral print midi dress and Abbie had to admit, grudgingly, that she looked cute and feminine. Day four, a mid-blue, short, sleeveless dress which accentuated her prettiness. Other days, she was in shorts and top which showed off her developing golden tan on slender arms and legs. Her Nick, note, her Nick, was looking mega handsome in shorts that revealed his muscular legs and shirts that hinted at his toned arms. Those arms she knew so well. The arms that she ached to be held by but would never hold her again. Oh God, it hurt s-o-oo much. Why had she been such a fool? If she had her time again with him, she would play it different. Not be so greedy in pestering him to pay for all the treats, the clothes, the meals out, the beauty treatments and so on. But her stupidity hadn't stopped there, as she blathered on about city breaks and holidays that they could take together without indicating that she was willing to pay her share. Using her body to keep his interest as this was the only way that she knew how to keep a man. She wasn't good at the emotional stuff with men, did not really know how to give and receive love. She had brought her 'A' game, all the tricks and magic from her witchery book of sexual spells. At first it seemed to work, he was hooked in, and addicted to, her power to thrill and excite him. But very quickly she had to acknowledge that his interest started to wane. Deep in her heart she knew that she had lost him after only a few weeks. His body engaged but she had never captured his heart. Just looking at the photos of Nick with her replacement, drippy Anna, Abbie could see that he was happy and relaxed. And possibly in love. Shit. And fuck. And shit.

'Let's have a look at the photos, then,' Russ asked, reaching his hand out for her phone. He took the phone and slowly scrolled down the photos, pausing here and there to examine a photo more closely. 'She sure is classy, that one. Looks real cute in the photos. All cool blue eyes, flowing hair and a beautiful face,' he commented, knowing it would rile Abbie up.

This was another thing. Abbie had seen this Russ about four times now over the last month. What was going on here? Part of it was the sex, full-on and frequent, and this man was very dominant in fulfilling his needs. Very attractive, all deep brown eyes that penetrated your soul and tapped into your own dark spirit. From her vast experience with men, she knew that this one would not commit, would take what he wanted until he was bored and then drop a woman without any guilt. She sensed a restlessness in him, a feeling that the routines of life were suppressing his needs and urges. That he had to fight hard not to unleash his full destructive power on the world. A couple of times when they were in bed, Abbie had experienced fear when his actions had been too forceful. As a natural risk-taker and deviant, and a bad-ass woman of the world, she had been shocked by her own fearful reaction to him. Still, what was life without excitement and so she'd let him come round for as long as he wanted her. Or she wanted him. The things they both liked to indulge in, the booze, the drugs and the sex kept her mind off Nick and the dull, persistent ache in her heart.

Now, having seen these photos, Abbie was determined to take her revenge on the two people causing her pain. Why should she suffer while they were displaying their happiness to the world? Abbie Steele was not a piece of trash to be discarded in the nearest bin. She was worthy of being worshipped for the goddess that she was. If idiots were to dismiss her, and humiliate her, then they were fools if they thought she would not seek revenge. As referenced in Biblical times, she may not have a sword to smite her foes, but Abbie would use modern weaponry to wreak her vengeance.

****

Russ observed that Luke's beloved, Anna, looked stunning in every single photograph. Relaxed, smiling, beautifully dressed for a summer holiday, her gently-waved hair skimming her bare shoulders and her eyes made bluer by a golden tan. Photos of female perfection. He gazed at the ex-girlfriend, Abbie, currently sat close to him on the sofa. Since meeting a month ago, Russ had decided that there were benefits to be gained by seeing Abbie, the provider of plentiful booze, lines of cocaine and raunchy sex. But physically, the Abbie at home was not the polished sexy siren that went out to pubs and bars. Tonight, she looked scruffy in skinny blue jeans and a white sloppy jumper. Her hair was pulled into a messy ponytail with strands falling around her face. She hadn't bothered with much make-up. Her skin was a blotchy red with a smattering of acne spots on her chin. Her face was puffy, a sign of a bad diet and too much booze.

Her snippy attitude also irritated Russ. He was used to being with Leanne who treated him as a guest and provided drinks and snacks. On arrival at Abbie's, her general instruction to him was, drinks in the fridge, snacks in the cupboard. Get your own. It was an attitude in women he didn't generally tolerate. Abbie was no housewife, that's for sure. For now he put up with her rudeness but that may change in the future. He handed the phone back to Abbie. 'Yes, she's proper fit that one, every man's type. I know I would give her one if I got the chance.' It was fun to throw a firework into the room and wait for the explosive reaction from Abbie.

A third cushion lost its place on the sofa and landed in his lap. 'Bloody give her one. What's wrong with you men, are you morons? Don't answer that, yes, you all are. I've got more spark in my little finger than she's got in her whole body. What can she possibly do for him?' She picked up the glass, glugged down more wine, and then refilled it from a nearby bottle. On her way to getting bladdered.

'Ok, Abbie, cut out throwing the cushions at me, ok?' Russ ordered, though secretly he liked it when she had a meltdown and her eyes raged with anger. It meant that when they hooked up shortly, she would be still fired up with fury, which when combined with lust made a potent combination. 'Forget this Nick, he's got a new girlfriend now and there's nothing you can do about it. He's not coming back to you, if he's got her.'

Russ snickered to himself. It was such fun to lay on the cruel comments, pour boiling water into the open wound. He'd decided to visit Abbie for as long as he tolerated her. The type of woman he liked and loathed at the same time. Liked her because she was needy, craving love and attention. Though she'd deny it if anyone said this to her. Generally, she got minimal input from men who cared little for her and were intent on sating their own needs. Loathed, as she had an overinflated view of herself; her sexiness, her beauty and her belief that all men should worship at her feet. Her false impression that she was the High Priestess of Sex and that every man should be eternally grateful for having access to her body. There were a lot of these women around these days. Those who thought that a man should sweat and break his back for the few crumbs thrown his way. That's why Russ avoided committed relationships with women. Very few had much to offer and he was never going to slave for a precocious princess.

Abbie stomped off to the kitchen to get a second bottle of wine and brought back a bottle of whisky, and a glass, for him. She lit a cigarette and then refilled her glass from the new bottle of wine. She resumed her cross-legged position on the sofa, facing Russ, drinking the wine and taking drags on the ciggie. 'You're right, Nick's not coming back to me willingly. But I will make him come back. And take out the simpering bitch. Once they're back in the UK they won't know what's hit them.'

Russ poured himself a large glass of whisky, feeling the fire as the liquid slipped down his throat. 'What are you going to do, you mad cow?'

Abbie glanced at him cautiously, a cold hardness in her eyes. 'I'm not saying. But she'll suffer, and so by association, so will he. He'll suffer emotional pain. But then he'll have to put all that aside when I drop my bomb on him.'

Russ shuddered, as he realised that Abbie was a formidable combatant, and Luke's beloved Anna was in danger. Russ felt conflicted. He didn't want Anna killed or maimed but he did like inflicting a little pain himself from time to time, so it would be hypocritical to deny Abbie her chance to get revenge. This type of game playing really excited him and for now he could be a bystander and see how things panned out. Life was good at the moment. He was alternating between Leanne and Abbie. Leanne, dull and boring, but a good provider of life's comforts and easily dominated. Abbie, crazy, psychopathic and sexually liberated, a tease and a torment and he felt exhilarated after their hook-ups. He and Abbie were two mighty warriors fighting their own personal battles against life's unfairness. Both seeking to win and take action against those that wrong them.

'Ok, looney tunes, put the fag down, cut the crap and come over here to do something you're good at,' Russ ordered her. She scowled at him, about to complain, but the hardness in his voice and the intensity of his gaze made her listen. She'd realised that there was no option but to comply. On a recent occasion he had shown her what happens if she played him up. Abbie extinguished the cigarette and shifted over on the sofa to sit astride Russ.

⁂

CHAPTER FIFTY FIVE

Tuesday 21ˢᵗ June 2022

Luke lurked around the fruit and vegetable section of the supermarket, hoping that Anna would come in to buy food. Russ informed him over the weekend that Anna, and her boyfriend, Nick, had been away on holiday to Dubrovnik over the last week. Russ had seen holiday photos, on Abbie's phone, of the couple looking happy in the beautiful Croatian city on the Adriatic coast. Russ had forwarded photos from Abbie's phone to his own, and then as a big favour, forwarded them to Luke. Luke had been blown away by the photos of Anna, looking absolutely stunning in sundresses or shorts and tops, as she walked in the city's Old Town. Photos of her in a two-piece blue bikini, which flattered her sexy figure, made Luke tremble at how awesome she was. She was the epitome of female beauty.

The downside of being privy to her holiday photos was that there were also photos of the boyfriend, in swimming shorts, looking super fit, exposing toned arms, and flat stomach. Luke gazed at the food in his trolley, sausages, bacon, burgers and a white sliced loaf. A round belly protruded over his jeans. He was flabby due to a diet of high fat meat and low quality carbohydrates. He knew that he was storing fat around his stomach and on his face which was not attractive to women. Eating too much of the wrong things made him pale, sweaty and prone to spots. Russ on the other hand could gorge on meat like a cave dweller, or consume a diet solely comprised of pizza and beer, and still retain a toned abdomen and chiselled features. Luke knew that if he left his job as a plasterer's assistant and became a full-time writer he would soon become a fat blob with a puffy, pale face, sitting in a chair, typing on a keyboard with sausage fingers. Yuk. He resolved to eat a healthier diet.

At the salad section, Luke's heart soared when he saw Anna walking down the vegetable aisle. She did not disappoint. Dressed in a blue/white floral frock which highlighted her golden tan, she looked fresh and beautiful. As she walked towards the salads, Luke pretended to examine a bowl of Greek salad. She stopped next to him, not recognising him, as she reached for a bag of rocket.

'Hi, long time no see,' Luke commented, feeling his cheeks pinken at the proximity of her. 'You are looking very tanned, have you been away on holiday?'

Anna turned towards him, taking a moment to recognise him. 'Oh, hello. Yes, I've been to Dubrovnik for a week. The weather was really warm and sunny. We had a great time.' She did not elaborate who 'we' were but Luke knew who it was.

'I'm pleased you had a good time,' Luke commented, revelling in the nearness of her and the gentle scent of her perfume. 'The weather here has been up and down but the forecast's good for the next few days. And did you know that it's National Ice Cube Day, today? So lots of ice in the G & T.'

She laughed, a genuine laugh, and not fake like a lot of people these days. It was rare these days for people to take time for others but she did always linger a little when they now greeted each other. People were always so busy, no time for anyone, too wrapped up in their own petty lives or hooked on their mobile phones. Not Anna, she did stop for a chat and showed genuine interest in him. 'National Ice Cube Day, how funny.'

'Yes, but there are national days for lots of foods all over the world. The 7th of June was National Chocolate Ice Cream Day in the USA,' Luke explained. 'I think it's very discriminatory to have a day just for chocolate ice cream. What about those left out, the less popular ones such as rum and raisin or mint.'

.'My personal favourite is salted caramel and my least favourite is Neapolitan. I wonder if there's a National Ice Cream Day in the UK?' she speculated.

Luke glowed as he informed her. 'After extensive research I can tell you that this year it's on 17th July. I will celebrate with chocolate chip ice cream. But all this is very unfair to other food stuffs so I decided to investigate further. There is a National Pizza Day UK on 9th February and a World Pizza Day on 17th January. We will have to wait till next year to celebrate these.'

'Yes, but a reason to eat pizza on two different days,' she commented.

'Indeed. But what of the much maligned Brussel sprout, is there a day for these neglected, despised, humble green vegetables?' Luke joked, as she shook her head at the madness of it all. 'Yes there is,' he continued, 'Eat Brussel Sprouts Day is on 31st January so sadly we will have to wait till next year and put a date in the diary. In theory, I hope everyone doesn't take part as the expulsion of gases from human bodies on that particular day, including methane and CO_2, could accelerate global warning.'

Anna was now laughing openly at all this silliness. Luke noted other men gazing at her whilst he was talking to her, their eyes skimming over her face and her body. In those moments, Luke always felt a rush of pure pleasure as he imagined that those men were wondering what he was saying to make the beautiful lady laugh.

'Anyway, I'd better get on with my shopping,' she added before picking up a bagged salad.

Luke felt he was floating on air as he continued with his shopping. He decided he would buy the food in his trolley today and consider a healthy eating plan in the future. Perhaps a fit body wasn't so important to Anna if he kept making her laugh.

After finishing his shopping, he sat in his car, waiting until Anna returned to her car so he could get a final glimpse of her. But his joy of seeing her evaporated as he recalled the conversation he'd had with Russ concerning the boyfriend's ex, Abbie. Apparently, Abbie had gone crazy on seeing the Dubrovnik holiday photos. She vowed to take revenge on both Anna and the boyfriend. Abbie did not give specific details of what she planned to do but it was all said with anger and hatred. Music from *'The Twilight Zone'* played in Luke's head as Russ recounted this information. Importantly, Abbie was going to take action very soon.

Luke felt shaky at the thought of what the lunatic Red Witch was planning. He'd urged Russ to visit her to try and find out her exact plans. Was it all talk, a few nasty tweets or a video on TikTok? Or would it be a physical assault which would cause his beloved harm? He'd witnessed Abbie's rage in the Frizzy Lion and reckoned she was capable of anything. But as of now he had no details to warn Anna of an imminent attack. All he could do was raise her awareness, to be careful of those around her.

He was pleased that he had sent that text earlier this afternoon. He prayed that she had read it.

⬦

CHAPTER FIFTY SIX

Tuesday 21st June 2022

Her first day back at work after the wonderful holiday was proving to be an ordeal for Anna. After opening the one hundred plus emails and getting a brief up date from one of her team as to what had been going on in her absence, there was an urgent meeting scheduled in her diary to meet with senior manager, Jack Buckner. A complaint had come from a high profile client that the May salaries of a number of employees had not been correctly calculated. This left people without the money they were expecting, with serious financial consequences for some of them. Jack detailed in his email to Anna, that there were payroll errors in terms of sick leave and maternity pay calculations, and failure to input bonuses to relevant personnel. The client had stressed to Jack that they wanted swift action taken to remedy the matter and to ensure that it didn't happen this month. The client reminded Jack that the contract was due for renegotiation shortly and there was the possibility they would take their business elsewhere.

It was now two p.m. and Anna was sat at a round table, with Jack, in his office. Jack Buckner was an imposing man, in his early-forties, who was confident and direct in his manner and expected high standards from those he managed. 'Thanks for coming, Anna. Did you enjoy your holiday?' he asked, his eyes assessing her face and arms. 'You obviously had good weather. Ok, I'm sure Kim has brought you up to speed on the Baxbase issue. I've spoken to Kevin Manns, he's irate as his best employee is threatening to hand in his notice if his salary is incorrect this month. Still being paid at sick pay rates when he returned to work two months ago. I want to know what's going on and for this to be resolved as a matter of urgency.'

Jack Buckner was always controlled in his manner when addressing issues of poor performance with his staff, generally not raising his voice but the cold, intimidating glare from his eyes did chill the blood.

Anna breathed in deeply to calm her nerves as she did not want to give an indication of her unease. She was not going to start with a grovelling apology but she needed time to assess what had caused the problem. 'I have not had a chance to fully examine what has gone on as I have just returned from holiday. I'll make it my top priority to look into this matter at the end of this meeting.' Anna had an inkling of what might have occurred but was not going to enlighten Jack. The employee who handled the Baxbase account, Jodie, had some personal issues which were impacting on her work and resulting in payroll errors due to her lack of focus. It was tricky, as Anna needed to establish what was going on without making Jodie the scapegoat in all this.

Jack leant forward slightly and his cool blue eyes were laser focused on hers. 'Jodie looks after the Baxbase account. I gather from sources that her work's been a bit erratic recently. I hope this isn't down to her. Anyway, I want an email from you about what's go on by four p.m. so I can assure Kevin Manns that we are putting things right. Is that clear?'

'Yes, it is,' Anna stated. 'Was there anything else?'

'No. My only concern, at the moment, is to ensure that we do not lose the Baxbase account or heads will roll.' He stood up and picked up his laptop and phone.

Anna walked behind him as he went towards his desk. But then he stopped abruptly and she almost collided into him. He turned slowly to look at her. He was now in her personal space, looking down at her, a well-dressed man who oozed confidence and smelt of expensive cologne. He continued to stare at her, as if he had lost the ability to move, or speak, as if in a trance. He muttered....'so beautiful.' He then blinked which seemed to break the spell he was under, and he added....'the weather.' And he went towards his desk.

Anna found this disconcerting. Had her boss just told her that she was beautiful or was she reading something into nothing? Olivia's assessment that the man fancied her was becoming a strong possibility.

Back at her desk, Anna settled to start investigating the payroll issues with the Baxbase account. A text pinged on her phone. '**Hi. Beautiful One. Dark forces are gathering against you. Those that wish to do you harm are getting closer and more determined. Be on your guard. Xan xxx'.** Anna exhaled loudly.

Olivia glanced over from her desk. 'You ok, Anna?'

Anna smiled weakly at her friend. 'Yes, just wishing I was back in Dubrovnik.'

Later on that evening, Anna concluded that her first day back at work after her holiday had been trying. She'd investigated the payroll errors on the Baxbase account and discovered they were errors due to Jodie's failure to adhere to payroll deadlines. Anna worked diligently on the Baxbase payroll all afternoon and assured Jack that she had corrected all the payroll errors for this month's salary run. Jodie's work would be closely supervised for the time being.

Having left work feeling deflated, Anna had been cheered up in the supermarket by Tulip Man and his funny account of National Food Days. She was beginning to like him for his unique take on life.

Her phone rang and it was Nick. 'Hi, my favourite travel companion, how are you after your first day back at work after our amazing holiday? It's been full-on for me, meeting with Eric, dealing with thousands of emails and scheduling performance review meetings with those I line manage. Still it's good to crack the whip, occasionally, to stop any slacking.' He paused, waiting for Anna to bite.

'Having had the work day from hell, I don't want to hear how you make your poor employees suffer under your tyrannical regime.' Anna tried to joke but it came out a bit snappy.

'What's up, my lovely, are you in trouble with the boss. Not a slacker, I hope?' and she could detect the humour in his voice as he teased her.

'No, but my boss, Jack, has been on the warpath due to payroll errors concerning the staff of one of our most valued clients. Not a great first day back at work. Plus, my boss is a bit too creepy for my liking.'

'Why creepy? Nick asked.

Anna outlined the comment made by him. 'Anyway, just forget it. What concerns me more is another text I've had from Xan. This one has freaked me out, big time.' She read the text to Nick.

'Holy shit,' he exclaimed. 'What does all of this mean? Who is behind these texts? We know it's not Connor Peterson as the police looked into it. Is this Xan a friend or foe, or just a weird creep? I think it's time that you logged these with the police and see if they can trace this burner phone. I know he sounds non-threatening but is he linked to someone, to 'the dark forces' he mentions.'

'I don't know about going back to the police. There's not much they can go on,' Anna commented, her voice shaking. 'But it's all very unsettling.'

Nick's tone was now serious and concerned. 'I wish I was with you to hold you close. Chase away your fears, my sweetheart.'

'I wish you were too,' Anna stated.

'Anyway, if you are free on Saturday, I am inviting you to meet the family. It's my granddad's birthday and he'll be eighty-six. My mum's organising a bit of a party. As he can't resist a pretty face, I expect he will be chatting you up but I shall put him straight if he oversteps the mark.'

Anna felt a bit rattled at the prospect of meeting his family, particularly as his sister Aylssa could be there. The number one fan in the Abbie fan club. 'Will Aylssa be there?'

Nick responded, 'Most likely. Alyssa is fine. It was Abbie who could bring out her bad side. Plus I'll look after you.'

CHAPTER FIFTY SEVEN

Saturday 25th June 2022

As Nick drove onto the drive of his parent's semi-detached house in the Myton area of Warwick, Anna had a thousand butterflies fluttering in her stomach and she felt nauseous and slightly light-headed. She breathed in deeply to calm her nerves and to delay the moment that she would have to leave the safety of the car and face a group of people that she didn't know but who all knew each other well.

Nick turned to look at her. 'Come on, it'll be ok.'

Anna smiled nervously at Nick. 'Do I look alright?' She was dressed in a short sleeved, V-necked mid-blue midi dress which was tied at the waist to accentuate her figure but was modest and tasteful. This was teamed with white sandals and two blue and white beaded bracelets. She was also wearing the blue teardrop earrings that he'd bought her as a holiday gift.

'I know this is an ordeal for you but honestly, Anna, you look perfect,' Nick stated, leaning across to kiss her right cheek.

They entered the large kitchen/dining room area with oak kitchen units, white quartz worktops, integrated appliances and light oak vinyl flooring. It was airy and spacious with an oak dining table with eight blue carver chairs. On one of the chairs sat an elderly man, who Anna guessed was the birthday boy, Nick's granddad, the famous, or should that be, infamous, Bill. A trio of balloons, one blue, one gold, and one blue with gold inscription of 'Happy Birthday' were nearby. A blue banner hanging across a wall proclaimed 'Happy 86th Birthday, Bill'. As Nick and Anna walked in, a woman in her late fifties, slim, with long fair hair, came to greet them.

Nick kissed the woman lightly on the cheek. 'Hi, mum. I'd like you to meet Anna. Anna, this is my mother, Sophia.'

Anna awkwardly extended her hand but she was soon embraced by the woman. 'It's lovely to meet you, Anna. Welcome to the Carlton family home. I know it's a bit tricky to meet all the family at once.' Sophia then accosted an older man standing nearby. 'Jeff, come and meet Nick's girlfriend, Anna.'

The man was tall and white-haired with an easy smile. 'Hello, Anna, great to meet you,' he stated, giving Anna a light hug. 'Just to let you know, Anna, I take all the credit for my son's good looks and brains.'

Sophia laughed. 'Watch it Jeff or I'll tell Nick who is real dad is,' as Anna giggled. 'What would you like to drink, we have wine, lager, spirits, a soft drink?'

Anna opted for her go-to drink of dry white wine. Taking a few gulps to give her courage, Nick took her hand to introduce her to Granddad Bill who was seated at the dining table, talking to Nick's brother, Ed. Bill immediately spotted Anna and stood up very quickly for a man with bad knees. 'Alright, our Nick, who is this vision of loveliness I see before me?'

Nick gave his grandfather a hug and wished him 'Happy Birthday'. 'Granddad, this is Anna, my girlfriend.' Bill immediately went in for a hug, squeezing her tight as Nick scowled at him. He addressed Bill. 'I've warned her that you are an old rogue and it being your birthday does not give you extra privileges.'

'Well, Nick, lad, she sure is a beauty. If I were twenty years younger I'd give you a run for your money.'

'That would make you sixty-six, granddad, which I still think is a bit too old for Anna,' Ed commented, 'try fifty years younger.'

'All women like an older, more experienced man, don't they Anna?' Bill winked at her whilst Nick slipped his arm around her waist. 'You don't have to answer that, Anna,' Nick advised her.

'There is a lot to be said for wisdom and maturity in a man.' Anna gave the older man a beguiling smile.

'Well, she won't find much of those two qualities in you, Granddad Bill, eh?' Ed quipped.

'I think you'll find that I have a vast experience of pleasing the ladies, as those in my little black book will testify,' Bill boasted, trying to avoid eye contact with Nick.

'Ok, I don't think Anna wants to hear about all your romantic escapades over the decades, Bill,' Nick firmly stated. I shall now take her out of your clutches to introduce her to the other family members.

'That's it, Nick, lad, take her away. I know you feel insecure when I'm around in case I steal her away from you.' To Anna, he added, 'If there's a bit of dancing later, pencil me onto your dance card, sweetheart.'

'Come on, Anna,' Nick stated, taking her hand to go and introduce her to other family members.

A while later, whilst eating a plate of buffet food including chicken drumsticks, dips and crudites, Anna was sat with a small group of Nick's female relatives, including Sophia, Sophia's sister, Diana, and Sophia's best friend, Janice. Diana and Janice scrutinised Anna intensely. It felt as if she was a young woman in a Jane Austen novel being assessed for her suitability to wed into the Carlton family. Diana had an aristocratic, high society air about her. 'I understand that your family are from Tewkesbury, what do your parents do?'

'My father is a senior manager at an engineering company in Tewkesbury. I have an older brother, who is ex-army, and now works as a self-employed electrician. My mother died in a car accident when I was ten-years-old. I miss my mother all the time but my dad has been a brilliant single parent.' Anna's voice faltered as she praised her wonderful father.

'I know the area around Tewkesbury quite well, whereabouts is your family home?' As Diana asked this follow-up question, Anna wondered if she was trying to guess her families wealth or lack of it. According to Nick, Diana's husband, Neil, was a cardiologist who did a lot of private work and the family were well off.

'My dad lives in a village, Bredon, just outside Tewkesbury.'

'Can be prone to flooding in that area which can devalue house prices, have you had much trouble?' Diana enquired, a sort of Austen's Mrs Bennett character and Anna wondered if Diana vetted all potential suitors who dated her daughter, Claire.

'Diana, Anna does not want to be interrogated by you on her family credentials,' Sophia commented. 'You'll send her scurrying off and make an enemy of my Nick.' The piercing look Sophia gave her older sister did manage to shut her up.

A while later, Sophia produced a large chocolate birthday cake with a number '86' candle on it, as everyone sang *'Happy Birthday'* to Bill. Ed quipped, 'We didn't put eighty-six individual candles on the cake in case you blew out your dentures, Granddad Bill.' The birthday boy was then toasted with champagne, the bubbles of which seemed to go to his head very quickly, making him naughtier as he tweaked Auntie Diana's bottom.

Ed was in charge of the music and had composed a playlist of Bill's favourite songs. *'Can't Take My Eyes Off You'* by Andy Williams started to play. Anna suddenly heard her name being called. Granddad Bill, having imbibed beers and whiskies, was walking unsteadily towards her with a twinkle in his rheumy old eyes as he made a beeline for her. He went up to where Anna was seated and extended his right hand. 'Please make an old man very happy on his birthday and give him the honour of a dance with the most beautiful woman in the room.'

Blushing slightly, due to all eyes upon her, Anna took hold of Bill's hand and followed him onto the dancefloor, aka the kitchen tiles. Nick shouted, 'I'm watching you, Bill, so behave' which made everyone laugh. Before Anna knew what was happening, Bill had his right arm encircling her waist, drawing her towards him, then he took hold of her left hand as they slowly circled the floor, in competent fashion. For an octogenarian, Bill was surprisingly strong and fleet of foot. He then tightened his grip on her waist and leaned in close to her and for a heart-stopping moment Anna feared he was going to kiss her. Instead, he sang the words of this seductive, beautiful song into her ear. During one turn of the dancefloor, she caught Nick's eye and noted that he was not looking happy.

****

Nick scowled, trying to get Bill's attention but the crafty old git was avoiding all eye contact. The next song played by Ed was 'Frank Sinatra's *The Way You Look Tonight*'. Before Nick had a chance to intervene, Anna was once again being swept around the kitchen floor by the nimble-footed octogenarian. When Bill moaned about his knees or back again when wanting a hand with his shopping, Nick would remind him of his spritely dancing. Nick stood close by, watching while Anna was spun away, then pulled back in by wily old Fred Astaire, using his great age as an excuse to get to grips with her. She was beautiful as her dress swirled around her lovely legs, giving flashes of golden thighs and she had a radiant smile on her face. The words of the song were really getting to Nick, he wanted to be the one dancing with her. He also knew that there was nothing he could do to stop himself falling in love with her.

A commotion in the room brought Nick out of his trance. His sister Alyssa, dressed in blue denim shorts and a white scoop-necked T-shirt, had entered the room and was greeting their mother and aunties as she headed towards Granddad Bill. 'Is Granddad having a good time? He'll be thrilled to see his favourite grandchild. Plus I've brought him a surprise to put a big grin on his face.' The 'surprise' dressed in a figure-hugging, green, mini dress, was Abbie who was holding a large blue balloon with 'old fart' written in white. Hand in hand, Alyssa and Abbie approached Bill on the dance area with a fuming Nick following.

Alyssa waved and shouted to Bill. 'Hi, Granddad. Look who I've brought to see you' as she pointed at Abbie. The song kept playing, and Bill continued to swirl Anna around, lost in the dance and the words of the song, as he sang loudly to Anna about 'never changing' and 'I love you'.

Abbie moved closer to the dancers, the balloon bouncing around. 'Happy Birthday, Bill,' she shouted.

As the song ended, Bill stopped dancing and noticed Alyssa and Abbie. He took hold of Anna's hand and walked over to the women. 'Hello, Alyssa, love. Hello, Abbie. This is Anna, who has made an old man very happy by dancing with him on his birthday. Isn't she beautiful?'

Nick noted, with some satisfaction, a flicker of annoyance on Abbie's face before she quickly composed her features into a smile. 'Granddad Bill, I've brought you a balloon' she said, kissing him on the cheek and giving him the balloon.

Reading the balloon's message, Bill chuckled. 'Where ever you be let your wind blow free has been my life's motto, so good choice. Are you ok, Abbie, girl? Keeping out of trouble?'

'Of course, Bill. I've always been a good girl.' Abbie stated, openly flirting with Granddad Bill. Nick cringed, as this was typical Abbie, capable of flirting with anything male including an eighty-six-year old man. But her eyes were on Nick, to get and hold his attention. It worked, as Nick said, 'Come with me and I'll get you a drink.' To Anna, he added, 'I won't be long.'

Sophia and Ed arrived at Anna's side and Sophia said to Ed. 'Can you put on some tunes that Anna and I can dance to.' Ed obliged by playing Abba's *Dancing Queen* and Sophia sashayed onto the dance area dragging Anna along with her.

Abbie followed Nick. 'Thanks for getting me a drink, babe. I'll have a sparkling water with slice of lime. I'm cutting down on the drinking. Great to be here on Granddad Bill's birthday. I think he always fancied me and occasionally pinched my bum, the old lech. It's great to see you, Nick.' She smiled at him, pouting her moist red lips. This was Abbie, using her sexy wiles to draw him back under her spell. Nick felt nauseated.

Taking a tumbler glass, Nick added ice, sparkling water and a lime slice and handed the tumbler to Abbie. She squeezed some lime juice into the drink, added a straw and sipped seductively, keeping her eyes locked onto Nick. 'Thanks, babe. See, I knew we could be friends if we try. I can still be part of the family as I'm Alyssa's friend.'

Nick regarded her sternly. 'You're only staying here tonight if you behave. If you start drinking to excess or upset Anna, I will pick you up, carry you out and eject you onto the driveway.'

Abbie wiggled in the green dress, a trick to draw his attention to her cleavage. 'If misbehaving means I get your hands on my body, then I might have to be a bit naughty, Nicky.' She winked.

'Stop playing games, Abbie. I'm not interested in you,' he said, in a loud, no nonsense voice. As Abbie glared angrily at him through eyes caked with layers of black mascara, Nick did note that she did not look as healthy as he remembered. Alyssa had commented recently that Abbie was overdoing the booze and putting on weight. This showed in her face, which underneath the make-up looked puffy, sweaty and pimply.

'Don't worry, Nicky, babe. I've moved on. Having a good time testing out lots of guys, you know, to see what works. One in particular is becoming a regular. Very good looking and very fit. He really gets what I like in bed, you know, the dominance thing, but at times he's a little scary. But nothing I can't handle.' Her hazel, feline eyes were locked on Nick's, waiting for a reaction.

Nick shrugged. 'Sounds like a match made in heaven. Anyway, you can stay here as long as you behave yourself. Stay away from Anna or you might find I'll be doing the dominance thing and causing you pain.'

Thinking this was some sort of come on, Abbie purred. 'Oh, Nicky, I knew you'd want me again after a few months with that drippy cow.'

'That's enough, Abbie. Stop it.' With that he left her to go and find Anna.

Once again, Granddad Bill had Anna in his clutches as they danced, very closely to '*My Girl*' by The Temptations. Nick wondered if it was ok to punch your granddad? To infuriate Nick more, Ed made a whistling wit-woo sound which seemed to encourage Bill to embrace Anna more firmly. Luckily the song ended and Nick went over to rescue her from Bill. 'Ok, Granddad, that's enough excitement for your heart for one day.'

Bill was listening to his tall, imposing grandson, but making a connection of what the words meant between his ears and brain was not happening. 'Look, Nick, lad, don't deny an old man a dance with this lovely young woman.'

Nick now placed his arm possessively around Anna's waist whilst glaring at Bill. 'Ok, Granddad Bill, the next person to dance with her will be me.'

'Is that so, Mr Nicholas Carlton,' Anna looked up at him, a feigned look of annoyance on her face which looked beautiful with a faint pink bloom to her cheeks from the exertion of dancing. 'I don't recall seeing your name on my dance card.'

'Give me the bloody card then and I will put my name in every place,' Nick tried to tease her but the anger still bubbling in him from the conversation with Abbie was still apparent in his voice.

Anna looked a little surprised at his tone. 'Are you getting a bit jealous of your older, handsome grandfather, Nick?'

'I'm getting annoyed with him as he never knows when to stop. I'm livid that Abbie has turned up uninvited. And I'm pissed off that I haven't danced with you yet so we will rectify that right now,' Nick insisted as he guided her to the dance area as the song he had just requested played, '*Amazed*' by Lonestar. As he took the most beautiful woman he had ever seen into his arms, and pulled her into him, his arm was securely around her waist as they slowly began to dance. He softly sang the song to her, gazing into her lovely eyes, knowing that every word of this song perfectly explained his feelings for her.

****

Abbie stood nearby, holding her non-alcoholic drink, and vaguely listened to something Alyssa was saying about going to the pub shortly. Yeah, the pub would be good where she could forget this charade of not drinking and get wasted. Not have to witness her Nick dancing, slowly and lovingly, with a woman she detested. As he gazed into the drippy cow's eyes, Abbie knew that he was absolutely in love with this woman. It hurt so bad. A stabbing pain in the heart. A twisting of guts. Abbie had not moved on. Russ was a temporary diversion. Her mission was to remove the obstacle in her way in order to get Nick back in her life. It should be her being held in those strong arms. It should be his flawless blue eyes gazing into hers. It should be his seductive voice singing in her ear. And later, in her fantasy, Abbie would have sex with the best lover in the world. But for her fantasy to become real, the bitch must go.

⚜

CHAPTER FIFTY EIGHT

Monday 27th June 2022

Luke hovered by the entrance to the supermarket, praying to all known gods, that his beloved would appear and he could start a conversation with her before she commenced her shopping. Today, he was planning to see if she would have a quick coffee with him and had thought of an idea which would convince her to spend a little time with him. Therefore, he was currently lurking by the first aisle nearest the door, gazing at punnets of strawberries and raspberries. Then he spotted her, dressed in blue floral knee-length dress and white sandals. She always looked so fresh and fragrant whilst everyone else struggled to keep cool in the summer months.

As she started to walk to the salad products, pushing a trolley, Luke sidled up to her. 'Hi, I'm glad I've caught you.' She smiled weakly, obviously a little surprised at his unexpected approach. Luke continued, 'I'm planning to do a dog walking challenge to raise funds for a charity for older people. Would you be interested in sponsoring me? If you let me buy you a quick coffee, I can give you some details.'

'Oh, ok,' she responded, 'of course I'll sponsor you. A coffee would be good.'

Twenty minutes later, and Luke was sat at a table in the café, drinking a latte and staring openly at his most favourite woman whilst she concentrated on filling out his sponsorship form. It was wonderful just to drink in her beauty as she looked downwards, flawless skin, with a sprinkling of freckles, revealed under a light make-up. Those perfect plump lips, moisturised by a rose-pink lipstick, that he ached to kiss. Realising that he was staring, she gazed up at him, and her spectacular blue eyes took his breath away. 'How long has your great aunt had Milly?' she asked.

For this sponsorship scam to work, to draw her in, he'd concocted a story that he was planning to raise funds by walking his great aunt's black cocker spaniel, Milly. Aunt Daisy was now struggling to walk her furry companion regularly and Luke had offered to walk it on a regular basis. 'She got the dog as a puppy and it's now four years old. Cute as can be as you can see from the photos.' Photos courtesy of Shutterstock. 'Auntie had a mild stroke a couple of months ago and isn't so mobile so I offered to help out with taking it for walks. Thought I'd raise a bit of money for Age UK at the same time. Charities for older people get overlooked a bit, in my opinion.'

'Yes, you're right,' she nodded.

'Anyway, I'm hoping to walk sixty miles in thirty days in July. Milly's quite lazy so I don't want the challenge to be too difficult for her. Having said that, my fitness isn't that great so she may outdo me. You can sponsor me whatever amount you like, such as 50p a mile or a total payment, say of a fiver or tenner. It's up to you. As you will see from the form; you are my first sponsor.'

'I'll pay you £15 if you do the full sixty miles,' she advised. 'It's all in a good cause.'

She passed the form over to him and Luke checked out what she had written. 'Thank you, Anna. I didn't know your name until now. I believe that Anna was originally a Hebrew name meaning He (God) has favoured me. I have to say He (God) has definitely favoured you with your beauty. I'm Luke by the way.' He noticed that she blushed, slightly, as he mentioned her beauty. This woman was just perfect in terms of femininity and modesty. Such a change from the ones on social media who pouted and preened, seeking validation. 'It's been great to have a coffee with you, we will have to do it again. I will keep you updated on how Milly and I are progressing, Anna.' How he loved to say her name to her face.

'Great. I hope Milly realises she is contributing to a good cause.'

After they parted company, Luke walked around the supermarket as if walking on air. He had spent a whole thirty minutes just being in her orbit. He was obsessed with her beauty but she definitely had other qualities as well. She interacted well with him, listened to what he said, and laughed at his jokes. Luke always felt that he was invisible amongst strangers. Due to his shyness he was often overlooked at family gatherings. At work, his dad was good at the jokey banter that kept the customers engaged. Russ never bothered unless there was a comely female to impress in the absence of her husband/partner and out would come what passed for social interaction in Russ world. Luke felt saddened that his own intelligence, creativity and wit were undervalued by the world in general. He felt sure that Anna would recognise his worth and give him the confidence boost he needed once they were in a relationship.

Outside of the store, the day was generally sunny, average high-teen temperatures for the month of June. Luke's car was parked close to Anna's and he was lingering by his car, further down on the opposite row, to watch her load her shopping into her car before she drove off. One last glimpse of her before he went home to his sweaty-sock, masculine home. Anna tended to park in the same area most of the time so it was easy to find her. Spotting her, he stood at the driver side of his car, pretending to make a phone call, but was actually going to sneak a few photos as she walked from her car to the trolley storage area. He would have a photographic record of the day when he had spent time with his beloved on a coffee date. As she halted by her car, and opened the boot, he took a number of shots of her loading the car with her shopping. She then stood on her toes to lower the boot door which drew attention to her gorgeous bottom and slender legs (this action was s-s-o-o cute it was heart-stopping).

At this point, an idiot in a white transit van called out of the window 'alright darling'. As the van drove off with its two knuckle-dragging misogynists inside, Anna crossed the path of the traffic to place the trolley in the storage area. She had sufficient time to cross as a white car came towards her into the supermarket car park to find a parking space. The white car progressed slowly, as normal in a car park, but then increased its speed as it came closer to Anna. Luke looked on, anxious that the car was travelling too close, and too fast, near to her. Surely it would slow down again in a moment. But no, the car increased its speed striking squarely into the trolley that Anna was pushing. The impact sent the trolley ramming into Anna, pushing her forcibly backwards, at such speed that she could not stay upright and her knees buckled, and she crumpled, sending her sprawling backwards onto the cold, hard asphalt surface.

Luke believed that he was watching a film in slow motion as first her body bounced upwards before the back of her head hit the ground. The trolley fell onto her before it toppled off her and onto its side. A scream was heard, not from Anna, but from Luke, as he rushed forward crying, 'no, no'. Quickly, Luke took a photo of the front of the white vehicle and captured its car registration number. He assumed that the car would now stop but instead it swerved around Anna, and the trolley, and raced off, tyres screeching. The car then turned left at the end of the row of cars to speedily find the car park exit.

Luke rushed over to Anna as a few more people gathered round to try to help.

A woman knelt down, assessing Anna, who was lying motionless on her back. The woman spoke to Anna, and gently touched her, but there was no response. The woman called 999. Luke looked on anxiously as the woman spoke to the operator. 'Yes, she's lying on her back, not moving. The back of her head is in contact with the road. Ok....' the woman paused in her conversation and leaned over Anna, checking her body to see if her chest was rising and falling. She placed her cheek near to Anna's mouth to check her breathing. Speaking to the operator, the woman confirmed, 'Yes, she's breathing but still unresponsive.' A man joined the woman, and knelt on the ground to offer his assistance, stating he had first aid training. Other people were taking control of the traffic in the vicinity to ensure that cars were not passing too close to Anna and to ensure that no new vehicles entered the area.

Luke gazed on, stunned. His body paralysed by the trauma of seeing Anna unconscious on the ground. His Astraea, his goddess, who he deemed to be immortal proved to be human, and of the flesh, after all. He could see grazes on the palm of her left hand and the ankle area of her left leg appeared bruised and swollen. The left side of her body bearing the scars of her impact with the surface of the car park. She looked so small and delicate, a broken doll, lying on the hard ground. He wanted to scoop her up and carry her away. To care for her, mend her, put her back together.

'Oh, poor love, she looks so vulnerable lying there,' an older woman standing next to him stated. 'How awful. I hope she'll be ok and the ambulance hurries up. Do we know what happened?'

Feeling tears prickling his eyes, Luke was fighting to control his emotions. In a wavery voice, he stated, 'She was putting her trolley away when a white car drove straight into her, knocking her down, and then drove off at speed. A scumbag hit-and-run driver. I think it was a woman driving. I hope they catch her, lock her up and throw away the key.'

'Did you get the number plate of the car?' the woman asked. 'It could help the police trace the vehicle.'

'No,' Luke replied. 'It all happened so quickly and to be honest I was so shaken up by watching it happen. Hopefully, there's CCTV that will help.'

The woman's kindly eyes looked at Luke. 'Yes, it's not good to witness an accident like this. You must go home and have a strong cup of hot tea. Lots of sugar.'

Going over the events that had just happened, Luke was convinced that this was no random accident. It was not a driver pressing the accelerator and not the brake, a driving error, and then cowardly rushing off to avoid owning up to what they had done. It did appear to Luke that the female driver had increased their speed to deliberately knock Anna down. The driver was a young, blonde female. This had the smell of witchery and the caldron about it. 'Eye of newt and toe of frog' to quote Shakespeare's '*Macbeth*'. The Red Witch, Abbie, in this case had stirred her witch's brew in a saucepan on the hob in her kitchen whilst placing a spell on her victim. Abbie had likely succeeded in getting her revenge on Anna, Luke was sure of it. He must send Russ to check out if she was the owner of the white car with the registration number he had recorded. If it was her that harmed Anna then retribution would follow. In real life and in fantasy stories, according to Luke's moral code, wrong doers had to be punished. When the time was right, Xandros would bring a divine retribution down on the evil Red Witch for causing pain and suffering to his beloved Astraea.

⚜

CHAPTER FIFTY NINE

Monday 27th June 2022

It was getting on for nine p.m. and Nick was relaxing on the sofa, drinking a decaf tea, and pondering why Anna was not answering his texts and calls. His mind wondered back to Granddad Bill's birthday on Saturday night. Bill declared he'd had a great time and was telling Anna that she could marry him if she got fed up of his grandson. Really, the old man was incorrigible and as slippery as a snake.

Nick was pleased that Abbie had behaved herself, kept away from Anna, stuck to mineral water and then left with Alyssa to go to the Frizzy Lion. It had been good to hear her say she had moved on and was seeing someone else, though, how she described this man as 'a little scary' was quite disturbing. Abbie was rarely phased by anything and was obviously indulging her sado-masochistic tendencies with the guy but for her to describe him as 'scary' meant that he may have a propensity for violence. Nick shrugged, it was her bed, let her lie in it. Not his problem.

But for now, he was feeling a little cross with Anna as she wasn't responding to him. He's sent two texts, the first one, **'How was your day? Had the greatest time with you after the party back at my house. Anna Louden you are so hot. N xxx.'** Having ignored that saucy text, he sent '**As Sinatra almost sang. I love the smile so warm on your sexy mouth. Your (bottom) cheeks so soft. You know what I want to do to you, darling. N xxx.** Still no response; which now puzzled him.

Nick started to watch a documentary about cops catching criminal drug gangs in the UK when his phone rang. He didn't recognise the number. 'Hi, Nick Carlton.

'Hi, Nick. This is Mike Louden, Anna's father. I'm sorry to tell you that she's been hit by a car in a supermarket car park and is in Warwick Hospital awaiting a CT scan.'

Nick felt a physical jolt to his body as he tried to process this news. He cleared his throat. 'How badly is she hurt?'

'Initially, she was unresponsive at the time of the accident but now she is conscious but very drowsy. Her heart rate and oxygen levels are being monitored. She sustained a blow to the back of her head, resulting in a cut, and some bleeding, which is now under control. The doctors have organised a CT scan to check for skull fractures, bleeding to the brain, or brain swelling.'

Nick jumped up from his chair. 'Mr Louden, I need to come to the hospital to see her for myself. I'm on my way now.' He ended the call before the man could object or tell him to stay at home. There was no way in hell that he would be diverted from finding out firsthand how she was. Nick rushed to the hall, put on his shoes and jacket, grabbed his keys, phone and wallet, and rapidly exited the house.

Luckily, the distance between his home and Warwick Hospital was barely ten minutes but Nick was determined to get there as quickly as possible thus he called out other drivers for pulling out too slowly at roundabouts or dawdling along at a snail's pace. He accelerated fast at traffic lights to squeeze through just before the light went to red, thus risking prosecution if a camera were present. This was the sort of driving that he would have described as erratic, bordering on dangerous, as a cop, and would pull over the driver. But now, he didn't care.

On arrival at the hospital, Nick parked and almost ran into the A & E. The waiting area was crowded with weary people, staring down at the floor or at their phones, enduring the long waiting times. As he joined a queue to make enquiries about Anna at the reception desk, an older man approached him. 'Nick Carlton? I'm Mike Louden, Anna's father.' He extended his hand and Nick shook it. Mike Louden was a tall, distinguished looking man, clean shaven, with grey hair swept back off his face. A face that looked tired and gaunt.

'I'd say it's nice to meet you but not in these circumstances,' Nick stated. 'Where is she?

'She's in a cubicle and we're waiting to see what happens next. They've done a CT scan so we'll see what that tells the doctor. It's this way,' Mike said as he led the way along the corridor past staff and trolleys till he came to a number of cubicles with curtains in the front. Mike Louden stopped at the appropriate one and went in.

Nick followed.

His beautiful Anna was dozing on a bed, dressed in a hospital gown. Small nasal tubes were supplying oxygen and a pulse oximeter on her right middle finger was measuring oxygen levels. Her face was deathly pale, and if Nick were a doctor he might recommend a blood transfusion, but there was no visible signs of injury to her face. Nick quietly approached the right side of the bed, trying to steady his breathing, and take the anxiety off his face so as not to alarm her. 'Hello, sweetheart. What trouble have you got yourself into now?'

She slowly opened her eyes to look at him but he could see that she was tired, her eyelids heavy. A tiny, weak smile touched her mouth. 'Hi,' she murmured.

Nick bent to kiss her forehead and gently took hold of her left hand. His voice broke with emotion as he joked, 'I thought I told you to be careful of cars.'

She tried to join in with the banter. 'Should've listened,' she whispered but she lacked energy and her eyelids closed.

There was a chair by the left side of the bed and Mike Louden sat down and gently stroked his daughter's right arm. Nick asked Anna's father, 'Do we know what happened?'

'According to a woman witness who was parked near Anna, she said that Anna was crossing the roadway to put her trolley away. There was a white car entering the row and driving slowly. As Anna crossed, the female witness thought that the car deliberately increased its speed and slammed into the trolley, pushing Anna backwards. The car then swerved around Anna, and the trolley, and raced off. A hit-and-run,' Mike's voice wavered as he spoke, as tears choked him. 'The witness thinks the car was being driven by a woman but she didn't get the registration number. The police are looking at the car park's CCTV to try and identify the car.' Mike continued to stroke his daughter's arm as he gazed, angrily, at Nick. 'What type of disgusting human being drives at someone, knocks them down, and drives off?'

Nick's response was equally vehement. 'A bloody scumbag. One that I will kill with my bare hands around their neck if I catch them.' To help cool his temper, he took a deep breath. 'Besides the head injury, is she hurt anywhere else?'

Mike pointed to a dressing on the palm of Anna's left hand, at the base of her thumb. 'That's a graze the size of a two pence piece that they've cleaned and dressed. There are grazes on her left shin, the side of her left knee and just below her left elbow from where she came into contact with the road surface as she fell. These have all been attended to. She also knocked her left ankle and there's some bruising and swelling. The doctor didn't think she'd broken the ankle but the CT scan was going to check this out as well. She won't be very mobile for a while. The main concern is whether there is any injury to her skull or brain.'

'Let's pray that it's nothing serious,' Nick added, choked to see the woman he loved, lying bruised and battered on a hospital bed. 'Have they said what happens next?'

'It's likely she will be admitted for observation, at least overnight, or longer, depending on the results of the CT scan,' Mike Louden stated, 'and when she comes out of hospital she will need someone to look after her for a while. I'll get some time off work and come and stay with her for a bit. She won't like it.

She can be a stubborn little madam and will insist that she can look after herself.'

Despite the situation, Nick laughed. 'You're right there. She's very independent and head-strong when she wants to be. We have many a tussle about who's going to pay what when we go out. I'd like to pay as I earn more than her but she won't let me a lot of the time. I paid for the holiday but she's set up a monthly standing order to pay me back.'

'That's my girl. I don't want her to be beholden to a man unless she's married and they share the money,' Mike sighed, wearily rubbing his forehead. 'That bastard Alistair, with all his swanky ways and family wealth, used money to control her. Too much money was his downfall, made him lazy, able to indulge in bad habits, booze, drugs and gambling, and abuse women. After Alistair, Anna vowed to keep her financial independence and avoid rich men. I understand that you have a bob or two, Nick?'

'I am a partner in a security company and do have a good income, Mr Louden. I am extremely fond of your beautiful daughter and would never intentionally hurt her or allow anyone else to do so, if that's within my power.' Nick's gravelly voice expressed his earnest intent to Anna's father. 'She told me what happened with Alistair. I'm truly sorry she got hurt like that.'

'So am I, son. I was truly shocked when I saw her after the attack. It took all my strength to stop her brother, Dan, from killing the bastard. I know she likes and trusts you, so please don't hurt her. Men want her because of her beauty but then don't cherish what they have.' Mike Louden's face looked ravaged with pain, ageing him in front of Nick's eyes.

After what seemed like an age, the doctor, a young female, came in with the results of the CT scan. She glanced at Nick but addressed Mike Louden. 'The head CT is clear with just minor bleeding and bruising at the site of the wound. But as a precaution we shall be keeping her in overnight for observation.

In terms of her left ankle, there is bruising but no obvious injury or tear to the ligaments. It will require rest and treatment with ice, compression bandage, and elevating the foot. She may require crutches for a short while until she can walk on the foot. I'll be back shortly when we've organised a bed for her.'

As Mike Louden went to fetch coffees, Nick sat beside Anna watching her sleep. Whenever he saw her sleeping, he was always blown away by her loveliness. Her face had a serene, flawless beauty that was other worldly, angelic. Lying on a bed, in a hospital cubicle, injured by the actions of another, she looked vulnerable and fragile. Nick's heart ached. He wanted to scoop her up, hold her and protect her. He then considered how she had become injured. A car was driven at her, knocking her down, and then driven off. A deliberate hit-and-run according to the witness. A white car with a female driver. An awful thought entered Nick's head. Abbie Steele had a white car. Was she the driver of the car that had deliberately driven into Anna? Hopefully, CCTV in the car park would shed light on the incident. If it was Abbie then Nick wanted the law to deal with her so that he didn't have to.

Anna's phone pinged a text message. Her bag was on the chair. He took the phone from her bag to access it and entered her six digit passcode which she had shared with him. The text read, '**Hi. Beautiful one. The evil one has struck. I pray that you are alright and your beauty is not harmed. Do not worry, there will be retribution. Evil cannot go unpunished. Xan xxx.**'

Fucking hell, thought Nick. Who the hell was this Xan? How could he (mostly likely) know about Anna's accident so quickly? Was he involved? It would be prudent for the police to investigate whether these texts are linked to the hit-and-run incident. The police may be able to trace the owner of the burner phone that this moron used.

The texts from this Xan, though weird and creepy, did seem to be from an individual that liked Anna and wanted to protect her. Nick shivered as he now considered that there were two individuals who were fixated with Anna. The female hit-and-run driver who had done her physical harm and who Nick feared could be Abbie Steele. The male stalker who seemed harmless but whose texts were a sinister intrusion into her life. The whole thing was getting too fucked up.

CHAPTER SIXTY

Friday 1ˢᵗ July 2022

Russ sat on a stool at Abbie's dressing table, looking forward to what was going to happen tonight. Abbie was definitely the Red Witch tonight, as Luke called her.

She greeted him at the door, dressed in red basque, thigh-high red stockings and high-heeled, black shoes. Already swaying slightly from too much alcohol, she guided him straight into the bedroom.

'I've put some booze over there. Help yourself to get into the party mood and then we'll take it from there,' she ordered. That was the thing with Abbie, she always assumed that she was in control. Russ knew this was nonsense. She climbed onto the bed and picked up her wine glass from the bedside cabinet. She sipped at the wine, licking her lips seductively, and flashed glimpses of red thong between her thighs. A full-on Abbie show to excite him. It did but she would never know that it angered him in equal measure.

A selection of drinks, wine, lager, whisky, were on the dressing table and Russ picked up the whisky bottle, poured a large measure into a glass, and drank a generous mouthful. He stared at Abbie propped up against the white upholstered headboard. The room oozed class with high quality, high thread-count white linen with gold border, oak wardrobe and dressing table, and a cream-coloured, wool carpet. This opulence was spoilt by the woman lying on the bed, a woman who reminded him of one that he had encountered years ago in a window in Amsterdam's Red Light district. The red basque accentuated Abbie's curves, a tiny red thong covered her crotch, and suspenders drew his eyes to the area of plump, golden thighs. Black, patent, four-inch stilettos were a sexy addition to highlight her slender legs. Her eye make-up was heavy: smoky grey eyeshadow, black eyeliner, black mascara on false eyelashes. Luscious, ruby red lipstick added a sensual, 'kiss me now' allure to her lips. Drinking her wine, she was sexually hot and ready, basking in his unflinching gaze. Russ laughed, 'What's got into you tonight? You should be out on a street corner, touting for business, flashing an old geezer that red basque underneath a fur coat. Giving him a heart attack.'

Abbie smiled seductively at Russ, a cat-like quality to her hazel eyes. 'Yeah, I'm stoked. Had a great week. I've dealt with a problem that's been pissing me off for months. People don't upset me and expect to get away with it.'

'What you do?' Russ asked, trying not to be overly interested. Keep things low-key, play it cool. He actually knew what she had done. Luke had given him the registration of the white car that had knocked down Anna. Russ had located the car just now parked outside on the road near to this property. A white VW Golf GTI with the registration number Luke had provided. On close examination, Russ found a few scratches on the front of the car near to the VW badge. Russ texted Luke to confirm that the white car did belong to his hated Red Witch.

'Let's just say a stealing bitch got taught a lesson she won't forget in a hurry. I brought her some pain for all the hurt she's caused me by taking my boyfriend,' Abbie gloated.

'How?'

'She was walking in a supermarket car park, pushing a trolley back to its storage place, and she was unfortunately hit by a car which left the scene pretty quickly. I'm sorry to say that she would've sustained some injuries. Shame but accidents happen. Hey-ho.' Abbie laughed, a tinkly, maniacal sound, as she grinned at Russ.

Russ now re-filled his glass, enjoying the burning sensation of the whisky as it slipped down his throat. 'I take it this is the new girlfriend of your ex that you're talking about?'

'Yes, her, the drippy cow.'

'You've knocked her over in a hit-and-run. How did you find out where she shops?' Russ asked.

'I got my friend, Alyssa, Nick's sister, to find out as much info as possible on the drippy cow from Nick's mum. This included where she lives and where she shops on a regular basis. Then I visited the supermarket quite often, got familiar with her shopping patterns, and then waited for my chance to get her,' Abbie explained.

'Won't the cops find evidence of it being your car from CCTV cameras?' Russ asked.

'I checked out the area. I couldn't see any cameras, so I think I got away with it. If I get caught, I'll say it was an accident and I panicked. But I don't regret it for a moment. I really hope she's dead but I won't get that lucky. Still, if I've damaged that pretty face so much the better,' Abbie cackled. 'Anyway, that was only part one of my plan. I've got the second part of my plan to implement. As in all good military campaigns, part one, disabling the enemy, has been accomplished. Now for part two. The enemy has been weakened, they must be stopped from re-grouping and be kept apart for good. This weekend I shall put in place part two of my plan. I will be contacting my Nick, to throw an enormous explosive into his life and scare off the girlfriend for good. Part two of 'Operation Fuck Them Over'.

Russ laughed loudly. 'You really are an evil bitch, aren't you?' He got up off the stool and walked to the bed, taking the whisky bottle and glass with him. 'I shall have some fun tonight punishing you for being a bad girl. That's why you've dressed in that outfit, isn't it?'

'Let's do some lines first to really get in the mood,' Abbie giggled, pointing to small plastic bags of cocaine on her bedside cabinet. Before she could reach them, her phoned pinged. She picked it up and read a text. The happiness that was on her face a moment ago faded. 'Holy shit, what does this mean?' she said, mainly to herself.

Russ noted her worried expression as she gazed at the phone. 'What's up, darling?'

She picked up her wine glass and gulped a large mouthful to calm her nerves. 'I've had a weird text from an unknown number. It says, **I know you knocked the girl down with your car. I have your car reg number. Bad girls get punished. Xan.**' I don't know who this Xan is but they could report me to the police.'

Russ pretended to feign sympathy. He knew who Xan was and what was expected of Russ tonight. Luke had tasked him to seek revenge on Abbie for hurting his beloved Anna. Russ was willing to oblige for the fun of it.

Abbie scowled at him. 'Have you just texted this? You did just call me a bad girl. Give me your phone.'

Russ did not normally like being told what to do by women but he handed over his phone so that she could check he had not sent the text. After a few minutes she handed the phone back. 'Satisfied are you? Obviously, someone else has sussed out your bad girl tendencies. Let's hope they don't give the car reg to the cops.'

The colour drained from Abbie's face, even under the heavy make-up. 'Jeez, I could be in big trouble. Who is this weirdo?'

Russ shrugged his shoulders. 'Who cares. Let's forget all that. As you've dressed up so nicely I think we should make things a bit more exciting.' Out of his pocket, he took out a small vial. 'A few drops of this GHB will liven things up.'

Abbie held out her wine glass and he put in a small amount of the liquid drug. Russ gulped down more of the whisky but kept his drink drug free. They started to kiss casually, a lazy meeting of lips, each to tantalise the other in anticipation of what was to come.

Russ picked up Abbie's favourite toys that she had placed on the bed; bondage rope and a black leather riding crop. 'Kneel on the bed.' Giggling happily now as the drug took hold, Abbie put down her glass and obeyed. Russ pulled her arms back and tied her wrists together, then gave her bottom a friendly smack to illustrate her vulnerability. 'Ok, Roxy, my favourite hooker?' he asked, as he noted the pleasure on her face. A wave of excitement flooded Russ's body as he examined the sexy sight before him. Her bum was presented to him perfectly, two white buttocks, each one with a red suspender crossing them to secure a stocking. Russ gave her bottom another smack but this was a hard slap which made her jerk and she emitted a loud 'oomph' noise. This was repeated three more times until her buttocks glowed a bright red.

After each blow, and after the sting of the slap had subsided, Abbie licked her lips, as her drug-glazed eyes focused lovingly on Russ. She smiled, and her flushed red face lit with excitement. 'Thanks, babe. Will there be lots more?'

Russ laughed inwardly, knowing that he was in control. 'Ok, Roxy, getting turned on, are you? But don't forget, it's the customer that dictates the action, not the hooker. All you need to do is to hold that position.'

Obeying orders, she wiggled to ensure that she was presenting her rosy backside as a perfect target for his next action. She was whimpering slightly but he knew it was from pleasure as he had not yet administered the level of pain that she was begging for.

Russ pulled off his black T-shirt, to reveal his toned chest, as he liked to be free of any clothing that could restrict his movements. He picked up the black leather riding crop and enjoyed the satisfying 'thwack' sound as he hit his left hand. Abbie groaned in anticipation of the pain that was coming. Russ trailed the leather flap of the crop along her back, and over the curve of her bottom, as her buttocks tensed ready for the first blow. 'Look at me,' he ordered in a deep, controlled voice which caused Abbie's buttocks to visibly tense as she awaited the whack of the crop.

Russ gripped tightly onto the handle of the riding crop, brought back his right arm, and slammed the riding crop down hard onto her quivering buttocks. Her body jerked violently and she screamed 'ouch'. From a nearby dresser, Russ's mobile phone was carefully recording every second of Abbie Steele indulging in her favourite bondage fantasy.

❖

CHAPTER SIXTY ONE

Saturday 2ⁿᵈ July 2022

Anna eased herself gently out of the passenger seat of Nick's car and placed her feet on the driveway to his house. Her left ankle was still bruised around the ankle bone and along her left foot, an artist's palette of red/deep purple and tinges of yellow, but the initial swelling had subsided. It was still painful to put her weight on, but the hospital doctor's instruction was to try to walk as normally as possible, without the aid of crutches. Nick got out of the car and walked around to her to try to assist.

'What can I do to help?' he asked, his anxious eyes assessing her.

'Can you hold my arm to help me up so I don't put too much weight on my left foot,' Anna instructed him, frustrated at how this type of injury can impact on your life. There was also the issue of the bang to her head. The area at the base of her skull, where her head had hit the car park, had been repaired with medical glue. This meant no hair washing or styling for the past five days and her hair had reverted to its wavy, slightly drier norm. The other injuries, mainly grazes to her left hand, arm and leg were healing, scabbed over, still with red and purple bruising. All her injuries could make her flinch from time to time, if she moved suddenly, or knocked them. She was still prone to low grade headaches but she had cut down on taking paracetamol to the occasional one or two.

Nick gently took hold of her lower arm and helped her stand. 'Ok, nana, let's go,' he joked as she slowly made her way into his house. It was early evening and she'd arrived in time for him to prepare dinner. Her father had been caring for her all week but she had sent him home this morning after insisting that she was now alright to look after herself. Dad was happy that she would now be staying at Nick's until at least Sunday evening.

Anna shuffled into the kitchen/dining area, going 'ouch' as she put weight on her ankle. 'Sorry,' she said, glancing at Nick, 'I sound pathetic making this noise when it's only a bit of bruising but it does hurt and makes me wince.'

Nick stopped to gaze at her troubled face. 'Hey, sweetheart, don't apologise. You've been hurt by some female maniac driving a car at you. Why don't you sit on a stool by the hob so that you can watch the master chef at work making his signature dish of beef tacos.' He pulled a stool away from the kitchen island and placed it to the left of the hob. Anna struggled to get onto the stool, cautious of knocking her ankle and suddenly strong arms lifted her up. As he placed her carefully on the stool, he leaned forward to kiss her, softly at first, but then with passion. It was wonderful to be in his arms, the sense of safety it brought her after enduring her week of pain, and if she were honest, of fear. In her rational moments, she believed that she had been unlucky, the victim of poor driving, and the driver had panicked and scarpered when they realised what they had done. In other moments, she thought about the anonymous texts she had received about 'dark forces' and wondered if what happened was not a random accident but that she had been deliberately targeted. Police were still investigating the matter including checking for any CCTV at the supermarket.

Breaking off the kiss, Nick's hands gently cupped her chin as he gazed into her eyes. 'I'm so glad that you're here. That I can see for myself that you are ok. I've been worried sick about you.' His right thumb gently rubbed her jawline as his eyes searched her face. Biting the inside of her lip, Anna was trying not to cry but the trauma of the past week washed over her like a tsunami and she started to sob. Nick held her tightly against him, as the tears flowed, and he gave comfort by stroking her back. 'It's ok, let it out,' he urged her.

After what seemed liked forever, she did manage to stop, but continued to hiccup, and she was still cocooned in the security of his arms. 'T-thanks, N-nick, for your support. It means a lot. I've tried not to cry around dad as I didn't want to upset him. Now, I'm upsetting you.'

Nick gently raised her head, ran his thumbs under her eyes to dry her tears, and stated, 'Anna, look at me. You've been badly hurt and things could've been a lot worse. You've suffered a number of injuries and had a massive shock. Do not think you cannot cry in front of me.' Once he was assured that she was ok, he went to the fridge to get wine and beer. 'Right, miss, I am offering wine but you will be going easy as you're still recovering from a head injury, ok?'

'Yes, boss,' she laughed, as she reached for her bag for a tissue and her powder compact case to try to discreetly repair the damage to her tear-stained face whilst he prepared the dinner.

Nick was soon chopping onions and garlic which went into a non-stick frying pan with a drizzle of olive oil and were softened over a low heat. 'Ok, my sous-chef, you can stir that whilst I chop the iceberg lettuce and tomatoes to accompany the tacos.'

Anna was pleased to have something to contribute after a week of lying around and inactivity under her father's strict regime. 'Thanks for letting me help. I love my dad to bits but I've been going mad as he wouldn't let me do a thing except lie on the sofa with my foot elevated. This was also to ensure that I didn't aggravate my head injury. I was not allowed to do anything but it's irritating when you know there are jobs that need doing around the house.' Once the onions and garlic were softened and slightly browned, Anna added the minced beef to the pan to be cooked.

Nick paused from chopping the salad items to address Anna, a stern expression on his face. 'Ok, Miss Louden, let's get one thing straight. Your father is a wonderful man who I totally respect. He has cared for you well all week but he has now passed that job to me. Under my regime, you will be taking things carefully, not aggravating your head or ankle injuries, not overdoing the alcohol, and definitely no jobs. Just keep stirring the pan, ok?'

'Yes, boss, again. And, my annoying Gordon Ramsey, head chef, in my humble opinion we now need to add the spices.' Anna enjoyed watching as he finished the dish by adding a mixture of spices including oregano, cumin, paprika, and chilli powder. Once the minced beef and ingredients were cooked, he loaded them onto taco shells, covered them with grated cheese, and placed them to bake in the oven. Anna sipped the refreshing wine and the food smelt spicy and appetising. It was the first time since her accident that she had felt hungry. All in all, being here with Nick, the wine and the food were truly comforting after her ordeal. He laid the table with placemats, cutlery and small bowls containing shredded iceberg lettuce, chopped tomato, chopped onion, grated cheese, sour cream and guacamole. He lit a white candle which released scents of peony, rose and honeysuckle into the room to do battle with the aroma of Mexican spices. Nick came over to Anna and placed his arms around her, his eyes carefully scrutinising her face. 'Are you feeling ok now?'

Anna nodded. 'Yes, I am. All this is really helping. I feel relaxed for the first time this week and it's great to be here with you, just the two of us.'

'Time to eat, I think. I am offering my restaurant's bespoke carrying service but only to my favourite and most beautiful customers.' To Anna's surprise and delight, he lifted her off the stool and carried her to a dining chair.

The tacos were tasty, a brilliant combination of browned mince, onion, garlic, piquant spices and melted cheese in crunchy taco shells with added extras of lettuce, sour cream, guacamole and so on. Anna managed two, the most she had eaten in a meal all week. Having finished the food, she sipped her wine, pleasantly full, though her ankle was beginning to ache and she'd need to elevate it soon.

Their peace was disturbed as Nick's phone rang. He said 'sorry' to Anna and went to turn it off but she encouraged him to take the call. 'Hello, Abbie,' he answered and Anna watched his face become angry. Anna could hear Abbie speaking as Nick listened, though Anna could not discern what Abbie was saying. Whatever it was, wasn't pleasing Nick, whose jaw tensed, brow furrowed and cool blue eyes turned icy. When he spoke, his voice was controlled but loud. 'Ok, Abbie. Stop talking. You're gabbling and I can't really get what you're trying to say. I hope that there is a genuine reason for this call and it's not some half-baked scheme just to talk to me and waste my time.'

Whilst Anna listened to Nick's direct approach, his probable boss-voice, she felt a little bit sorry for Abbie. But then why was she calling?

As Abbie prattled on, Nick interrupted. 'Right. You want to speak to me in person? I haven't the faintest idea what this is about but if the matter is that urgent then you can come over here tomorrow evening, about eight p.m.' This designated time seemed to suit Abbie and the phone call ended quickly after that.

'Well, what the hell does she want?' Nick asked, more to himself than to Anna. 'God, that woman is a complete pain in the ass. She told me at Granddad Bill's party that she had moved on. She has a new boyfriend, deluded fool that he is. What can she possibly want?'

Anna didn't really want to comment. It was none of her business really but she hoped it wouldn't affect her relationship with Nick. Anna could not deny that she was developing strong feelings for Nick Carlton. But she still felt fragile after the fall-out from her relationship with Alistair. She was really scared of getting hurt again, even if it would only be emotionally this time. This Abbie seemed to be having a hard time letting go of Nick and Anna didn't want to be the one discarded if he decided to return to his past girlfriend.

Nick must have noticed the anguish on her face as he commented, 'Anna, do not worry about her. Hell would have to freeze over before I took that woman back in my life. She's the biggest mistake I've ever made. Now, I'm going to clear up in here. You can go in the sitting room, rest your ankle, and drink your wine. I shall once again offer the restaurant's bespoke service of carrying customers to their destination.' Before Anna could object, he had picked her up off the chair.

'I only bruised my ankle on Monday, I can still walk you know,' Anna chided him but secretly she loved to put her arms around his neck as he carried her to the sitting room. 'I think it's just a ploy to get your hands on my body.'

As he kissed her softly, he responded, 'You got me. You know I always want to make love to you whenever I get the chance but tonight we may need to put that on hold. I wouldn't want to hurt you whilst you're recovering from your injuries.' In the sitting room she was gently deposited on the sofa and he placed her left foot on a cushion. 'I'll be back shortly.'

Anna picked up the television remote control and flicked through channels absent-mindedly looking for something to watch. But she couldn't concentrate as she thought of Nick meeting with Abbie tomorrow. It probably wasn't anything but Anna could not shake off the feeling that Abbie's phone call, and subsequent meeting with him, was going to bring more trouble to their door.

CHAPTER SIXTY TWO

Sunday 3rd July 2022

Having driven Anna home half an hour ago, Nick sat on the sofa, staring at his phone, waiting for Abbie to arrive. His sole objective now was that Abbie should arrive on time, discuss whatever the issue was, and get her to depart quickly. His phone alerted him to her arrival and he went to open the front door. He greeted her in a neutral tone, not wanting her to think he was pleased to see her. 'Hi, Abbie. Come in.'

Nick escorted her into the sitting room. 'Take a seat.'

Abbie was dressed casually in grey, zip-front sweatshirt and black jeans. Her appearance was more subdued than normal, no false eyelashes and talon nails. There was little evidence of make-up as her skin was pale with a sprinkling of pink spots. There was a puffiness to her face and her hair was greasy. She sat on one end of the corner sofa and smiled, weakly, at him. 'Hi, Nick. Good to see you.' She glanced over, then looked away. The usual Abbie confidence seemed to be absent.

As he gazed over at her, Nick now had to control any anger he was feeling, but it was hard. He wished that this woman would take the hint and disappear out of his life for good. 'Ok, Abbie, cut to the chase, what do you want?'

She sighed deeply and bit her top lip. 'I've got something to tell you and I don't know how you'll take it.' Another deep intake of breath before she spoke, 'I've recently found out that I'm pregnant, Nick, and it's your baby.'

This declaration sent a seismic shockwave through Nick. 'Pregnant? We've not been together since April. How many weeks pregnant, are you?'

'About thirteen weeks. I had a scan last week which confirmed it. This would put the date of conception to the beginning of April which was when I was with you,' she confirmed and a hint of a smile touched her lips.

'As I recall, you have frequently referred to your dislike of babies and children. What do you propose to do about this pregnancy?' Nick asked. It was a difficult question for him. If this baby had been conceived with a woman he loved, a woman like Anna, he would be over the moon at the prospect of being a father. To be linked by parenthood to a woman he despised was a truly chilling possibility. But at the heart of this was a baby, a child, that was a part of him, and he did not think he could abandon it.

Abbie fixed her eyes on him. 'I don't know. You are right, I'm not fond of kids. The thought of having to bring up one on my own fills me with dread. It will be hard to do my job with a kid to care for as a lot of my work is at weekends. I doubt if I can rely on my mum for regular support. I've not made my mind up on whether to keep it or not. Basically, I've come here to find out what you think.'

Nick rubbed his forehead, already feeling a headache developing. 'I don't know what to think. It's all a big shock. Sure, I like kids and if it's my child I would want to help look after it.'

The placid expression on Abbie's face disappeared instantly. A brightness touched her eyes. Nick could not help but think that this plan of hers had now born fruit. 'That's good to know, Nick. It will help towards making my decision as to whether I keep it or not. Are you talking about financial help?'

Typical Abbie, thinking that money was the most important thing in all of this. 'Yes,' he responded, 'money would be one way that I would want to support my'... he paused to emphasis the word 'my'...'child but I would like to be a hands-on dad and have some involvement in its upbringing.' This declaration of his intent may be a little bit premature at this early stage of the pregnancy but Nick wanted to be clear from the start what he thought his parenting role would be.

This seemed to please Abbie. 'Of course, Nick, I would not stop you from seeing your child. I'm sure we can work everything out.'

'Yes, Abbie, this is all very civilised. The big question is, how have you got pregnant? We discussed contraception during our relationship and you were taking the pill, so how did this happen?' Nick asked her, ready to watch how she reacted.

Abbie's face flashed, momentarily, to show anxiety as her brow furrowed. 'I must have missed a couple of pills, perhaps due to overdoing the booze at the time. I then carried on taking the pill as usual, not realising that I was pregnant. I admit to feeling a bit off over the last few months but I put that down to the fallout from the end of our relationship. I've been tired, putting on weight through eating badly, and my skin's terrible but I thought this just related to feeling miserable.' She now gave him a weak smile and Nick guessed that this was her ploy to make him feel sorry for her. 'I only decided to do a pregnancy test recently when a friend suggested that this could be what was wrong with me. We'd been discussing my general lethargy and fat stomach.'

'You say that you've had a scan?' Nick commented. 'Have you got a photo?'

This caused her expression to go to one of annoyance. 'What's up, Nick, do you want proof? Typical of you men, don't mind sticking your cock into a woman, but then don't want to believe it when that action has consequences.' She picked up her bag, took a photograph out of it and leaned over to give it to Nick.

As Nick took hold of the photo his hand shook. The black and white scan photo, dated 27-Jun-2022, showed a twelve week fully formed baby-to-be. The scan photo was from Warwick Hospital and mother-to-be, Abigail Steele. This in front of Nick's eyes was possibly his son or daughter. This should be the most joyous moment of his life and he did feel emotional but also conflicted. There were a lot of reasons not to trust Abbie. Had she slept with other men besides him when they were together? Was this a real scan photograph of his baby or fake photo she had got off the internet? The bottom line was that he did not trust Abbie one little bit. Nevertheless, it didn't stop him feeling like he'd had a real kick in the guts as he gazed at the scan photo. If this were real, it would alter the course of his life. And forever tie him to this woman who he did not even like. It could also seriously affect his relationship with Anna. They were still in the early, fragile days of their budding relationship but he knew, without doubt, that he did not want to lose her.

Nick handed the photo back to Abbie. 'Was the baby's physical development ok for this stage of pregnancy? I know from Alyssa that you've been drinking a lot recently and any alcohol can seriously affect a baby's development. You were drunk and abusive on Alyssa's birthday at the Frizzy Lion. And you were smoking outside the pub before you went in. If you decide to keep this baby, all the drinking, smoking and cocaine need to stop now.'

Abbie scowled at him. 'Fucking typical of you. Wanting to control me. But I cut out all the bad vices once I found out I was up the duff.' She then slipped across the sofa to sit nearer to Nick. 'As I said earlier, I've not made a decision about whether to keep it or not. If I do keep it, it may be the push we need to get us back together. We could be a little family unit, you, me and baby Carlton. If it's a boy I like the name Aristotle, so that he grows up brainy. For a girl, Serenity.'

Nick cringed inwardly. This was typical Abbie, giving a child the burden of a ridiculous name. He joked, 'With a name like Aristotle, let's hope little Ari is bright. Let's hope Serenity is calm and not a hot-headed diva.'

Abbie giggled, not realising he was mocking her. She gazed fondly at Nick. 'A hot-headed diva, just like her mother. See, Nick, we can still have a laugh together. And I know you'd make a great dad.'

Standing up now, Nick went to close down this discussion and get her to go. 'You need to seriously think about whether you want to keep this baby or not. This is a massive issue, Abbie, and not one to be taken lightly. If you do keep the baby, I would fulfil my financial responsibilities and would like to be involved in its upbringing. But Abbie, to be crystal clear, there is absolutely no chance of us being together as a couple. None. Make your decision based on what is best for you, as a single parent. Let me know what you decide and we can take it from there. Anna is in my life now and I do see a future with her.'

This mention of Anna riled Abbie. She picked up her bag and got up off the sofa but then winced in pain, letting out an 'ouch' sound.

Nick felt compelled to ask, 'What's up with you?'

Abbie's avoided eye contact with him as her face flushed red. 'N-nothing. Just a bit of an overenthusiastic session with my new man and the riding crop. He's very dominating.'

Nick shook his head in disgust. 'For God's sake woman, you've just told me you're pregnant. I think you need to lay off the kink stuff for the sake of the baby.'

'Thanks, Nick, for the advice,' Abbie sneered. 'Changing the subject, I heard through Alyssa that your girlfriend had an accident. Not too badly hurt, I take it?'

Nick felt anger flooding through him as he noted the dismissive tone in Abbie's voice. 'No, luckily, she's was not too badly hurt. She was the victim of a hit-and-run by a white car driven by a female driver in a supermarket car park.' As Nick gave the details to Abbie; he watched her face closely to gauge her reaction. Was it his imagination or did she blush slightly? 'The police are checking the CCTV in the car park to try to identify the car and driver.' Nick knew this wasn't exactly true as he had been to the car park to check out any CCTV cameras in the vicinity of where Anna was hit. There were no cameras in that area. 'I'm sure the police will soon know who knocked her down.'

'G-good,' Abbie stuttered, and Nick was sure that she blushed more deeply. 'Yeah, tough shit, getting knocked down.'

'I'm not sure it was tough shit, as in bad luck. A witness at the scene informed the police that the driver seemed to deliberately drive into Anna and then sped off. When this person is caught, I hope they are charged with ABH and dangerous driving. A nice stay in prison is just what they need.'

The redness in Abbie's cheeks suddenly paled and she gulped. 'Anyway, I'd better go. I'll be in touch when I've made a decision about the baby. Knowing that you would support the kid will be a big factor in this decision.'

His eyes bore into hers as he stated, firmly, 'I don't want any of your bullshit with this, Abbie. For you to get my support, you need to be straight with me. No lies. And I will repeat myself again, you and I will not be getting back together.'

'Ok, Nick,' Abbie sighed, 'I hear you. Don't flatter yourself. I'm actually getting into my new man. You're not the only fish in the sea. So, suck it up you arrogant bastard.'

After Abbie had gone, Nick thought about the hand grenade she had thrown into his life. For now, he would accept what she was saying but he did not trust Abbie one bit. Was she pregnant? Was the baby his? Yes, he did want a child in the future, but he wanted a child with a woman he loved. That would not be Abbie.

CHAPTER SIXTY THREE

Monday 4th July 2022

Anna felt exhausted after her first day back at work after the car incident. Sitting at a desk all day was tiring and a headache developed mid-afternoon. She cleared it with her boss, Jack, to leave early. But she did not feel like pushing a trolley around a supermarket and made do with baked beans on toast for dinner. Her ankle was now swollen and she was sitting propped up on the sofa with a cushion under her foot. Waiting for Nick to arrive. He had texted earlier that he wanted to speak to her about Abbie's visit to him, yesterday. This all sounded a bit ominous to her. Was he coming to say that he was resuming his relationship with Abbie? She didn't think this was likely but why did the most ludicrous ideas pop into your head when you were anxious?

Anna's phone alerted her to his presence and she went to let him in. Nick was dressed in white, long-sleeved shirt rolled up to the elbow, with cream trousers. She was surprised at his slightly dishevelled look; crumpled shirt, his beard not quite so trimmed, and a greyness around his eyes. As he entered the hallway, he looked at her, pulled her to him and pecked her cheek. This was all lovely but his usual greeting was a passionate kiss not this 'saying hello to grannie' version.

'I need to talk to you,' Nick stated, as he led the way into her living room. Anna hobbled along behind him as her ankle was now painful after a long day. Nick sat on her sofa and she sat next to him but not touching. Whatever he was going to say didn't feel as if it was a time for intimate contact. He turned to look directly at her, a sadness in his eyes. Clearing his throat, he said, 'Abbie informed me yesterday that she's thirteen weeks pregnant with my baby, apparently.'

'Apparently,' Anna mimicked, 'what do you mean?'

'That she was with me at the time the baby was conceived at about the beginning of April,' he stated, rubbing his forehead gently. 'I say, apparently, as I do wonder if she was completely faithful to me for the time we were together. She liked to brag about men she met at parties. It was a tactic to make me jealous which never worked. I suppose it boils down to the fact that I just don't trust her.'

'Oh dear, Nick,' Anna shook her head. 'What is she planning to do, is she going to have the baby?

'She hasn't made a decision yet. An abortion could still be on the cards as Abbie is not exactly the maternal type. She came around yesterday to give me the news and find out my reaction. I told her that I would offer financial support and would want to be involved in the care of my child. I've got to be fair to this baby who didn't ask to be born,' Nick sighed loudly, running his fingers through his hair. 'But it's all a bloody shock and a mess. This is not the way I planned to start a family. I had an old-fashioned plan of being in love with the child's mother at the time.'

Anna felt she could cry at seeing the anguish on his face. He was truly conflicted. Nick was a good man, wanting to fulfil his parental responsibilities to his own child, but he knew that the child would bind him to Abbie for the rest of their lives.

'Abbie was strongly hinting that she hoped we could get back together for the sake of the baby.' He laughed hysterically. 'We'd be a family, me, Abbie, baby Aristotle or Serenity. There's no way on God's Earth that a son of mine will be called Aristotle or a daughter will be called Serenity.'

To try and take some of the despair out of the situation, Anna joked, 'I've always liked ancient Greek names, Achilles for a boy and Persephone for a girl.'

'Remind me not to have a kid with you then,' he teased but this comment obviously took him back to the nub of the situation he was in with Abbie, if the sadness on his face was anything to go by. 'Come here, Anna,' he requested as he pulled her into his arms. He cupped her chin with his fingers, his eyes holding hers, as he kissed her tenderly. 'As far as I'm concerned this doesn't change what we have. There is no way that I am getting back with Abbie.'

The kiss made Anna's heart ache with love for him and she felt a longing in her belly. He went to kiss her again but she pulled away. 'It will change what we have. If our relationship continues, there will be two more people in our lives for good. Your child and its mother.'

'Yes, I know, Anna, but it's you I want to be with,' Nick insisted, looking concerned and a little cross as she shifted away from him on the sofa.

Anna could feel tears welling in her eyes but she was not going to cry. She wanted to be with this amazing man but he was going to have a child with another woman. It may be best all round that she allowed him some space to think things through and give him the opportunity of resuming his relationship with Abbie for the sake of their child. 'I love being with you, Nick. I'm really happy when we spend time together. But you must think of the baby. I know that lots of single mothers do a great job but a child does benefit from having two parents who live together. Perhaps you should reconsider your relationship with Abbie for the sake of your child.'

'Hold on, Anna, you're letting this run away with you,' he stated, lightly holding her hand to get her attention. 'Firstly, Abbie could simply have an abortion and this will all go away. This is very likely as a baby would seriously limit her hedonistic lifestyle. Secondly, even if she decides to have the baby as a way of keeping close to me, I will never resume a relationship with her. If I get involved in caring for the child, I would keep my contact with Abbie to a minimum.'

'That might not be as easy as you think. Abbie is a very single-minded individual and I think she will use the child as a way of getting back into your life,' Anna commented, a sadness touching her eyes which he noticed.

'She can be manipulative but as I keep stressing, I will never go back into a relationship with her,' Nick emphasised, 'I don't care for her or like her.'

'Yes, but you will be in regular contact to discuss child care issues. She'll be contacting you when the baby's ill, about medical appointments, nursery pick-ups, and so on. You'll be a dad and mum sharing the parenting responsibilities for their child. Your feelings towards her may change,' Anna said, then partly regretted it. It was as if she was doing her best to drive him away even before the baby was born. A self-protection mechanism to stop herself being hurt in the future.

'Oh dear,' Nick groaned, 'This baby hasn't arrived yet and it's already coming between us. I want to be with you, Anna. Please understand that.' He moved closer to her, leaning over her to kiss her softly and gaze into her troubled eyes, 'it will always be you, Anna.'

Anna felt her treacherous body respond to his exploration of her mouth. Emotionally, she was not ready to make love as thoughts of Abbie and her unborn child plagued her mind. Images of him having sex with a laughing, smirking Abbie to conceive this baby flicked through her head. Anna stopped responding to him and disengaged from his kiss. 'I can't do this at the moment, Nick. There's too much to get my head around.' She could not avoid seeing the hurt in his blue eyes.

He moved away from her and they both sat on the sofa, not touching. 'I'll go in a minute. You're probably exhausted after your first day back at work. How was it by the way?'

'I worked till about four p.m. but by then my head was aching so I asked to leave early. It was ok, overall. But I'll admit to being tired now,' she stated, feeling genuinely ready to go to bed, alone.

Nick gave her a soft kiss on her mouth. 'Don't worry about Abbie and the baby, nothing is going to happen for a long time.'

After he had gone, Anna knew that she had handled the whole conversation about Abbie and the baby all wrong. He was right, she was getting troubled about a baby that may not even be born. But Anna had to admit that the thought of a child connecting Nick and Abbie for eternity was not an easy prospect to consider. Abbie made her dislike of her crystal clear on their first occasion by drenching her in wine and, on the second encounter, by trying to do the same thing again. Anna concluded that Abbie was aggressive and unstable. This was not a great endorsement for a mother-to-be and someone who Anna would want to have on-going contact with through Nick, if Abbie gave birth to their child.

◆◆◆◆◆

CHAPTER SIXTY FOUR

Tuesday 5th July 2022

For Luke, the last eight days since Anna's car incident had been an awful time. He missed her so much. The anticipation of seeing his beloved Anna at the end of a tiring and boring working day was the tiny bit of joy in a lacklustre life. Knowing that she had been injured by a car and taken to hospital meant that she would need time off work to recuperate. Thus she would not be calling at the supermarket for her food shopping. Yesterday, Luke hoped that she might be back to her normal routine but there was no sign of her. Maybe today would be the day. He had been irritable all last week to the extent that Russ threatened to punch him and his father was tempted to throw him out of the house.

Today, Luke was hanging around the fruit and vegetable section, praying that she would come in. After a half an hour of loitering near the cucumbers, and celery, he had to move on before curious shoppers called security to have him removed for having a fetish for hard, green vegetables. Then he spotted her, dressed in a short-sleeved, red/floral dress, looking as fresh and summery as a poppy field. Luke's heart leapt with joy. A bright smile illuminated his face. He'd worked out how he was going to approach her and was not going to hesitate in case he lost sight of her in the store. Turning his trolley around, he strolled towards her. 'Hi, Anna. I've not seen you for a while. Everything ok?'

A welcoming smile touched her pretty blue eyes. 'Oh, hi. Yeah, I've been off work for a bit,' she explained. 'I was knocked over by a car, in the car park here, last Monday.'

Luke had to feign surprise but the shock in his voice was genuine. 'I'm so sorry. What happened?'

'A car entering the parking area drove into me as I was putting the trolley away,' Anna stated, 'but I don't really remember much until I came round at the hospital. A woman witnessed the whole thing and thought that the car drove at me deliberately. A female driver in a white car who then drove off without stopping.'

Luke could feel his cheeks redden with anger as she described this. 'Well, I hope the police catch the scum that did it. Were you badly hurt?' His eyes scrutinised her face, looking for signs of bruising or scabbing but her beautiful face did not appear to have been marked. Thank goodness.

'I hit the back of my head as I landed and bruised my left ankle. Luckily, neither injury was too serious. I was left with some cuts and grazes to my left hand, lower arm and left leg.' She turned over her left hand and he could see yellow bruising with areas of purple below her thumb.

'Head injuries can be very serious, are you ok now?' he asked, distress apparent on his face.

'Yes, thanks,' she smiled having noted his concern. 'I was lucky that it was a minor bump and there'll be no lasting damage. Some may say that there's little left to harm,' she joked.

'They would be idiots as I know you are very bright,' he teased. 'Anyway, I'm really glad that you are ok. Now, could you spare me ten minutes as I need to update you on my charity dog walking with little Milly? Perhaps I could buy you a coffee again?' Luke noted that she hesitated before agreeing. 'Would you like a latte like the last time?'

In the café, Luke was quickly back with two lattes as the place was nearly empty. He sat opposite her so that he could enjoy her perfect beauty as she drank her coffee. There was a little white heart etched on the top of the coffee and he hoped that she'd recognise it as a token to demonstrate his love for her. She took a sip of the coffee and a trace of the white froth remained on her upper lip. This looked so cute and so enticing that he yearned to lick it off. He wished that he could take a photograph to gaze at later. 'Ok, about walking Milly. I'm afraid that the challenge is off. Poor Milly was attacked by another dog at a local park and is out of action. This brown mongrel, off a lead, rushed up to Milly. It snarled at her, she yelped, and the dog bit her on her front left leg.' Luke showed Anna some heart-melting photos on his phone that he'd found online of 'Milly' looking sad-eyed due to a bandaged leg and a plastic cone. Luke watched carefully as Anna's lovely face registered her pain for Milly's suffering.

'Poor Milly. Neither of us had a good week. We should form a survivors club,' Anna laughed, 'and you can be an honorary member.'

Luke continued to stare at her, then commented, 'I would be the loyal carer to two beautiful females. You and Milly.' He noticed Anna blanch a little at this remark, so he changed the subject. 'Anyway, dog walking is now not an option to raise funds for Age UK. I am now going to try to raise funds with another event. My family's garden will be open to the public on Sunday, 17th July. A number of gardens in the nearby village will be open and people can have a mooch around all of them. I can't claim to be the gardener, that's my dad's area of expertise, but he's decided to go away on holiday and I said I'd do the garden opening, as planned. Admission is by ticket and I will be selling cakes and white wine as well. Any money raised will go to Age UK.'

Anna looked mildly interested. 'I can't say that I'm a keen gardener but I do love flowers and plants and it's for a good cause. Where do I get a ticket?'

'You can get a ticket at my garden which will admit you into all the other gardens,' Luke explained. He took out of his pocket an information sheet that he had prepared about the 'Sherbourne Open Gardens event on Sunday, 17th July 2022. It invited those interested to visit a number of delightful, mature gardens stocked with flowering plants, herbaceous borders, roses, vegetable patches etc. Details of ticket prices, programmes, charity beneficiaries and refreshments available were all given. Pictures of roses, lavenders, sweet peas, cornflowers and sunflowers all added authenticity to the information sheet. 'It would be lovely to have your support for a good cause. Hopefully, Aunt Daisy will bring Milly for a short visit. Give me your phone number so I can call you if it's called off for any reason. Save you a wasted journey.'

'Yes, ok,' Anna commented. 'It's a shame my boyfriend can't come as he's working over that weekend and would not be available. I'd have to come on my own.'

Luke's elation at the prospect of her visiting his house/ garden on that Sunday, on her own, made him giddy with excitement. He smiled pleasantly at her. 'Don't worry about being on your own. There are lots of single ladies who come along to admire the gardens and have a sneaky glass of wine. You won't be out of place. Anyway, it would be lovely to see you on the day. And don't forget you may get to meet Milly.'

They quickly finished their coffees and went back to do their shopping. Luke continued to watch her as she went over to a display selling strawberries and cream to help celebrate the Wimbledon fortnight. As she selected a punnet of strawberries to place in her basket a handsome man with brown hair and beard stood very close to her and started a conversation. A rush of jealousy ripped through Luke's body. He hurried over, near to the strawberry section, to listen to what was being said.

The man said, "You must be a strawberry because you're so red hot.'

Anna shook her head slightly, as the man gave her his best cheeky smile. 'That's a bit corny,' she joked before putting a punnet of strawberries in her basket along with a small carton of single cream.

'Yeah,' said the man, 'but it got you talking to me. And you do look like a delicious strawberry in your pretty dress. Come on a date with me and I'll feed you strawberries all night.'

'A date would be great. Just buy enough strawberries for three so that my boyfriend can come along as well,' Anna stated, as she smiled at the guy. The man's expression changed from hopeful to defeated when he heard this.

'Well, I'm Max. If you get bored with him you know I'll take you out. Once you have heard all my best fruit and veg jokes, you will be begging me for more. If I give you my number will you promise to kale me?'

Anna laughed and walked away to continue her shopping. Luke sidled up to the man as Anna headed off. Picking up a carton of cream, he eased up the top and then pretended to lose his grip on the carton, sending single cream over the man's shopping in his trolley. 'Oops, sorry,' Luke said, noting an angry scowl on the man's face. 'The top was loose. I'll go and get something to clean this mess,' before he quickly headed off in another direction. Luke was chuckling to himself that he had seen off a rival. Idiots who tried to move in on his beloved would be dealt with.

⚜

CHAPTER SIXTY FIVE

Saturday 9th July 2022

A Saturday evening and Russ was out with Abbie at a town centre pub in Leamington Spa. It was one of only a few times when they had actually gone out as a couple. The day had been hot and sunny, and the evening was warm, so the outside area was rammed full with pub goers, some seated, but most were standing close together, jostling for space. Abbie was dressed in blue denim micro-shorts and dusky pink T-shirt. Her hair was all golden wavy tresses and her makeup was bold, with over red plump lips, that she kept licking, which suggested recent lip fillers. They were both seated on stools at a high table, Russ with a pint of lager, Abbie with white wine from a bottle she had purchased. This was a very animated Abbie who, Russ suspected, had been drinking before she came out. Casually smoking a cigarette, she caught the attention of men in the surrounding area and lapped it up as they gazed at her. All this wasn't really pleasing Russ. 'What's up with you this evening? You're acting as if you've suddenly won the lottery.'

Abbie gave him a smirky look. 'Maybe I have. I went round to my ex's house last Sunday and dropped my bombshell on him. I told him that I'm thirteen weeks pregnant with his kid. God, it was great to see the surprise and confusion on his handsome face.'

Russ eyed her across the table as he supped his lager. 'Pregnant? Is this a scam or what? You're sat here drinking from a bottle of wine and smoking a fag. I know that pregnant women should avoid booze, fags and drugs. Are you deliberately putting the kid at risk?'

Abbie gave Russ an innocent look. 'Scam? I've shown him the twelve week scan photo of little baby Carlton. I think he fell in love with it straightaway. Says he'll give me financial support and help with childcare. What more could I ask for?'

Russ shook his head. He'd met some crazy women in his time but this one must be the craziest. 'I really don't know what you're playing at. Are you pretending to be pregnant to get his attention? Or are you really pregnant and hoping that this will get you back with him?'

As she was showing signs of intoxication, her eyes squinted and she wagged her finger at him. 'Wouldn't you like to know, Russie, babe. But at least I've taken my revenge on him and the drippy cow in two ways. Firstly, I caused her to have a little accident. Secondly, there might be a howling, pooing baby on the way to disturb their cosy existence. Good old Nick will do the decent thing and want to help support his baby. The drippy girlfriend will have to put up with me disrupting his life at a moment's notice with childcare-related emergencies. All good.'

Russ scowled at her, still not sure what she was doing. 'Well, that's up to you. It might mean the end of us as I don't want anything to do with a squawking kid.' So far with Leanne he had avoided any real contact with her two boys, though he had met them on one occasion for an hour before their nan picked them up. After ten minutes of them trying to show him their toys and get his attention, Russ had escaped to the garden for a smoke.

To Russ's surprise, this seemed to upset Abbie. 'Don't worry, Russ. It won't be anything to do with you. And we've always agreed, we're just fuck buddies, that's all. Just in it for the sex. We're cut from the same cloth. We don't do commitment, don't like people much and take what we can get. Live for the here and now, not the future.' This was all said with an air of defiance but Russ could not help but note a sadness in her eyes.

Russ laughed. 'Well, I'm no fortune teller but if you are pregnant then I predict the next eighteen years are going to be pretty busy.' Russ finished the last of his pint and got off the stool. 'I'm going to get another drink. I see you're ok with the wine.'

Inside the pub, it was heaving, and trying to get served at the bar was a nightmare which didn't improve Russ's temper. What he wanted with Abbie was a good time, no hassle, and no fricking baby. Especially a baby that was conceived with a man that Russ could definitely hate. Nick Carlton was not only good-looking but according to Abbie he ran a successful business, owned a large, detached house and drove a flash Audi. He was also dating the beautiful Anna.

Eventually, Russ struggled back to the outside area with a pint and whisky chaser. Sitting on his stool was a male talking to Abbie, who was listening intently to what he was saying and laughing at the appropriate place. The male was mid-twenties, fair-haired, which was short at the sides and a flop of curls on top. A spider tattoo crept out of his T-shirt and up his neck. Russ plonked his drinks on the table and addressed the man. 'Shift. I was sitting there.'

Abbie recognised the anger on Russ's face and quickly said, 'Russ, this is Josh. He's a DJ I know from my work in events planning. Got a night off, haven't you, J?'

Josh moved off the stool and stood close to Abbie. 'Yeah, it's great not to be working, as it's been non-stop for weeks. It's also good to see my favourite party girl.' He winked at Abbie who flashed him a smile with a lot of pouting due to the lip fillers. 'Remember that party at the house in Stratford for the son's twenty-first. We kept meeting up to snort a line in the downstairs toilet. The last time we went to go in, the door was unlocked, and the birthday kid's dad was inside shagging a woman. OMFG.'

Abbie shrieked with laughter and nearly over balanced off the high stool. 'God, yeah. Gross. Do you remember the one where the birthday kid was so hammered he fell on the buffet table and landed face down in the chocolate fountain. Just stayed there licking it up.'

Russ gazed at his phone as Abbie and DJ Josh kept the stories going. Abbie drained the last of the wine from the bottle into her glass, then placed it on the table. 'Hey, Russ, babe. Get us another of these, will you.' Lips pouted and eyelashes fluttered to positively assist her request.

'If you're going to the bar, get us a lager, mate,' Josh requested, a cocky smirk on his face.

Russ slowly looked up from his phone. 'Go and get your own drink. Do I look like your fucking servant.' He got off the stool and said to Abbie. 'I'm going to the bog.' When he came back, Russ would be sending this muppet on his merry way.

On arriving back at the outside table, Russ discovered that Abbie and the DJ had disappeared and two people were sitting at their table. Russ's eyes searched the pub for Abbie but she wasn't in the immediate area. Anger flooded him, not because he missed the little bitch, but because she'd swanned off without telling him.

⸺◈⸺

CHAPTER SIXTY SIX

Saturday 9ᵗʰ July 2022

Nick had just texted Anna that he was waiting for her outside the Frizzy Lion so that they could get a cab together. He'd been out with Ed, Ethan, Justin and a few others for a curry night and avoided the Frizzy Lion afterwards to give Anna time out with her friends. The pub was closing at just past midnight and people spilled out in pairs or groups, all boozed up, and in a party mood. Nick lingered by the door of the pub, enduring a few wolf whistles and leers from young women who passed by.

'Hi there, babe,' a young dark-haired female addressed him, as she wiggled towards him in short pink miniskirt, low-cut white top and white, high-heeled shoes. 'Wanna go for a drink with me?' Very long black lashes batted at him whilst she pouted with all the might of her lip fillers. Her mate, blonde and petite, in white vest top and wide-legged red trousers, offered her own sexy invitation. 'We can get a cab, the three of us, and have some fun.'

Nick was thinking never in a million years but smiled politely at the two temptresses. 'Thanks for the offer girls, another time perhaps.'

The dark-haired one fluttered the bat's wings again. 'What a shame, babe. It would've been amazing with us.'

Nick grinned. 'I don't doubt it. I'll think about you in my dreams.'

As they wobbled away in the high shoes, the pub door opened and Anna's friends came out. Kate came first carrying two pink balloons with 'Happy Birthday' on them as well as carrying birthday gift bags. A tall, well-built man was with her who hovered by her side as Kate smiled nervously at him. That awkward moment when you've just met in the pub, like each other, but don't know how to progress from this point. Hold hands, kiss, say goodbye? Next out was Georgie with a brown-haired guy who Nick had not seen before. These two were not having any awkward moments as they stopped on the pavement for a full-on snog. After a few seconds, they broke off the kissing and walked in Nick's direction.

Georgie spotted him. 'Hi, Nick. Anna's on her way out. She's being chatted up by Mitch's (nod to her male friend) mate, Owen, a real, gobby type. I think he really fancies her.'

From what Anna had said about Georgie, Nick knew she played games with people to taunt them and get a reaction. Nick responded, casually. 'Oh, really. Thanks for the heads-up.'

Kate and her man joined the three of them as Kate heard what Georgie said. 'Don't worry, Nick. Anna's trying her best to keep him away. I know he's not her type. He's a manager in car insurance claims, the sort of role that I do, but apparently his company's far superior to my tinpot outfit. Sam here works for him and says he's a real jerk.'

Just at this moment, Anna, Olivia and two men emerged from the pub, one of them standing very close to Anna. The male was of medium build with bleached blond hair cut in a sharp style with on-trend quiff. He was dressed in a tight white shirt which looked as if the buttons were about to pop. Olivia spotted Nick, waved and walked towards him. Anna went to follow but was stopped by the male in the white shirt whose arm wrapped around her waist. Nick watched as the man pulled her towards him with the obvious intention to kiss her. Leaving the group. Nick walked up to Anna. 'What's going on?' he asked.

The man gave Nick a cursory glance. 'Nothing to do with you, mate. Piss off.' To Anna, he said, 'Let's get a taxi and go back to yours, eh?'

Nick's voice rippled with anger. 'I think you'll find that this has everything to do with me as she's my girlfriend. There won't be any taxi rides back to her place.'

The male looked between Anna and Nick. 'I think we'll let her decide, shall we?' A smirk developed on his impish features as he winked at Anna.

Nick knew these types, smallish men who overdosed on their own bravado. 'Ok, mate. I'm playing nice for now but that can change at any moment.' Nick towered over him, his blue eyes, cold and glacial, boring into the man. Deep furrows between Nick's eyebrows registered his anger.

Anna moved to the far side of Nick away from the man but he took hold of her hand. Anna pulled her hand free. 'Look, Owen, it's been fun meeting you but I need to go now.'

'It's been fun meeting you, babe. You're so beautiful. I'll be looking out for you in the future.' Owen added, giving Nick a dismissive look.

Nick directly addressed Owen, disciplining himself not to wrap his hands around the arrogant idiot's throat. In a deep, slow voice, he said, 'Ok, Owen. My fist is going to connect with your cocky face if I hear you speak to her again.'

For the first time, Owen recognised Nick's determined tone and his gloating face drained of all blood as he gazed up at a formidable Nick. Muttering, 'Sorry, mate, she led me on,' he backed away from Anna, to walk away from the pub with his male friend.

This 'led me on' comment further spiked Nick's anger as he turned his attention to Anna. 'I hope that's not true.'

Anna looked upset at being asked this. 'Don't be ridiculous. The four men joined us for a drink and got chatting, that's all. It's great for Kate as the guy she was talking to, Sam, seems friendly and they've really hit it off. Georgie was also happy as she's clicked with one of the others, Mitch. Olivia and I were just being friendly with the other two.'

'Owen obviously picked up on your friendly vibe and thought he was in with a chance,' Nick commented caustically, still angered by the whole thing. They shared a taxi with Olivia, who tried to disperse the tension between him and Anna by telling funny stories until she got out of the cab at her house. The atmosphere in the taxi on the way to Anna's was frosty despite it being a warm evening.

They walked in silence into Anna's house and she offered him a drink, whilst getting a large glass of water for herself. They then sat on her three-seater sofa, each at the opposite end, a space between them. Nick gazed over at her as she sipped the water, trying to re-hydrate after drinking. Anna looked at him, trying to judge whether his anger had abated. 'About that guy, let me explain.'

'Go on then', Nick demanded, his eyes fully focused on her face. The phrase 'this had better be good' sort of lingered in the air, unspoken.

Anna took a deep breath, then spoke. 'The four guys were standing near to us in the outside area of the pub. They spotted us and came over, led by Owen. He asked if they could join us and Georgie gave him the go ahead. They bought drinks, we bought drinks, it was good fun and Georgie and Kate were getting on well with two of the guys. It would be great for Kate to have a boyfriend.' '

'Wonderful,' Nick retorted, his earlier irritation with her rising again. 'Let's cut to the chase, here. Owen's comment that you led him on.'

Anna gulped down more water, presumably to quell her nerves. 'Nick, I hope you know me well enough now to know I wouldn't do that. Owen kept pestering me to go out with him but I made it very clear I had a boyfriend. Owen is an arrogant type who will not take no for an answer.'

Nick knew from what she said that it was Owen who was the wrongdoer in all this. But he was still feeling mad at her for somehow encouraging the man. Even though she hadn't. 'Well, Anna, I came very close to flattening that Owen. Can you please stay away from trouble?'

Anna now looked hurt by this and Nick wondered if he'd gone too far. Her voice was now flecked with justifiable anger. 'Honestly, Nick, I no way encouraged him to ask me out. He wouldn't listen. What is it with men and me? This is the type of thing that happened with Alistair when he accused me of encouraging men. Now you're doing it as well.'

Part of Nick wanted to remain angry with her for a little longer so that she got the message that he wasn't happy about her and Owen. But Nick had to accept that it wasn't her fault. It was due to her beauty that men were drawn to her and wanted to be with her. The arrogant, often good-looking types, who thought they deserved a beautiful woman like Anna. Yet they never changed their self-centred, cocky attitude to make themselves worthy of her. In fact, these types of men often acquired these women, and instead of treasuring them, they treated them badly and hurt them. Nick's voice softened as he spoke to her, 'I know you didn't encourage that idiot, Owen. Come over here, Anna. Let's talk about us.'

She moved across the sofa to sit next to him. 'Have you stopped being cross with me?' she asked, anxiety still apparent in her lovely blue eyes.

Nick pulled her against him and kissed her with love. The feel of her in his arms, the softness of her skin beneath his fingers, was arousing his senses. His eyes scanned her face, drinking in its delicate beauty. Her eyes the colour of sapphires, priceless jewels. The perfect symmetry of her flawless features. Her luscious red lips that he could never tire of kissing. 'I'm sorry for being annoyed at you as I know that it was not your fault. Problem is, Anna Louden, you are so beautiful that the swaggering Owen or Connor types want you. It makes men, like Alistair, jealous, and scared of losing you.'

Anna looked away from his intense gaze, perhaps feeling a little shy at what he was saying. 'Would it sound conceited to say that I do find it difficult at times, to have a lot of male attention? I know lots of girls love it but I can find it tiresome. Does that sound very ungrateful as beauty is deemed by society to be the greatest human asset?'

'No, Anna, it doesn't, if it means that you get unwanted advances from men. A lot of men are not emotionally mature and act on their urges,' Nick stated, his worry for her obvious in the anxious tone of his voice.

'My dad calls it the 'beauty curse' as I have been pestered by men from my early teens. Being chatted up and asked out all the time at work, at uni, in shops and pubs. Men following me. Being harassed on social media. Random assaults where I've been grabbed, and kissed. Boyfriends getting jealous of the attention men give me. All culminating in Alistair's attack on me which he justified was because I lead men on and I need to stop doing it, basically. It's happened tonight with us. You were angry at Owen but also at me as he said I led him on. Run for the hills, Nick.'

Nick could hear that she was struggling not to cry. Nick pulled her into the protective circle of his arms. He wanted to place a ring of steel around her or find a property on a remote island away from men with their lecherous eyes and bad intentions. 'Don't worry. I'm not going anywhere. I'll get rid of the liberty takers.' He kissed again, wanting to make her completely his but was this wrong of him? Was he as bad as the rest of them by wanting to own her? 'Ok, my beautiful Anna, I think that I need to speak seriously to you about how I feel about you and this relationship.'

'Ok,' she muttered, and he could see that she was going to say more so he placed a finger on her lips to silence her.

'Shush, for a minute. Firstly, don't let Abbie's bombshell about the baby unsettle you. I will not resume a relationship with her once the baby is born. That we'll drift back together as a couple, united by our parenting responsibilities. I never want to be with Abbie again, baby or no baby.' Nick stopped speaking and noted that Anna wasn't convinced, given the anxiety in her eyes. 'It will never, ever happen because of the difference between my relationship with her and the one I have with you. I will admit, coldly, that with Abbie it was only about the sex and if that makes me heartless, then I'll wear the badge. With you, it's a whole lot more. The sex is amazing but I feel a real connection with you, so it's emotional as well as physical. I love you, Anna, in a way that I have never loved a woman before. I want you fully in my life, if you'll have me.'

His eyes gazed at her face as she registered what he said. She smiled at him through watery tears. 'I will have you, Nick Carlton. You are a wonderful man and I have the best time when I am with you. And to be clear, I don't want any other men. I only want to be with you so you have no need to punch anyone,' she asserted, whilst leaning to kiss him.

'Ms Louden, I will reserve the right to punch any chancer I think is becoming too forward with you. Be prepared as there may be blood,' Nick joked, as she gave him a worried look.

But the time for talking was over. Nick pulled her silky hair away from her face, allowing him to kiss her neck and bare shoulders. His right hand then explored downwards, over the curves of her bottom to explore her thighs under her very sexy summer dress. His own voice, made gravelly by lust, whispered in her ear, 'I've told you how much I love you. Now I'm going to show you, Anna.'

⊷⊶◁❮❯▷⊷⊶

CHAPTER SIXTY SEVEN

Sunday 10th July 2022

Mid-morning on the next day, Russ got up, clear-headed from not drinking, but still seething due to Abbie's behaviour last night. He sat at the kitchen table opposite Luke, eating toast and drinking strong tea, a scowl on his face. 'Pass the butter' was the brusque instruction he gave to Luke.

Luke smiled at his brother. 'Please, I think you mean. What's rattled your cage more than normal?' Luke passed the tub of butter to Russ.

Russ slathered the butter over two slices of toasted white bread. He bit into one slice with the same ferocity that Ozzy Osbourne might bite into a bat. 'Nothing, just pissed off with a woman, that's all.'

Luke's expression was curious on hearing this. 'A woman? Women don't normally get under your thick skin. Which one's upset you, Leanne or Abbie?'

'Not Leanne, she's sweet, does as she's told.' Russ paused to eat the toast. 'No, it's the other one, your so called Red Witch. We were out at a pub in Leamington last night, having a drink. I go to the bar and when I come back she's flirting with some bloke she knows, a DJ. He's a total wazzock who's full of himself. Has the brass neck to ask me to buy him a drink.'

Luke chuckled. 'As you're not known for your generosity, I guess you politely said no to that.'

'Too right I did. The tosser can get his own. Anyway, I went to the bog and when I came back, the two of them had disappeared.' Russ breathed heavily to control his temper before drinking his tea. 'She's messed about with the wrong bloke, I can tell you.

And she was all excitable and drunk about knocking Anna over. She's also told the ex-boyfriend, Nick, that she's pregnant and it's his kid. I'm not sure I believe her but he's willing to support it, the dickhead.'

Luke's jaw dropped as he heard this. 'What? This is all being done to hurt my beloved Anna. How dare she? I thought we'd agreed that we'd take action against this woman.'

'We have. You have the evidence of the white car and its registration number that was driven at Anna. We know that Abbie was the driver. I've recorded some videos of her dressed in red basque and stockings enjoying some bondage fun. It will be great to circulate these photos on social media when the time's right. Right now, I'm pissed off that she went off with that DJ jerk,' Russ growled. He picked up another slice of toast and buttered it. 'I'm not going to let it pass.'

Lying on his bed, half an hour later, Russ rang Abbie's phone. It was answered by a gravel-voiced Abbie, presumably just waking up from a sleep. 'Yeah, Russ, ok?'

Russ could hear the muttering of a male voice in the background. Good old Josh, the DJ, had obviously stayed the night. The anger was red hot and scalding in Russ but he would control his rage for now. 'Abbie, where did you get to last night?'

'Yeah, sorry, Russ. Josh and I went back to his to do a line or two. I should've told you.' She squealed then, presumably as the DJ pinched her. Weren't the two of them having fun?

'Yeah, you should have but instead you left me in the pub looking like a right loser. I don't like being messed about by women, Abbie. ' Russ kept his voice even and controlled but inside he was fuming. Abbie started to giggle as the bed-sharer was trying to distract her from the phone call.

'Sorry, sorry, again, Russ,' she managed to say whilst pre-occupied with the attentions of Josh. 'I'll make it up to you in my own special way next time we meet.'

'Is somebody there with you, Abbie?' Russ asked, smirking to himself as he awaited her reply.

'No, Russ. I'm on my own. I think you can hear the telly,' Abbie lied. 'Speak to you soon, babe.'

Abbie ended the call, as Russ seethed. He really didn't care that much for Abbie but he did not like to be taken for a fool by a woman. Leaving him in the pub and going off with another man whilst she was supposed to be with him was beyond rude. Now she'd lied to him that she was alone when it was clear she was not. This woman had now disrespected him, twice. Russ could not let that go.

CHAPTER SIXTY EIGHT

Thursday 14th July 2022

Russ shoved in the door as Abbie opened it and strode into the hallway. Abbie flinched as he walked into the living area and she quickly followed. As this was an unexpected visit, and the day was warm, she was dressed in khaki shorts and white vest, hair tied back in a ponytail. Russ sat on the sofa. 'Get us a lager and we'll talk.'

Abbie stood, hands on hips, glaring at him. 'Nice to see you too, Russ. This is not a pub where you give your orders to the bar staff.' But on seeing the harsh look on Russ's face, she relented and went for the drinks.

Russ glugged on the lager, as he stared at her, safely seated on an armchair away from him. 'I'm not happy with you after Saturday night. Going off with that DJ and leaving me looking like a loser in the pub. And then ending up in bed with him.' Anger blazed in Russ's brown eyes. He noted that the glass of wine she was holding was shaking in her hand but there was a defiance in her eyes as she stared back at him.

'As I told you, I went back to Josh's to score some lines. He lives nearby. I was going to come back to the pub but we got pissed and, well, yeah.' Abbie shrugged, a gesture that really sent Russ's rage soaring.

'Oh, that's ok, then,' Russ sarcastically stated. 'What am I? A useful idiot to buy you drinks and then throw aside when you get a better offer. I bought you that bottle of wine.'

'Do you want me to give you the money, then?' Abbie asked, a flash of red burning her pale cheeks. 'Let me remind you that I provide the drinks when you're here and a lot of coke. That's about the first drink you've ever bought me as you're a tight wad. And FYI, I didn't end up in his bed.'

Russ aimed a hard kick at the chrome leg of the coffee table which sent a cream candle toppling onto the floor. 'Cut the crap, Abbie. I know you slept with him as I could hear him messing about with you the next day when I called.'

'What, you jealous, babe?' Abbie asked, a smirk on her face. 'I thought we didn't do that. I do what I do and you do what you do. Ask no questions, tell no lies.'

'Yeah, it's not jealously, it's about showing me respect. If we go out to the pub together, I don't expect you to go off with some jerk and then go to bed with him.' Russ glowered at her. He had come here to call out her behaviour and ensure that she said sorry. Instead, her attitude was one of defiance which was winding him up all the more. 'Get this straight, Abbie. I don't let women make a fool of me and you did just that the other night.'

'Honest, Russ, I wasn't dissing you. It started off as wanting to do a line of coke with J and I lost track of time.' She smiled weakly at him. 'Anyway, you give off this couldn't care less vibe in the way you treat people. Don't like it so much when it happens to you, eh?'

'As I've just said, I don't like being messed about by women and that includes you.' Russ's tone of voice was now harsh and loud. This conversation was not getting anywhere but it was really stoking his anger.

Flinching in her chair at the volume of his voice, Abbie looked visibly shocked. 'Ok, Russ. Let's calm it down shall we and have a few drinks. I won't do that to you again. Let's just carry on being friends with benefits, no complications. I'll get you another lager.'

As she went to the kitchen, Russ drained the last of the lager out of the bottle. He couldn't decide whether he wanted to see this woman again or not. Yeah, the drink, drugs and sex were all good but he liked women who were compliant, not argumentative. Abbie was head-strong and riled him up. Plus there was all this issue with the real or fake pregnancy which was a complication he didn't want messing up his life. Abbie returned with another lager for him and a topped-up glass of wine for herself. This baby was going to be an alcoholic before it was born.

Abbie sat next to Russ and leaned over to kiss him. 'Friends?' she pouted.

'We'll see,' Russ replied, not responding to her mouth as she explored his. 'I'm still angry with you. I haven't decided yet if I want to see you again after tonight.'

She pulled away from him slightly, a panic in her hazel eyes. 'Don't say that Russ. I like what we have. I'm sick of guys using me and discarding me.'

'I'm not using you. This is a mutually beneficial thing between us. But I won't be made a fool of,' Russ stressed, a coldness in his eyes which made Abbie shiver.

Abbie got up off the sofa, taking her glass of wine with her. 'Ok, I get the message. Stay or go, I don't give a shit. I'm off to bed, you can join me or go home and we'll forget the whole thing.'

Watching as she disappeared out of the room, her curvy bottom and firm thighs displayed temptingly in the shorts, Russ thought that he would take advantage of the bedroom offer, even if this was the final farewell.

⸙

CHAPTER SIXTY NINE

Taking his lager with him, Russ followed Abbie to her bedroom. Abbie was lying on top of the duvet, sipping her wine and scrolling through her phone. Though the whole casual relationship with Abbie had been exciting, he knew that it was time to knock it on the head. The stunt she had pulled with the DJ was something he couldn't forget. And, when drunk, she would whine and cry about missing her ex, Nick, which wasn't something Russ wanted to hear after putting the effort in to give her a great sexual experience. Russ didn't expect her to love him, or even be faithful to him, but he did not want another man's name mentioned when he was present. Russ Milner was not a man to be disrespected by any woman. Tonight, there would be one last good time, indulging her favourite pleasures, and then that would be it.

Russ stood for a moment, gazing down at her, seeing her for the final time. Wavy blonde hair, freed from the ponytail, framing her good-looking face but without all the make-up she normally wore she was not a stand out beauty. Her face was puffy and spotty, possibly a consequence of her early, was it 'fake', pregnancy. Russ was determined to find out the truth of this once and for all. 'What are you doing, just lying there? I think you've got some making up to do after going off with the DJ jerk. Go and put on one of my favourite sexy outfits, put on some makeup, and hurry up.' Abbie vacated the bed. Russ took her place, sat propped up against pillows and drank whisky from a bottle she'd brought upstairs.

Abbie went to the wardrobe to extract an outfit from a box of choices. And rushed into the bathroom to get ready. Russ edged off the bed to get a few items out of her box of tricks for his entertainment before he returned to the bed. He positioned his mobile phone on the dresser to record the next instalment of their bondage sex tape. Abbie was soon back, a spicy red lipstick staining her smiling lips, hair falling loosely, as she sashayed towards him. The outfit, a black, lacy, thigh-skimming chemise with black stockings emphasised her curves. 'Will this do?' she whispered as she edged towards him on the bed. 'Will you make me pay for being a bad girl?'

'What do you think?' Russ commented as he picked up the riding crop. 'You know what to do. Come over here, and kneel, face down.' His voice was harsh, and Abbie giggled nervously. But she did as instructed as Russ pulled her arms behind her back and secured her wrists together with bondage rope. The satiny material of the chemise rode up her back exposing her naked bottom which Russ gave one hard slap. Abbie reacted with an 'ouch' before giggling again. 'Thank you, Russ.'

Russ pulled off his shirt and positioned himself at the side of the bed. 'Look at me,' he ordered as he tapped the crop against his left hand. Abbie's eyes were wide in anticipation of the first blow and she licked her lips, nervously. 'Ok, Abbie, I've told you that I was displeased with your behaviour with the DJ jerk. What do you need to say to me, Abbie?'

Biting her lip in a conciliatory way, she whispered, 'I need to say sorry for disrespecting you, Russ. I will never do that again.'

'Good,' Russ stated, as the riding crop thrashed across the bare flesh of her buttocks leaving a raised, red line. 'What do you say, Abbie?'

As the pain stung, she breathed deeply to gain her composure. 'Thank you, Russ.'

Russ took position, standing with legs apart, enjoying the sight before him, the red welt in contrast to the whiteness of her bottom. 'What happens Abbie, when you tell me lies?'

'I get punished, Russ,' Abbie stated, as her bottom tensed, ready for the next lash of the crop. It came quickly, and it came hard, causing Abbie to almost leap upwards off the bed before she tried to stifle her crying in the duvet. 'Thank you, Russ,' was said through watery tears.

Russ stopped for a moment to admire the criss-cross of welts on her pale skin. 'I expect some level of loyalty if I spend time with you. And I don't like women who play games.' Russ tapped the crop under her chin to gaze into her worried eyes before stroking it along her back. He guessed that her arms were beginning to ache due to her wrists being tied together. In anticipation of the next blow, she tensed her bottom. Russ didn't disappoint and two more whacks of the riding crop hit their pretty target. 'I think this little session is being very productive. We'll carry on for a bit longer until I'm sure you have been thoroughly punished. Are you having a good time, Abbie?'

A while later, Russ and Abbie were sat up in bed, as he drank more whisky. She had finished crying as a result of the punishment session which he knew had hurt her. But as the pain subsided she'd welcomed the pleasure of having sex. Now, she was gazing lovingly into his eyes before kissing his mouth. 'You taste of sweetness and smoke. Thank you, Russ, for an amazing time just now. It felt difficult to endure at the time but now I feel really mellow and content after our session.'

Russ chuckled to himself. This was a new version of Abbie, as the wildness had been tamed, and she seemed content for the first time he'd known her. 'I bet your bum's not feeling so mellow,' he teased, as he glided his hand down her back to her bottom where a red heat still radiated off it.

Abbie moved slightly to get more comfortable which was difficult due to the pain. She focused her tear-stained, mascara-smudged eyes on his. 'Russ, I know you don't like commitment but I do feel we have a connection. I want to forget Nick and concentrate on you.'

Russ chuckled. 'That may be difficult due to the fact you are pregnant with his kid.'

Abbie now ran her fingers down Russ's bare chest before leaning in to kiss him, a passionate onslaught of moist mouth and tongue. On stopping, in her breathy sexy voice, she added, 'I'm not really pregnant. It's all a scam to get him back and drive them apart. I'd like to carry on with the deception for a while to make him suffer. Get rid of Leanne and we could move towards an exclusive relationship.'

Removing the roving hand, Russ shook his head, then clasped Abbie's chin to focus her eyes on his. 'Abbie, I thought we'd made some progress tonight but you never learn. Let me remind you. I don't do relationships, period. I'll decide who I see and who I won't. Leanne does not have the whore factor like you but she is good enough.'

Abbie's eyes filled with tears as she heard the harsh reality of his words. 'Sorry, Russ. Forget what I just said.'

As Russ watched her, tears rolled down Abbie's cheeks. In between sobs, she managed to say, 'We can just carry on as we are, no commitment. Just casual hook-up buddies. I want you in my life, Russ.'

Russ felt the wetness of the tears on his chest but it made his heart harder. 'I came tonight to tell you that I won't be seeing you again. I've had my fill and it's time to move on. You showed total disrespect to me by going off with that DJ at the pub and then sleeping with him. I don't care who you fuck but don't tell me lies when I phone and ask if he's there with you. Don't tell me how to run my life and who I can see. I don't do relationships. I don't like you snivelling about your ex-boyfriend. I don't like needy women. All I ever want is a good time of sex, drugs and booze and I step away if a woman starts to get needy.'

Abbie could no longer control the flow of tears cascading down her face, as her eyes pleaded with him. 'Please, Russ, don't go. I don't want Nick. I want you. We can both change, have a proper relationship, and you could move in here with me.' Her arms coiled around his neck as she covered his mouth with hers for an all-consuming kiss.

Russ pushed her away and started to edge off the bed. Abbie focused her attention on moving her mouth down his body, a trail of saliva, tears and damp hair. 'Stop now, Abbie. I'm going. I don't like needy women.'

Abbie moved off him, and crawled across the bed, sobbing uncontrollably into her pillow as Russ got dressed. As he re-sat on the bed to put on his shoes she tried to compose herself for one last attempt to stop him going. She sat up, pushed out her breasts to display their pertness in the lacy chemise. She drew her legs up to draw attention to the sexy black stockings and her lack of underwear. Running her fingers through her tousled, blonde hair, she pouted, before licking her lips. 'Russ, don't just give up on this sexiness. It's here for you at any time.'

Russ walked to the door but stopped before exiting. 'The desperation is now getting cringy. We're over.'

As he closed the door, a loud thump was heard on the other side, presumably as her wine glass hit the door. Loud, loud screams, and full-on sobs were heard as Russ went away.

CHAPTER SEVENTY

Saturday 16th July 2022

Luke could not supress his excitement as he made arrangements for tomorrow. The day that was going to be the best day of his life. He was really pleased to have the house to himself. Dad was away on holiday with Angie in Lanzarote and would be away for another ten days. Russ was currently staying at Leanne's for a few days. Russ had been in a weird mood for the last two days, flipping between anger and sarcasm, so Luke was relieved to have him out of the house. This meant he could concentrate his thoughts on the preparations for his special guest.

Luke had finished cleaning the house, having paid particular attention to the downstairs living areas, his bedroom, and the upstairs bathroom. He liked this family home but he wished that his dad would refurbish it. Though the property was originally a farmhouse, it was refurbished in the 80s, and had an old-fashioned rustic style. The kitchen/family room was large with natural oak fitted units, taupe-coloured, laminate worktops and terracotta tiled flooring. To Luke it looked dated, with white-fronted dishwasher, free-standing white fridge/freezer and old-fashioned oval pine table and six chairs. Luke nagged his father to bring the kitchen into the twenty-first century with handle-less units in trendy colours such as graphite or marine, integrated appliances, and a kitchen island with pendant lighting. Jez Milner's response was that if Luke paid for it, he could have it.

Anyway, thought Luke, we are where we are. At least the house was clean and hygienic, most suitable for his VIP female visitor. A large glass vase on the table displayed pink and white roses, white lilies, white antirrhinum and green foliage. The distinct smell of the lilies dominated the air. Luke was going to lay on refreshments for his guest and had placed white porcelain/ gold rim small plates, cups and saucers on the table ready for use along with white paper napkins with a gold floral design. Cutlery of knives, teaspoons and cake forks had been inspected and shined. His hope was that she would indulge in a glass of white wine, so wine glasses had been washed and polished. Luke enjoyed doing all these preparations, taking the utmost care to ensure that everything was just right. It was the attention to detail that a host would undertake if they were entertaining Her Majesty, The Queen. To Luke, his beloved, Anna, was worthy of the same attention to detail.

Luke wanted the conversation to flow and to say things to make her laugh. He'd been looking up funny stories and snippets on-line to keep her entertained. His greatest joy was to see a smile on her beautiful lips and a sparkle in her blue eyes. To hear the wonderful sound of her laughter.

He had also spent time fretting about what he was going to wear. Shorts were not an option. His pale, skinny legs were not his best feature thus he opted for dark blue chinos which would be relatively cool on what was forecast as a hot day. The trousers would be worn with a loose-fit, white shirt which skimmed over his small belly and would not draw attention to his flabby upper arms. It was a look that he hoped would make him look fresh as he was prone to sweating profusely in hot weather. Also, any blotchy pinkness to his face due to the excess heat would be added to by his tendency to blush at times of nervousness and anxiety. His brother Russ in a white shirt, blue chinos combo would look mega sexy as the shirt tightened across his muscular chest and dipped down to his slender waist. The tight-fit sleeves of the shirt would display toned biceps, a look which women swooned over. Add in a pair of sun glasses and many a female would dissolve in a puddle of lust. Luke could never emulate his brother's hot sexiness so he was hoping for a cool allure vibe.

Thus, tomorrow, Luke did not want Russ anywhere near the house. If Russ were to see Anna, he would definitely lay on thick the charm to entice her away from him. His other tactic would be to try to undermine Luke by pointing out all his faults to make him look inferior. At the same time, Russ would be boasting of his success with women and how they all fell under his spell. Subtlety was not one of Russ's virtues. Luke was a realist. If most women had a choice between Russ and himself, they would all choose his handsome, arrogant, womanising brother. Russ bragged about his sexual prowess and Luke knew that this was not idle bragging as Russ could deliver what he promised. Even sweet Anna might be tempted to try out the chance of a night in bed with Russ.

Anyway, Luke hoped that he had dealt with the problem of keeping Russ away from home and Anna. He'd explained to Russ that he was opening their garden as part of a local open gardens initiative to raise money for charity. Their garden would be full of elderly couples, gardening enthusiasts, and mothers and daughters, all having a genteel afternoon of admiring flowers and plants and indulging in refreshments of tea, cakes and wine. Russ had shown a slight interest when hearing the word 'daughters' as it might give him a source of new casual girlfriends. Luke took the mischievous smile off Russ's face by describing the 'daughters' as unmarried types in their fifties. All this guaranteed that Russ would stay away.

After all his hard work, Luke sat on a chair at the kitchen table, sipping a small beer. All his plans for tomorrow would come together as long as a number of things happened.

The weather was warm and sunny as predicted so there would be no reason to cancel the open gardens. Russ kept out of the way. His beloved, Anna, would come as promised without her boyfriend. Luke placed his hands together and prayed to a deity that believed in pure love between a man and a woman. A deity that would deliver to him the woman of his dreams.

CHAPTER SEVENTY ONE

Sunday 17th July 2022

Anna brought her car to a halt at her destination, a property on a country lane, just outside of a small village, in South Warwickshire. As she got out of her car she did note that this was a property in a semi-rural area without immediate neighbours either side. It did give her a pang of anxiety. But she reassured herself that in approximately thirty minutes there would be lots of people all enjoying the garden. It was for a good cause. And she had now chatted to Luke on a number of occasions and he seemed a genuinely pleasant young man.

Luke had texted this morning to notify her that the open gardens were still on and as it was a glorious day he was expecting a good turnout. A follow-up text made her chuckle. '**I am regretting this as I don't know my Shaggy Soldier from my Knobweed. All real plant names. See you at 1.30 p.m. for a VIP tour before the crowds arrive. Luke.**'

To suit the garden vibe, Anna had on a pretty pink dress with floral design, which was V-necked, short-sleeved, flared to the knee and ultra-feminine. As she walked towards the front of the property, she noted a laminated sign stating '**Garden Open from 2.00 p.m. Refreshments available.**' There was a deep pink honeysuckle plant growing up the wall by the front door and she paused to inhale its sweet scent. For a moment she hesitated about being here alone, but she took a deep breath, and pushed the solid brass doorbell.

After a few minutes, Luke answered the door. A brilliant smile lit up his round, slightly pink face. 'Hi, Anna. So glad you could come. It's so hot, I think we will all melt. Come in, come in, before you do.' He held open the door and led her through the hallway into a large kitchen/dining room area. The room was cool, a bonus on this hot day, as French doors and windows were closed, and an air conditioning unit pumped cool air into the room. 'I'm keeping this room nice and chilled so that I don't melt into a puddle and to help with my hay fever. Not the best advert for opening a garden, am I?' he joked.

Anna moved near to the air conditioner to get the benefit of the cool air. 'Well, you will have to venture outside when the public arrive.'

He bit his lower lip, then sighed before he spoke. 'Actually, I received notification two hours ago that the whole thing is cancelled. Six gardens, including mine, were due to open but five people from our group of gardeners have come down with a nasty stomach bug. They all went out for a curry last night and have got food poisoning. So that's four out of the six gardens out of action and the whole thing is off. I did send you a text.'

'Oh dear,' Anna stated, 'I don't recall seeing it. What a shame. I'm sure everyone has to do a lot of hard work to get the gardens up to the required standard.'

Luke sighed. 'Yes, they do. Our garden is quite ordinary compared to some who have exceptional spaces of raised flower beds, water features, pergolas, veg patches, statues and garden art designs. And gnomes. Ted and Jen have a great collection of gnomes, some a little rude, including a naked couple, and a gnome on the loo. And my fav, drunk as a skunk gnome.'

Anna pulled a face. 'I won't miss seeing them. Call me a snob but I really can't take to gnomes.'

Luke didn't take much encouragement. 'Snob! But I jest, I can't stand them either. Anyway, as the open garden event is cancelled, let me offer you some refreshments to make up for your wasted journey. I've got quite a selection of cakes as I had hoped to sell them this afternoon. Name your favourite cake and I'm sure I'll have it. Also, please take a seat.'

Anna sat down on a chair at the kitchen table. She noted that it was laid out for two people with two plates, two cups and saucers. Cutlery and napkins for two. This all seemed a little odd if he had been expecting a lot of visitors outside. 'I like most cakes, who doesn't, a lemon drizzle or Victoria sponge are two favourites. I expect that you've been doing the baking all morning.'

Luke went over to a cupboard and brought out two cakes on plates, covered with kitchen paper sheets. 'Here we are, a Victoria sponge and a lemon cake. I've got carrot cake as well. Would you like tea, coffee, lemonade or orange squash?'

After placing all the cakes on the table and providing lemonade for Anna, Luke sat down. He poured an orange squash for himself. Anna selected a slice of Victoria sponge, a three-layered cake with separate layers of raspberry jam and vanilla buttercream. 'This is delicious, thanks,' she enthused as the moist sponge and smooth buttercream tantalised her tastebuds.

Luke did not immediately help himself to any cake. He sat quietly, watching her eat. To Anna this scrutiny felt like she was an animal in a zoo, a cute large-eyed marmoset nibbling on a piece of fruit while the public gazed at her. It was a bit disconcerting. She asked, 'Aren't you having any cake?'

His cheeks flushed a slight pink. 'In a minute. It's great to see you enjoying it. I have some strawberries if you'd like a few to go with the cake?'

'Yes, ok,' she said, 'I love strawberries.'

He was soon back with a bowl of strawberries and a jug of single cream and she added both to her plate. 'I saw you buy strawberries the other day in the shop. I noticed that you gained an admirer who tried to chat you up.'

Anna frowned, then remembered the guy who said she was red hot. 'Yes, he asked me out on a date but I insisted my boyfriend would have to come along as well. Oddly, this seemed to put him off.'

Luke helped himself to a few strawberries and nibbled them slowly. Quite a bit of lip licking was involved. He then pointed his cake fork at her. 'You see, Anna, and I hope you don't take offence when I say this, but you are truly beautiful. The most beautiful woman I have ever seen. And today you are looking exceptionally lovely in your summery dress. S-so feminine.'

This was now starting to get a bit awkward and Anna decided to ignore the personal comments. 'It's difficult to know what to wear when it's hot. I thought I would be out in the sun so this was the best choice. We should go out into the garden shortly so I can admire your father's hard work.'

'Yeah, maybe,' he muttered. 'For now, let's enjoy our little tea party, just the two of us. I'm borrowing you from your boyfriend, who is a lucky man. Tell me about him?'

'He's called Nick, he's thirty-years-old, and is a joint partner in a security company. He's quite successful which is a sign that he's a hard worker and a good business man. Plus, more importantly, he's intelligent, caring, kind and funny,' she added, blushing slightly as Luke scrutinised her face.

Luke bit into his last strawberry, a little of the juice dribbling on to his chin. He used a paper napkin to get rid of it. 'Well, he is very successful in the scheme of things as he ended up with you. I bet he's very good-looking as well?'

She placed down her cake fork and dabbed her mouth with her napkin. 'I have to admit he is easy on the eye. I'm very lucky and very happy.'

'How long have you been together?'

'We met four months ago when my car broke down in a layby. We started going out about two months ago. We are getting close now, I think,' she confirmed and her face lit up as she remembered last Saturday when he told her that he loved her. And their very special time making love throughout the night. In a way she had experienced a level of joy she had never had in her life before.

·Luke was now gazing intently at her again. 'Your face lights up and your eyes sparkle when you speak of him. He is a very lucky man.' Luke continued to stare at her as if drinking in every detail of her face.

Having finished her cake and strawberries, Anna decided it was probably time to go. 'Thanks for this, Luke, it's been lovely. It's a shame that the gardens weren't open.'

'Don't go yet. Stay and have a glass of chilled white wine with me,' Luke insisted. 'I bought it for Aunt Daisy but she and Milly couldn't make it. Anyway, before you go I want to tell you about my hobby of creative writing, if you're interested.'

Anna hesitated. She was driving but one small glass of wine would be ok. 'I could have one very small glass of wine before I go. Creative writing, what type of things do you write?'

Before she could change her mind, Luke was up out of his seat. He took a bottle of wine out of the fridge, unscrewed the top, and poured the wine into two glasses. 'There you go, a New Zealand Sauvignon Blanc,' he said, handing her a glass. 'Cheers, to beautiful Anna,' he stated, before clinking her glass with his. 'I write magical tales of faraway kingdoms with beautiful women, handsome men, warring armies and fantastical creatures. You, Anna, are my inspiration for my perfect woman, my goddess, who possesses exceptional beauty outside of the human realm.'

'Oh, shit,' she thought, 'that's a weird comment'. An inspiration for his stories. Anna was beginning to get uncomfortable with all these compliments about her beauty and the intensity of his scrutiny of her. Time to drink a little of the wine then leave. She drank a couple of mouthfuls and was disappointed with the taste which wasn't the dry, crisp, zingy flavour she expected. This tasted a little off, a slight soapy flavour which lingered on her tongue. 'Thanks for the wine.'

After about ten minutes, Anna was hit by a wave of nausea as if she was about to be sick. The nausea quickly faded but then her whole body became super relaxed as if she needed to go to sleep. Then everything went black.

CHAPTER SEVENTY TWO

Luke watched as Anna slipped into unconsciousness, slumped sideways on the chair and was about to slip off. He managed to catch her before she fell as he did not want her to fall and hurt herself. As she lay against his chest, he placed his left arm around her waist and his right arm under her thighs and he scooped her off the chair. He had anticipated this moment when he had made preparations to drug her wine. Not being the strongest of men, he wondered if he would be able to pick her up to carry her to where she was going to go. He need not have worried. She was petite and light and easy to carry. This did not stop his legs from trembling. Not from her weight but from his being overwhelmed by the sheer joy of holding her in his arms for the first time.

Her glorious hair fell away from her face and he was free to stare intently at her without any restriction. Her eyes were closed, and she looked to be in a dream state, and he was able to admire her lovely eyelashes. His eyes traced downwards, taking in her straight nose with its subtle upturn and a sprinkle of freckles on her nose and on her cheek bones. Then, he scrutinised her mouth taking in the detail of the plump, pink symmetry of those perfect lips. Lips which were now placed in a position so close to him, ones that he had imagined kissing every single day since he had set eyes on her. He moved his left arm to behind her neck, to raise her head. He edged his mouth nearer and nearer to hers, certain that he could detect the sweet smell of strawberries and wine on her breath. Luke brushed his lips across hers, a tiny delicious taste of the delectable honey. This sent him into a sensory overload; the taste of her mouth, the scent of her perfume which was the one he loved, the touch of her soft skin under his fingers and the sound of her soft breathing. And overall the sight of her physical perfection as he held her in his arms.

As part of his plan, Luke must now take his beloved to the special place he had prepared for her. Walking out of the kitchen area, he climbed up the stairs, along the landing and into his bedroom. His beloved was sleeping in his arms and did not stir. Gently, he placed her on his double bed, on top of a new crisp white duvet cover and rested her head on two white pillows. He settled her, ensuring that her dress was pulled down to protect her modesty. He arranged her hair so that it flowed, silkily, around her face and down to her shoulders. The shiny mid-brown colour of her hair highlighted against the stark whiteness of the pillow case. Though it was hot outside, a gentle breeze wafted through the open window and touched the exposed skin on her arms and legs. Luke watched as her chest moved up and down as she breathed.

Luke took his mobile phone from his pocket and proceeded to take multiple photos of his captive beauty. Full body shots capturing her slender legs and thighs, the curve of her hips, her slender waist, the rise of her rounded breasts and the enticement of the dark valley of her cleavage. Click, click. Shots of her face, her mouth, her closed eyes as she remained in a drug-induced sleep. Some selfies, where he lay next to her on the bed and gently tilted her towards him, the phone in his right hand so that he could pull her towards him. Two lovers embracing in bed. Two lovers, lips touching lips.

After he was satisfied that he taken enough photos, he drew up a chair and sat next to her by the bed. It was pure bliss just to sit and stare at her as she lay still and perfect, the only movement the rise and fall of her breasts as she breathed. But a little trickle of anxiety sent a shiver down his back. Had he given her too much of the liquid drug, GHB? Was she going to wake from this slumber? Luke knew that Russ used the drug from time to time and had found two vials in Russ's bedroom drawer. From what Luke had read online, the amount of liquid drug in the vial was about the right amount to administer. Enough to relax Anna so he could go forward with his plan. But now Luke worried that she was too relaxed and panic started to overwhelm Luke. She could not die on him. One, he was terrified of being charged with murder and going to jail. Two, she was the love of his life, his soulmate, and he did not want her to die. He could not bear to live with the knowledge that he had taken her life.

Out of a bedside cabinet, Luke took some bondage equipment, borrowed from a box in Russ's wardrobe. He secured her wrists together with metal handcuffs, then looped a metal chain through the left cuff to secure her to the metal headboard by a padlock. Luke was conflicted in doing this. He didn't like to clip the wings of his beloved Astraea but he didn't want her to try to escape either. His intention was to secure her for a short time until she realised that he was a true friend who she could trust. Their loving relationship would then develop and she would willingly want to stay with him forever.

After securing her to the bed, Luke leaned over and gently tapped her face. 'Anna, please wake up.' Fortunately, she did stir, and moan, but then fell back to sleep. He tried again. 'Anna, wake up, it's Luke. Let me get you a drink of water.'

This time she did slowly open her eyes, and blink, to take in her surroundings. Luke took a glass of water off the bedside cabinet, helped her to sit up slightly, and placed the glass to her lips. A tiny drop of water moistened her mouth and she spluttered. She was now more awake and lucid. Her eyes searched the room, the bed and Luke's face. 'What's happened? Where am I?'

Luke placed the glass back down on the bedside cabinet and sat on the chair.

'It's ok. You were drinking the wine and came over all faint. I brought you up here to help you recover. How are you feeling now?'

Anna tried to lift her head off the pillow. 'Odd. Weird. I can't explain it. A bit like I've drunk too much but I know I haven't. I feel quite nauseous and giddy.' She moved her right hand to try to rub her forehead and noticed the handcuffs. A panic swept her face. She noticed the metal chain through the left handcuff and quickly realised that she was secured to the bedframe. 'Oh my God, what's going on? Get these off me,' she cried.

Luke had the grace to look apologetic as she struggled and shouted to free herself. He tried to shush her, to make her calm down, in the way one might do in trying to placate a toddler having a tantrum. 'Calm down and don't be afraid. I won't hurt you. I just want you to get to know me better and then we can be friends.'

Anna lifted her head off the pillow and pulled on the metal chain to try to get free. 'Friends? Are you crazy? How can we be friends when you have tied me to your bed. Let me go now.' An anger raged through her and she tried to lash out at him with her legs. Her blue eyes were flashing with fury and her cheeks pinkened as she struggled. If anything, she was growing more beautiful in front of his eyes. 'You'll never get away with this. I will report you to the police.'

'Relax. Chill. Take in your surroundings. The lights over the bed. The high-quality bed linen I bought especially for you.' He took a lighter out of the bedside cabinet and lit a candle. 'The blurb with this candle is that it is calming and comforting. Let the scent notes of juniper berry and ylang ylang drift over you, to relax you, and bring you peace, my lovely Anna.'

'I am not your Anna, you freak. Untie me and let me go,' she cried. She wrestled with the metal chain to try to break free.

Luke pulled the chair nearer to the bed and Anna edged away from him, fearful that he was going to touch her. 'I think I mentioned downstairs that I am a writer of fantastical tales. My females are always the most stunning women in the world, the universe, the cosmos. Exceptional faces, flowing locks, blue eyes with long, natural lashes, the most perfect noses and the plumpest of lips. Bodies that have all the allure of female excellence with rounded breasts and slender waists that lead to shapely hips. They are the ultimate female form designed by the Gods.'

'I don't want to hear about your fantasies. I want you to let me go,' Anna insisted, straining her arms to try to release the restraint.

'On our earthly plane I have searched for the ideal woman. The one that would fire my imagination and arouse my senses. But I was forever disappointed in my search. The vast majority are average or below. Pale, spotty, snaggle-toothed, numerous facial imperfections. Lank, dry or frizzy hair. The bodies are awful. Thin and spindly with no curves or definition. Or large and unfit, rolls of flabby fat on bulging arms, gigantic tummies or thunder thighs. There are a few diamonds amongst the rough but I've never found my goddess. My Astraea. Until I saw you, my Anna...' he paused as she looked at him as if he were crazy...'You. On my wall.'

Luke pointed to a portrait on the wall opposite the bed. A beautiful woman with flowing locks of brown hair, piercing blue eyes, a luscious mouth and a body of sexual perfection. She was dressed in a tight-fitting white gown which displayed flawless skin. A golden bodice emphasised her pert breasts. A golden headdress with a central diamond adorned her head. She was surrounded by blueness and light in a place outside of planet Earth. The portrait was labelled, 'Astraea'. Anna's eyes widened as she gazed at the portrait. 'Is that based on me?'

'Of course,' Luke smiled, beguilingly. 'I have many, many photos of you, beloved one. Look around.'

Her eyes searched the room, to the walls left and right of her, and the opposite wall, all of which were covered with photos of her, mainly at the supermarket. At her car, putting her shopping away. Pushing the trolley. Photos of different seasons with her in winter coats through to summer dresses. There must be hundreds of them. Anna gasped loudly. 'Oh God. You're a stalker.'

Ignoring this, Luke explained. 'In ancient Greece, Astraea was the virgin goddess of justice, innocence, purity and precision. One day she is expected to come back to Earth to bring the return of a Utopian Golden Age. But my Astraea is not of the Greeks but of the Universe, a magnificent creature that captures the essence of the feminine. She compliments the warrior, Xandros, who encapsulates the strength and power of the masculine.' Luke's gaze drifted away from Anna, his thoughts lost to the fantasy world of his creation.

Anna ceased all struggling and pulled herself up to sit against the headboard. 'This gets worse and worse. You're Xan, the nutter who has been sending me those weird texts, aren't you? You've got my portrait on your wall. You have me tied up on your bed. I have been such a fool. I thought you were a kind, funny and harmless guy. But you're not. You are a stalker at best, a predator at worst.' She slumped slightly as if all energy had left her body. Luke noted that there were now tears in her eyes which trickled down her beautiful face. His heart hurt to see this as he did not want to make her cry.

Luke wanted to get on the bed to take her in his arms and comfort her. Make sure that she knew he was a friend and not a foe. But not yet. She needed time to sleep, to heal. He took a glass, a vial, and a bottle of wine out of the bedside cabinet. Mixed the drug and the alcohol together in the glass and stood over her as she lay on the bed. She tried to shift away from him but she was hampered by the restraining chain. Sitting next to her, he pulled her firmly to him and brought the glass up to her lips. She tried to fight him, rigorously moving her head left and right, but Luke was now more assured of his strength. 'Drink this, my beloved, and sleep, and you will awake refreshed and calm.' The majority of the liquid went into her mouth and he gripped her face tightly to stop her spitting it out. Quickly, she stopped struggling. Luke held her, his own body in a state of ecstasy, as he luxuriated in the feel and smell of her. 'Go to dreamland, my angel.'

CHAPTER SEVENTY THREE

Monday 18th July 2022 – early hours

Hours later, Anna awoke and once again could not make sense of where she was and what was happening to her. She forced her eyes open, even though her eyelids were heavy. All around was darkness, except for the faint glow of string lights across the headboard. She felt groggy, as if she had spent a night drinking heavily, and was now suffering the mother of all hangovers. There was a dull ache in her head. It was a persistent mugginess that stopped her from truly understanding what was going on. Her stomach felt achy and nauseous and there was a vile, oily taste in her mouth. Slowly, she moved her arms to relieve the stiffness in them but quickly her movement was restricted by the chain securing her to the bed. It was now dark and she must have slept for hours but she had no idea what time it was. The sheer blackness across the room away from the low glow of the lights suggested it was very late into the night.

With the physical discomforts to her body, it was hard to focus on what to do to get out of this ordeal. The man, Luke, who she believed to be a friendly acquaintance had obviously lured her here under the guise of a charity event. And was holding her hostage. This level of drowsiness was a concern, an overall lethargy she was feeling in her body. As far as she could think rationally, at the moment, it did suggest that he may have drugged her, not once, but twice. What was all his talk about a goddess and a woman called Astraea? That she, Anna, resembled this Astraea, his idea of the perfect woman. The many photos chilled her blood. It was clear that he seemed to have some weird obsession with her. But what was he planning to do? He could not keep her tied to the bed forever. She did not get a sense that he was violent, but he was a fantasist, and possibly mentally unstable, so it was not possible to predict his behaviour.

Where was he now? Anna lay very still on the bed and tried to listen for any sounds. Her rising fear and panic caused a pounding noise in her ears which made it hard to discern other sounds. But there was another noise in the room, the rhythmical sound of someone breathing. He was in the room with her, lying on the floor beside the bed. The sense of terror that now tore through her was paralysing. Her body froze as any sound or movement from her was in danger of waking him up. Not being able to see due to the darkness of the room and not being able to move due to being restrained, left her completely vulnerable and terrified. A man she didn't know was holding her against her will and there was no way to escape or summon help. She had not planned to see Nick. Would he have any clue that she was missing? Her breathing was getting shaky now and she wanted to cry but she bit on her lip to stop the tears as she did not want to wake her captor.

Suddenly, a bedside light was turned on. The mattress sank as Luke sat down next to her on the bed. Anna shifted away from him, to the far side of the bed, as best she could. She pulled herself to sit up, leaning against the headboard, trying to ignore him. His hand lightly touched her right hand before she pulled it away. 'How are you, Astraea? Can I get you water or anything?'

In as forceful voice as possible, Anna commanded him. 'You can release me from this bed and let me go home. You have no right to keep me here. This is a serious crime of false imprisonment and will lead to a prison sentence. I suspect that you have drugged me so that will add to your criminal offences and lengthen your jail time.' Her voice though did lack authority as she was still very shaky with fear.

Anna did not want to turn to look at his baby-face which belied a twisted character. His left upper arm touched her bare right arm which repulsed her. This closeness of him was likely to send her spiralling into panic.

Luke spoke softly. 'I won't hurt you, Astraea. I just want us to spend some special time together. To get to know each other and be friends.'

'I don't think the best friendships prosper when one person is holding the other captive, tied to a bed,' she said with a hint of hysteria to her voice.

He sighed, loudly, a sort of blissful sound. 'It's wonderful to have you here. I've dreamed of this for so long. Just you and me. Sharing our hopes and dreams.'

Anna stared ahead, her eyes frequently gazing at the portrait of herself on the opposite wall. For the moment, he wasn't making any moves to touch her for which she was grateful.

In a lot of ways, this Luke was like a teenager, as there was a childlike quality to him due to his round, rosy cheeks, smiley expression and lack of facial hair. But this was no child; he was a grown man. At the moment, he was acting calmly and gently. Could all this change? He had already contrived to get her here, spiked her drink and was holding her against her will. Thankfully, he was acting in a non-violent way. But she had no idea what he was capable of.

'Hold, on,' he declared, suddenly moving off the bed to take something out of the bedside cabinet. He then resumed his position, sitting next to her. A spray of perfume scented the area and dampened her skin. 'This perfume is the one you wear. I bought a bottle to spray on me at night so I can think of you whilst I fall asleep.' His left arm slipped awkwardly around her shoulder as he pulled her against him. The mating ritual of an inexperienced teenager with his first girlfriend. 'This is bliss, isn't it Astraea?'

Anna tried to escape his grasp. 'Get off me, get off me,' she ordered but his fingers dug into her upper left arm to secure her to him. This was the first move of physical contact. Anna knew distinctly that he was not as benign as he appeared and guessed there were no limits as to what he could do.

⚜

CHAPTER SEVENTY FOUR

Luke could not believe his luck. This wonderous moment in his life was the pinnacle of all his hopes and dreams. He'd achieved them all. This perfect woman, Astraea, was in his bed, and he holding her, enraptured by the closeness of her body and the scent of her perfume. His devious plotting had delivered her to him. He yearned to kiss her perfect lips. But he lacked the courage to do so in case she was disappointed as he was not experienced in this sort of thing. Not like Russ who had likely kissed hundreds of women and would instinctively know what to do. Luke had watched a lot of YouTube videos about kissing and practised kissing his hand to try and get it right. Now, when the moment had come, he was too cowardly to try.

Anna wrestled to break free from his tight hold on her, still shouting 'get off me'. This now riled Luke and it fired him up. He moved over her, took hold of her chin and kissed her lips, very briefly. He sighed. 'That was perfection, Astraea, as I knew it would be. You have the loveliest of mouths and taste of the sweetest nectar.' He continued to stare at her in a lovesick trance.

A look of pure loathing spoilt Anna's attractive face. 'Stop it you moron. I am not Astraea, as you keep calling me. I am Anna and I do not want your disgusting kisses. DO YOU HEAR ME? GET AWAY FROM ME.'

Luke flinched at the harsh words. 'Dearest beloved. Do not shout. Don't spoil the tranquillity and joy of our time together. We are the perfect couple, Astraea and Xandros, and our delicate kisses will seal our relationship. In time, we will unite our bodies after we are joined in wedlock.'

Luke released his hold on Anna as he did not want to upset her further. She scrambled away from him as far as the restraining metal chain would allow. Luke was the opposite of Russ who believed that sex was the only thing that bonded him to a woman. Luke could wait to marry his Anna before they consummated their love. In reality, he was a little scared of doing the sexual act with a woman. He had only ever got to the kissing stage with Imogen and no one else. Thus, he was a twenty-six-year-old virgin. He remembered the many porn films he'd watched that made it all seem so easy. He liked the men in those films who were confident and controlled the action with the women. Anna's boyfriend, Nick, would surely be a master in the art of lovemaking. On their wedding night, Luke wanted Anna to take him on a journey to sexual fulfilment.

Anna turned to face Luke and shouted. 'This has to stop now. I am not Astraea, I'm Anna. You are not Xandros, some warrior king. You are a sad, deluded fool. We will not be joined in wedlock. You're seriously weird, a mix of young boy and fantasist. Not of the real world. But you need to leave this fantasy world of yours and face reality. Reality will mean police, courts and prison if you do not let me go. NOW.'

Ignoring her rant, Luke gazed at her face. 'Do not fight what is between us, Astraea. We are destined to be together for eternity. Forget the real world of pain and disappointment. I, your true love, Xandros, will be your provider and protector. We will build a home in a meadow with flowers in springtime and snowflakes in winter time. We will have beautiful babies, a girl, Caprice, a French name meaning 'whimsical' and 'impulsive'. Our own little fairy. A boy, Marcellus, meaning 'young warrior'. Our own little fighter.'

As she held his gaze, she seemed to lose all energy, and in an exhausted tone said, 'Just let me go.' Her beautiful blue eyes held his. Luke gazed into their depths, hoping to find love but all he could see was defeat and despair. This wasn't going to plan at all. Luke had hoped for a connection once they were alone together and she discovered the magic of him, his kindness, his gentle personality and his intellectual genius for storytelling.

Luke sat back, to lean on the headboard. 'I don't want to upset you, Astraea, I mean, Anna. Things will turn out fine. Let me get you a drink.'

Anna stated. 'Yes, I could do with a drink of water and I need to use the bathroom.'

'Yes, the bathroom,' Luke mumbled. He realised that this was the moment she would try to escape. He got off the bed and unlocked the padlock securing the metal chain to the bedframe but left the cuffs on so that her hands were secured in front of her. 'You can't be serious, how am I supposed to go to the toilet?' she asked, incredulously. Luke gently eased her off the bed, and she stood up, her legs a little shaky either through fear or lack of movement. Taking hold of her upper right arm, he guided her out of the room and towards the bathroom. He opened the door, removed the cuffs and pushed her inside the bathroom. Closing the door, he remained on the other side.

Luke tried to focus his mind on what to do next in terms of his control of her. Anna was right, he could not hold her hostage forever. In his plan, he believed that over a short time they would bond and fall in love. This wasn't happening, she was resisting massively, and seemed to despise him. A sense of panic swept through him. His heart was beating so fast that he thought it would explode and he was sweating profusely. If he could not win her over, what was he going to do with her?

He heard the toilet flush and the sound of running tap water. She would be out in a minute. His rising anxiety was such that he felt a panic attack coming on like the ones he'd experienced in his teens and twenties. He recalled her words. Police. Court. Prison. Luke quaked with fear at the horror of going into a stinky prison cell to be greeted by a six-foot-five, tattooed, hairy cellmate. Gulp. Gulp. He must try harder to win her round. Convince her of his love and devotion. That he would be her soulmate in a union of perfect, harmonious bliss. Astraea and Xandros for eternity.

His hysteria abated as he was distracted by the sound of the front door closing and the sound of heavy footsteps climbing the stairs.

'Oi, idiot. What you doing standing guard duty outside the bog?' his brother, Russ, sneered, a quizzical look on his handsome face.

CHAPTER SEVENTY FIVE

Anna ran the tap and scooped the cool water into her mouth. She was so thirsty and was desperate to get the persistent soapy taste off her tongue. Though it was a warm night, she was shivering with cold, and absolutely unable to think how to get out of this hideous situation. She knew that the weirdo would be standing outside the bathroom door. On leaving the room, she may be able to force her way past him, and rush down the stairs. But then what? Exit the house, barefoot, and run to a nearby house or try and flag down a car? If it was late into the night, everyone in nearby houses would be asleep and there was the likelihood of no cars on the roads. She must rush into the kitchen to grab her shoes and her handbag with her car keys and phone inside. Make for her car. No time to over think it now. Open the bathroom door and rush at him to push him out of the way. Anna drew in a deep breath, to steady her nerves and aid her courage. Pulling open the door, she sped forward, ready to knock into Luke. Whoosh. Bang. She ran into the hard chest of a man in a blue polo shirt. This winded her and she jumped back, trying to make sense of things. This was not Luke's flabby chest in a white shirt. This was another man. Slowly she looked up, dreading who she would see.

'Well, what delights have we got here?' the man asked, as he stood, his arms on his hips. 'This is a big surprise. I didn't know you could pull such a beautiful woman, brother. Still waters run deep, eh?'

Anna shivered, rubbing her arms with her hands to generate some heat in her body. She was trapped between the bathroom door and the landing by this imposing man. Luke was standing to the side, looking smaller and weaker, next to his brother. A man that she recognised but where from? The Frizzy

Lion? The supermarket? Somewhere else? He stood staring down at her, his muscular physique dominating the small space of the landing. There was a smirk on his lips and his cold, dark eyes took in every detail of her face and body.

Anna stared directly at this newcomer. 'Your deluded brother has not pulled, as you put it. He is keeping me here against my will. He is living in some sort of twisted fantasy world and I am somehow part of it in his sick mind. You need to help me to get away from him.'

The brother laughed loudly. 'Wow, brother. She sure is feisty, giving out her orders. Look her cheeks have gone red.' The man clasped her chin with his right hand, his fingers digging into her flesh. This action also pulled her closer to him. His eyes thoroughly scrutinised her face and then gazed downwards to the front of her dress. If Luke was physically weak and timid, this man was the exact opposite, strong, muscular and arrogant. If her hopes had been raised about fleeing this nightmare, they were now dashed. This man was not going to be her saviour. But then his next words surprised her. 'Perhaps I can help.'

'Thank you,' Anna stated, her eyes lifting to meet his, momentarily. She did not continue to hold his gaze as his hard stare sent icicles up and down her spine.

'That's ok, darling. Anything for you.' His hand now left her chin and started to play with her hair, pushing it back behind her ears. 'It's great to get the chance to look you over properly. And you certainly don't disappoint. You are gorgeous. I can see why our Luke developed a massive crush on you. Any man would want to be with you.'

Anna stepped forward, praying that the two men would step aside to let her go downstairs, to get her shoes and her bag, and let her go to her car. But the brother still blocked her way. 'It's time I left,' she commented in a matter-of-fact way to encourage his co-operation.

'What's the hurry. The three of us should have a drink together so that I can get to know you, darling. If you are Luke's new girlfriend then you need to get to know the family. I'm Russ but we've actually met twice before. In the supermarket where you frequently shop and at the Frizzy Lion. You weren't very friendly either time, as I recall.' Russ now took a step nearer to Anna, towering over her.

Anna did remember him from the pub. He'd offered to buy her a drink and she'd declined. 'Sorry, I don't recall meeting you.'

A coldness touched his eyes. 'Not memorable enough for you, stuck-up bitch, eh? But I'm not one to bear a grudge. We'll have a drink now and let bygones be bygones,' he smiled at her, a false, fake one that made her shiver. To Luke he said, 'Go and get drinks. Whisky for me.'

Anna was now fed up of all of this. 'I don't want a drink. I just want to leave. Get out of my way.' She pushed forcefully at his chest to shove him aside.

He laughed loudly at her feeble attempt to move him out of the way and lightly tapped her face, a non-verbal warning not to do it again. 'Turning down my offer of a friendly drink for a second time, are you? I don't think so.'

Before Anna could object, he had picked her up, slung her over his shoulder and was carrying her back into Luke's bedroom. He flung her down onto the bed and sat down next to her. His left hand clasped around her shoulders, fingers digging into her left upper arm. A grip so powerful that it felt she was in the coils of a python. Anna was imprisoned by him and could not move. This man was the opposite of his brother. His face was all planes and angles. Sharp cheekbones, well-defined brows, straight nose, hawk-like brown eyes. A harsh haircut, undercut at sides, slicked back at the front exacerbating his imposing features. Unlike Luke's, his body was muscular with toned arms and chest, and broad shoulders. Hard brown eyes, displaying a hint of cruelty, now assessed her face. Paralysed with fear, she could not speak or move.

The man took hold of her face to gaze at her up close, scrutinising every detail. 'You know, babe, Luke and his stupid stories have always been a joke to me. Dad and me indulge him as he struggles to live in the real world. But all credit to him this time. He has picked a female of utter perfection to be in his stories. You.'

Anna struggled to break free of his vice-like hold. 'Take your hands off me.'

Russ sniggered, clamping his left hand at the back of her head to pull her closer and then brought his mouth down on hers. His mouth devoured her, licking and biting gently, as he relished in the kiss. Anna's could not free herself from this onslaught, and was overwhelmed by the taste of sour beer and the smell of stale cigarettes. Anna squirmed to try and escape but to no avail. In his own good time, Russ ended the kiss. 'Babe, that was amazing as I knew it would be.'

Anna pushed at his chest to try to free herself but there was no way he was letting go. 'Let go of me. I don't want you or this. You've no right.'

Russ ignored all this. 'Just relax and enjoy yourself, babe. Don't fight the chemistry. We'll have those drinks and get nicely pissed to get you in the mood. To be honest, babe, a woman as gorgeous as you is never going to be satisfied with Luke. He's not man enough for you.'

Defiance radiated out of Anna's eyes at this egotistical man. 'And you're a man I would never look at in a million years. You and your brother are two pathetic losers.'

Russ laughed, a harsh cackle. 'Losers? I suggest, babe, you watch what you're saying. You've no say in any of this.' With a smirky smile, he clamped her chin and kissed her again. It was a show of dominance, to reinforce that he was in control.

The door banged open and in came Luke carrying a plastic bag containing the drinks which he placed on the bedside cabinet. From the bag he took out bottles of whisky, white wine, lager and glasses. He scowled at Russ who was still holding Anna. 'Russ, Anna is my guest. Let go of her.'

Ignoring Lukes's instruction, Russ pulled Anna closer to him. 'She's enjoying it aren't you, babe.' He picked up the metal chain lying on the duvet. 'Great to see the bondage gear, it should come in handy, later..'

Luke poured whisky into a tumbler glass and gave it to Russ. Luke scuttled back and poured a glass of wine for Anna, then tried to hand it to her. She refused to take it. Anna was parched, her throat dry from lack of liquids over the last hours but she really didn't want to drink the wine. Keeping a clear head was necessary to escape this nightmare.

This didn't please Russ. 'Ok, babe. Take the wine, that's a good girl. We're having a little party, so play nice.' His nails dug into her upper left arm, making her wince in pain, until she obeyed and took hold of the wine glass. 'Cheers, darling..'

Reluctantly, Anna took small sips of the white wine.

Luke took the top of a bottled lager and dragged his office chair to the side of the bed near to Russ. He glowered at his brother; his eyes so full of hot rage he could start a forest fire.

Russ chinked his glass against Luke's bottle. 'This is great, a party. Just the three of us. It's a shame you've haven't got a woman, bro.'

'As I keep saying, Russ, Anna is my guest, not yours. She is not one of your usual skanks to be used and discarded. She is a beautiful woman who I hope to develop a relationship with over time.'

'Poor Luke, this woman will never be in a relationship with you,' Russ mocked, watching as his brother's face went the colour of the ripest tomato. 'She wants a man who knows his way around a woman's body.'

Sipping her wine, Anna listened to their banter. It was hard to imagine they were brothers. One was immature and weak, living a fantasy life to escape the harsh realities of the real world. The other, a womaniser, who believed that he was the world's most gifted lover.

'I don't want either of you. This is not a party and I wish to leave. NOW,' she shouted, her eyes flashing with rage as she addressed the two men. She flung the remaining wine at Russ's face and then pushed hard at his chest to break his hold on her.

Wine dripped down Russ's face, and he wiped it away from his eyes, but then quickly clamped his hand on Anna's arm as she tried escape. Flinging her down on her back, on the bed, Russ loomed over her. 'You'll pay for that, bitch.' Anger distorted his facial features into an animalistic rage as he lashed his right hand hard across her face. The left side of her face throbbed with pain. A liquid trickled down from her left nostril to her lips and the metallic taste of blood filled her mouth. A second, harsh blow followed, as Anna whimpered in agony and fear.

Russ roared at her, his face contorted to a snarling, salivating beast. 'Ok, darling. Try that again and you'll be in a whole world of pain. You owe me.'

Once again, he was kissing her, but this kiss was brutal and raw. Anna flinched as his strong mouth clamped over hers, stinging an area of her lower lip where the second blow had landed. Anna's ears were assailed by his laboured breathing, as he crushed her on the bed by his powerful body. It felt to Anna that she was confined in a coffin, while soil piled in, robbing her of sight, and sound, as she slowly suffocated. His right hand slide downwards to her left breast which he kneaded forcefully.

'GET OFF HER NOW, 'Luke shouted and Anna felt Russ's weight pulled off her as he was dragged backwards by his brother's grip on his polo shirt. Russ sprang off the bed, breaking free of his brother's hold. Anna slowly moved to a sitting position on the bed, to watch, terrified, as Russ faced Luke with a raging anger in his eyes. Luke's usual podgy, pink cheeks quickly drained of colour. Luke froze, as in 'deer in the headlights' fashion. Russ swung back his right arm and landed a hefty punch at Luke's non-descript features. The fist glanced off Luke's chin but slammed into the left side of his upper lip, blood spurted out and trickled down his chin. As Luke staggered in shock, a second, lightning-fast punch to his abdomen bent him double.

Anna watched with horror at this one-sided physical attack. Luke was now whimpering, down on his knees, clutching his stomach. Russ towered over him, legs apart, rage and lust making him into an all-powerful, testosterone-fuelled adversary. If this carried on, Luke would end up dead.

Catching his breath, Russ laughed, 'There you go, brother. I've helped to bring to life one of your little stories where the super villain, let's call him, General Zod, crushes the forces that come up against him. All this blood and pain will be great for you to understand the agony of a real battering.' Whoosh, Russ brought his clenched fists down, hard, between Luke's shoulder blades sending him sprawling onto the carpet.

Anna screamed from the bed. 'Stop. You'll kill him.'

Ignoring her, Russ hauled Luke to his feet. 'Ok, moron. Get out of here now and leave me with her. If you come back into this room in the next two hours I will kill you.' Russ opened the door, grabbed a blubbering Luke by his shirt, and pushed him out of the room. Slamming the door, he leapt back on the bed. Anna scooted back across the bed away from him, her face white with terror. 'Ok, darling, let's get back to where we were.'

He dragged her body underneath his as she cried and screamed. 'Don't mess me about or things will turn bad.' Her body quivered under him but she did stop fighting and shouting as she noted the harshness in his eyes. 'That's better, darling, if you behave like a good girl, things will go well. I've wanted you for the longest time.'

⊷⊶◖▷⊶⊷

CHAPTER SEVENTY SIX

Luke wandered up and down the kitchen area, the terracotta tiles cool under his feet, as he considered what to do. He was holding a damp tea towel against his cut lip to soothe the soreness and stop the bleeding. His abdomen and shoulders throbbed from the powerful punches delivered by his raging brother. Russ had always been strong, even as a child, and being pummelled by the grown-up man, it was like being in a boxing match with a kangaroo. But Luke had to put his own injuries to one side and concentrate on what he was going to do. Now. He could not allow his beloved, Astraea, be violated against her will by an out-of-control monster. Even though that monster was his own brother.

Luke knew he had only minutes to act. Russ was fully turned-on and nothing short of an earthquake was going to stop him. As it had just been proved, Luke was no match for Russ in a fight. The only options he had was to arm himself with a weapon and launch a surprise attack on a distracted Russ. Luke looked around the kitchen area. The knife block held the most obvious choice, six stainless steel, sharp knives of which the carving knife was the longest. Panicking as time was running out, Luke hopped slightly on the spot as he contemplated stabbing the knife into his brother's back. He doubted he'd have the courage to do it. Even if he did, he might only hit muscle or bone without inflicting enough damage to stop him hurting Anna. If he ended up slightly wounding Russ, they would all be in greater danger. No, a knife wouldn't do. Time was running out. Focus, Luke. Then his eyes hit upon the rolling pin. A heavy wooden object, not unlike the baseball bat he had successfully swung at the man that had hurt Anna. Picking up the rolling pin, he rushed out the room, pelted up the stairs, his heart racing and his breathing laboured from exertion and sheer terror.

Luke slammed the bedroom door open as he dashed clumsily into the room. Russ was on top of Anna, but he could not see her, so overwhelmed was she by his brother's weighty body, broad shoulders, firm buttocks and strong thighs. A muscular, predatory beast subjecting the fragile prey to its all-powerful attack. There was no way she could fight him off.

Luke took in this terrible sight, as he stood, legs trembling, by the side of the bed. Cold fear lodged in his throat. He felt the solid weight of the rolling pin in his hand and remembered how he'd whacked the man's body. This time was different, his opponent was a dangerous pugilist who had honed his fighting skills over many years. If he failed to stop Russ, he and Anna could both be dead. Remembering that he loved Anna, helped to fire his rage. 'Russ. Stop, get off her,' he ordered.

'Go away,' growled Russ, ignoring Luke, as he ran his fingers along Anna's waist and hips. 'I said I'd kill you if you interrupted us.' As Russ lost focus on Anna, she used all her power to hit out at him, catching her hand across his face. Anger flared in Russ. 'Fucking bitch,' he shouted, and he knelt over her, bringing his right arm up ready to slap her across the face.

In the next second, Luke had raised the rolling pin and slammed it down on the back of his brother's skull. For a second, the blow seemed to have no impact on Russ, as his arm hovered ready to hit Anna. Luke's hands were shaking uncontrollably and sweat was making his grip of the rolling pin almost impossible. Should he hit him again? Luke looked over at Anna and her terrified eyes stared back at him while they both waited, silently, to see what Russ would do. What he did was slump forward onto Anna's body and lay still.

'Oh hell,' she said, as the solid weight constricted her movements. 'Have you killed him?'

Luke dropped the rolling pin and stood fidgeting by the side of the bed. His heart was pounding in his chest like a bass drum in a marching band. Russ lay sprawled over Anna, pinning her down into the bed, as a trickle of blood stained the back of his polo shirt. Edging nearer to Russ, Luke observed that he was breathing and he pinched his left earlobe to see if he responded which he didn't. Luke's hand trembled as he placed his index and middle fingers to the side of Russ's windpipe to check for a pulse. 'He's breathing and has a pulse so at least I've not killed him,' Luke said, his body shaking visibly as he stared at Anna. 'I've always joked that Russ has a thick head.'

'Just get him off me before he comes to,' Anna ordered Luke.

Luke fanned his face frantically with his hands to try to cool his sweating brow and reddened cheeks. 'If he wakes up we are toast. I'll get him off you.'

Anna sighed with relief, believing that her ordeal was coming to an end. 'He's really heavy and I'll be the one not breathing shortly.'

Luke gazed into Anna's lovely eyes. It hurt him to see her trapped by the weight of his pig of a brother, particularly after what he had tried to do to her. Luke's heart ached as he recognised the terror in her eyes and the fear she must be feeling due to his brother's actions. He must remember his original objective, to love her and keep her safe. 'Hold out your arms,' he requested, as she gave him a puzzled look.

Taking hold of the metal cuffs, Luke went through the process of securing her wrists and then used the metal chain to secure her to the bedframe once again. 'What are you doing? Get him off me and let me go,' she begged him.

Lightly stroking her forehead to bring comfort, he muttered, 'It's ok, my beloved Astraea. I will remove Russ from the room and then we will be alone together again.'

Anna jolted her head away from him to escape his touch. 'For goodness sake, you idiot. Stop this. It will not end well for you as you have now injured your brother as well as imprisoning me against my will.'

Her sudden movement caused Russ to groan softly and Luke feared that he was waking up. Grabbing hold of Russ around the waist, Luke manoeuvred him off the bed and he landed on the carpet with a thump. He then took hold of Russ's legs and pulled him, face down, towards the door. Huffing and puffing, and bright red in the face, Luke dragged Russ across the landing into his own bedroom. It would take too much effort to haul him on the bed. He rushed to the wardrobe to get Russ's box of bondage gear and took out a pair of handcuffs. Luke rolled Russ, pulled his wrists together in front and secured the handcuffs on him.

Chuckling to himself, Luke could see the humour in the situation. Russ was always boasting of the times he had restrained women with cuffs and ropes as part of his sex fun. It was a shame that he was currently unable to enjoy the pleasure of them being used on him. Russ now started to slowly move his head and groan. It was likely that he was waking up. In Russ's box of tricks, amongst the paddles, whips, blindfolds et al there was a roll of bondage tape. He grabbed the roll and rushed to secure his brother's ankles together with the tape before he started to come to. It wasn't easy, Luke was sweating profusely to do the job quickly as further moans came from Russ. Luke then ripped off a piece of tape to cover Russ's mouth before the moans turned to shouts. Looking down at his brother's restrained body, Luke imagined a fully conscious Russ trying to crawl or hop out of the room. To stop this, Luke dragged Russ across the room to lean him against the radiator. Taking a further set of cuffs from the box, he secured one cuff around Russ's left wrist and one to the radiator valve. This was a priceless moment for Luke. The master of bondage games trussed up like a chicken. If only he hadn't left his phone in his bedroom. Luke contemplated getting it but resisted as it would be a further distraction from returning to Anna. Instead, he patted Russ lightly on the head. 'Sweet dreams, bro.'

Luke went back into his own bedroom. Anna was lying still on the bed, her eyes closed. Amazingly, she had fallen asleep. Luke drew his chair closer to the bed to take this unique opportunity to gaze at her without hinderance. He noted that the whiteness of the linen intensified the paleness of her flawless complexion. Perfect eyebrows, long black eyelashes but a smudging of black eyeliner and mascara under her eyes only added to her loveliness. Her lips were free of lipstick but they still had an enticing rosy pink plumpness. Luke was thumped in the chest as he stared at her awesome beauty. She was ethereal, of nature, of water, of wind, of clouds, of other realms. Truly his Astraea. But would his incarceration of her affect her vitality and spirit. Would she fade, become as mist or fog, and slowly disappear before his eyes? If he kept her here, away from the light and the air, would she diminish altogether until she was no more?

It was a warm night but Luke gently pulled the duvet up to her waist to protect her modesty. It was not his intention to hurt her but he could not let her go. For now, until the need for sleep overcame him, he would sit on the chair and drink in her beauty as she slept. He, Xandros, had his ideal woman in his life for all eternity. He would write more stories about beautiful Astraea now that she was close by to inspire his imagination. His books would be published and film companies would be fighting to make movies of his thrilling tales about Xandros and Astraea. Luke and Anna would become rich, buy a magnificent house, and then fill it with children to make their family complete. It was the dawn of his new life. People would treat him differently, with more respect, when they saw the loveliest of women had chosen him as her husband.

◄◊►

CHAPTER SEVENTY SEVEN

It was early Monday morning and Luke was sat at the kitchen table; his hands clutched around a hot mug of tea, as he listened to Russ's rant. He didn't want to listen to this as it spoilt the cosy, warm feelings of earlier having spent the night with his beloved. The most incredible time of his life had occurred in the last few hours and he wanted peace and tranquillity to savour every single second. After watching Anna whilst she slept, Luke had curled up on the carpet by the bed, and fell asleep dreaming of adventures in a make-believe world. When he woke up, Anna was still asleep so he had taken more photos for his collection. A photo of her lovely brown hair fanning out on the pillow whilst her exquisite face was restful in sleep. Up close photos of her face, her well-defined cheekbones, her luscious mouth, the gentle 'V' of her jawline. Modest photos of her shoulders, arms, and rise of her breasts, as her golden skin was drenched by the early morning sun in the room. He'd sneaked a few selfies as he lay next to her sleeping form, photos that forever would be a record of his perfect night.

His bubble of happiness was now popped by the ugly face of Russ, growling and shouting at him, across the kitchen table. Luke had been startled to find Russ in the kitchen after he had secured him with handcuffs and tape last night. It was a relief that his brother was still alive after the blow to his head but an angry Russ was not easy to deal with. Luke asked, 'How did you get out of the handcuffs? Are you some sort of Houdini?'

Russ scoffed at this, leaning back in his chair, a gloating expression of his hard features. 'What brother, are you upset to see that I am alive? No, I am not a skilled escape artist. You left the bondage box within my reach and I found a spare key to undo the cuffs.'

Luke pouted his lips, in a way that he always did over the years, to try to soothe his brother's rage and win him over. 'Sorry, Russ.'

'Ok, numb nuts, stop looking all down-trodden and pathetic, and listen to me,' Russ snarled; his face contorted with anger. 'I've not forgotten what you did to me last night by battering me across the head. And that you stopped me from getting it on with the goddess. You will pay in due course. But for now you have got bigger things to worry about than a thrashing from me. What are you planning to do with your little problem upstairs?'

Luke felt that as he was still in a state of sleep deprivation he couldn't make sense of what Russ was saying. 'What do you mean? I've haven't got a problem. In fact everything is wonderful. Today is going to be perfect as I am going to spend it with my beloved.'

Russ laughed loudly, throwing his head back which caused him to flinch with pain. 'I mean, your problem of Anna, or your beloved, or whatever she's called. What are you going to do about her?'

At the mention of her name, Luke felt that warm, fuzzy glow he always experienced when he thought of her. 'Oh, what? Yes, I'll let her have a shower and she can use some of the expensive shower gel I bought for her, jasmine and rose. Then, I'll make her breakfast – scrambled eggs, wholemeal toast, honey or jam and a mug of coffee. After that we can go for a walk, perhaps have a cream tea at a quaint coffee shop. Later I'm going to do salmon, new potatoes and salad with a nice white, delicate Chablis.' Luke sighed loudly as he visualised the perfect day ahead.

Bang. Russ's right fist hit the wooden table hard, making it vibrate and spilling their coffees. 'Cut the crap, Luke. You brought her here under false pretences, drugged her, and handcuffed her to your bed. She will not be up for a day out with scones and jam.'

'But Russ, you don't understand. She is my girlfriend, my beautiful Astraea. She wants to be with me. We are soulmates,'

Luke explained, hurt that his brother was not trying to understand that he was now with Anna for life.

Russ rubbed his hands at his forehead, still suffering a headache after the blow to his head. 'Fucking hell, Luke. Wake up. She is not your girlfriend or your soulmate. She does not like you. She wants to go home to her boyfriend. She will report you to the police and you will be arrested. You will go to court and be sentenced to prison. You will share a cell with a big hairy ape who decides that he's missing his girlfriend but will make do with his pasty-faced cell mate for rumpy-pumpy. You. So, Luke, I ask again, what are you going to do about her?'

Luke felt a hot flush of anxiety rush through his body and his cheeks flamed a vibrant red. 'No, Russ. You are wrong. She will grow to love me after we spend time together.

'For fuck's sake, Luke. You need to consider your options and quickly. People will start to miss her when she doesn't arrive at work and she's not answering her phone. The boyfriend will be looking for her. And to be honest, when he catches you, he will whip your arse worse than I intend to.'

Luke could feel a knot in his stomach as fear clutched him in its tight claws. 'She will just tell him that she's with me now and it'll be ok. He'll respect what she says and leave us together.'

Russ leaned forward and slapped his hand across Luke's left cheek. 'Listen, idiot. Option one, you let her go but she goes straight to the police and you will be arrested. Option two, you continue to keep her here, chained to the bed, indefinitely. This will work out fine until dad gets back. He won't be happy to find a woman shackled to your bed. He will force you to let her go and she will go to the police, blah, blah, blah. Option three, you get rid of the problem permanently and lie through your teeth to the police when they come looking for her. I think your best bet is option three.'

Luke's mouth fell open, before he stuttered, 'Option three means I have to kill her, right?'

'You've got it, bro. Don't start researching online how to kill then dispose of a body or you'll be up shit creek, pretty quick,' Russ snickered, a cruel hardness to his dark eyes. 'You write all those stupid stories so you must have an idea how it all works.'

Luke was feeling really peeved with his brother's attitude now. 'They are not stupid stories, they are fantastical tales. There's lots of slaying and deaths but a CSI team doesn't turn up to gather forensic evidence. An apex predator or flesh-guzzling beast normally takes care of the bodies. So, actually this is not my realm of expertise. Anyway, you are not an innocent in all this as she will report you for sexual assault.'

Russ drank his cooling coffee before answering. 'Yeah, that's a fair point. Basically, we're both screwed every which way but option three seems the best one. How to do the kill without leaving forensic evidence? Answer, it's difficult but we should steer clear of methods that leave a lot of DNA evidence such as stabbing, strangulation and blow to the head. Drowning's a possibility, particularly if we dispose of the body in water. My preferred option would be to give her a high dose of the GHB as it doesn't stay in the body long, then dispose of the body in the Avon.'

The coffee that Luke had just drank was now in danger of re-appearing as he listened to Russ's practical approach to murdering his beloved. 'Russ, we cannot do this. We just need time to think it through. I'll go and bring her down here and give her some breakfast. When she realises that I genuinely love her I'm sure she'll see sense. We'll let her go off home with a cheery wave.' Luke got up out of his chair and went over to the bread bin for bread; eggs, butter and orange juice out of the fridge and honey out of the cupboard. 'Do you want some eggs?' he asked Russ.

'Yeah, ok. Do some bacon as well. With your stupid plan in place, we might as well enjoy a last meal before we're forced to eat prison slop,' Russ joked. 'I'll go and wake up our sleeping beauty with a kiss. I'm the handsome prince in this story, as you bro, are the pale, warty frog.'

As he took the heavy-based frying pan out of the bottom of the oven, Luke ordered Russ, 'Oh no you don't. You'll end up doing more than a kiss. I'll go and you cook the bacon and eggs.' Luke tapped the frying pan against his hand to emphasis his point, hoping that he wouldn't have to give Russ another whack to incapacitate him. Realistically, this could lead to his own brains chilling on the kitchen floor.

Russ got up and came over to the hob and took the pan out of Luke's hand. 'Don't think you'll get another chance to knock me out, bro. Go and bring Sleeping Beauty down here.'

CHAPTER SEVENTY EIGHT

Anna lay on her back, motionless, staring at the ceiling. She was in the most frightening situation of her life but she was at a loss as to how to get out of it. What to make of the two men involved and what were their intentions? The man, Luke, had planned to get her here, drugged her and was holding her against her will. Was the brother, Russ, involved or had he just stumbled across what Luke had done and used all this as a chance to attack her? Her assessment of Russ was that he was an opportunist, a man who would use violence to achieve his objectives, and a man who used women. Luke had stopped the assault on her by his brother by bashing his skull with a rolling pin. On balance, it did seem that Luke did not want to physically hurt her but still had no intention of letting her go. But she could not work out what he would be prepared to do to keep her with him. And his attack on his brother indicated that he was capable of violence. What was his ultimate plan as he could not keep her captive indefinitely? If he released her, he must know that she would go to the police. Was he capable of murder to ensure her silence? It was all too awful to think about.

The room was warm, and she was covered by the duvet, but she felt cold due to the icy pit of fear in her stomach. She had no idea of the time but guessed that it was about seven or eight a.m. on Monday morning. There was a working meeting at eight-thirty and her boss would be irritated if she did not attend. Would Olivia try to phone her to find out why she wasn't in work? Nick would have tried to contact her last night, would he be worried about her lack of response?

One good thing, Luke had left the room. Anna felt drowsy with a persistent low-level headache that never seemed to shift and hindered her ability to think clearly. Her mouth was dry due to lack of water and the nasty taste that persisted. She had not wanted to sleep but she had slept fitfully, as her body and mind were exhausted from the trauma. As she was still shackled to the bedframe by the handcuffs there was no way of getting free. Luke would surely come to free her shortly as she would need to go to the bathroom and this may be her chance to escape. This time the tall, muscular brother was out of action, at least one obstacle removed.

Anna heard someone entering the bedroom and opened her eyes to see her friendly-faced captor gazing down at her. With his twinkly eyes, rosy cheeks and smooth skin, he looked like a character out of an Enid Blyton story but this cheery goodwill persona was all facade. Beneath the boy-like innocence there lurked a cunning man who was not concerned about breaking the law to achieve his goals.

He reached out with a pale, chubby hand to stroke her forehead which made her cringe. This was not the hand of a typical monster, one with hair and claws, but it had the same effect of chilling her to the core. 'Astraea, beloved, time to wake up.'

Anna tried to shuffle away from his hideous, unwelcome touch. 'I am not your beloved. You need to end this now and let me go. Things will only get worse for you as time goes on. I will be missed at work. My boyfriend will be worried. They will report me missing to the police.' She stared into his anxious eyes. 'Luke, I know that you are not an evil person but what you are doing to me is wrong. Help yourself by letting me go.'

Luke took out the keys to remove the metal chain and the handcuffs and took her arm to ease her out of bed. 'Come on, Anna, you can use the bathroom and Russ is preparing breakfast. You must be hungry. We can then discuss our plans for the day.'

This information spooked Anna. Firstly, the psycho brother was up and about. Secondly, this deluded fool, Luke, was talking of breakfast and plans for the day. As if this was a perfectly normal Monday.

As she got up on trembling legs to vacate the room, she gazed around at the hundreds of photos of her on the surrounding walls that an obsessed Luke had taken. Photos over many months. A lot of the images were of her upper body and face but others concentrated on her body. He liked to take shots of her back view, her bottom, as she leaned into the car boot to put away her shopping. Another favourite was of her standing on tiptoes to close the car boot, photos zooming in on her legs and thighs revealed by a short summer dress. But she gasped as she noted other photos, not just of the supermarket car park. Many photos of her entering and exiting her house generally in the evening. It freaked her out to think he had been in his car, outside her house, watching her. A few photos caught her eye, photos of the Connor Peterson incident, including the arrival of the police and Peterson's arrest. This man had been stalking her for a number of months. 'Oh my God, you've been stalking me at my home.' The shock of this almost stopped her breathing and she had to focus on taking deep, controlled breaths to stop a panic attack.

Luke looked sheepishly at her. 'Er, yes, but only to make sure you're safe. With Russ's help, I punished that weasel who attacked you. We brought him here and gave him a good thrashing with a baseball bat.'

Anna had to sit down on the edge of the bed to stop her legs buckling under her. 'It was you and your brother who assaulted him? Holy shit. You are unbelievable.'

Staring at her with loving eyes, Luke tried to take her hand. 'It is my duty as Xandros to protect you, Astraea, and to wreak vengeance on those that hurt you.'

Anna shuddered with fright. This man, with a boyish face, had originally seemed benign and friendly. In truth he was a stalker, a fantasist, who plotted to take her captive, drugged her and tied her up. He was prepared to use violence on those that sullied his fantasy world where she was the goddess. This included Connor Peterson and his own brother. How far would he be prepared to go to keep her with him? Anna stated, in a wavery voice, made weak by exhaustion, 'You are in all kinds of trouble.'

Ignoring this, Luke took hold of her arm to pull her up off the bed and guided her out of the room. 'Come on, Anna, breakfast is waiting.'

Anna allowed herself to be led towards the door, at least it meant escaping this room. But then another collection of photos caught her eye. Photos that recorded her accident when she was knocked down by the car at the supermarket car park. The photos showed a white car driving towards her and then an image of the car's impact with the trolley. A photo of her lying on her back on the ground after the impact, the trolley toppled over onto its side. But the most interesting photograph was the front of the white car including the car's registration plate. This was the car that had knocked her down. Luke had witnessed the incident, recorded it on his phone and captured the evidence. There was also a photo of the car's rear number plate as the car rushed away from the scene.

'Oh God. You've got photos of my hit-and-run including the registration number of the car that hit me. This is vital evidence we can pass this to the police.' Even though her head was aching and her brain felt like mush, she mentally recorded the car registration number. 'Did you pass this on to the police?'

Luke avoid her eyes as she stared, hopefully, at him. 'Er, I am intending to. I just forgot.'

Anna guessed that he had not passed this evidence to the police. Why? Because he did not want to become involved with the police as it might bring his stalking behaviour to their attention. But for Anna she was relieved that at least the police would be able to trace the evil person who had knocked her over and driven off, leaving her injured in a supermarket car park.

CHAPTER SEVENTY NINE

Ten minutes later, Anna entered the kitchen area, to be greeted by a smirking Russ who was frying bacon in a pan. In a second pan he was stirring scrambled eggs. 'Morning, gorgeous. Take a seat over there.' He pointed at a chair at the end of the kitchen table. To Luke, he said, 'Take over here. I'll make our guest comfortable.'

Anna sat in the chair as instructed. Russ came to stand next to her, his physical presence crowding her personal space. Despite the heat in the room due to the warmth of the day and the gas hob, she had to try to stop her body from shivering. Russ placed his hand on her left shoulder and bent down to speak to her, his abhorrent face close to hers. 'Sit and eat your breakfast. Afterwards, me and you have unfinished business. Don't think that my bozo brother is going to help you again. If he tries anything, I will kill him, then I will kill you.' The menace in his voice as he uttered this threat was bone-chilling.

On the table there was cutlery, toast, butter, honey and marmalade. Luke brought over a plate with two rashers of bacon and scrambled eggs and placed it in front of Anna. 'Tea or coffee,' he asked and she requested coffee with milk. The smell of the greasy bacon was churning her stomach but at the same time she was hungry as she had not eaten in hours. This was like some weird daydream where outwardly she was staying in some rural B & B with English breakfast included. In reality, there was no charge for the bed and breakfast, you just swapped your freedom to be held against your will by the Brother's Grim.

Luke brought over the mug of coffee and placed it in front of her. 'There you go, my beloved. You must eat or you will be ill.'

Russ sat on the chair to her left side and Luke gave him his plate of food. Russ buttered three slices of toast, covered his eggs and bacon with tomato sauce, and then ate hungrily. Swigs of coffee aided his digestion. 'Great grub. We'll eat up and make polite conversation. Isn't that what we do when we have a guest, Luke?'

Luke sat down with his food and a mug of coffee. 'We do, Russ. Though you're normally very monosyllabic when you're eating. You can't seem to eat, and talk, at the same time.' He gave Anna a cheeky smile. 'Russ is not a fully developed male in terms of human interactions. How he manages to get so many women is beyond me.'

Anna nibbled at a slice of buttered toast and ate a few mouthfuls of the eggs. The food was bitter and tasteless in her mouth like eating ash from a grate. She sipped at the now cooling coffee to take the taste off her tongue.

Russ's eyes focused fully on Anna. 'Talking of women, I've been seeing an insatiable slut recently. You might know her. Abbie. She used to go out with your boyfriend.'

Anna spluttered on a mouthful of coffee. 'What's that, you've been going out with Abbie? How did that happen?'

'I met her at the Frizzy Lion, the night she tried to throw wine at you but your boyfriend stepped in. I've been seeing her since then. Your bloke must've had some stamina to go with her. She never lets up. Loves all the kinky stuff, you know, whips crops, paddles, handcuffs, gags, blindfolds, you name it she's up for it.' His cold, dark eyes locked onto Anna's. 'What about you, are you up for that stuff? Does you boyfriend get you under his control, sweetheart?'

Anna decided to ignore this pathetic questioning and attempted to eat a little more of the scrambled egg as a distraction from his intense gaze.

Russ resumed eating the last rasher of bacon and the remaining scrambled egg. 'You are very ungrateful, sweetheart. After what I've done for you. You see that Abbie, she was the one who knocked you down with her car. To get revenge for taking her Nick, she said. She's one spiteful bitch if you cross her and she really had it in for you.'

Anna was too stunned to speak. The knowledge that Abbie had driven that car at her was beyond awful. To get revenge for taking Nick. It had been no accident, Abbie had meant to harm her or kill her. A wave of emotion swept through Anna, tears filled her eyes, and she struggled not to sob in front of these two men.

Luke noticed immediately and paused in eating his breakfast. 'Do not get upset, my Astraea. Xandros has not let her actions go unpunished.'

Anna's chest juddered as the unshed tears threatened to overwhelm her and having to endure his continual crazy talk was making matters worse. This was a hellish nightmare with no escape. She wanted to cry but drank more of the coffee to try to ease her emotional trauma. It was beyond endurance to allow these two to witness her pain.

Russ gazed at her, interested in her reaction but unmoved by her tears. 'I'm really glad that I never get attached to women. I can't stand the tears, the neediness, the acting up and disobedience. Anyway, I've punished her for her bad behaviour including knocking you down in that car.'

The man wiped his mouth with his hand and dragged his chair nearer to Anna. Placing his hand behind her head, he pulled her towards him so that he could kiss her mouth. Flavours of bacon and tomato sauce overwhelmed her tastebuds and Anna believed that she may be sick. The man kissed powerfully, fully controlling her mouth, until he decided when the kiss should end. Incredibly, he winked at her. 'Well, babe, that kiss was my first reward from you for dealing with your Abbie problem. She overstepped the mark with me. Thinking she's so clever and that I'm a lapdog that will bow to her every command. Disrespecting me by going off with some loser in the pub. Telling lies. She told me of her scam of telling your boyfriend that she's pregnant with his baby and getting a fake scan photo off the internet to back up her story. That bitch ain't having no kid. It's a way to bring him back into her life and get rid of you. I don't care about all that but I won't be lied to or made a fool of. As I said earlier, she's learnt the consequences of her bad behaviour.'

Placing her head in her hands, Anna groaned with pain. 'What have you done? She did hurt me physically but I don't want you to be some avenger on my behalf. I want the law to hold her accountable for her actions.'

Russ snorted and shook his head. 'I never bother with the law. I deliver my own justice to those who cross me and Abbie got what she deserved with her favourite instrument, the riding crop. The session started with the normal level of sting she was expecting but it ended with a high level of pain being delivered. It taught her not to cross me, I can tell you. But, there's another sting in the tail, or should I say, her tail.' Russ paused, for Anna to appreciate his little joke. 'I recorded some of our bondage sessions on my phone and have sent them to everyone on her social media, including her blonde mate, Alyssa, and your boyfriend. I've also sent Luke's photos of her car leaving the scene of your accident in the supermarket car park, including the registration number, to everyone. I expect the police to be contacting her shortly. Anyway, I've done all this as she pissed me off by disrespecting me. I've done it because Luke wanted revenge on her for hurting you. So now, you owe me, babe. We'll go upstairs so you can pay your dues.'

The man dragged her out of her seat, the grip on her upper arm so strong that she thought he would cut off her blood supply. 'Let go of me,' Anna ordered as she struggled to escape his grasp. Pulling away from him and then trying to kick his legs, earned her a powerful slap to her face which made her left ear ring. His hand caught the side of her nose and she experienced a wetness which trickled down onto her upper lip. The wetness penetrated her lips and the metallic taste of blood tainted her mouth. Russ re-took hold of her upper arm.

Luke, who was sat close by squealed, 'Oh my God, you've made her bleed. Leave her alone, Russ.' Luke jumped up from his seat and went swiftly over to the gas hob and picked up the largest frying pan. The greasy oil in the pan dribbled onto the tiled flooring.

'Don't you fucking dare try to hit me with that, brother,' Russ ordered, pushing Anna ahead of him but still clasping her arm.

Walking with determination, Luke pressed on towards Russ. 'Let her go. I love her with all my heart and soul and you will not hurt her.' Luke kept pressing forward, firmly holding the frying pan. Russ let go of Anna and went towards his brother. Luke swung the heavy pan through the air with the intention of landing a blow on Russ. In seconds, the pan was wrestled from Luke's hands and Russ was holding it.

Luke backed away from a snarling Russ but he was soon walking on the greasy bacon fat on the tile floor, which caused him to slip, and he smacked down on his bottom. 'Oomph,' he exclaimed as the breath went out of him. His angry brother loomed over him, gripping the frying pan handle so tightly his knuckles went white.

'This, brother, is going to be your thrashing for battering me last night,' he bellowed, a full on raging bull. Anna watched, frozen on the spot, as Russ swung his right arm backwards, his biceps bulging beneath his blue polo shirt, before he brought the pan slamming into the left side of Luke's head. Luke screamed, his body absorbing the thud of the heavy pan as it connected with his skull and facial bones. A loud 'ouch' was uttered by Luke as he clutched his injured face. Droplets of blood sprayed the air around Luke's head from the gash to his temple near to his eyebrow. Russ towered over him, his face distorted by fury, as he raised the pan in his hand a second time.

Anna came out of her trance, sickened by the attack on Luke. But this was her chance to get away. Seeing her bag on the kitchen worktop she grabbed it and sped towards the French doors that led to the garden. Luckily, they were unlocked and she pushed them open. Quickly scanning left and right, she ran to the left over a patio of grey flagstones towards a building that she recognised as the garage at the rear of the property. Running over grass in bare feet was fine but as she exited the garden, via a gate, walking on a gravel driveway was more of a challenge. She ran to where she had parked her car then gasped in horror on seeing that her car was gone. Had it been moved into the garage/workshop to conceal it? At the front of the building there were two large timber doors. Anna pulled at the doors to try to open them but they were both closed and locked. She'd noticed another door to this building, on the garden side, thus she re-entered the garden. This door opened, and her eyes searched frantically around the garden area to see if Russ was following her, before going inside the garage where she found her car parked behind a work's van. Anna's breathing was juddery as fear threatened to overwhelm her. With shaking hands, she took her phone out of her bag, switched it on and prayed it was not out of charge. Logically, she knew she should ring the police first but she really needed to speak to Nick and hear his reassuring voice. One thing was certain, this nightmare had to end.

⊷⊶◈⊷⊶

CHAPTER EIGHTY

Nick stretched at his desk, his back muscles and shoulders were aching from the exertion of demolishing his father's old garden shed and laying down a concrete base for the new shed, yesterday afternoon. There had been a lot to do including clearing the shed of all tools and gardening equipment before they could get cracking. Ed had been roped in to help but was useless as he was recovering from a hangover and his main contribution to the work was moaning and groaning. For a man who made a living out of landscape gardening he was also very low on ideas and helpful suggestions to make the job easier. He'd texted Anna a couple of times during the afternoon and evening. Text one: '**Hi sweetie. Hope you are enjoying the open gardens. Relax and eat cake. I am sweating buckets. Thinking of committing fratricide as Ed is proving to be lazy idiot. Speak to you later. N xxx.**' Text two, two hours later: '**Hi Anna. Nearly finished doing the concrete base. Ed buried underneath it. Hope you got home ok. I'll ring you later. N xxx.**'

Now, at eleven a.m. on Monday morning, Nick was getting worried and annoyed in equal measure that he had not heard from Anna. When he rang her later yesterday evening, she didn't answer. Another text this morning had gone unanswered. A follow-up text an hour later was ignored. It was not like her. She usually responded quickly to his texts except when she was at work. Nick ran through in his mind their discussion on Saturday night. The intensity of their love-making had taken their intimacy to a whole new level and it was what he had been searching for all his life. When he'd told her that he loved her, it was meant with the depth of love and emotion that a man can have for a woman. He was honest and sincere, opening his heart to her. But now she was not responding to his texts or answering his calls. Had his declaration of love for her been too premature? Had he scared her off? There was a fragility to Anna due to her past bad experiences with men. Was she now withdrawing from him, curling into a ball, to protect herself from getting hurt again?

It occurred to him that he wasn't really sure of where she had gone yesterday for this open garden event. She had mentioned a village, south of Warwick. She was going first to the garden of someone she regularly chatted to at the supermarket. From that first garden, she would move on to the other gardens that were open. Nick wondered who this person was that she chatted to at the supermarket as she had never mentioned them to him. Were they male or female? Would it be a problem if they were male? It was now worrying Nick that Anna was not responding to his texts. A worry that something was wrong. To put his mind at rest he decided to contact her directly at work to satisfy himself that she was ok. He rang the main telephone number for her payroll company and asked to speak to Anna Louden. He was put through to Olivia, Anna's friend.

'Hi, Olivia, I was trying to get through to Anna. I'm assuming she's in a meeting?' Nick asked.

'Hi, Nick. Nice to speak to you. Anna's not in a meeting. In fact, she hasn't come into work today and no one has heard from her. It's very puzzling and not like Anna to just not phone in.'

Nick's worry was now growing to a major concern. 'She's not at work and not phoned in sick?' he clarified.

'No. I've texted her a few times and she's not responding. I'm assuming she's dying quietly under her duvet. Jack Buckner's not happy as there was an eight-thirty briefing she missed. Still, he'll love it when she gets back and he can take pleasure in giving her a bollocking.' Olivia's voice reduced to a whisper as she said this.

'This is all very worrying. She's not responded to my texts and calls since yesterday afternoon. She went off to some open garden event in South Warwickshire and there's been no contact since,' Nick clarified.

'So you guys were ok following the incident on Saturday night with that Owen idiot. It was a bit icy in the taxi on the way home,' Olivia commented.

'Yeah, he was an utter idiot. But yes, Anna and I were fine when she explained what had happened. And it was remiss of me to be angry with her. We talked things through and we are both happy with where our relationship is going. Happier than ever, I think. Thus it all feels really off that there's been no contact since yesterday. I'm going to go over to her house to check on her.'

'Oh yeah, I forgot about the open garden thing,' Olivia stated. 'I was surprised that she wanted to go to that. It's to do with some guy who always speaks to her in the supermarket. A bit of an awkward loser type. I think he's got a big crush on her and could be a weirdo. He bought her tulips at Easter. Recently, he asked her to sponsor him and his aunt's dog on some dog-walking charity thing. Then the dog hurt its leg and that was all off. So he invited her to this open garden thingy for charity. This guy's in his twenties and is doing an open garden event for old ladies who drink tea and old men who grow veg. Give me a break. Definitely oddball, in my opinion,' Olivia added, emphasising the word 'oddball'.

Nick couldn't actually speak for a while. He had absolutely no idea about this man at the supermarket and his approaches to Anna. He did remember her receiving the tulips at Easter and they'd jokingly called the person 'Tulip Man'. The reason the man had given Anna the tulips was because she was the most beautiful girl he'd ever seen. Nick had absolutely no idea that she was still speaking to this man three months later. 'Well, Anna's not told me about her ongoing contact with this man. Sometimes she's a bit too kind and doesn't like to hurt people's feelings. I'm not liking that she's gone off alone to the house of a man who may have a crush on her. And we've not seen or heard from her since. Shit.'

Olivia sighed loudly. 'This guy does definitely sound persistent and she thinks he hangs around the supermarket waiting for her. He always makes a point of having a chat and recently he's started to buy her a coffee. I did tell her to be careful about going to his house. She insisted it would be fine. She wasn't going to his house but to his garden and there would be lots of people around.'

'Buys her a coffee? Does this person have a name?' Nick could feel a tightening of nerves in his stomach as he heard about Anna's interactions with this man.

'I think he's called Luke. He says things to get her to talk to him. The dog-walking was a bit sus as the dog was quickly out of action. Then it's another charity event to raise funds for Age UK. For a young guy, he's got the interests of a pensioner, gardening and charities for oldies.'

Nick now felt an extreme urgency to check that Anna was at her house and was ok. 'Right, thanks, Olivia. I'm going to go over to her house now.'

'Great. Please let me know she's ok. Don't tell her Jack's on the warpath or it may hinder her recovery if she's ill,' Oliva commented.

'I won't. But if he upsets my girl he'd better watch out,' Nick joked. 'Bye, Olivia.'

Olivia's assessment of this Luke as being a bit creepy was getting to Nick. He picked up his keys and phone and went to tell Eric he'd was leaving work due to a personal matter.

Fifteen minutes later, Nick pulled up at Anna's house. Her car was not on the driveway. He rang the video doorbell and waited but there was no response. Once again he texted her: **'Anna. I'm at your front door. Olivia's told me you're not at**

work. I'm getting worried about you. I need to check you're ok. N xxx.'

Nick stood patiently on the doorstep, waiting to give her time to read his text and let him in. There was still no response. If she was really poorly, she could actually be asleep. Then he remembered the next door neighbour, Ben, the parcel guy. He knocked on Ben's door and he quickly answered. Nick explained the situation regarding his concerns for Anna and was given Anna's spare key.

Nick rang the doorbell again and on getting no reply, he let himself into Anna's house. He quickly checked the downstairs area but there was no sign of her and everything looked neat and tidy. Taking the stairs, two at a time, he arrived at her bedroom door and knocked gently. 'Hi, Anna, sweetheart. It's Nick.' Again, there was no response. He eased open the door and entered, speaking softly so as not to alarm her if she was asleep. 'I've come to check on you as you're not answering my calls and I'm worried about you. Olivia says that you're not in work...' He stopped talking abruptly. Anna was not in bed. The bed was made and the room was tidy. Where the hell was she?'

Nick's next option was to ring her father to find out if she'd gone to visit him for any reason, a family emergency or such like. But if this were the case why couldn't she just respond to his texts so that he knew that she was ok. He texted her again: **'Anna. I'm in your house having got the spare key from Ben. Where are you? I'm seriously worried about you. Just let me know that you are safe. I love you. N xxx.'**

⚜

CHAPTER EIGHTY ONE

Sitting in his car on Anna's driveway, Nick was completely perplexed as to where she was and what was going on. He immediately telephoned Anna's father, Mike Louden. 'Hi, Mike, it's Nick here. Is Anna with you?'

Mike Louden coughed to clear his throat. 'No, son, she's not here. She went to an open gardens event in South Warwickshire yesterday afternoon and I've not heard from her. I sent her a text yesterday evening to ask her how she got on but she's not responded. I would've gone with her if I knew that she was going alone as I like a garden. Did she have a good time?'

Nick felt there was a bit of censure in Anna's father's voice that he had allowed his daughter to go alone. Nick reckoned that he got along ok with Mr Louden but felt that high standards were expected of him in return for the privilege of dating his only daughter. Nick now felt that he had failed to reach the approved standard as the man's beautiful daughter was missing and Nick had a prevailing sense of unease that something had happened to her. 'I don't know, Mike. She's not responded to any of my texts or calls since yesterday afternoon. I've contacted her work but she's not reported in. I've checked at her house but she's not there. Too be honest, I'm worried about her.'

Mike concurred. 'Yes, this is truly concerning. Anna does not play games and will always respond to text and calls from close family and friends. Do you know anything about this open garden event. Who told her about it?'

Nick gave Mike all the information he had gained from Olivia concerning this Luke who had invited her to this charity event. A man that seemed to have a crush on Anna and who in Olivia's opinion was a 'weirdo' and an 'oddball'.

'Good grief. This does not sound right,' Mike Louden snapped down the phone. 'It is of the utmost concern that she has not texted you or me. That's just not like Anna as she knows that I always text to check she's ok if she goes off on her own. I know she's a grown woman but I'm always anxious about her safety.'

Nick agreed. 'Yes, this is very worrying. She's gone alone to the house of a man that she didn't know and we've not heard from her since. Holy shit.' He didn't mean to swear to Anna's dad but his fear for her safety was turning a knife in his gut.

Mike's voice trembled with emotion as he spoke, 'I think we are right to be worried. This kind of situation, Nick, is something I have dreaded happening to her since she was a young teenager. She has always been catnip to men due to her beauty. Does it sound remiss of me to say that sometimes I wished that she was more homely looking so that they would not pay her such attention?'

'I know what you mean, Mike. I've only known her for a short time and it's not been plain sailing with rogue males after her,' Nick stated, drawing in a deep breath to focus his mind. 'We must concentrate on trying to find this property she went to yesterday. All I know is that it's in South Warwickshire.'

'Well, that's where I can help, Nick, son. We do a family sharing on Find My App on her iPhone which will give us her location. Hang on whilst I check it out,' Mike instructed. In a few seconds he was back. 'Yes, it's an address of Pitsdown Lane, Sherbourne. I'll set off now and I should be there in about an hour. Can you go there now?'

'Yes, of course. I'm only about twenty minutes away. I'll update you once I get there,' Nick stated, then ended the call.

What should've been a straightforward journey via A429 was turning into a disaster. A minor collision between two cars on the A429 resulted in a damaged car blocking the road and required a recovery vehicle to remove it. Drivers were having difficulty trying to go round the broken down car and so a long queue had backed up. Nick crawled along and cursed frequently. His phone rang via his blue tooth device. 'Nick Carlton.'

A faint, shaky voice responded. 'Nick, it's Anna. I'm in trouble and I n-need..,' her voice broke at this point.

'Anna, sweetheart. Are you ok? What's happening? Nick asked. Though he would be eternally grateful to hear her voice, his tone with her was terse to the point of bluntness. His first priority was to get details of her situation as fast as possible in case she was cut off. Nick, back in cop mode. She paused and he feared that he had lost her call. 'Anna, speak to me.'

In a raspy voice, she said, 'I'm at a house in Pitsdown Lane, Sherbourne. I've been h-held captive against my will.'

Nick could hear her voice waver and a sob filled the car. 'Ok, Anna, I know your location. I should be there in about fifteen minutes but there's a breakdown on the A429 holding up traffic. Where is this man now?'

The sound of her crying now tore at Nick's gut. 'T-there are two of t-them. Two brothers. One has been injured by the other who....' sob, sob, 'is violent. I'm in the garage where my car's been parked....' her words faded and all Nick could hear was a male voice shout 'come here, bitch, you owe me' before the phone went dead.

Fucking, fucking hell. Nick banged his hand on the steering wheel as he imagined that the violent brother had now got hold of Anna. This was a nightmare of monumental proportions. His precious woman was in the clutches of a dangerous individual and he could not get to her. He could now see the broken down car. Nick's level of impatience was off-the-scale with nervous drivers who didn't over take the broken down vehicle when it was safe to do so. A bloody snail could overtake faster than some of them.

Nick steeled himself to focus on clearing this road obstacle and getting to Anna. The man who had just called her a bitch would be in for the biggest trouble of his life when Nick arrived. He vowed that if he had hurt her in anyway it would be the devil's own job to stop himself from killing this prick.

CHAPTER EIGHTY TWO

Anna struggled ferociously as Russ grabbed hold of her from behind as she was on the phone to Nick. Russ clasped one hand over her mouth to stop her talking on the phone which he then snatched out of her hand. The phone was dropped on the floor, he stamped on it a couple of times before kicking it, sending it skidding under some shelving. His right arm clamped around her waist so that she was firmly held in his iron grip. She tried her best to struggle and flay her arms at him but there was no way she could shake him off.

Sheer terror now filled Anna's brain as this strong man dragged her further into the interior of this garage/workshop. The area was large with a central area given over to equipment and tools of the plastering trade, as far as Anna could tell. On the left wall of the garage, there were shelving racks containing numerous clear plastic boxes filled with various tools including hammers, spanners, chisels, screwdrivers and so on. Smaller plastic boxes and tin boxes presumably contained nails, screws and all the usual stuff found in a workshop area. Also on the shelving were power tools, including cordless drills, planers, a jigsaw, a nail gun and others she didn't recognise. Anna's mind was not undertaking an inventory of a workshop but trying to focus her tormented brain on finding a way of escaping from this ordeal. All in all, this workshop contained an assortment of lethal weapons. Would she be able to get hold of a weapon to see off her attacker?

Anna continued to struggle until he slapped the left side of her face. He ordered her, 'Stop fighting me or there'll be more of that.' The harsh sting of the slap subdued Anna and for all her battling with him, he was inordinately strong. He was now dragging her along, her feet not touching the floor. Nothing she was doing was halting his progress to the place he wanted to go. The workbench. Once he got her on there, she knew what was going to happen.

When he reached the workbench, he turned her to face him, his left hand clamped on her chin as hard fingers bit into her jawbone. His right hand grabbed hold of her left upper arm, as cold eyes radiated his anger. 'Time to pay your dues.'

Anna tried to shout 'get off' but it came out as a muffled groan so she kicked him hard in the left shin. It was satisfying to hear him yelp in pain but then her punishment for this was another sharp slap to her face. She winced but tried not to let him show he had hurt her. This was hard as the pain stung her cheek and brought tears to her eyes. There were some dirty pieces of rag underneath the workbench and he picked one up and roughly shoved it into her mouth. A second piece of rag was tied over her mouth to keep the first one in place. The rag smelled of wood polish and an acrid taste tortured her tastebuds. All the time he was tying the rag, Anna was fighting hard to kick and punch him away from her.

'Enough,' he barked, his voice loud and commanding.

Ignoring him, Anna continued to make groaning noises as her arms flayed about. But she knew that she was unlikely to win the battle as he threw his right arm backwards before landing a hefty punch from his fist into the side of her head. It felt as if she had been whacked by a sledgehammer and an explosion of pain erupted in her head. As he had let go of her, she crumpled to the floor, not able to stand as her whole being was focused on waiting for the pain to subside.

'Right,' he stated, 'I've had it with you. Like I said, you owe me for battering that moron who Luke saw at your house and sorting your Abbie problem. It's time to pay the piper.' He ran his hand over the top of the workbench to clear it of a few wood shavings and chips of wood. Dragging her upwards by her right arm, Anna was lifted onto her back on the workbench with her bottom positioned at the front edge.

Russ placed his left hand behind her head so that the focus of her terrified eyes were on his own. 'I'm going to remove the gag but if you scream you'll regret it.' He removed the gag and replaced it with his own mouth which fully ravaged hers. He bit on her lips and probed her mouth with his tongue as the stubble of his beard scratched her skin. Anna felt that dying would be a good option at this moment. After a few minutes of this he stopped, his hawk-like eyes scanning her face. 'God, you are so beautiful. It feels wrong for our first time to be in a smelly garage but I've been messed about too much. This'll do fine for now.' The weight of his body immobilised her as she was pressed into the hard wooden workbench. The sound of his heavy breathing filled her ears as his right hand started to explore downwards to her breasts, squeezing and pinching, before moving down to raise her thin, flimsy summer dress above her thighs. Anna tried to free herself but an immovable heavy boulder was holding her down. Absolute terror threatened to overwhelm her and the continued pounding in her head from the severe blow was impeding her ability to focus on trying to escape.

'This is so good, baby,' he murmured as his hand moved over the shivering flesh of her thigh. His off-the-scale arousal was apparent in his panting breath and mounting groans, so lost was he in his own gratification. Anna frantically searched with her right hand for something that might help her. Her hand alighted on an item at the back of the workbench. Her fingers quickly examined the item, part wooden handle, part steel blade, a slim chisel with a hard edge.

Anna tensed as she felt his hand reach for her underwear. This was her last chance to save herself. Closing her eyes, she lifted the chisel as high as possible and, despite her confined state, she brought the steel end of the chisel down into the left side of his upper back. She had no way of knowing if she had penetrated muscle or bone but it had an impact as he yelped in pain, stopping the assault on her. He stumbled backwards, groaning, and shouting, 'Fucking hell.' Whilst he was focused on his agony, Anna dropped the chisel and jumped off the workbench. She pushed at his chest to throw him further off balance. Running barefoot, she could feel sharp bits of wood and shavings under her feet, causing her pain, but she had to concentrate on escaping her assailant. Fleeing towards the garage door, she was aware that he was not mortally wounded as he was now stumbling after her, shouting, 'Come here, bitch.'

Anna turned briefly to look at him. From the front he looked uninjured but there was a fierce anger on his hard features. He was an angry bear, snarling, grunting, open-mouthed, teeth-bared, and spitting saliva. In his right hand he carried the blood-stained chisel that she had so carelessly discarded. Running with heavy, long strides he was closing in on her as she headed for the door that led back into the garden. 'I'm going to kill you,' was roared from a voice getting closer to her by the second.

◦•◦●◄《》►●◦•◦

CHAPTER EIGHTY THREE

Nick identified the property where Anna was located on Pitsdown Lane. He gazed across at the detached property, the driveway, and a garage that was set back away from the road. He slowed his car almost to a halt but parked further along the road, out of sight of the house. Getting out of the car, and closing the door quietly, his approach to the house was concealed by trees and bushes along the lane. Stopping to take in the view of the house and garage again, he noticed at first glance the place looked deserted. There were two cars parked on the driveway, a dark blue Ford Focus and a grey VW Golf. Nick paused to listen for any sounds, and after a car had passed by, all he could hear was the chirping of birds on this warm summer day.

Suddenly, the shout of a loud male voice focused Nick's attention. Though he could not see anyone; the voice was very close by. He ran quietly over to the property, noting a laminated sign, attached to a wall stating, '**Open Gardens, Sunday, 17**[th] **July 2022 from 2.00 p.m.**' Nick knew he was at the right place.

It was hard to say whether the loud voice had come from inside or outside the property as most of the house windows were open due to the heat of the day. A six foot wooden gate led to a garden and Nick eased himself up to scan the garden area. He could not see anyone, so he climbed over the gate, landing quietly on the other side in the garden. Concealing himself behind bushes, he glanced around the garden but he could not see or hear Anna or the man. Nick noted that the rear door to the garage was slightly ajar. He crept over to it, eased it open to allow him access, praying that it wouldn't squeak. It was dark inside compared to the bright sunlight outside and smelled of plaster and sawdust. There was no sign of Anna. He glanced around, noting a large van, and Anna's car. He wandered over to a workbench and on the floor he saw a splatter of red droplets which were likely to be blood. A maelstrom of utter fear and anger churned in Nick's stomach. Turning swiftly, he picked up a two foot section of copper piping from a nearby shelf, and rushed to exit the garage. He tapped the piping against his left hand, gleefully imagining it was the skull of the bastard that had seemingly attacked Anna.

Outside of the garage, Nick once again took shelter behind bushes as he contemplated which way to go, the garden or the house. A comment of 'I'm coming for you, bitch' from the garden area answered Nick's question. A tall man was on the far side of the garden, searching behind shrubs and bushes, stabbing an object into random greenery as he went along.

The man stopped the poking and started to swing his arm forcefully backwards and forwards as if he were scything long grass. Then, abruptly, he stopped. 'Come out, now,' he ordered. Nick watched as he dragged Anna out by her right arm from behind a massive pink buddleia shrub. As he pulled her, she stumbled before standing on her bare feet. Despite the warmth of the day, she was trembling and her flimsy pink summer dress added to her vulnerability. Fear was etched on her beautiful face as she gazed with terrified eyes at the man. Nick could now see that the object the man was holding in his right hand was a chisel. On the back of the man's blue polo shirt there was blood which had soaked around an area near his left shoulder blade. It looked as if Anna had managed to wound him. The man held the chisel near to her neck, as he snarled, 'You've pissed me off enough. Kneel down on the grass.' With that he pushed her forwards onto all fours.

Nick knew exactly what the man was intending to do next and he needed to be stopped. Nick sprinted across the garden; the copper piping firmly held in his right hand. 'GET AWAY FROM HER, NOW, YOU BASTARD,' Nick roared, 'OR I'LL KILL YOU. Nick slapped the copper piping into his left hand to emphasis his intention.

Anna slumped forward onto the grass relieved that she was no longer alone. 'Nick,' was all she could whisper.

'What the hell?' the man exclaimed as he turned his full attention on Nick and clenched his hand tightly around the chisel. 'You can fuck off or I'll kill you. And I'll then do her in all the ways I've dreamed of before I finish her off.'

'I don't think so, you scum.' Nick addressed him full-on, shoulders squared, muscles tensed to face his adversary. This was going to be the fight of his life. But he had to be quick and fierce so as not to allow the man to take Anna as a shield for his protection. Nick slammed the copper piping hard against the man's left upper arm then as he flinched, a powerful follow-up slug landed in his stomach area. This winded him, and he drooled saliva, but he was soon standing, and roaring, as he stabbed the chisel violently towards Nick. The man's face was contorted by hatred as he charged at Nick. Swinging the copper piping like a baseball bat, Nick slammed it into the man's lower right arm, sending the chisel spinning out of his hand.

'Fucking hell,' he yelled as he dived at Nick, flinging his fists around to land a punch. A punch skimmed Nick's chin. He dropped the piping and countered with three harsh punches to the man's head. Blood spurted from a gash to the man's left eyebrow and spilled from his left nostril. He snorted and wiped his nose, slightly dazed, but then landed a kick on Nick's thigh. Nick wrestled him to the ground, his full weight upon him, as he landed further blows to the man's head. The man struggled and growled to throw Nick off him which sent them rolling about the grass, lost in a volley of punches thrown and landed, bone smashing bone, as each used their strength to subdue the other. Grunting loudly, Nick got the male on his front, and slammed his clenched fist into the wound on the man's left shoulder blade which made him bawl with pain. Lifting the man's head by his hair, Nick delivered another hefty punch to his head.

Nick got up off him, not convinced that he was truly out of it, but edged away from him, all the time watching in case he got up. He didn't have to wait long. The man pushed himself upwards, rubbing his head, as he struggled to pull himself upright. In the precious moments of calm, Nick scrutinised his opponent, a tall, muscular male, with hooded dark eyes and strong features who was reminiscent of a warrior in ancient times. He lunged at Nick, bellowing, 'I'll have your head off,' before slamming into Nick and landing him on his back.

Nick pushed fiercely at him, rolling him off, leapt to his feet and smacked a fist into the man's face. Panting from exertion, Nick waited as his opponent stood opposite him, his face bloodied, as he prepared to attack again. Roaring loudly, he swung his fists at Nick before landing a punch to the side of his head. Nick shook his head to recover from the impact then countered with a kick to the man's groin, quickly followed by a swift, hard kick to his abdomen. The male collapsed onto the grass, moaning in agony, and clutching his stomach area. Trying to get onto his knees, he glared at Nick. 'I'll finish you off and then I'm shagging her.'

Standing over his assailant, Nick could see that his fighting energy was depleting as blood flowed more freely from the wound on his left shoulder, spreading a large patch of red across his polo shirt. 'I don't think so, you prick.' Nick stated as he slammed the side of his right hand into the side of the man's neck which sent him sprawling onto the grass. Overcome by his own exhaustion, Nick took a moment to catch his breath. The silence was filled by the sound of a police siren as a car pulled up, blue lights flashing.

Straightening up, Nick walked over to Anna. She was sat on a two-seater garden sofa, head in her hands, but she stood up as Nick came towards her. As he stared into the depths of her blue eyes, all he could see was the pain from what she'd been through.

And as yet he did not know the detail. He was scared to know the details. He gently took her face in his hands and examined her. She looked ghostly pale even though it was a hot day. There was a greyness under her eyes due to smudged makeup and exhaustion. The only colour on her face was a redness to her left cheekbone and at the corner of her left eye, suggesting that she'd been hit. A scabbing at her left nostril and traces of blood on her upper lip, once again, evidenced that she'd been punched.

Anna's large blue eyes focused on Nick's face as he examined her. 'Thank you for coming. It's been a nightmare.' The words were said listlessly, as her body slumped and he guided her to sit back on the chair. He sat next to her, holding her, whilst she lay against him, silent and numb.

'Police. Anyone here?' a female voice asked, as a police officer entered the garden, followed by a second male officer. They stopped to take in the scene of an injured man lying on the grass and a couple sitting on a sofa. The male officer went over to attend to the injured man. The female officer addressed Anna and Nick. 'I'm PC Blakemore. 'Who are you and what's gone on here?'

As Anna failed to answer, Nick responded. 'I'm Nick Carlton and this is my girlfriend, Anna Louden. Anna didn't return from an open garden event at this property yesterday afternoon. She was not answering my texts, or those of her father. She didn't go to work this morning or report in sick. Consequently, I've been very concerned as to where she is. She had a family sharing location app on her phone which showed this location. On my way here, she phoned me to say she'd been held captive by two men, two brothers. As far as I'm aware, one is injured and, probably, in the house. The other is on the grass over there. When I arrived he was holding a chisel to her neck and was about to sexually assault her. I had to stop him and a massive fight ensued.' Nick pointed at the man lying on the grass. 'I was not going to let him hurt her. Anna will need to tell you the full story of what's happened to her since yesterday afternoon at the hands of these two men.'

The male police officer radioed for an ambulance for the man now sat upright on the grass, bloodied and groaning softly.

PC Blakemore scrutinised Anna for signs of injury. 'Anna, I can see that you've got injuries to your face, do you have any other injuries?'

Anna had now regained some energy and sat up straighter on the sofa. Her voice trembled. 'I've been slapped on the face and punched in the head. That man, Russ, has sexually assaulted me and just tried to rape me. I was lured here yesterday by his brother, Luke, who has been stalking me for months and has photos of me all over his bedroom wall. This Luke drugged me, chained me to his bed, and held me captive. Russ sexually assaulted me last night and this morning as well. Luke did try to stop Russ by threatening him with a frying pan. But Russ overpowered Luke, took the pan off him, and hit him around the head. I haven't seen Luke since. He must be in the house, injured or worse. Whilst this was going on I ran out of the house and called Nick. In all, I've been drugged, tied up, sexually assaulted and beaten. I've been terrified and thought I was going to d-die.' She could not speak further. Nick could see that she was physically exhausted and it was all too much for her. She started to sob, loud, juddering sobs which racked her body. These were followed by a torrent of tears that cascaded downwards, streaking her face, and skimming her chin. Nick held her securely in his arms and let her cry.

PC Blakemore asked Anna and Nick to remain where they were. The female officer updated her colleague of what she had been told and then she went into the property, presumably to check on Luke.

After her sobbing subsided a little, Anna looked up at Nick. 'It's all a m-mess'...hic...'will you be arrested for attacking that Russ? Will I be arrested for stabbing him? I only did it in self-defence as he was seconds away from r-raping me.'

Nick ran his thumbs gently under her eyes to wipe her tears. 'I doubt they will bring charges against you, in the circumstances, as no jury would convict you. Me, I'm not so sure as I did give that scum a good battering. Still, they're lucky they haven't got a dead body on their hands.'

Anna's body started to shake and she was soon crying again. 'I'm s-so s-sorry, Nick. There's other b-bits to t-this nightmare,'...hic....and she paused to catch her breath...'Luke writes f-fantasy novels and I am his h-heroine, Astraea, and he is Xandros, Xan, the sender of the texts. Luke and Russ b-beat up Connor Peterson for me, apparently. Luke has hundreds of photos of me including my hit-and-run incident showing a white car and its registration number. Russ has b-been seeing Abbie who told him about knocking me d-down in her c-car.' Anna paused, as a further wave of crying overwhelmed her.

Easing Anna gently away from him, Nick stared at her tear-ravaged face. 'Oh my God, that evil witch knocked you down. Just don't let me lay eyes on her or I will wring her scrawny neck.'

Rubbing her eyes and fighting to stop her tears, Anna drew in a deep breath to help her speak. 'Abbie told him that the p-pregnancy is fake, a scam, to get you back and split us up. Russ claimed he'd dealt with Abbie and for this I owed him, s-sexually.' This was all too much for Anna and she cried again as if her heart would break.

Nick just held her, stroking her hair, trying to comprehend the ordeal she suffered, inflicted by these two brothers. Luke, a weirdo stalker who'd developed a massive crush on her. Russ, the psycho, violent brother who took advantage of Luke's fantasies to lay claim to Anna. But a third person had caused her pain, his crazy, deluded ex-girlfriend, Abbie, who he should never have brought into his life. The whole thing was completely nuts and would take time to full comprehend.

After a while, Anna's father was escorted into the garden by PC Blakemore. Initially, Mike Louden was walking alongside the police officer but when he saw Anna he ran towards her. 'Anna, my beautiful girl, you're ok. Thank God.' Anna stood up and went to her father, who was struggling to hold onto his emotions, as he folded her into his arms.

Nick watched as she cried into her father's chest as he held her, tightly. But then she pulled away slightly to say, 'Yes, thank God. But also thank Nick. He saved me.'

Mike Louden nodded his head and smiled at Nick. Nick felt that he had perhaps taken a small step towards winning Mr Louden's approval.

CHAPTER EIGHTY FOUR

Forty-eight hours later, Anna was now feeling a little more recovered from her ordeal. She had spent the remainder of Monday afternoon at the hospital being checked over and physically she only had bruising to her face, a red/purple colouration under her eye and across her cheekbone. There was also a small cut to her left nostril which was healing but tender to the touch. Yesterday, she had spent a number of hours at the police station, giving a full detailed account to a DI Fiona Meriden about what had happened. A Senior Investigation Officer, a DCI Ravi Chabra, was over seeing the case which had a number of strands including the wounding of Luke Milner by Russ Milner.

Anna's father had spent Monday and Tuesday night at her house, bringing her food and drink, ensuring that she rested and tried to sleep. Anna loved her father, but he did have a tendency to fuss, and talk too much, when all she really wanted was some time to try and process what had happened. She also yearned to see Nick, spend some time with him, as she was missing the comfort of his arms. He too had spent a number of hours at the police station being interviewed by DI Meriden. He had briefly stopped by her house to see her yesterday, late afternoon, but had then left so that she could spend time with her father. Now, she was sat on the sofa, dressed in silky pyjamas, her legs under her, trying to eat a bowl of granola with milk, but the food was sticking in her throat. After a few mouthfuls she leaned forward and placed the bowl on the nearby low table. She picked up her mug of cooling coffee and sipped at it.

'You need to eat, Anna, as you've not really eaten since Monday,' her father stated, as he sat on the sofa, gazing at her with troubled eyes. 'I hope Nick can make you eat something when he gets here. As soon as he arrives, I'll get off as I know he will look after you. He's a great bloke and really seems to care for you.'

Staring at her father's tired face over her coffee mug, Anna said, 'He is a great guy. I really like him, dad. He's so different from Alistair who was a selfish, lazy, rich, entitled idiot. Nick is really kind and loving. I feel safe with him. But perhaps he'll want nothing more to do with me after all this. I keep bringing chaos to his life, dad.'

Mike Louden moved nearer to his beloved daughter and wrapped his arm around her to give her a hug. 'Don't be daft, Anna. That man loves you, I can see that. None of this was your fault and some of it involved his loony ex-girlfriend.'

Anna glanced shyly at her father. 'Yes, I know, dad. But we've only known each other a short while and there's been all sorts of trouble including Connor Peterson, and now the Milner brothers. I don't need a boyfriend; I need a bodyguard.'

'Well, I think we can retire your sibling from his bodyguard duties as there is a new man to take over the job. Your very own, Frank Farmer, you know, Kevin Costner from '*The Bodyguard*', Mike chuckled.

There was a notification on Anna's phone that Nick had arrived. 'My Kevin's just outside, if you'd let him in,' Anna asked.

Mike Louden let Nick in and she could hear them have a chat in the hallway. The two men then entered the lounge. Anna's heart skipped when she gazed at Nick who looked cool and handsome in dark blue chinos and light grey polo shirt. He had some bruising to his face, on the left side of his forehead, down his left cheekbone and under his chin, a result of his fight with Russ Milner. As he smiled at her, Anna looked away, suddenly feeling shy around him and the chaos she had brought into his life. Nick leaned over and kissed her on the head. 'How are you today, trouble?'

Mike laughed. 'You're right there, son. She is trouble without meaning to be. Keeps causing me a lot of headaches, I can tell you.'

This was all meant as jokey good humour but Anna felt the burden of all the pain she had brought her family. 'Sorry, dad, Nick.' As was common over the last two days, she started to cry and quickly leaned over to grab a tissue out of a nearby box.

Anna's father then addressed her. 'Come on and see me out as I don't want to get caught in the rush hour traffic. I am leaving Nick in charge, so do as you're told, young lady. I will come back to see you at the weekend.' Anna went out into the hall and said a teary farewell to her father. Nick slipped past them into the kitchen and she heard the sound of the kettle boiling. She stood at the door, waving her father goodbye, then went back into the sitting room and sat on the sofa. Nick was soon back with two mugs of hot coffee. He gave her a mug as she sat on the sofa and tucked her legs under her. The warmth of the coffee mug on her hands was comforting as she allowed the steam to heat her face. The lovely aroma of the coffee aroused her senses. 'Thank you,' she whispered.

After a few quiet minutes of sipping their coffees, Nick placed his down on the coffee table and studied her face. His right hand gently caressed the area of redness on her cheek and under her eye. 'I hate to see those injuries to your lovely face. If there's any consolation, Russ Milner will be sore and bruised as he sits it out in a police cell. Have you heard from the police how his brother is?'

'According to DCI Chabra, he is in intensive care and in a stable condition,' Anna explained, pausing to sip her drink. 'Obviously, the police won't tell me much. I feel very conflicted about him. I don't want him to die and hope he recovers. But on the other hand he has traumatised me by holding me captive, drugging me, and handcuffing me to his bed. He's stalked me for months and invaded my privacy by taking many photos. These are not the actions of a sane, rational person. He lives in a fantasy world and I was his beloved, Astraea.' A sob left her mouth and despite her determination not to cry, the floodgates were open once again.

Nick placed her coffee down and drew her into his arms, stroking her hair as she cried against his chest. 'The actual ordeal is over now. You are safe. But it will be a long time before you forget.'

After a few minutes of crying, her eyes were red and her face was wet with tears. 'I know,' she muttered, her breathing impeded by sobs and hiccups as she mopped her tears.

He took a soggy tissue out of her hand and replaced it with a dry one. Then he gently cupped her chin with his hand to ensure her attention. Anna couldn't be sure but she felt she detected a sternness in his gaze. 'There is one thing about all this, I need to say. This man, Luke Milner, has been making contact with you for a number of months in the supermarket and has recently been buying you coffee. Why didn't you tell me about him?'

Anna felt uncomfortable under his gaze and rubbed her nose with the tissue to deflect his attention. 'It wasn't a big deal to me. He seemed a genuine person. A bit shy and unworldly and I was just being friendly. I try to see the good in people and I am not suspicious of everyone. Though, with hindsight, I should've seen that he wanted more than friendship due to the many compliments, the tulips, and asking me out on a date.'

'A date?' Nick said bluntly, as his eyes widened with surprise. 'This gets better and better.'

'Yes, that was quite a few weeks ago and I told him I had a boyfriend but it didn't put him off. In fact he'd got bolder recently. He bought me a coffee whilst he talked me into sponsoring him for doing a charity dog walk. I'm now sure that was a scam. There's probably no dog called Milly. Then, he put in place his plan to get me to his house for the open garden's event and that's when my nightmare began.' Anna felt herself getting tearful again.

Nick's serious expression faded and he smiled softly at her. 'In the future, I do want to know if you are getting any unwanted attention from men. And that includes the Luke types who appear all nice and pleasant. I'm in no way trying to curtail your freedom but I think we have to recognise that you are a target for men because of your beauty and I don't want something like this to happen to you again.'

'Ok, I will let you know if I get chatted up. But please be aware that I do not encourage them. I will continue to be polite but I will be a bit more cautious of those that come over as too friendly.' Nick nodded in agreement as Anna added, 'I will be very clear that I have a boyfriend. I'll tell them that he's five-foot-seven, very weedy, and couldn't knock the skin off a rice pudding.'

Nick raised one eyebrow in mock amusement. 'Couldn't knock the skin off a rice pudding? Five-foot-seven and weedy?' He pulled her close to him and scrutinised her face. 'I think you are talking about yourself but I must correct your height, at five-foot-four.'

She was fully in his arms now as he leaned in to kiss her. 'Maybe I'm not too tall but watch your step as I can be lethal with a chisel, Nick Carlton.' This was meant to be jokey but her voice was flat and humourless. It was really all too early and she was too raw after her ordeal.

'Hey, Ms Louden,' he stated, drawing her body against him. 'You are perfectly formed. And I love you in these sexy pyjama shorts and shirt.' His mouth found hers and he kissed her softly before gazing into her eyes. 'We can just kiss and cuddle for now. And I'll hold you. Give you some time to recover and feel safe again.'

But then the tenderness in his blue eyes evaporated as he looked at Anna's damaged face. 'Luke and Russ Milner have a lot to answer for but so does Abbie. I wish with all my heart I had never met her as it would've stopped you getting hurt because of me.'

Anna sighed. 'At least you know that the baby was not real, just a con to get you back. It was a mean thing to do to you. I feel sorry for the pain she's caused you.'

Anger was now blazing in Nick's eyes. 'I'm so relieved that the baby wasn't real. But I'm not letting Abbie off the hook that easy. I shall be visiting her so that she can tell me to my face it was all a scam. And I shall be calling her out for knocking you over. She's lucky she's a woman or I would be giving her a good hiding.'

Anxiety flushed Anna's face. 'Please, Nick, don't do anything rash. There's been enough trouble, let the police deal with her.'

The hardness in Nick's eyes did not soften. 'She's going to have her reckoning with me, I can tell you, Anna. I will not be thwarted on this.'

⋯⋖◈⋗⋯

CHAPTER EIGHTY FIVE

Abbie smiled widely at Nick as she opened the door to allow him to enter her home. 'Great to see you, babe,' she simpered, fluttering her eyelashes at him. 'I could really do with a friendly face at the moment. Things aren't going so well.'

Nick gently closed the door behind him as he entered her hallway. Concealing the furnace-hot anger that was burning in him, he gave her a dismissive look. 'Things not going so well... 'he parroted. 'What a shame.' He took a couple of steps towards Abbie who's hazel eyes widened with expectation that he was about to caress her.

'I knew that you'd come back one day, Nicky.' She reached up to touch his face with the intention of kissing him and he noticed that she was shivering in anticipation of their touch. Touch they did, as Nick picked her up off her feet and slammed her against the wall in the hallway. The impact jarred her back and she let out a loud 'oomph'. His right hand held tightly under her chin, forcing her head upwards, so that her puzzled eyes stared into his icy cold blue ones. She struggled to speak as his hand constricted her throat. 'B-babe, you're hurting me.'

Nick smiled softly, glorying in her predicament, as emotions of anxiety and fear played on her face. 'Am I hurting you? But you like these games, don't you? You like the juxtaposition of pain and pleasure. It was always your thing.' Nick kept his grip on her throat but pressed his body into hers to take the weight of her. 'I seem to remember that grabbing your throat was one of your favourite things. Amongst others.' He loomed over her, snarling as a wild beast, as his anger raged. 'What was one of the other things you liked? Oh yes, a bit of a slap, eh?' He smacked her face hard with his right hand, leaving a red mark on her left cheek. 'That good, was it?'

Abbie registered the sting of the slap on her face as she still tried to work out if this was play or punishment. She struggled to speak due to the continued grip on her throat, but she panted, 'It hurt a b-bit.'

'Ter-ri-fic,' he barked, the rat-a-tat sound of a machine gun. He flung his right arm back to strike again and Abbie squirmed as she realised this would not be play. Nick's hand slammed into the wall just to the left side of her face, making her body jump in shock. He kept the grip on her throat and lifted her higher off the floor before letting go so that she crumpled onto the oak flooring. 'Right, get up,' he ordered as he took hold of the back of her T-shirt, gripped it tight, and dragged her into the living room. She was thrown face down onto the sofa then Nick pulled up a chair to sit near her.

Abbie curled into a ball on the sofa and held onto a cushion. All the blood drained from her anxious face as she stared at a raging Nick. 'I'm s-sorry, b-babe,' she stuttered, trying hard not to cry.

The anger that was flowing through Nick at this moment was so fiercely hot it could melt an ice cap. 'Sorry, for what Abbie? I want to hear and don't tell me any lies because I know what you've done.'

Abbie blinked but this did not stop tears from falling down her face, streaking her eyeliner. 'I w-was the p-person who d-drove the car at your'...pause for breath.. 'girlfriend. I'm s-sorry, Nick.' She started to sob and Nick did not know if this was due to feeling genuinely sorry for Anna or herself.

Nick moved suddenly towards Abbie, and she jumped back on the sofa, fearing another blow to the face. Instead, he gripped his fingers on her chin, making her wince in pain but ensuring that her terrified eyes were focused on him. 'I could happily kill you at this moment, Abbie. Take your riding crop and lash you repeatedly before crushing your windpipe with my bare hands. Your two favourite sex kinks to end your worthless life.' He eased off the hold on her chin and lightly tapped her face. 'But I'll let the law deal with you as photo evidence of your car deliberately running into Anna, including its registration number, is now with the police.'

'I know, the police have been in touch,' Abbie stated, 'and I'm due to be interviewed at the police station for possible assault charges. My Solicitor thinks I could be charged with GBH in accordance with Offences Against the Person Act 1861. Section 20 carries a prison sentence up to five years or Section 18 up to life imprisonment. The difference is based on intent. What have I fucking done?' Her body juddered as fat tears cascaded down her cheeks.

Nick eased out of her personal space and sat back on the chair. 'Prison, I hope so. Your bad behaviour has been escalating for a while, particularly under the influence of alcohol. You deliberately knocked Anna over, so I hope you get convicted and incarcerated.'

Abbie swallowed to help stop the crying, then wiped her wet, tear-stained face with her hand. 'God, Nick, you're so cold. How did that happen?'

'It happened when you threatened my family with a knife. It happened when you tried to pretend you were having my baby to worm your way back into my life and cause trouble with Anna. But mostly it happened when you tried to kill the woman I love,' Nick informed her, feeling absolutely no sympathy for this woman.

Abbie leaned over to a nearby table to grab a tissue from a box. 'Alyssa told me what happened to Anna with that man, Luke, who stalked her and tied her up. It turns out I've been going out with his brother, Russ. I met him in the Frizzy Lion when I went to throw wine over Anna and you stopped me.' Abbie paused as she saw the anger once again flare on Nick's face. 'The thing with

Russ started out as casual fun, you know, no strings, great sex, but I started to really like him. Then I ballsed it up as usual.'

'Let me guess which one - drunken bad behaviour, getting clingy or cheating on him? Nick asked, as Abbie gave him an almost childlike pout to feign innocence.

'Er, I suppose it was technically cheating but Russ and I weren't a couple, just fuck buddies. I was with Russ at a pub when I bumped into a DJ friend of mine. The DJ offered me some coke back at his, so I disappeared off with him, leaving Russ, and then ended up at the DJ's overnight.'

Nick could not now hold back from laughing. 'You are priceless, Abbie. But I'm not laughing with you, I'm laughing at you and your ongoing stupidity. This Russ has been arrested and charged with offences of ABH and sexual assault against Anna so he isn't a pussy cat. How did he react to your disappearing off with another man?

'Not well,' Abbie commented, and she looked to be on the verge of tears again. 'I don't think he cared a toss about my infidelity but he didn't like being disrespected. When he visited me after, and we played our sexy games, he really laid into me and I couldn't sit for days.'

Nick guffawed. 'Great result for you all round then.' But then all humour left him as he recalled the pain and fear that Russ Milner had subjected Anna to. 'Yeah, the bastard likes to inflict pain on women but I gave him a beating he'll never forget after hurting Anna.'

Abbie started to cry again and gripped the cushion for comfort, as she gently rocked back and forth on the sofa. 'He recorded two bondage sex sessions with me on his phone and posted them on social media, Facebook and IG. All my family, friends, and business associates have seen them. Have you seen them?'

'Yeah, I have. And the whole of my family. Not your finest moment. Don't worry some people started off with sex tapes that went viral and have become rich and famous off the back of them,' Nick stated, as he looked at Abbie's ravaged face as she snuffled and hiccupped. This woman was now paying a high price for her bad behaviour including lack of boundaries, drinking, drugs, greed, neediness and impulsiveness. Her out of control behaviour when drunk. Playing games with a man like Russ Milner, making a fool of him, and not realising there would be severe consequences. Her lies and deceit in faking a pregnancy to disrupt his life and his relationship with Anna. The calculated way she deliberately drove a car at Anna to maim or kill her. 'You've made a complete mess of your life, Abbie. And it's all your own fault.'

'I know. It all went wrong when you finished with me, Nick.' Abbie locked her watery eyes onto his, hoping for sympathy. 'You were the best thing to happen to me, Nick. I wish I could turn back time and not mess it up with you. I love you, Nick. We could have had a great future together if you hadn't met.. the bit..' She stopped before completing the word, noting the fury returning to Nick's face.

Nick's hand whipped out and landed a light slap on Abbie's face as she shuddered with fear. 'Don't say that word when referring to Anna or I will kill you. Anna did not destroy our relationship, as you seem to think. You did. You were lazy, materialistic, pushy, rude to people and have an overinflated opinion of yourself. Anna is everything you are not. Very beautiful, sexy, intelligent, hard-working and kind. I am truly grateful to have Anna in my life and my intention is to marry her in the near future. Raise a family.' With that he got up to leave.

As Nick walked by her, she took hold of his left arm to halt his departure. 'Please, Nick, we could try again.' Abbie placed a hand on his waist which then moved to his belt. Large hazel eyes locked on his face as she gave him a wanton smile and licked her lips. 'Let me do your favourite thing, one last time, Nicky.'

Forcefully slapping her hand away, Nick regarded her with pity. 'Take a hard look at yourself, Abbie. You disgust me.' As he strode out of the room, the sound of sobbing filled the air.

CHAPTER EIGHTY SIX

Saturday 24ᵗʰ September 2022

The property that Anna and Nick were staying at for three nights in Bourton-on-the-Water in the Cotswolds was actually breathtaking. A two-storey, spacious, modern barn conversion of beamed ceilings, oak flooring, open plan kitchen/dining area with high spec units and equipment, leading into a comfortable sitting area with 'L'-shaped sofa, log-effect electric fire and large Smart TV. Upstairs there was a high-quality bathroom with vanity sink, walk-in shower and free-standing bath. A super king size bed dominated the main bedroom. Arriving early on Friday afternoon, they had taken full advantage of soaking in a lavender foaming bath before retiring to the spacious super king bed for a little afternoon delight.

Today, Anna's twenty-sixth birthday, Nick had arranged for a three-course meal to be delivered and he was to be the chef, doing the necessary, but minimal, cooking and placing food on plates. They were sat at a dining table for two, looking out on a small courtyard, adorned with clay pots containing blue asters. The dining table was laid with a white linen cloth scattered with rose petals. A centrepiece of three ruby red candleholders emitted a red/orangey glow as their tealights flickered and wafted a honeysuckle and rose perfume into the room. Anna was blown away by the ambience of this romantic setting.

A delicious starter of baked feta cheese, drizzled with honey and sprinkled with a few flakes of chilli, had been consumed. They were waiting for the main course of salmon en croûte to finish cooking. Anna was savouring her glass of dry white wine and thinking that this was the most perfect birthday of her life. She was dressed in a red/polka dot, V-necked, sleeveless dress that suited her perfectly. As this was a special meal, she had taken extra care with her hair and make-up. On her right wrist was the white gold, diamond tennis bracelet that Nick had given her earlier as her birthday gift.

Nick, ultra-handsome in navy trousers and tight-fit white shirt with sleeves rolled up, was gazing at her hungrily as if she were the next course of the meal. 'Anna, sweetheart, I wish that you weren't looking so damn gorgeous as I can't decide which to eat first, the meal or you.' He gave a sexy wink which made her laugh.

'Stop it, Nick. You've got a one-track mind. I want to enjoy all of this lovely food so you are not going to distract me with your come-to-bed antics, ok?' Anna teased him, 'And I was hoping you'd be exhausted after all our frolicking yesterday and this morning.'

'Frolicking? What sort of medieval word is that to describe my first class love making. I will give you a good frolicking later, miss, if you're not careful,' he teased, a determination in his steely eyes.

Luckily, for Anna who was hungry, the oven timer pinged to indicate the salmon en croute course was cooked which Nick served with new potatoes and tender stem broccoli. The sumptuous meal was finished with a dessert of lemon posset, sliced strawberries and a heart-shaped shortbread biscuit.

After eating, they sat at the table, drinking the last of the bottle of wine. Nick drained the last drops into her glass. 'Well, that's dead but I've got a very expensive bottle of champagne to continue the celebrations. Won't be a moment.' He took away the empty bottle and the ice bucket and was soon back with a bottle of Dom Perignon champagne, two flutes, and the bucket with fresh ice. He then picked up his phone. 'I think we need some romantic music to set the scene,' he said.

Anna watched him with amusement in her eyes. 'You are really spoiling me today. I shall expect this for every birthday.'

She looked at the beautiful bracelet on her wrist. 'Thank you again for this bracelet, it is truly lovely. And now champagne, I am a lucky girl.'

'One more thing,' he stated as he rushed over to the kitchen worktop and picked up a plate with a small cupcake on it. A sparkler was in the cake which he brought over to the table with a cigarette lighter. 'Ok, Anna Louden, I'm ready.' He touched the phone and the Frankie Valli song, *'Can't Take My Eyes Off You'* started to play. Nick lit the sparkler and moved to place the cupcake in front of her.

Anna's face was a mix of shock and excitement as she gazed at the cake. On top of the vanilla icing on the cupcake, a red, heart-shaped decoration had the words 'Marry Me' written in white. Anna was mesmerised by the sizzle and crackle of the sparkler and its flashes of yellow before she fully realised the meaning of the message on the cake.

Nick knelt on one knee next to her chair and she turned towards him. There were tears in Anna's eyes as she looked at his handsome face. Nick Carlton, usually so confident, was now nervous as he took a small, red velvet jewellery box out of his pocket. Taking Anna's left hand, he studied her face. 'Anna Louden, I know that we have not been together long, but I love you to the moon and stars, and beyond. I love you for your beauty, your sense of humour, your intelligence and your kindness. I believe that you are the perfect woman for me and I will strive to be the perfect man for you. I would like to spend the rest of my life with you. Anna, will you do me the honour of becoming my wife?' He opened the box to reveal a white gold, three stone diamond ring.

The beauty of the ring and the surprise of this proposal stunned Anna. She had not expected this. She had not anticipated getting married at any time soon but staring into Nick's loving eyes she knew that she would never meet a better man than him. A man that was funny and kind but also confident, caring and made her feel safe. He was consistent in his treatment of her, in a loving way, and was not arrogant and selfish like other men she'd known. As he patiently waited for her reply, getting more anxious, Anna smiled to put him out of his misery. 'Nicholas Carlton, I would be very honoured to be your wife. I love you with all my heart and want to share my life with you, forever.'

Taking the ring out of the box, he placed it on the ring finger of her left hand. It slipped on nicely and fitted well. Anna stared at the sparkling ring as light hit the diamonds and bounced from one facet to another to give rainbow colours and white light. Anna gasped. 'It's so beautiful, thank you so much.'

On Nick's proposal playlist, Chris Young's '*Who I Am With You*' was playing as he helped her to her feet, to enfold her in his arms and kiss her passionately. 'I will always try to be a better man for you, sweetheart,' he promised, echoing the words of the song. They danced slowly, as he held her closely in his arms.

Anna realised that she didn't know what love truly was until this moment. 'Thank you for making my birthday so very special, Nick.'

'You are very welcome.' Nick gently took her face in his hands, to drink in her beauty, and take possession of her mouth again. Then he stated, 'I did ask your father if I could marry you and he gave me his permission. His words were along the lines of, it was great to find a deluded fool willing to take you off his hands.'

Anna punched Nick lightly on the arm. 'No, he didn't.'

Nick chuckled as he noticed the peeved look on her face. 'No, you're right. It was if I hurt you he would put my balls in the vice in his garage. So I'd better behave.' Anyway, Ms Louden, soon to be Mrs Carlton, I suggest we take the champagne to the bedroom and celebrate our engagement.' He picked up the ice bucket, placed two champagne flutes inside, and took hold of her hand.

Anna was guided out the room but did comment, 'I suggest that we leave the discussion about our married name for another day, Mr Louden. And perhaps we should have a ban on sex from now until after the wedding,' she joked.

Nick turned to give her a quizzical look. 'I don't think that would be possible unless we get married tomorrow.'

CHAPTER EIGHTY SEVEN

Early October 2022

Luke lay on his bed, staring ahead at the bare walls. The police had removed all the photos of his beloved as part of their evidence gathering to bring his case to court. His most treasured possession, the beautiful portrait of his goddess, Astraea, had also gone, along with his mobile phone, laptop, and his writing notes. The bedroom was sterile, devoid of any comfort, and the walls needed painting to take away the faint outlines of his precious photos. When he had complained to his father that it was unfair that he had been stripped of his priceless belongings, his father had reacted with anger. Along the lines of, 'get used to it, son. Your prison cell will not be a four-star hotel room with ensuite bathroom, large telly, cosy cushions and water colour paintings on the wall. It will be a tiny room, with white-washed walls, a shared toilet, a sink, bunk beds and a cellmate. Let's hope he's a friendly type.'

Luke's heart thumped in his chest every time he thought of the possibility that he was going to jail. Correction, he knew he was going to jail as he had been charged with three offences. One, a charge of false imprisonment of Anna Louden, under common law. Two, a charge of illegally drugging Anna in accordance with Offences Against the Person Act 1861. Three, charged with stalking in accordance with the Protection from Harassment Act 1997. All offences carried lengthy prison sentences if found guilty. He was currently on remand awaiting trial in Crown Court. His Solicitor had urged him to plead guilty to all charges to reduce his sentence but Luke had refused.

Luke was emphatically not guilty. He had acted entirely out of love and caring for his beautiful woman, Anna. His Astraea.

On the recommendation of his solicitor, he had been visiting a psychiatrist to discuss what was termed as his 'mental health issues'. All a waste of time and money. There was nothing wrong with Luke. His intentions towards Anna were genuine, from a place of love. He was merely trying to build a relationship with the woman who would be his wife and have his children. Luke now got off the bed, as it was time for dinner, and his father would be annoyed if he didn't go downstairs. One tiny speck of joy over the last three months since he had lost his beloved was that his appetite had diminished. Food was only necessary as fuel for his body and he didn't enjoy eating anything. Consequently, he had lost a stone and a half, so his belly had shrunk and fat had disappeared off his face, giving it more definition. He'd not yet achieved Russ's chiselled cheekbones but Anna would be impressed with the change when she next saw him.

In the kitchen area, Russ was sat at the kitchen table, eating sausages and mash with green vegetables. Russ was also out on bail awaiting trial for charges of ABH for his attack on Luke and charges of ABH, charge of threatening with an offensive weapon and charges of sexual assault on Anna.

At least in one area, Luke and Russ were given a break. Neither he nor Russ had been charged for the attack on the wanker, a Connor Peterson. They had both been question by police due to the photos taken of Peterson's arrest by Luke but there was no forensic evidence directly linking them to the assault.

A plate of sausage and mash was awaiting Luke at the table and he pulled a face before sitting down. 'Getting fed up of sausages now that I'm eating healthier and losing weight.' But he sat down and started to eat the meal.

Jez Milner sat at the table and added a slice of buttered white bread to his plate to soak up the rich gravy. He gave Luke an angry scowl. 'What's that, sir, the cuisine is not to your liking. I will consult with the chef on your next visit to try to meet your dietary requirements.' Pausing to eat a piece of the juicy pork sausage, he added, 'I've heard that those chefs in the prison kitchens are of Michelin star competence.'

Russ laughed, on seeing his brother's peeved expression. 'Brother, the least of your worries will be the quality, or not, of the food. It will be coping with the hard nuts in there when they get a glimpse of your boyish face that goes bright pink at the slightest thing. You'll need to toughen up, act more manly, and never, ever, cry.'

Seeing Luke's troubled expression, Jez glowered at Russ. 'Leave him alone, Russ. We know you'll be cock of the walk in no time. Let's just cut out the prison talk for now. It gives me indigestion at every meal when I think that two of my sons will soon be in prison. It's very difficult to hold my head up around this town and it's affecting business. In practical terms, with you two inside, I won't be able to do the plastering by myself.'

Luke did feel a twinge of guilt when he gazed at his father's face which seemed to age significantly in the last few months. Puffiness under his eyes due to sleep deprivation, more wrinkles to his brow and around his eyes, and flare-ups of eczema resulting in a red blotchiness to his cheeks. 'You'll have to employ an assistant to take our place for the time being. I'm sure I won't be in long. I never intended to hurt Anna and I protected her from Russ. I'm sure the jury will be sympathetic and see I acted out of love.'

'Oh good God.' Jez commented, shaking his head in despair. 'We've been through all this with the solicitor. You need to recognise what you did was wrong and not based on your deluded idea of 'love'. That young woman was not feeling the love when you lured her here under false pretences, drugged her, and chained her to your bed. She didn't want your love. She doesn't want you. You need to wise up, Luke, because if you keep spouting this dribble to the jury you will be found guilty, no question. It would be better all round if you pleaded guilty. At least we'd be spared the indignity of a trial where you make an utter clown of yourself.'

Russ helped himself to bread and butter and mopped up the gravy on his plate. 'Yeah, too right. Should've pleaded guilty.'

Jez turned his attention to Russ. 'You can shut up, Russ. Don't give him advice that you won't take yourself. You should plead guilty as well. At least in his defence, he didn't intend to cause the woman physical harm, unlike you. And battering your own flesh and blood with a frying pan, it's beyond crazy.'

Russ shrugged, chomping on a sausage on his fork. 'Got to take what's coming, do the time and then start out again in a few years.'

'Yeah, good idea,' Jez agreed. 'Clean slate when you get out. Come back and work for me. Think of settling down with Leanne and having a kiddie of your own.'

Luke now almost choked on his food. 'Well, he's certainly having a good time on dating apps for a man who knows he will be deprived of female company for a few good years. How many dates is it this week, Russ?'

'A couple so far,' Russ stated, hard eyes glaring at Luke. 'Mind your own business. But I might as well store up some pleasant memories to think about when I'm in that cell with an ugly, snoring cellmate. I'm still keeping it going with Leanne and I'm going to move in with her when I get out of the nick. See other tarts on the side.'

Jez shook his head. 'Poor Leanne. I hope she finds a decent man who is worthy of her. She's a good sort.' He got up off his chair and took his dirty plate to the sink. 'I despair. Two useless sons. One is obsessed with women and having a good time like a rampant rabbit. The other is obsessed with one woman who he can never have. All this will be the death of me.'

Luke got up off his chair, took his plate to the sink, to rinse it before placing it in the dishwasher. Russ dumped his plate, leaving Luke to clear up. As Luke set about this routine task, his mind drifted. Regardless of what everyone said, his father, brother, solicitor, psychiatrist, Luke knew that he and Anna were destined to be together. Part of his bail conditions were to keep away from Anna but this was not possible as he had an uncontrollable urge to see her. She was living with her boyfriend and no longer went to her local supermarket. Luke now went to her work place to take sneaky photos of her when she got into her car after work. He was lucky, there was a wall along one side of the car park where he could crouch down, dressed in baseball cap, hoodie and sunglasses, to take photos of her. Anna was as stunning as ever with her lovely brown hair falling to below her shoulders in flowing waves. During the remainder of the summer, he'd taken lots of photos of her in thigh-skimming pretty dresses displaying slender legs in summer sandals. Now, in autumn, it was photos of her in short skirts, black tights and black boots. All recorded on his new mobile phone. Making memories for when he was in his tiny prison cell where he would have time to write new stories of Astraea and Xandros in the magical, other world kingdom of Corinthius.

Luke was happy. Harmony was restored when he caught glimpses of Anna and recorded them on his phone. Only one tiny jot of anxiety spoilt Luke's world. A rival male, of slick suit and weasel features, frequently waited by his car in the car park, for Anna. Exiting the office, and immediately lighting his first, post work cigarette, the man always found an opportunity to speak to Anna as she went to her car. Warning signals went off in Luke's head as he observed the man with her, all oily presence and false smiles. In Luke's fantasy world this man was an enemy, a despoiler, a ravenous beast in human form. Luke did not trust this man near his beloved and wished that he could warn Anna of this man's evil intent.

CHAPTER EIGHTY EIGHT

Mid-October 2022

The noise level in the room was high as everyone stood around, chatting and drinking, as Anna and Nick tried to circulate to meet all the guests at their engagement party. Anna had not necessarily been sold on the idea of a party but had been persuaded by Nick's mother, Sophia, to have one. It had been organised by Anna with guidance from party planner, Alyssa. This had turned out to be a good idea as it allowed Anna and Alyssa to get to know each other and start to develop a relationship which had really pleased Nick. After finding out that Abbie had deliberately targeted Anna in the hit-and-run, Alyssa had cut all ties with her. When it later emerged that Abbie had deceived Nick in believing that she was pregnant with his baby, Alyssa was mortified that she had befriended such a person.

The party was at a delightful bespoke venue for engagements/weddings, in a spacious room with large windows. The room was dominated by a giant balloon arch of varying size white balloons interspersed with foil balloons in white, rose gold and silver. A large banner in white with rose gold lettering announced 'Anna & Nick, Engagement party, 22nd October 2022'. Round tables were decorated with white table cloths. Each had a centrepiece of a glass jar with fairy lights and faux greenery, faux rose gold and white roses. A DJ was hired to entertain the guests once the buffet had been served.

Before mingling with other guests, Nick drew Anna to one side and pulled her to him to kiss her softly. 'I know we will be separated shortly by our guests. I just want to say that you look spectacularly beautiful tonight. I am the luckiest man on this planet to have you in my life.'

Anna was wearing a deep V-neck, long-sleeved red/glitter evening dress which defined her waist before flaring to her knee. Recently, she'd added subtle caramel highlights to her brown hair which gave it a warm glow as it cascaded to below her shoulders in a gentle wave. Her make-up was more 'eye-catching' than usual as Olivia had applied brown eyeshadow, black eyeliner and lashings of black mascara. 'You scrub-up well, too, my handsome fiancé.' Nick did look handsome in dark grey, slim-fit chinos and white long-sleeved shirt. She did love him, in a lustful way, in a white shirt.

Sipping her go to drink of white wine, Anna was now talking to Nick's mum, Sophia, and her sister, Diana. 'Well, Anna, I cannot say how pleased I am that you are engaged to my son. He is looking particularly happy this evening and it's great to properly welcome you into the Carlton family.

Diana ran her eyes over Anna's face and body as if assessing her for breeding purposes. 'Yes, you will be a great asset to the family with your good looks. The babies will be very cute. It's a relief that he did not father a child with that hussy, Abbie. A truly awful person. Knocking you over in a deliberate hit-and-run and pretending to be pregnant with Nick's baby. Truly evil.'

'Diana,' Sophia said sternly. 'Anna does not want all that dragged up at her engagement party. Abbie is in the past and I'm sure Anna doesn't want to be reminded of her ordeal. We must be grateful that you weren't badly hurt, Anna, love.'

Diana, sipping on a G & T, was warming to the topic. 'Well, Alyssa tells me that Abbie's been charged with GBH and dangerous driving which could mean a prison sentence. Well-deserved, I'd say.'

Anna sighed, heavily. 'All I can say is that I'm glad I will not have to see her again and she is away from Nick.'

Diana was nothing, if not persistent. 'Yes, but then there's those ...' Diana looked left to right before she whispered, 'sex tapes... that are out on social media which were made by that psycho man who attacked you. My Claire showed them to me. Who does that sort of thing in the bedroom though the hussy did look to be having a good time,' Diana commented. 'I don't think this family has had so much excitement since Aunt Flo was found to be married to two men at the same time.'

'Oh for goodness sake, Diana, can you put a sock in it. Anna's here to enjoy her engagement party,' Sophia scolded her sister.

'Yes, I know. But it's good to know of any skeletons in the closet that could tarnish the family name.' Diana added, 'and that all this trouble is in the past.'

Anna felt her hackles rising at this comment. 'I can assure you that I did not seek out any of what happened to me. I would not wish any of it on my worst enemy.'

Ed joined the group and noted that Anna was looking a little upset. He gave her a friendly hug. 'Are you ok, Anna? Are they giving you a lecture on how privileged you are to join the Carlton clan?'

Sophia glared openly at her sister. 'Your Aunt Diana cannot stop speaking to Anna of things she wants to forget at her engagement party.'

'That's ok, mum,' Ed commented. 'I'll take her away to chat to Granddad, he keeps asking where she is. Going on about putting his name on her dance card. It's like watching an episode of '*Bridgerton*' and Granddad Bill is old enough to have been around in the Regency period of the early 1800s.'

After the buffet had been consumed and before the DJ started, the guests were given glasses of champagne. Anna's father, Mike, proposed the toast. 'I'd like to thank you all for attending this happy occasion of the engagement of Anna and Nick. I have loved my precious and beautiful daughter from the day that she was born, and after we lost Caroline, our wonderful wife and mother, I have been more aware of my role to love her and keep her safe. As recent events have proved, this has not always been possible. Like all dads, I worried about the type of man, or woman, my daughter would choose as their life partner. Therefore, I am overjoyed that Anna has chosen Nick, a man who has proved how much he cares for her by his recent actions. I know that he truly loves her and will strive to make her happy. It's wonderful this evening to get to know Nick's family, dad Jeff, mum Sophia, and everyone and I welcome the joining of our two families. Please raise your glasses and join me in a toast to Anna and Nick.'

Nick and Anna stood together, hand in hand, as Nick responded, 'Thanks, Mike. On behalf of Anna and myself, I would like to thank everyone for coming to celebrate our engagement.' He gazed at Anna and slipped his arm around her waist. 'I think I fell in love with this beautiful woman from the moment I met her and I am so grateful that she has agreed to be my wife. I can assure Mike that I will love and protect her to the best of my ability, always. And that includes making sure that Granddad Bill does not try to whisk her off home with him. Anyway, everyone, drink, dance and have fun.'

After much clapping, the DJ started with songs from the 60s and 70s. Sure enough, Nick was not surprised to see Bill rushing over, an Exocet missile, locked on its target, Anna. 'Hello, Bill, I don't need to ask what brings you over here,' Nick commented, smiling at his granddad's choice of blue floral mix shirt.

Bill greeted Nick, all the time his eyes on Anna. 'I've come to claim my dance with your beautiful fiancée. You wouldn't deny an old man a little pleasure, would you Nick, lad?'

Nick shook his head at the audacity of his elderly relative. 'If Anna wants to dance with you, that's up to her but I will be watching you, so behave.' To Anna, he asked, 'Anna, do you want a dance with my old reprobate of a granddad in his garish shirt?'

In reply, Anna took hold of Bill's extended hand, and said, 'I love an older man who can rock a floral shirt. Come on, Granddad Bill, let's kick up a storm on the dancefloor.'

****

Nick shouted at Bill, 'go easy on your dodgy hip that prevents you from using the lawn mower.' Bill moved very briskly to the dancefloor to display his dancing ability to *'You Sexy Thing'* by Hot Chocolate. Ed joined Nick to watch their granddad shake off at least thirty years of age as he swung his hips in a rhymical way to the song. Ed sipped his bottle lager and commented, 'I wouldn't have liked to be out with him in the 50s and 60s in the dance halls and clubs. We know he was a right ladies' man. Probably caused a few fights, I imagine.'

Nick watched as Bill placed his arms around Anna, whispering in her ear to make her laugh. 'There will be a fight here with me in a minute, if he doesn't watch it.'

A tall, well-dressed man was now standing next to Nick, drinking a bottled lager, and staring at the couples on the dancefloor. Nick didn't recognise him but guessed he might be a work colleague of Anna's.

The man turned to Nick to introduce himself. 'Hi, I'm Jack. I work with Anna. I must say she's looking particularly stunning tonight. Mega hot. Unless she's bagged herself a rich sugar daddy, I'm guessing that old boy is not the fiancé. If we're all getting the chance to dance with her, then count me in for a slow one.'

Nick immediately knew who this man was, Anna's boss, Jack Buckner. The man who was fond of reprimanding her but was now speaking about her in a way that indicated he fancied her. Nick extended his hand to Jack. 'Let me introduced myself, I am Nick Carlton, Anna's fiancé. You're her line manager, aren't you? She's mentioned you from time to time.'

Jack was now trying to take the lustful look off his face as he shook Nick's hand. Nick could also tell that the man was feeling uncomfortable after what he'd just said. He spluttered slightly, as he stated, 'Yeah, right, I am her boss. Anna's a great asset to the team and the company. Let me offer my congratulations on your engagement.'

Nick gave him a sarcastic 'thanks' for the congrats before adding, 'Let me give you some advice. I suggest that you tone down your less than professional assessment of Anna or you'll be facing two things. One, an Employment Tribunal. Two, me. I will deal with those that upset Anna. Anyway, go and enjoy the party.' It was wonderful to watch Buckner scurry off to join his work colleagues with a pained expression on his weasel-like features.

****

The next day, after sleeping to mid-morning due to excess alcohol the night before, Anna was cuddling up to Nick, her head resting on his shoulder. Her head was muzzy from the drinking but she felt contented that the engagement party had gone well. She lifted her head to gaze at Nick and he kissed her lightly.

Nick started to laugh. 'The party went well, on the whole. No major incidents. Bill behaved and managed not to steal anyone's wife and cause a fight. I think he has a major crush on you, though. How many dances with him did you have, as I barely got a look in?'

Anna leaned up, noting the peeved expression on his face. 'Only three or four. He does tire after that, thankfully. But he is quite a good dancer and very entertaining.'

'Well, I shall be watching him carefully from now on. And that boss of yours who was eyeing you up, and commenting about you, without realising he was talking to your fiancé,' Nick stated.

'What?' Anna asked, in a shocked voice. 'What did he say?'

Nick repeated the brief conversation. 'His comments made it very clear to me that he fancies you. So, I've set him straight.'

Anna stared at Nick, her annoyance radiating out of her. 'I wish you hadn't. I hope that he doesn't find a way to get back at me for that.'

'I don't think he will. The guy's all bluff and bravado. And he didn't get the chance to dance with you as you were dancing very energetically with all your friends and family,' Nick added. 'I, on the other hand, did not get my fair share of dancing with you. Still, you are now within my grasp.' With that he lay over her, and she noted his eyes intensely scrutinising her face before he caressed her. 'It's all this beauty that's a magnet for men. Your lovely face, large blue eyes, perfectly pert nose, and smoulderingly hot mouth. Not to forget your soft, wavy brown hair. And lest we forget the sexiest body on planet earth.'

Anna knew that he loved the way she looked but these comments actually made her tearful for a moment. 'Yes, I am grateful for my looks but they have resulted in a lot of trouble over the years. It leads to a lot of unwanted attention, all the time, and then attracts the wrong kind of entitled men to try to lay claim to me, as in Alistair, Connor, Russ Milner who've all physically hurt me. Then, there have been the weird ones that developed crushes on me over the years, at school, at university, at work. Culminating in the super-weird Luke Milner. Alyssa said that Abbie was angry that I was good-looking and this meant she wouldn't be able to get you back. The beauty curse, my dad called it, when I had trouble at school with jealous girls and persistent boys. On one level, it's exhausting, on another level, it's resulted in terrifying experiences. I hope now that I'm with you, things will settle down a bit. If nothing else, your physical presence and annoyed expression can help to keep unwanted men away.'

Nick brushed away a stray tear. 'Hey, sweetheart. We can do things such as online shopping or shopping together. We will spend more time as a couple though I want you to still have time with your girlfriends. I don't want you to be a beautiful bird in a gilded cage, shut away from the world, for your safety.' A gentle kiss caressed her mouth before a smirky smile touched his lips. 'Anyway, in a few years all this beauty will fade, you'll get wrinkles and get fat. I will trade you in for a prettier, younger model.'

Anna tapped his smug face lightly with her hand. 'I knew you were really shallow, Nick Carlton. It's a good job I know your true intentions before I take my wedding vows. I will also point out that you will age as well. If you get a receding hair-line and a paunch like your dad, I will trade you in for someone younger. I'll have to do this very quickly in the few years that I retain my beauty. Excuse me whilst I get Chris Hemsworth's phone number.'

'Chris Hemsworth, eh, madam? I thought you said someone younger. The man's older than me.'

'Yes, but I'm sure he has a lot of physical attributes that will appeal to me,' Anna stated, looking at Nick coyly.

Nick now laughed loudly. 'Is it Thor's big hammer that attracts you, Miss Louden? I know I can give him a run for his money in that department?' Nick goaded her, forcing her to lie on her back as he started to kiss her with passion.

Anna sighed as he explored her body with his eager hands and mouth. Nick Carlton was handsome, loving and sexy, and had many other great qualities. She was grateful for the day they met when the Angel in Charge of Laybys had come to her aid and found her the perfect man.

⸙

Get Help - If you are being stalked or harassed

This novel is purely a work of fiction concerning Luke Milner's obsession with Anna Louden. Luke created a fantasy in his head that he was in love with Anna. He believed that Anna would fall in love with him when she got to know him. He plotted to bring her into his life. His obsession escalated leading him to commit serious crimes of stalking, false imprisonment and illegal administrating a drug to endanger life.

In the real world, many people fall victim to stalkers. Stalking is characterised by a perpetrator's fixation or obsession and may escalate to other crimes. Stalking and harassment both involve repeated behaviours, such as unwanted contact online or in person, that cause alarm, distress or fear of violence in a victim.

In UK law, stalking or harassment offences can be found in sections 2, 2A, 4 & 4A of the Protection from Harassment Act 1997 (PHA 1997) & section 42A(1) of the Criminal Justice & Police Act 2001.

Get help (UK) National support organisations:-

National Stalking Helpline – 0808 8020 300. This helpline offers practical help for anyone who has been affected by stalking or harassment.

Protection Against Stalking (PAS) A national charity raising awareness of stalking and harassment and supporting victims and their families. If you feel you are being stalked and in immediate danger – call 999. If you believe you are being stalked, but not in immediate danger, contact support@ protectionagainststalking.org

Suzy Lamplugh Trust – campaigns to reduce the risk of violence and aggression.

Paladin – National Stalking Advocacy Service – 020 3866 4107 and online.

Alice Ruggles Trust – raises awareness of coercive control and stalking to help victims seek help sooner.

Karma Nirvana – a specialist charity for victims and survivors of so-called 'honour'- based abuse in UK.

Acknowledgements

To Martin, from Agatha Crusty – thank you for your ongoing support for my writing. The cups of tea are still very welcome when I am working away on the laptop.

To Dave. Once again, you have created a wonderful design for the cover of my new book, 'The Beauty Curse'. It truly captivates the image I had in mind for the book cover. I really cannot thank you enough for this. Your design for my first published book 'Wife Number Three' has been widely praised and deservedly so.

To Mark – thanks again for all your ongoing support for helping me with any IT problems. I am still as not as technically advanced as most people but I have now thrown the quill pen and ink into the bin.

To Lauren, Frankie and Max. Thank you for your support and love.

To Margaret, Debbie, all dear friends, family and neighbours who have all shown their ongoing support and interest in my writing.

To my readers of 'Wife Number Three'. It has brought me the greatest joy to know that you enjoyed this novel. It was wonderful to have individual feedback and to discover which characters captivated your imagination. Often it was the ones I didn't expect, such as young Alfie or sexy Natasha. Obviously, the world's most obnoxious man, Gary Anderson, was deservedly singled out for being the devil's spawn.

Also by Rose Horobin on Amazon
Wife Number Three

Contact author – Rose Horobin
Email address – writezbook@outlook.com